Imaginings

Stories that
Stay with You

Imaginings

Stories that
Stay with You

Stanley Jones

A Red Robin Book

Imaginings
Stories that Stay with You

Library of Congress Cataloging-in-Publication Data:

Imaginings—*Stories that Stay with You*—Stanley Jones

Contents: Fiction. 22 illustrated short stories:

A Fanciful Interpretation—The Overcoat—Bowsey Wood—Jesse James—Across the Crystal Sea—A Desirable Fare—One Hundred Eight-Six Thousand Miles per Second—Incident on the Road to Kabul—The Chatterer—They Came Running—A Misjudged Approach—The Replacement—Paranoia—An Alluring Enigma—Rabanus—The Sentence—A Retaliatory Measure—The Intruders—Bear Attack—A Short-Lived Affair—The Faker—Mrs. Crouch

ISBN-13: 978-1492333944
ISBN-10: 1492333948

Printed in the United States of America
First Printing

Cover & Interior Design: Red Robin Books
Text set in Palatino Linotype
Titles set in Oswald Light

Cover: *Wordsmith* (artist unknown)

For Jean

Contents

Contents

Not that the story need be long, but it will take a long while to make it short—Henry David Thoreau

A FANCIFUL INTERPRETATION

Joey Martin was not a man who you would think could kill. Other than, say, to put an injured farm animal out of its misery, or, possibly, to entice a rat to step into a lethal trap. You only needed to have observed the farmworker taking a shortcut, striding purposefully across a meadow he'd soon be soon be cutting for winter hay, to sense that compassion, that goodness of heart, as others did. At least the few who knew him. "A country boy at heart," they would tell you; "sweet, humble, and honest through and through."

The grass was soaking wet from days of heavy rain, the pastoral landscape cloaked in the haze of an early summer evening. A scarlet sky seared the western horizon. The fiery display foretold of much-needed drier weather in the days ahead.

"Red Sky at Night, Shepherd's Delight," Joey muttered. His wellington's glistened with moisture. The knee-high rubber boots squeaked as he pushed them through the tall grass. He was coming from the direction of a rain-swollen river where he'd been repairing a fence along the bank. He felt somewhat downcast. A cow had been lost the day before. A section of the old wooden barrier had collapsed, taking the animal with it.

Muscularly lean from long days spent in the open fields, Joey's tanned, healthy glow belied twenty years of toiling on the land. His sun-burnished hair furled onto his shoulders. In the setting sun the filaments took on the hue of amber held up to light. He was most comfortable in work clothes: washed-out, dark-blue, twill trousers tucked into his wellies and a black waistcoat—a remnant of his father's wedding suit—unbuttoned over a flannel shirt. He hadn't much in the way of best wear. He'd never had need for it. Other than to attend his father's funeral.

As usual, at the end of his workday, Joey's thoughts turned to the evening ahead, to his mother's wave from the front room window that would greet him, and to a hot bath he would take to cleanse away the day's toils. After his meal, when he'd cleared the table and settled his mother with a cup of hot tea, he'd take out a journal from a chest beneath his bedroom window. Hunched over a blank page, in the creamy glow cast by his bedside lamp, he would let the events of the day unwind from his pen. What he'd done. What he'd seen. What he'd thought. The words wouldn't come at first, then, like a freshly plowed furrow, they would flow across the page. Five other journals lay in the chests' deep drawer. His spidery writing filled both sides of the pages. It pleased him to put into words his thoughts about the land upon which he labored. His mother was the only person who knew of his literary passion. As far as he knew, even that knowledge was scant. Joey preferred to keep his daily accounts of farm work to himself, for he liked to embellish each piece such that it read a little like fictional narrative. He'd rather that no one read his writings, not even his mother. He just didn't think his work yet good enough.

He'd call at Benson's Bakery on the way home. That's why he was taking the shortcut across the hayfield. It meant his mother would not have to go out for bread in the morning. After her stroke, she was not as strong as she used to be. Joey didn't have money with him, but he knew Mrs. Benson would hold a loaf on account until he was paid on Friday. He was used to striving to make ends meet. Even when his dad was alive, the family had been poor. The pittance his mother got at the wool mill had helped for a time—before she became ill. Now they had to make do on his wage alone.

Before working on the riverside fence, Joey had raked fertilizer over a nearby pasture. High on a Fordson Major, a steel rake in tow, he'd thought about his dad who'd once sat in that same seat. He'd wondered what *his* thoughts had been, traversing that same field.

He felt fortunate to be working for such a fine man as Mr. Atkinson. The farm owner had taught Joey everything he knew about the land. When the farm came on hard times, as it had recently, it never crossed Joey's mind to take another job—even a better-paid one. The lifestyle suited him at Atkinson's, just as it had his dad before him. The heavy-set, wavy-haired farmer once told Joey's mother, Peggy, "Your son is the damn, hardest-working, most honest man I've ever met in all my forty years on the land. I'd double his wages, treble them even. Take him on as a partner tomorrow, I would, if I could see my way clear."

Mr. Atkinson's blue eyes had blazed defiantly from his pockmarked face. It was one Peggy Martin thought attractive in a craggy sort of way. She well knew what Mr. Atkinson's remarks meant. He'd been looking for someone to share the burden for some time. Trouble was, neither she nor Joey had any money to offer. And that was what the farm needed most.

Bullied at school, Joey had become inhibited by those around him. The result was a shy, overly sensitive man, one who would sooner stare at a patch of ground in front of him than look a person in the eye. Then there was his stammer. When it came on, as it would when under pressure, he'd pretend a coughing fit. Somehow, he would get the words out even when seeming to choke on his own spittle. Boys in his class were always a step ahead. Most were now carpenters or electricians. Some even had their own business. Many had left the village to prosper in nearby towns. But Joey had turned inward, taken a job on the local farm, as far away as he could get from the likes of them. Only with his mother did he feel comfortable. He could look her unflinchingly in the eye. Sometimes he felt like he wanted to be back in the womb, to be cozy and warm, protected from the outside world—a world in which he found it difficult to compete. There were a few compensations. He got fresh eggs and vegetables to take home when he needed them that helped buffer his lowly wage. And, at Christmas time, Mr. Atkinson would give him first pick out of the turkey pen. Joey's subordinates were the farm animals: cattle, pigs, and strutting chickens. He knew like no other how to get the best out of them.

As Peggy cut into the fresh Benson loaf, she wondered what her son would write about that night. Earlier, she'd glanced into his bedroom to see Joey standing by the open window, seemingly deep in thought. Arms folded, he'd been gazing out over the moonlit fields. *"Thinking up what fine words to put down,"* she'd decided. Pride welled within her when she thought of her son as a budding writer. She couldn't quite believe it. At one time, he'd never touch a pen; now every spare minute he seemed to have one in his hand. Sundays too. The only day he finished at the farm early. Most of the afternoon, he'd sit with a dictionary in his lap, or with the dark-blue thesaurus, she'd bought him earlier in the year for his thirty-second birthday.

Joey didn't know his mother examined every word he wrote. That she went over each passage several times. That she envisaged what set him about writing it. That she sometimes stroked and kissed the pages, imagining them to be a manuscript. That she dreamed of his book one day being on display in stores around the country. A beautiful bound volume of her son's work.

Early the next day, as soon as Joey had left for the farm, Peggy read the prior evening's journal entry. Her son had written long into the night, so she was more excited than ever at the prospect. The pages quivered in her trembling hands, but she persevered. A bit of shake, as she put it, was not going to stop her from reading her son's work. She read slowly, savored the chosen words. The sentences, she thought, were crisply constructed, like a real writer's. As she read, tiny gasps escaped her. Her lower lip drooped slightly, as if a small weight was attached at its center. Her eyes widened and her brows rose up to form twin arches, smoothing a frown between them. When she paused to reflect on a story, as she often did, the shake subsided a little. Now the quiver had almost entirely ceased, so strikingly fanciful did she find the writing. Her son had written quite a piece. No wonder, she thought, that he'd needed so much time contemplating.

Joey had written:

Needed to go to Benson's after work today, so took the shortcut across the hay meadow. It was the first time since I sowed the seed. The dark-green grass was lushly wet. Being so, it smelt sweet as honey, as if freshly cut.

The massed rippling fronds reminded me of the sea. The soft breeze wafted them about a bit, first one way then the other; swathes of jade and mother of pearl, swaying, swishing, gossamer soft.

Halfway across the field, I came upon a bag, a square of chestnut leather lying deep in the grass. A satchel I suppose you'd call it. Such an unexpected find, so out of place, I wondered how on earth it got there. It was bulged out quite a bit, by whatever was packed inside. It lay not upon the surface of the soil—as one might expect, had it been carefully placed, or even lightly dropped—but partly embedded in the ground as if hurled there with great force.

Two brass buckles, each one tightly laced to the leather body, secured a fold-over top. The whole thing was bound with a tough fiber string that my thick, muddy fingers had trouble undoing. A brass ring stitched into each side showed that at one time there'd been a shoulder carry strap of some sort attached.

There was no name or address anywhere that I could see. Inside, a grease-paper wrapped package contained several smaller packages, each individually wrapped in the same type of paper, all enclosed in a plastic bag. The bag was sharply folded and held tight with adhesive tape. Evidently, whoever packed it, intended that the contents survive intact, even if the satchel was submerged in water.

It took me quite some time to get to the contents. When I finally did, my first thought was that I'd come upon a child's game; the kind that trades properties with pretend money, for the plastic bag was stuffed with twenty-pound notes. I counted fifty banded packages. A quick thickness comparison showed that each bundle contained a hundred notes—one hundred thousand pounds in total!

I was stunned. The notes looked and felt so real: purple overall in color, the Queen emblazoned on one side, a statue of William Shakespeare on the reverse, and they had a distinctive linen-feel about them.

Instinctively, I crouched low to the ground, in case someone should see me—I must have looked quite startled. I stared long and hard at the wall of stems, any moment expecting someone to burst through, to claim my find.

But the wall didn't part. The stalk barrier remained intact. The only sound, apart from my heavy breathing, and I might add, the pounding of my heart, was the whisper of fronds and the caw of a crow wheeling overhead.

A closer, more careful look confirmed the notes had a quality look and feel about them that strongly suggested they were genuine. I was astounded at the thought of such a possibility, that such a huge amount of money should be lying in a farmers field. One Hundred Thousand pounds in Thomas Atkinson's hayfield!

I remained low in the grass for some time, flipping the edge of the notes with my thumb, like I'd seen people do with cards. Dumbfounded, I didn't quite know what to do. I suppose you could say I was in a quandary. I'd barely ever handled a twenty before, never mind crisp hundred-note wads of them.

My first thought was to go to the farmhouse, hand the lot over to Mr. Atkinson. He'd know what to do. Someone out for a walk had obviously dropped the satchel. Maybe even him. Although, I found this highly unlikely since I knew he hadn't two pennies to rub together.

The odd thing was there were no footmarks other than mine in the immediate area. The grass around the satchel was quite undisturbed. And the leather was embedded a bit in the soft ground. I had a good look at that, for I was lying in the grass alongside the thing for some time. I decided the bag could only have flown itself into the middle of the field.

Or been flown!

That's when the thought first struck me that the satchel most likely fell from a plane.

Not wanting to bother Mr. Atkinson; my excitement being what it was might trigger a stammer fit that would make it difficult for him to understand what I was on about, I placed the packages back in the satchel and brought it home wrapped in an empty fertilizer sack that I found at the edge of the field.

On the way, I stopped by the shop to get a loaf of bread. Old Mrs. Benson, bless her kindly soul, told me I could pay for it on Friday, while there's me, standing before her — like a beggar looking for a handout — holding a sack full of money!

Peggy placed the journal back in the drawer. Quite overcome, she removed her glasses, wiped the beginnings of tears from the corners of her eyes.

"At last," she whispered. "Joey's embellished his account of a workday on the farm with a piece of imaginative fiction writing."

A year earlier, he'd barely been able to write. Now here he was, surely a novelist in the making. She was consumed with Joey's story. All that day, the fine lines around her eyes clenched and unclenched as different parts of her son's journal entry illuminated her mind. Later, when shuffling her fragile frame around her garden, she almost fell over a crumpled sack lying on the path. She held it up to see *"Midland Farm Fertilizers"* emblazoned across the front in dark green stenciling.

"My goodness," she said, dropping the empty sack with a start. "Where will Joey get his ideas from next!"

The eiderdown on Joey's bed was covered with stacks of twenty-pound banknotes. He held a single note up against the bedside light to study a vertical line that appeared within the paper. Each one he picked up bore the same line. He'd read somewhere that such lines showed that a banknote was genuine. He whistled softly, collected up the money, and put the bundles back in the plastic bag. The bag he then stuffed back in the satchel—just as it had been when he'd first found it. He dragged a large suitcase from the top of a wardrobe, and placed the satchel beneath a piece of curtain material already in the case.

Satisfied, he returned the suitcase to the top of the wardrobe, pushing it up against the wall where someone entering the room would not easily see it. He decided he wouldn't say a thing about his find. Not even to his mother. He hadn't heard any mention of lost money on the local news. Nor had he seen anything about it in Mr. Atkinson's newspaper, which he'd quickly leafed through at the farm. He decided that he would return the money to its rightful owner, only when he knew for sure who that was.

The black van was back. Peggy had noticed the vehicle as it went up and down the road a time or two during the morning. Parked now by the roadside, it hadn't moved for quite a while. Next to it, a man was struggling, trying to extricate himself from a hawthorn hedge. He appeared enraged as he tried to free his trousers from the thorns. A second man sat inside the van, reading a map. Every now and then, the man in the van cursed the one trapped in the hedgerow, who in turn cursed the man in the van. Peggy didn't like that one bit. She had seen the two men across the fields earlier in the day and had assumed that they were surveyors out looking for some reference point on the landscape. Now she was not so sure.

About noontime, the van moved off. She watched it turn up the lane to the farm, past a cowshed she knew Joey to be mucking out. *They've gone for advice about the area, she decided. Perhaps even from her son.*

Joey had seen the van too. He'd watched it go past, through the open gable of the cowshed. Mr. Atkinson had stepped out and spoke with the two men inside the van, waving his arms about as he did so. Joey thought he was telling them how to get to the hayfield. They're after the satchel, he decided. He felt his face flush. He looked down at his shovel. He lightly tapped it a time or two with the side of his boot. Later, after the muck had drained some, he'd shovel it onto a trailer. After that, he'd take it down to the heap to add straw.

As he scraped, hosed, and brushed, Joey decided he didn't like the looks of the black van, or the men in it. He also decided that if they asked about the money, he'd tell them nothing.

He didn't have to wait long.

"Ay, there," came a sharp voice. Like the crack of whip, Joey thought.

He looked up into the stubbled countenance of the stockier one of the two. The man peered down at him through a broken grating in the side of the cowshed. The man's face was moon-like, fleshy, and lit up with interest. It was as though he'd come upon a long-lost friend. Joey took in the man's pallor, stained teeth and baggy, blood-shot eyes. He lowered his gaze back to the concrete floor.

"Joey, isn't it?"

Joey nodded, coughed, tapping his heel against the side of the shovel.

"I'm lookin' for somethin' that fell from a plane," the man said. "Don't laugh, I'm serious. It fell over there somewhere." He pointed in the general direction of the hay meadow.

"Day before yesterday. Midafternoon time it would 'ave been. A bag. Might 'ave been quite large. Your boss seemed to think you might 'ave come upon it…"

"Jed! Over 'ere." The thickset one swiveled to direct the taller man to where he was.

Jed strode toward them. He was long, and skinny legged, wearing black trousers so tight that Joey at first thought they were stockings.

"No, over 'ere, stupid," Jed said to the stockier man as he strode past him to the front of the cowshed. "Idiot. We can't talk to 'im through that fuckin' gratin'."

"Now, Mister...?"

"Martin."

"Hi. I'm Jed. This fool 'ere's Morton, but you can call 'im Moron if you like, as I do." As Jed spoke, he broke into a whinny of a laugh that reminded Joey of Nellie, Mr. Atkinson's pony.

Morton stepped over to the other side of the cowshed, where he appeared to be examining its structure. *"For any place that looked like it might hide a bag of money,"* Joey thought.

"Well, Mr. Martin," Jed said, leaning toward him conspiratorially. "D'ya think you could 'elp us with this matter, eh? 'Ave you seen anythin'? Like a bag lyin' around? Such as a kid would take 'is books to school in, only a bit bigga'?"

Joey doubled over and broke into a cough. "No, can't say I've seen anything like that, Mister," he spluttered.

"Mr. Atkinson told us that day before yesterday you worked down by the river. We just thought you must 'ave seen it come down."

Jed's close-set eyes were as small and near to jet black as Joey had ever seen. He shuffled his feet. He'd never come across someone like this before—someone so...well, evil looking. Jed clearly was the leader of the two. This man had also referred to the bag as having "*Come down.*" So, it had been dropped from a plane, just as Joey had thought. He propped the shovel against the wall of the cowshed and picked up the brush. He swept an imagined patch of muck, lightly kicking its bristled head.

"Well, did you or didn't you?"

"As I've said, Mister, I don't know anything about a lost bag. I'd been on a tractor, fertilizing the pasture down there and was fixing a fence by…"

"You don't sound very sure of yourself, Mr. Martin, if you don't mind me sayin' so," Jed interrupted.

"Johnny, isn't it?" He continued with a grin.

"Joey."

"Joey, then."

"It fell from a plane. Would 'ave come down with quite a thump, I would imagine. So, you would surely 'ave 'eard it. D'ya remember the plane then? We were told it was red. Surely you must 'ave seen it. A small, single-engine type."

"With the roar of the river an' all, Mister, I might not have heard it, had the plane itself come down," Joey said, stifling a cough.

"Good answer, son," Morton said. He'd rejoined Jed from across the other side of the cowshed. "You can still walk us down there though, can't ya? So we can take a look around. You wouldn't mind that surely, would ya? Ya boss said you'd 'elp us in any way you could. Isn't that right, Jed? Jed, isn't that right?"

"I suppose I could do that, seeing as I've more or less finished up here," Joey said. "Mr. Atkinson will need to give his permission first, though. He may have other work for me around the yard."

"If you take this lane here," Joey pointed his brush in the direction of the river; "it'll take you down there. I'll follow soon as I can. After I've seen Mr. Atkinson."

Dignified, even in his shirtsleeves, Thomas Atkinson sat hunched at his kitchen table. His thick fingers drummed on its solid-pine top, every now and then pausing to stroke the wood-grain. The only other sound in the large, high-ceilinged room was the solemn tick-tock of a grandfather clock by the hallway door. A big man, even for a farmer, he looked older than his forty-five years. His wife's death a year earlier had brought a silvery sheen to his hair and turned his blue eyes a shade paler. It had come as a great shock, as had a sharp downturn in livestock prices soon after.

"Joey," he said, with a bang on the tabletop from his huge fist, "I tell you, I don't care for these men. Tell the buggers anything you want. Just get rid of them. Don't know what they asked you, but they questioned me about some bag or other they claim fell from a plane. Desperate to get their hands on it, I would say; a pair who'd stop at nothing. I thought I might call the police. Bring them in on it. See what they have to say."

Joey looked out the window. Across the cobblestone yard, the muck pile steamed in the cowshed like a smoldering bonfire. The tractor he'd used the previous day stood in an open-fronted shed next to it. The fat tires showed traces of fertilizer he'd used on the riverside field.

"Don't call the police just yet, Mr. Atkinson," Joey said quietly. He cleared his throat, discretely, behind a cupped hand, for he was inside the farmhouse where he didn't go very often. It was a large Victorian, a residence that reminded him of a church: cool, dimly lit, a place where footsteps echoed on quarry-tile floors.

"Let them have a look around," Joey added. "They'll be off then, since there's nothing there for them to see anyway."

The farm owner looked across the table at Joey, who sat askew from him, his chair pushed back. A rag-like cloak, which Joey wore when mucking out, hung down from his shoulders to drape across his boots onto the tiled floor. His clean-shaven face—fresh as a pippin apple,

Thomas's wife once said—was sideways onto him. The eyes, Mr. Atkinson knew, were hazel, those of a trustworthy, hardworking man. One who pondered, who took his time. One who carefully weighed things up. One who could be implicitly relied upon.

The farm owner pushed back his chair. He stood up from the table, straightened to his full six-foot height. "Go on down with them then, Joey. But be careful. Don't give an inch. Maybe what they're looking for dropped in the river. Tell them that. Tell them their precious bag might be twenty miles downstream by now."

Joey caught up with the two men just short of the meadow. The tall grass was still wet, so he suggested they walk around the edge where it wasn't so deep.

"Nice try," Morton said.

"But we cut straight across."

"The field lies along the path the plane took. The pilot told us that after he landed. Didn't he, Jed? Told us just in time. Since we 'ad to put 'im down. Didn't we, Jed?"

"Bastard imbecile! Can't you ever keep that big trap of yours shut?" Jed yelled.

"Take no notice of 'im, farmer-boy. Moron goes nuts like that every now and then. He misstates things."

But Joey had taken notice. It seemed the pilot of the plane, after completion of the mission, had been summarily executed. Fearful now, he gathered himself to make a dash for it. He hated to bother Mr. Atkinson, but he couldn't allow this to go on. He'd run back to the farm and tell him about the money. The farmer would then call the police.

"Now don't you think of doin' somethin' silly, farmer boy." It was Morton. "I can promise you'll be more than sorry if you do. The pilot told us the bag 'ad been let go north of the river in an area of dark green grass. Since this is the only field we've found that fits that description, the bag must either be in it, or close by. Isn't that right, Jed? Jed, that's right, isn't it?"

"It could well have dropped in the river," Joey said. "Could be miles downstream by now."

"Yes it could, but it didn't, did it?" Morton shot back.

"You would've crossed this field on your way back from the river. Where you'd been workin'. Your boss told us that. Didn't he, Jed? Jed, didn't he tell us that?"

"'Ere's where we found the grass disturbed," Jed said. They had come upon a flattened, muddied area of the field.

"Right 'ere," Jed pointed in triumph, "is where I'll bet it landed. Washed out a bit now, but anyone can see somethin' dropped 'ere with 'ell of a force."

Joey looked down at the smashed stems, and at the depression in the muddy soil that outlined where the satchel had been. The two men looked on, grinning at each other.

"Tell you what, Joey," Jed said. He studied his watch, holding it up close to Joey's face. "I'm goin' to be real generous. You've got ten seconds to own up to stealin' our money. Ten seconds to tell us where the fuck it is. Ten seconds and I set Moron on you. Let me tell you country boy, from long experience, once Moron starts, there's no way anyone can stop 'im."

Joey cleared his throat. Hands on his knees, he stooped, breaking into a hacking cough. "Then if I did happen to know where your bag was," he managed, "you'd never find it."

"Well," Jed said, "if the man doesn't have a tongue after all. And a clever one at that."

Joey turned to run, but Morton was too quick. He grabbed Joey, forcing his arm high up between his shoulder blades. Joey winced with pain. Morton's foul breath wafted across his face. Joey resisted with all his strength, but was easily overcome. Morton held him in a steely grip, the likes of which he'd never felt before. Sickly looking the man may well be, yet so unyieldingly powerful that Joey was swiftly rendered helpless.

Peggy could hardly wait for her son to come home. The previous evening he'd not written anything at all. He'd spent the whole time rummaging in his room with the door closed. She sat in the front room, looking out at the hayfield, to where she'd seen Joey go earlier in the day. The men in the black van had been with him. The figures had slowly shortened as they moved down the slope toward the river. Eventually just their heads had floated above the grass, until they too had disappeared. She sighed, wondering what the surveyor men wanted to know. Something to do with maps, she decided.

Jed cursed, he hated mud. *"Too much like shit,"* he thought. Now, here he was squelching through it like some village yokel. By right, the drug money was his. Even Morton's share. He'd make sure of that too in due course.

"Now! Where is it?" Jed yelled. He pinched his long bony fingers hard into Joey's nape.

The roar of the rain-swollen river drowned out all but shouted words.

"Yes, where is it?" Morton screamed.

"I've 'ad enough farm crap," Jed said. 'Ad enough to last me a fuckin' lifetime. Been traipsin' around in this shit three days, I 'av."

Morton yelled for him to "shut the fuck up."

Joey's stomach churned. He'd endured the pain from Morton's arm lock until he'd felt sure it would break. "Okay, okay, just let go my arm," he'd finally gasped out. Denied use of it, he'd be even more helpless. He knew he could never take them anywhere near his mother's house. Back to the farm was an option. But imperiling Mr. Atkinson could also end in disaster. He decided they'd need to break every bone in his body before he'd do either. He also wouldn't tell them he had the money, ill-gotten gain though it seemed to have been. He'd realized that should they happen to learn where it was, his usefulness to them would expire, as he had no doubt, so would he. The only thing he could think of was to lead them further away. His mind raced. Things had moved too quickly, too fast for him to grasp. All he could do was hope. Wait for some opportunity.

They were now walking parallel to the river, approaching the place where he'd been working on the fence. He pointed to a post he'd dug out and beside it, the pile of fresh soil. Lying against the post was the spade he'd used.

"It's there, buried by that post," he blurted.

Morton let go of his arm and pushed him roughly to the ground. "Well, there's the spade Joey-boy. Dig. And make it quick," he said.

Jed moved around to stand between Joey and the river. The leer had returned to the man's face. Jed's arms hung limp and low, like an ape. Joey felt the beady black eyes on him. "*Just try and make a run for it*," they said. Morton stood upslope, with hands on hips, solid as a rock pillar.

He should have said he'd hidden the bag back at the farm after all. Slowly, Joey rose to his feet. He picked up the spade. He could hardly feel the handle, his arm and hand were still numb from Morton's lock. He needed to work at it for a while, to restore circulation. As he loosened up—with shoulders powerfully muscled through years of farming the land—he built up into a rhythmic scythe-like motion, as though he was readying to throw the hammer at a sports event.

Jed's face froze just as the spade hit him. The flat of the blade struck across his half-raised arm. Joey had delivered the blow with all his strength. A force he felt through his upper body, a satisfying tingle that rippled through his arms, into his wrists; hands. The blow knocked Jed backward, over the edge of the bank into the torrent, to be sucked down amid the churn of flotsam, and the tumble of an uprooted tree.

Morton froze. He yelled out obscenities. Squealing like a stuck pig, he jumped on Joey, the weight of his solid body knocking the farmworker flat to the ground. The impact pitched the spade clear to follow Jed into the river. Winded, Joey struggled to his feet, to totter, dazed, on the brink of the bank. Morton lunged hard at him, but Joey managed to clutch onto a fence post—one of the new ones he'd dug in the day before. He pivoted around the upright, causing Morton to miss. The impetus of his charge not fully expended, Morton grasped a post too, but a rotten one was all that was in reach. For an agonizing moment, it looked like the wood might withstand the onslaught.

But Morton needed to lever against the old post, to add a fraction of extra force, to gain traction on the slippery grass, when it abruptly gave way, leaving him helpless on the lip of the bank, an armful of rotted stump clutched to his chest. He let go of the wood and dropped to his knees, clawing at the grass. He screamed oaths the like of which Joey had never heard before. Unable to find handhold or footing, Morton went over the rim of the riverbank, slithering inexorably down the muddy slope into the racing flow.

Joey leaned over the edge of the bank, his arm still in touch with the post that had saved his life. His mind whirled. He fought to collect his thoughts, to decide what he should do. Shocked, yet relieved, he looked about for signs that either man had snagged a hold.

Gouges left by Morton's scrabbling hands ran down the face of the bank below him. Those, along with pieces off the shattered, rotten post, were the only indications of the deadly struggle. A moorhen sailed past, twirling skillfully in the fierce current to hold in an eddy by the far bank. Joey pushed himself upright. He backed away from the edge. The brutality sickened him, yet he knew that it had to be either them or him. He walked shakily downstream to the first bend, examining the banks as he went. Onto the second. The third. The fourth. There was neither sight nor sound of the two men, only the churning brown flow: a roiling, foam-flecked conveyor of mud and debris.

Peggy placed the journal back in the draw. She had crept out of bed the minute she'd heard the latch drop, the metallic clink signaling Joey had left for the farm. He'd been so intense the previous evening. He'd written long into the night. She'd never seen him so eager to write. After the first read she'd been quite taken aback. Her son had not written about such viciousness, or used such strong language before. Neither though, had he been so cleverly fanciful in his storytelling. Still, she thought, the subject matter had been well imagined.

Snug back in bed, Peggy wondered what might be in Joey's next chapter. She allowed that even the best of writers go through such an over-fanciful phase from time to time. It happens, she decided, when their imagination runs wild. The thought comforted her, brought an enlightened look to her pale gray eyes.

THE
OVERCOAT

In this manner did it all come about—Nikolai Gogol

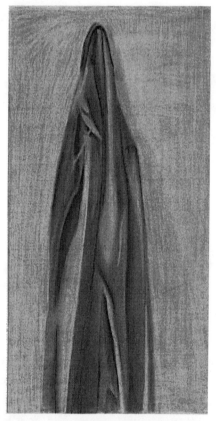

The façade of the railway station shimmers in late afternoon heat. It is the first warm, sunny day of an otherwise cool, cloudy English spring. Business commuters, caught by the unexpected burst of warmth—shirtsleeves furled, ties loosened; jackets, raincoats, slung over shoulders—crowd the platform, awaiting the arrival of the Liverpool train. Noticeably, Jamaluddin Wahab Mangoosh, standing at the periphery of the throng, has not shed any clothing, not even slackened the tightly buttoned overcoat with turned up collar he wears.

He is a tall, gaunt young man with lank, dark hair that
drapes like a scarf about the material encircling his neck.
Between the wings of the high collar, a pale, chiseled face
peers out at the world as though from between parted curtains. The few friends, who claim to know the youth, identify him as Jama. A quiet, pious individual they will tell
you. One who keeps himself to himself, to the point of an-
onymity. Conscious of the curious stares, being clothed for
a winter's day, he barely resists doing something other
than stand motionless, like a statue, as he's been instructed
to do. Though mindful of the command, he cannot help
but worry a frayed edge of the lapel in the hope such fidg-
eting gives the impression the overcoat hides some kind of
neck brace—a plausible enough reason, he feels, for not
taking the garment off. But the stares continue and the
stress of enduring them intensifies, such that he finds himself forced to lower his eyes, to the concrete slab he happens to be standing upon, to whirls left long ago by a
builder's trowel, to a flattened cigarette end, and to a
brightly colored KitKat wrapper.

As he takes in the trash-littered platform and his laced-
up boots astride it, he recalls his mother speaking about
the overcoat. About how over the years it had not only
been used by his father, but also by others within the
Mangoosh family for ceremonial events, weddings, even
funerals. He remembers too the navy-blue garment hanging from a hook on his bedroom door, that in certain lights
his boyish imagination filled with a body ghoulishly hanging there. Now *his* body occupies the space within the
overcoat, in circumstances so unspeakably dreadful that
back then, even in the most horrific of nightmares, they
would never have entered his mind. He tries to remember
the overcoat on happier occasions: long ago, the garment
being used as an eiderdown on cold nights when he would
dare extend an arm outside its inner warmth to insert a

hand into a seemingly bottomless pocket, or of the coat
being held by his father, ghostly lit one frigid night, slowly
releasing it's warming heaviness upon his bed.

Despite his need to vent the stupefying layer of heat
trapped around his body, he dare not take off the overcoat
or even loosen it about his neck. It's not that he would
have found either task difficult, or that he would not have
hesitated a second to shed the garment had his circumstances been normal. To undo the shiny black buttons
would be simple enough. Although the one he was instructed to sew on only that morning, fastened high up
beneath his chin, may not be so easy. This button differs
from those below it by having a thinner, curved edge that
complete with a bulging knot of hard twine, now presses
irritatingly against his windpipe. The discomfort forces
him to risk hooking a finger over the top edge of the lapel
to ease the pressure at that spot; for fear that he might
choke. He does this despite having been told that the light-
est of tugs at the material, or excessive jerkiness of movement, might generate enough static electricity within the
folds of the woolen material to jeopardize the holy-order
rite for which he's been ordained.

To minimize movement, he walked painstakingly
slowly to the platform from the beat-up Toyota that
dropped him off at the station. So anxious was he to avoid
jolting the fabric, he adopted a kind of foot-dragging gait,
causing several travelers to stop and stare. Arrayed in such
heavy clothing, they must have thought he was putting on
some kind of comedy act. The odd effect would not have
been as noticeable during the previous week's unusually
cold, wet weather, when everyone, it seemed, was trudging around clad as if it were January. Others possibly supposed the tentative motion was not humorous at all. The
somewhat bloated appearance, the need to shuffle in that

strange way—they might have decided—was the result of a defect in the youth's skeletal structure.

Though each scenario carried with it a ring of plausibility, the reason for the largeness and for the need to lessen movement is so shocking that those same onlookers would have fled in terror had they at the time been aware of it. For beneath the overcoat, strapped from throat to waist, making it appear several sizes too small for its occupant is a canvas satchel. The bag consists of an eight-pouch explosive device, wherein each compartment—arranged, he's been told, equally around the back and sides to maximize spread of charge—are packed nails, ball bearings, and jagged pieces of steel, embedded in a volatile mix of nitroglycerine and wood pulp, the whole laced with calcium carbonate. Jama has also been told that when he presses a button concealed within the left front pocket of the satchel—against which he now feels the hammering of his heart—his whole being will be blown to smithereens, comprised of such fine particles that the lens of a high-speed camera would capture it as an expanding reddish cloud interspersed with sizable chunks of shattered bone.

After a week of preparation to transform him into a human bomb, the faction leader, following an inspection of the assembled explosive outfit, had declared Jama to be *ready, able, and willing to commit carnage for the sake of Islam*. Final confirmation of *hallowed eminence* occurred when the tall, ashen-faced, bearded man—whom Jama thought had the look of one who had recently died himself—stated that although any survivors of a given slaughter may see a being instantly cease to resemble Jamaluddin Wahab Mangoosh—or anything resembling the human form, the body for the most part being vaporized by the blast—he need not concern himself, since at that same instant his mortal soul would be gloriously reincarnated before Allah.

Jama stands at the edge of Stafford's Platform 1, awaiting the arrival of the two-minute past five from London. A ticket clutched between his clammy fingers in a pocket of the overcoat tells him his First-Class seat is, as has been usual, in the center of Coach B, the second compartment behind the engine. Twenty minutes after the crowded Liverpool-bound train has departed the station, when hurtling through busy Crewe at seventy miles per hour, he is to detonate the bomb, destroying—he's been told—himself, everyone else in Coach B, an untold number of others throughout the train, a good part of the station—along with severely damaging its NW Junction Switching Center—and the up and down electric lines to London.

The Spiritual Leaders were concerned as to whether their young recruit would be able to summon enough steely nerve to enter martyrdom. After all, when conscripted from a downtrodden area of nearby Birmingham, he was only fifteen years old. To counter this, to bolster his commitment, they repeatedly stimulated their *Chosen One* with reminders of the reward that awaited him. The compensation to those entering such a hallowed state would be immense. This goading drove Jama to avoid rejection.

When the time came, he would do all he could to gain such a sacred state, even though it required that he die in order to achieve it. To this end, Jama made a show of being radicalized, infinitely more so than he knew himself to be.

From the Scriptures given to him, Jama has learned that one who sacrifices soul and blood in order to bring victory to the cause *will be henceforth the cream of the cream of the cream.* Moreover, at the first spurt of blood, *he shall be gifted seven special favors, including having all his sins forgiven and being married to seventy-two Beautiful Maidens of Paradise.*

The prospect of such instant, magnificent gratification at once appealed to him. When he compared such glorious prospect to the squalid, jobless, father-less, girl-less life he led, no question about it was left in his mind. So, at the re-cruiters insistent badgering, he'd accepted. He then quickly passed through indoctrination—supposedly brainwashed of all normal thought regarding safety of human life.

Jama knows the carnage will be immense. And, as his learning has taught him, among the rubble, the gore, there may well be the blood of unknowing non-infidels, believ-ers like himself whose posthumous reward will also be to gain entry to Paradise. He has accepted *deep into his mortal soul*—during weeks of chanted oaths and sworn allegiance rituals—that it is the purpose of the operation to which he's been assigned to kill as many nonbelievers as possible, along with any infrastructure such infidels happen to be occupying at the time.

The prospect of immediately being transported to such celebrated status had at first sounded fantastically dream-like, albeit tempered with an abject fear of sacrificing his life in order to get there. Compounding this dilemma was his increasing suspicion of whether forfeiting his young life—unfulfilling though it was—would end in such glori-fication. He had come to realize that the sect leaders, el-ders, instructors, and recruiters—despite having served with the faction for years compared to his mere months—had evidently not been given the same martyrdom oppor-tunity as he.

He felt that to counter this state of mind, signaled, he supposed, by the distrustful look that he knew had been creeping over his face—a disbelieving expression that, try as he might, he'd been unable to prevent—a scripture had been given to him in which a highlighted paragraph stated: *"An assignment given immediately upon completion of Learning & Understanding could be viewed—depending on the degree of dedication demonstrated prior to selection—an exalted personal beckon from The Almighty himself."*

He had greeted this order with disbelief at first, for he'd previously been led to believe that he would not reach *Assignment Status* for years, possibly decades; indeed, if ever. Significantly however, in one scripture was the statement: *"Howsoever unlikely it is that you will be called upon, nonetheless, the Holy Leadership require you to be prepared and available should an unexpected opportunity arise."*

Dying for a cause, of which he had become less convinced, worried him enough to want to tell the *Martyrdom Leader*—a wizened, serious-looking man in a long, flowing robe, whom he most startlingly thought, when first introduced, might be a Holy Prophet—that he'd made a monumental mistake. He didn't understand the reasoning behind the sacred order. In essence: why should newcomer Jamaluddin Wahab Mangoosh be the one to bring it about? But it was not in him to ask such a question.

Still, even at this dreadful hour, standing upon this ghastly, inert slab—as if an execution rostrum—he ponders why earlier in his indoctrination he didn't just walk away from the faction. Why didn't he just tell the leader that he could not go through with what he'd committed to do? There would be serious repercussions for such an admission. He had learned of consequences that included the *suffering of loved ones.* Since *loved one* for him meant *mother,* the implication was all too clear.

He pushes the overcoat cuff back off his wrist. So large is the sleeve's bore relative to his thin forearm, the appendage appears like a protruding rod. He studies his watch, a plastic-rimmed digital timepiece gifted by his mother for his sixteenth birthday a week ago.

She had handed it to him with a kiss on the cheek. "Those who keep good time," she whispered in his ear, "will live timely." He'd laughed at this, answering more primly than he intended that he always kept good time and that she should know that better than anyone. As he spoke, he held onto her embrace, fighting an urge to tell her about the religious group he'd joined and the pledge he'd made. He wanted to tell her that he had sworn to uphold an exalted allegiance. In his youthful way, he'd felt there might still be a chance his mother could intervene, protect him as she always had. But he didn't say a word about his assignment, for it was too secret even for a mother to know. Should she ever learn of it before the event, her life would be in mortal danger. So within the aura that had enveloped him—like a warm, soap-scented cloud—he'd hung on to the motherly body, blinking tears from his eyes in utter silence.

It is less than ten minutes before the train is due. Twice before during the past week, albeit each time in more temperate weather and with newspapers stuffed into the satchel in place of bomb material, the express had been on time. He had dutifully boarded the train during each rehearsal. Seated in his ticketed Coach B seat, as instructed, he'd pressed the timer button concealed in a pocket of the overcoat, as the train sped through Crewe.

Doubt continues to plague him. What if, instead of Gates of Paradise, there is *nothingness*? Not even that, since the word implied *existence* in order to perceive it. As he'd increasingly begun to imagine, perhaps the affect would be no different than what in life he assumes it to have been for the untold eons that had elapsed before he was born. Or even the time he lay anesthetized, to reset a fracture of his right femur, suffered during a boyhood football match. It had been a lapse, as far as his awareness was concerned, that could have been a single second or a thousand years. Would the explosion bring about such nonexistence? His young mind struggles to visualize such impenetrable possibilities.

As the orange digits on the black face of his watch click off the remaining minutes, his dark brown eyes take in details of the edifice in which he stands. It is a building that he's become familiar with during the test runs. In the platform waiting room, a woman and three small boys are sharing a sandwich. Through a large window of a snack bar, a waitress slops steaming, hot liquid into a circle of cups. Nearer to him, the yellow-tiled entrance to a gent's toilet gleams in a sea of artistically tooled Victorian stonework. His gaze finally settles on the perfectly round face of a well-built man seated directly across the tracks from him on Platform 2.

The man's presence concerns him. Along with being filled with dread at the thought of his mother seeing him, caught by a Closed Circuit TV camera, the man jars his mind. He now recalls this same confident-looking person sitting on that same seat yesterday. And the day before that. And possibly even the day before that. He is dressed in a black pantsuit that fits his athletic body like a glove. Yesterday, Jama was sure the man wore a similar suit, only maybe it was green. Three days ago he wore a black sweater and jeans.

On the seat beside the man is a folded, yellow cloak atop a backpack. The scene reminds Jama of *Subterfuge Instruction* in which a similarly dressed, innocent-looking man turned out to be a highly trained police commando equipped with a Heckler MP5. The powerful submachine gun was secreted within the folds of a similar plastic sheet. But then again, maybe it is just that Jama is overwrought. If the man *had been* tipped off about his mission, why would he sit, waiting on the other platform? Surely, he is probably nothing more than an innocent traveler.

Even so, in addition to the pounding of his heart, Jama now fears that the shaking that has started throughout his body will soon give him away. His throat is so dry that it is as though he'd swallowed sawdust. Hot urine leaks its way past his tightly compressed bladder sphincter to be surely staining his crotch, if not dripping onto the platform between his feet. His armpits, he fears, are wet enough to dangerously dampen, if not trigger, the explosive mix.

Whereas initially he'd thought himself to be an ardent believer, an adherent of Islam, willing to sacrifice life and limb for the cause, in recent days, acute attacks of nervousness have seized him, involuntarily twitching various parts of his body. His lips seem to demand constant licking, as if they were in danger of sticking together. Now, on the day of all days, when according to his teaching he should feel light enough to sense himself hovering haloed above the ground, he finds himself so highly strung he can barely breathe. The abject dismay that had gripped him when he first arrived on the platform has now ballooned to almost stifle him completely.

Just when he thinks he might press the button to escape his misery, rushing prematurely to The Almighty, a sign, which previously updated the arrival time of his train, now displays in flashing, red capital letters: *Service Cancelled.* The effect is electrifying. Irritated would-be passengers, who had stood silently fuming in the abnormal heat, quickly morph into an unruly mob. Howls of disgust greet the sign change. Jackets are flung out at arm's length in contemptuous gestures at the flickering image. One enraged traveler is so driven he hurls his briefcase to the platform, with such force that there is the unmistakable sound of glass being smashed within it. Others dash about grimacing at each other, or shout profanities at the sign, as if the inert, metal-framed contraption could be to blame.

One woman, feverishly thumbing buttons on a cell phone, only to find the device's battery has apparently run down, compresses the hapless instrument between the palms of both hands in what seems to be a futile attempt to crush the innocuous gadget.

Others mill about, wearing expressions of disgust. So agitated is one man, he almost knocks Jama off the platform into the path of a nonstop express that hurtles through the station with a thunderous roar. The train vacuums the KitKat wrapper into the air, where it floats about like a small red kite before dropping back to the platform in front of the yellow-tiled toilet.

The paper acts as a marker. Jama uses the pandemonium to slip slowly away — and he hopes largely unnoticed — into the bathroom. Locked into a cubicle, he presses his hot, sweaty forehead against the smooth plastic door. The coolness of the surface, like an ice-cold poultice against his head, helps sooth his anxiety. After a short interval, he is able to carefully undo enough of the lower coat buttons to allow him to relieve pressure on his pent-up bladder.

Any second Jama expects the explosive device to activate, or the man from Platform 2 to burst open the door and for him to meet his maker as a failed disciple accompanied by a hail of bullets. But nothing untoward happens. As seconds become minutes, bedlam from the crowded platform subsides. Fewer people rush in and out of the toilet. The sound of doors being slammed closed and wrenched open subsides. He supposes that passengers have either left the station to seek bus or taxi transport home, or have moved to another platform for an alternative train.

Jama recalls his instruction: *"Should any unforeseen event happen that would jeopardize success of your assignment, you are to set off the explosive mixture immediately, amid as many infidels possible. Failing that — other than if the explosive mix fails to ignite — you are to continue on to Liverpool where you will be met off the train."*

Very shortly, if not already, he knows his superior elders will learn that the train service has been cancelled. They will be aware that there was no agreed-upon contingency plan for such eventuality. They will of course know he has not detonated.

Jama warily opens the remaining buttons on the overcoat. He struggles with the chin fastener until it finally releases. Before he takes off the coat, he takes out the Liverpool train ticket. It is the only identification on his person that proves he'd ever been at Stafford station, or indeed anywhere else. As instructed, he rolls the ticket into a tight ball, vigorously chews, and swallows. He unbuckles the waist and chest belts that strap the explosive harness around his body and carefully lowers the now uncoupled satchels beside the toilet bowl.

On the now almost-deserted platform, he sees that the seat once occupied by the 'commando man' on Platform 2 is empty. It had been his imagination after all!

With relief he removes the overcoat. But as much as he would like to be freed of the garment's unwieldy size and heavy weight, he cannot find it in him to discard the only remembrance of his father into a trash bin. Instead, he drapes the coat across his arm. Not knowing what to do, or where to go, he heads in the opposite direction, away from the stations exit sign. Being prepared for the glory of martyrdom is one thing. But an unfulfilled mission is an invitation to meet The Devil. Already, they will be after him. A car will pull up outside the station any minute, if it has not done so already.

He takes an overhead bridge that routes him to a deserted platform further still from the station entrance. Resisting the impulse to run and thus draw attention to himself, he walks as calmly as he can to the far end of the platform, down a concrete ramp and across the rail lines via a workers' walkway. Sidestepping signaling equipment, he scrambles up a steep dirt embankment and clambers over a perimeter fence to find himself in a street thick with traffic.

It has started to rain. Isolated spots splatter the hot, dry pavement, quickly linking together into overall wetness. Pedestrians run for shelter. Tires hiss over steaming asphalt. Jama is arranging the overcoat as shelter over his head, when his attention is drawn to the plight of a frail-looking elderly woman. She is standing at the curb, holding an umbrella; a white stick clutched in her other hand. The traffic continues to flash past. Each time she steps off the curb, the cane is held out at arm's length in front of her. Unseeing of vehicles braking—no doubt confused by the multitude of sounds against the gathering roar of the downpour—she repeatedly steps back and forth onto the curb, each time more visibly shaken by the experience.

Jama drops the overcoat. Impulsively, he rushes forward to place a hand beneath the woman's elbow and proceeds to escort her across the busy street. She shuffles alongside him with such agonizing slowness that traffic backs up for some distance in both directions. Drivers are impatient; angry they should have to stop at a place they otherwise never would. Those at the rear of the line cannot understand why those in front have come to a halt.

It is then, amid the din of tooting horns, the angry revving of engines, the woman now safely across the street, tap-tapping on her way, that he remembers the overcoat. And it is then, his mind a whirl of conflicting dogmas, when crossing the busy street to retrieve it, running hard into the pelting rain, that a fast-accelerating car hits him. Such is the vehicle's closing impetus; his slight body is cartwheeled through the saturated air like a rag doll, over the vehicle's hood, windshield, and roof, to drop in the gutter beside the overcoat.

Supine on the oil-slicked roadway, on which imprints of his boots still faintly record his last steps, Jama feels not pain, but a pleasant coolness spreading through his being. He takes pleasure from the rain splashing on his upturned face, even when drops fall into his eyes, his mouth. Vehicles brake. Doors slam. People yell. The growing wail of a siren sounds.

In the teeming rain, a ring of anxious faces peer down at him. A young girl, blond hair plastered to her forehead, holds the hand of an elderly woman who is crouched alongside a youth about his own age. The young man leans close. So near, Jama can feel his hot breath, bringing with it the smell of apples.

Another woman, whose dark, sad eyes remind Jama of his mother—her face contorted with concern, hair alight with moisture—stoops to wipe his brow. She holds a shopping bag before her, out of which protrudes the tip of a baguette. She reaches outside his line of vision and pulls over the overcoat, to gently pillow the garment beneath his strangely aching head. As the softness of the material cradles his face, as he takes in the familiar woolen odor, he attempts to lift a hand, intending to squeeze a thank you on the woman's arm, to tell her to protect her bread from the pouring rain.

BOWSEY WOOD

The woods are lovely, dark and deep. But I have promises to keep, and miles to go before I sleep—
Robert Frost

It was Lilly who'd decided they should go for a walk. A pleasant, leisurely taking of steps, she thought, with never an inkling it would be anything but.

"We'll go down Rackers Lane to the river, then across the field past Bowsey Wood. It shouldn't be as muddy down there," she said.

Pale, thin, hair neatly gathered and pinned, she had about her the air of a schoolmistress. Yet beneath the graying bun, that made her look older than her sixty years, behind the shell of outer sternness, there rested the quiet sadness of one whose life had been a disappointment.

"And that means *all* of us," Lilly added, looking pointedly at her daughter, Gwen, who sat at a table in the front room of her mother's house, eyeing Arthur. Lilly couldn't bear the thought of *them two* being left alone in the house together. She sighed. If only she'd found the right man, instead of Bradley drunkenly finding her. The father Gwen had never seen. A man she herself had glimpsed only once, dimly, one summer's night twenty years ago. A furtive union nonetheless, which produced the jewel that is her offspring. Ever mindful of such good fortune out of such shamefulness, Lilly was determined that the divine creation of the sordid event not be entrapped by similar circumstance.

Gwen flinched. It hurt to have her most passionate thought bared. Especially in front of others in the room. Of course Arthur was on her mind, her eyes had hardly left him since he'd arrived at the house earlier in the day. Her mother's mere mention of a walk had caused the thought of being left alone with him, to immediately spear her — sharper, she'd thought, than a tongue of fire that happened to have spurted from a coal in the room's cast iron grate.

The house stood on its own amid open farmland. Inherited from Lilly's mother, it had for years been the abode of farm laborers: strawberry pickers, potato diggers, and pea gatherers. One still cooked, ate, and lived in its square front room. Its window overlooked a small flower garden, beyond which, a mile down leafy Ashburn Road, lay the village of Brampton.

Inside, when backed up against the brightness of the window, one looked upon three walls. The one facing had the table pushed against it. Gwen sat there, head propped on a jackknifed elbow. Arthur was sprawled on a seat in the room's right hand corner, beside a wide-open door that led to a tiny kitchen. A black, polished iron fireplace, its grate cherry-red with the coal fire, took up most of the left-hand wall. Bare chestnut cupboards flanked the fireplace from floor to ceiling. Easy chairs positioned either side provided focus for the room. Lilly rose from the chair facing the window to tidy her hair in a large bevel-edged mirror that hung above a walnut sideboard set against the right-hand wall.

"And we can come back the long way," said Tom. Lilly smiled her approval at her friends willing face reflected in the mirror. He was thickset with black hair, even blacker eyebrows, and an eager-to-please manner. He sat beside Gwen at the table, absentmindedly sweeping the back of a hand over the wood grain, back and forth as though to disperse shed cigarette ash.

"Around Bowsey, over Denstone Bridge to the main road," Tom added, his shiny, freshly shaven pink face lit by the thought as if illuminated from within.

"If we keep to the riverbank, it'll not be much further than it would be along the road," he added, gushing with friendly persuasion.

A northern light flooded the room. Through the partly open window, the fragrance of wallflower and jasmine drifted in from the garden. The scent mingled with perfumes of rue, mint, and parsley, fresh bunches of which sprouted from water-filled vases on the sill. The table was half-draped with a folded, white-linen tablecloth set with jade-green Wedgwood crockery: a teapot wearing a pale lemon cozy sat alongside cups, saucers, and crumb-littered side plates.

The solemn tick-tock of a grandfather clock, the creak of the room's rug-covered, pine-boarded floor, and a faint aroma of apples—Granny Smith's laid between sheets of brown paper in the lower sideboard drawer—further authenticated the sense of old-world charm.

Tom looked at his wife, Beth, as he spoke, as was his habit even when talking to someone else. But Beth turned away to look out the window, beyond a towering elm across the road—beneath which she had played as a child—to a terraced house crowning the top of a hill. She allowed a slight nod to indicate agreement, at the same time feeling the need to change her sad expression to one of curiosity, as if estimating the tree's height. The walk would do her good, she decided, even taking the longer route as her husband had suggested. It would get Martin out of her mind, for one thing. Remembrance of the farm-worker caused a frown to pucker her small, elfin face. He was in Brampton all day, supposedly overnight at his brother's place. Was he really there, she wondered, ignoring her husband's puzzled look reflected in the glass.

She studied her own image, the thin lips, pale-blue eyes, straight-cropped mousey hair, which Martin said gave her the appearance of a schoolgirl, an image she knew he found alluring. She admitted she was not beautiful. Unlike Gwen. Attractive, possibly, she allowed. As anyone looking at her a second time might conclude. Even so, the thought of Martin spending the night with some Brampton floozy made her bite down hard on her lower lip.

"I don't have proper shoes to go out in all that muck," Gwen said. She knew it to be futile, but she had to say something, if only to dispel her mother's insinuation left hanging in the air. Resigned now to the walk, Gwen seethed and fidgeted at the table before collecting the dishes together. Rolling her eyes at Arthur, she moved over to the window to stand beside Beth.

Her movement didn't escape Arthur. He languished against the sideboard, long legs stretched out across the wide-open kitchen doorway. Sunlight from a small window above the kitchen sink played across his unshaven face. The dark-green shirt he wore picked up the color of the flecks in his hazel eyes. It was unbuttoned almost to the waist, and the sleeves were rolled high and tight around his biceps. Unruly wisps of dark hair that folded over his ears completed the almost gypsy-look about him.

He had stopped by the house to look at a kitchen cabinet Gwen's mother had asked him to paint. "Gloss white, Arthur," Lilly had said. "To match the back door. Nice and shiny to reflect the window light." But all he'd done was look at Gwen, at the dusky softness of her apple-pink cheeks that he'd kissed so ardently only the night before. And at the full lips, smeared light coral—the color of her dress—that had been pressed so hard and warmly against his mouth.

"Don't be such a baby, Gwen," Lilly said. "The fields will have dried out by now. Anyway, a bit of muck never harmed anyone, least of all you."

Gwen thought in fact the garden path looked quite dry. But she wasn't going to tell her mother that. Instead, she remembered a year ago. It was when Arthur startled her. Not long after the painter and decorator had begun making regular visits to the house to paint the outside doors. Two years earlier, his wife had died in a road accident. He'd ignored Gwen at first. And on reflection, she supposed, she had also ignored him. But on that day he'd handed her a gift, for it was her seventeenth birthday. As he did so he leaned over. She remembered his looming head. She tasted the tartness on his breath from the apple he'd been eating as he kissed her. So suddenly she had no time to arrange her lips!

Her mother, Gwen was sure, thought she'd been given a harmless peck on the cheek, as anyone would give a pretty girl on her birthday. But Arthur had carefully placed himself so as to screen what he had long dreamt of doing.

In fact, Lilly clearly saw the chemistry. Later, she reminded her daughter that when she reached Arthur's age, he would be into his sixties. "And that fine head of hair you're so fond of," she said, "will be gray as a badger."

Lilly stood at the back door herding everyone out into the garden. Tom was already in the field, broad shoulders hunched within his blue denim shirt. He needed a moment with his thoughts. *What was up with Beth?* He wondered. *And what should I do about it if it's that Martin fellow again?* Last time Beth had promised him she'd keep away.

That was after Tom had followed his wife up the hill to the cottage. He'd watched her disappear through the darkened doorway where he would later confront them. He'd thumped his fist hard against its middle panel until it split, demanding to know what was going on. Martin hadn't answered. Beth ran home in tears. Instead of slamming his fist into Martin's face, he too had turned away. Too passionately disappointed. Too hurt to do anything.

When would they ever learn to suggest things for themselves? Lilly fretted as she closed the door. Had she not said anything, she was sure they would have spent the whole day languishing. She liked to be out and about. Most Fridays, she and Beth took the bus to Derby, where they looked around the shops. Or they would go to nearby Uttoxeter to share a pot of tea together and nibble on crisp ginger biscuits at the Crest Café by the bus station. Then they'd go see a film at the Odeon.

Last week's picture had been about an elderly woman who'd run off with a younger man. It reminded her that she'd done it the other way round. Dennis Robinson was a frail, kindly man who had collapsed and died their first night together. That had been five years ago. Yet people still whispered over the coroner's report: *Heart attack, induced in part by wedding night excitement,* was stated as the cause of death.

Gwen was incensed even though the farm lane was firm and dry. Imagine, her mother speaking to her like that, and not asking properly as she did with the others. A baby, she'd called her too. And in front of Arthur! She should have stood her ground. Declared that it made more sense to walk into the village than over the muddy fields. Now she would dawdle in protest. She'd pretend to be looking at the wildflowers that grew in profusion around her. Through the tangle of vegetation, she could make out Morris's ivy-covered farmhouse where dark-haired David tended the cows and pigs for his dad. She thought of the time his muscular arms had encircled her. So tightly it brought tears to her eyes. Tears she later realized stemmed from excitement.

She turned to see the others almost disappear out of sight down the lane, below the crest of the rise that hid a view of the river. It hurt to know she'd not been missed. No one had cared, it seemed, even had she returned to the house.

Except Arthur. Dear Arthur, she thought. She adored that lost look that crept into his eyes. And the stubble he liked to keep on his chin, the feel of which she so enjoyed against her skin.

"Where's Gwen?" Arthur asked. They were at the point where the lane petered out into a field that bordered the river. If he was out for a walk, he wanted her with him. Otherwise he might want to go find her.

"She'll be here directly," Tom answered.

Down the slope Lilly and Beth laughed at each other's attempts to skim flat stones off the surface onto the far bank. Tom thought how once he and Beth had so happily done the same thing.

"I think she's in bit of a sulk," Arthur said. He chose to think of them as childlike spasms, a trait that attracted him even more. She hadn't as much looked at him all day. But then she did have to watch out for her mother. He understood the need for that. Plain and simple, Lilly was hard against him being with her. A casual friendship was acceptable, it seemed, as long as there was nothing "going on." Gwen, of course, was old enough to do whatever she wanted. He knew she was loath to do that, unless, he thought with a reflective smile, her mother didn't know about it.

It was just then that Gwen came into view. She shouted for him to wait for her. Arthur caught sight of her as she crested the rise, auburn hair held back from her face with a raised hand. The coral summer dress was filled out about her. It felt so good to hear her speak his name.

She came up breathless, pushing herself between Arthur and Tom, complaining they'd not cared a damn fig about her. "It was a test of loyalty," she said, slipping her arm easily through Arthur's. She laughed then, loud and heartily, helping to release the tension. Tom said her name had been on their lips the moment before she'd walked up. "It must have been your ears burning," he said. They all laughed at this. And Arthur pressed his arm tightly against hers. He needed contact. To know she was his.

It was Beth who suggested they cut through Bowsey. They had been following the edge of the wood for some time. Warily, it seemed to Arthur, as if circling an unfenced pit. Every now and then, they had craned to get a glimpse of what was on the other side of the crowded mix of hawthorn and blackberry that formed the hedgerow surrounding the wood. They had continued for some distance along the strip of pasture that separated the dense stretch of woodland from the river before they came upon a break. It was spanned with post and wire.

"There!" Beth said triumphantly, pointing to the gap. Tom was a little taken aback. His wife's eagerness for adventure surprised him. "We always walk around Bowsey, so this time why don't we just cut through it?" she said.

"Agreed everyone?"

Lilly's shouted "Yes" spoke for them all.

Except Gwen.

"It's too spooky in there," she said, holding back with feigned cower.

"After the happening there."

But the others were already in the wood. Tom held up the wire for her to follow. Rabbits hopped about and a pair of partridges took off in alarm to hurtle in low flight across the field—all within earshot of the familiar murmur of the river. Despite this, and seeing Arthur disappear, Gwen did not want to be left alone—there of all places—so she had no choice but to follow.

The edge of the wood was so crowded with rampant vegetation she could barely manage to see how she could follow the others who had already disappeared. She hesitated, unsure of whether to turn back. Tom pointed out to her that indeed there was a track, revealed by him parting the layer of outer greenery. Little more than a rabbit track, Arthur had thought. As the most agile of the group, he was in front. In part to impress Gwen, he'd vaulted the fence the same moment as Lilly's shouted agreement.

Lilly was at Arthur's shoulder, followed closely by Beth. Gwen and Tom brought up the rear. Gwen was struck by how quiet it was. She felt she was intruding in someone else's space that she should tiptoe back out of. Even the splash and rumble of an upstream rapid on the river had faded after a few steps. A fly buzzed briefly about her head. She swatted it away with a sweep of her hand. Thickets of birch lined the path. Their slender trunks arched around her. Numerous firs she didn't know the names of were set further back. In places the canopies entwined to form a bower through which the path threaded. Thick leaf mold muffled their footsteps. Gwen felt as though she were treading on a plush carpet. She noticed the light too, how soft it was after the glare of the open field. In place of the harsh glint off the river were blotches of soft green and brown, lanced here and there with the white bark of the birches. The vegetation hemmed her in so closely she felt squeezed along the path further into the wood. Red Admirals and Cabbage Whites silently zig-zagged in slants of sunlight that managed to penetrate the thick canopy. And not a sound! The tumble of water over stone, the caw of rooks, the cries of pewits in the fields were suddenly absent.

Beth was similarly taken aback. She stood breathing the woodland dankness deep into her lungs. She sensed the earthy sharpness vitalize her; her fingers tingled with it. Not the rustle of a single leaf disturbed the utter peace-fulness. She thought it quite uncanny. She turned to look back along the path at Gwen, who had stopped to pull seed heads off long-stemmed grasses. Scattered, they float-ed off in small clouds like swarms of tiny insects. Caught in a ray of sunshine, the drifting motes turned to gold and sparkled briefly before being extinguished by shadow. She waved at Gwen, for to speak would shatter the silence. She thought how strikingly lovely Lilly's daughter looked.

Tom, who had been walking just behind Gwen, an-swered Beth's wave mistakenly, as he thought his wife meant it for him. Beth saw the ever-so-slight downturn of his face, so she made her wave more vigorous so it was clear she intended it for him too. Not satisfied with this, she then shouted out to him—exploding the silence no dif-ferently than had she thrown open a door to a noisy room—"Slowcoach, get a move on, catch me if you can," repeating the taunts several times until they took the form of a ditty, all the while marveling at how lucky she was to have snared such a wonderful companion in the first place. For there had been plenty more attractive women he could have had, many with money. Yet, he chose her, a farm la-borer's daughter. One who cheated! The thought knifed her; so much that she vowed as soon as they got back she would go see Martin. She'd tell him they were finished—this time for good. Then somehow, she didn't know how, or where, or when, she would make it up to her Tom. Why, she might admit to it outright. On her hands and knees, she would beg his forgiveness! She was so startled with the burst of goodness that flooded her; she held his anxious gaze until the woodland blurred, until the trees morphed into a wash of browns, yellows, burnt umbers, and dark greens.

Arthur didn't look back. Oblivious to the natural beauty, he barely had the sense of where he was. His mind was consumed with Gwen. How he wished she wasn't twenty-five years younger than him, that she would be more like Beth. More mature. That she would calm down and lose some of the childishness that beset her from time to time. It could come upon her like a fit.

There hadn't been much opportunity for them to be alone together. He whistled tersely through his teeth at this thought, for he knew it wasn't for the lack of trying on his part. Her energetic freshness is what drove him. Achingly. As it did now.

The woodland itself was conducive to affection. The fresh air was romance in itself. It made him think of peeling off Gwen's summer frock, undoing the buttons one by one—with a practiced flick of finger against thumb—down its front until the flimsy sheath, held now only by the cloth belt, fell away to reveal the delicate layers beneath. He imagined clandestinely being with her again on the hard wooden floor of his parents' high-roofed porch. Or in their favorite place, the backseat of his father's prized black Austin, conveniently parked in the unlit garage to protect its mirror finish from the weather. They'd lay stretched out on the leather seats, which in the heat of the moment gave off a faint animal odor. With her sweet perfumes and his sharp underarm odor, the mixed fragrances heightened the intimacy. He recalled them having each other in that place forbidden for two adults to occupy at the same time, to build from their previous encounter there, when desire stoked a need to press together, hard against the cool glossy wall, through which intricate outlines of bricks and mortar showed. The flush of the toilet helped drown out the soft grunts and breathed whimpers he was sure that his parents must still hear, even above the radio that blared incessantly in the front room.

His parents had come to dislike his wife almost as much as he had. A divorce was on his mind the day of Anita's accident. They had grown unsuited to each other. Simple as that. Still, her death had come as a shock. It was two full years before he could as much as look at another woman. Then, he had set eyes on Gwen.

"Arthur, for Christ's sake. Are you deaf?"

It was Lilly.

"What!"

They had all come together where the path widened to form a small clearing.

"I was asking you, Arthur, where they found the girl's clothes. It was supposed to have been somewhere in this wood, wasn't it?"

She had sensed his preoccupation, the subject matter on his mind. But there was little she could do about it.

"Here somewhere, I suppose, yes," Arthur managed. "Exactly where I don't know."

"It was twenty-eight years ago. I do know that," Lilly said. "Mid-August 1955 it would be. Very close to today's date if I'm not mistaken. I was thirty, while you, Arthur, would have been a skinny, pimply-faced youth. And my dear Gwen wasn't even born."

"Did they ever find them?" Arthur asked, determined to appear not to notice Lilly's pointed reminder.

"Beth, did they ever find those three girls?" Lilly asked.

She was just glad to see her friend more relaxed, after being so worried-looking all day. Like almost everyone else, Lilly had heard rumors of Beth's affair with Martin Sadler. Now semi-estranged man and wife were looking lovingly at each other. Most delightfully precious, she thought, was the sudden change that appeared to have beset them.

"Not that I'm aware of," Beth said. "In the end, people spoke of them being spirited away. Like in that movie."

"Picnic at Hanging Rock," Tom said, tightening his arm around his wife. Beth gripped his thick fingers. Squeezed them against her waist. At the same time she looked away, to hide brimming tears. Tom was just thankful she'd come out of it. Whatever state it was she'd been in.

"Yes, what happened, Beth? Do tell us," Gwen said with embellished wonder. She stood now beside Arthur, transfixed upon a particularly dense part of the wood. She was trying to imagine in her mischievous way what it would be like to be lost in such entanglement. She wondered what might be hiding in a particular spot that lay beyond the clearing. It was a place seemingly little different than the rest of the wood, a thatch of undisturbed peeling branches, slivers of bark, twigs and leaves. Ideal, she thought, for someone or something to hide, to pounce, to seize. She idly half-muttered, half-smiled to herself as she stood spellbound with enchantment at the scene.

"It was thought they drowned," Beth said. "Never proven, mind you, as there were no bodies. All that was found were clothes, neatly folded, and stacked in three piles. It was as if the girls had gone for a swim, yet so far from the river that the idea was thought unlikely."

"It's not that far, Beth," Gwen said. She was enjoying holding hands with Arthur. Defiantly, in full view of her mother.

"If you were going for a swim, Gwen, wouldn't you want to change as near to the river as possible?" Tom asked. "Or at least just inside the wood. I mean, why come all this way? It must be all of a ten-minute walk to the fence. It just doesn't make sense. Another thing that doesn't fit, is if they drowned in the river why didn't their bodies wash up somewhere? You would have thought at least one of them would."

"We don't know that it was exactly here though, Tom," Lilly said. "It could have been closer to the river, at the edge of the wood, possibly even where we came in. That appears to be the only place one could enter or, indeed, leave."

"It could have been further away," Arthur said. He was enjoying the feel of Gwen's hand clinging onto his.

Lilly looked away. Her eyes spoke of being the odd one out. She realized she envied her daughter. At the same time, she found that she could not dislike Arthur. At least, not as much as she had at one time thought she could. She sensed a bond developing.

"They're still listed as missing, as far as I know," Tom said. "The police scoured the countryside. They came from all over. Hundreds of men were walking in line at a snail's pace. Strung out side by side, they examined every inch of the wood. It was weeks before they gave up the search. Yet the police came up empty. Those girls vanished into thin air. Damn weird, if you ask me."

"What?" Lilly asked. She stared exaggeratedly open-mouthed at Tom. "They found *nothing*? Nothing at all? Not even a footprint? Surely, there must have been *some* sign."

"Only the bashed up hedgerow," Beth said. "I remember that bit in the paper. It appeared to have been charged into, like if an angry bull had been let loose at it. I suppose it could just have easily been a frightened deer or even an enraged badger. Then again, the hedgerow could have always been caved in like that."

"Or a cow, Beth, what about that? A stampeding, mad cow," Gwen said, laughing at her choice of words.

"Nobody really knows," Beth said. "Except that the damage seemed to have been done by something trying to get out of Bowsey instead of in."

"Right, enough morbid talk," Lilly said. She held her hand out to Beth, shaking it impatiently. "Come on. Let's get going, or we'll be too late back. Remember, we have strawberries and cream. After, there's the cricket match in the village. For sure there'll be another way out at the end of this path. If not, we'll just turn around and come back."

"Yes, come on, Gwen," Beth said. "We've been in this spooky wood long enough."

Gwen took Beth's offered hand. She gripped the extended fingers tightly. She too had heard the rumors. But Gwen trusted her friend. She was sure things would turn out right for her one day. And just maybe today was that day.

And so Lilly, Beth and Gwen, linked like a daisy chain in the manner of skipping chorus girls, jigged down the path to where it curved, to where its line became lost in innumerable verdant shades. To where the birches, the firs, the tall grasses met. Into which the dancing figures disappeared, leaving behind only the sound of their voices.

Until they too faded.

The abrupt departure of the women had left the two men so profoundly alone they could but gaze about, not quite sure in which direction to look, there being so much to see, yet so little to focus on, so blended was the woodland scene. Tom likened it to a piece of fine mahogany. Close up, he reasoned, he would see the whorls, knots, crevices, each defect exquisitely detailed, yet further away the discrete images would blur so it would be impossible to discern any feature at all. It was therefore understandable under such circumstance that the two men should seek the comfort of familiarity that they should at the same time turn toward one another.

That was when Arthur first detected unease in Tom's face. Normally perkily fresh, a countenance he knew only too well: rounded, on the pudgy side perhaps, but with an enviable smooth jaw line that sleekly became neck. The familiar pockmarks were there, as were the puffed-out, vein-streaked cheeks that gave Arthur the impression something was concealed within the mouth. But Tom's eyes had widened to be out of proportion to his forehead, while his mouth unmistakably gaped. It was as though an important memory had been recalled.

And Tom saw changes in Arthur's taller, gaunter face, with its familiar bushy eyebrows, raised like tiny humpback bridges. They were now too closely knitted. And his head tilted upward, as if he were sniffing for dangerous scents, as would an alert dog.

Then there was the quietness. More total, more absolute than before, when the weighty silence, broken by the occasional girlish yelp, was so distinct. It was a hush that pressed heavily upon them, as though the belly of a dense cloud had sagged upon the canopy, stifling all sound.

The giggles, the chatter, the banter were gone.

Arthur stirred first, as if from a stupor, ostensibly to shake off a sense of morbidity that had suddenly come upon him. At first, he continued his country stroll, ambling along the path in a loose gait. Being so long-legged, it was more of a lope, trailing a hand to brush the grass fronds as he went. But he soon felt the need to quicken, imperceptibly at first, and then to demand increased pace, as if rain was threatening and he'd spied shelter ahead. The pressure to move faster built until he felt it in his hands, legs and shoulder blades. At the same time he tried not to appear to be in a hurry.

"I mean, why should I be?" he gasped incredulously.

But he was soon into a jog, then more astonishing still, a run that accelerated with each stride until he was leaning forward, head back in the manner of a sprinter about to breast the tape, racing madly toward the thicket-shrouded corner, unable to understand what it was that made him want to get there so frenziedly, other than a desire to see around it! To confirm that he was not the last person in the world, let alone in Bowsey Wood. And to verify that it was merely a trick of light that caused the scene ahead to remain the same, such that the apex of the curve was an equal distance away, no matter how he strained, or how furiously he threw his body toward it, or pushed his protesting legs to go faster. Faster still when the thought of never seeing Gwen again struck him!

And now Tom, who had watched speechless as Arthur sped away, felt the urge to move too, quickly, through his loins, spreading like pins and needles, such that there was no time even for a last glance up through the green tracery into what in that instant was broken cloud fronting a cerulean sky—so hurried was he to find out what had beset Arthur. It was in this state of bewilderment that he realized he should never have let Beth out of his sight, not even for the time it took her to move behind a single intervening tree! So rapt was Tom with this thought, he built pace even faster than Arthur had, to reach the bend quicker, only to see nothing beyond it, other than dense vegetation going on and on, seeming endlessly, always the same length of path ahead as appeared with each fearful glance snatched backward, such that after a few minutes of frantic running, he felt he'd arrived back at where he'd just left!

It was only when near the end of their tether, legs on the point of collapse, arms flapping to pump more air into protesting lungs, that the path straightened to reveal in all its sun-drenched richness, a hawthorn and blackberry blossom-festooned hedgerow. Embedded invitingly in this riot of color was a post and wire fence section, similar to what had been encountered when they had first entered the wood. Lilly stood beyond the fence, hands on hips in the buttercup-and-daisy-dotted meadow, a sliver of silver river as backdrop. She was uncertain whether to openly laugh at the two men charging neck and neck toward her or to cry. The look of consternation stole over her face, as would the shadow of a cloud creeping across a sunlit field.

"Are they being chased?" she laughed disbelievingly. "A swarm of bees perhaps? Or have they inexplicably decided to race each other?"

Beth laughed too, albeit weakly, her expression tinged with worry at the sight of her Tom in such a flustered state, a wild, almost crazed look in his bluebell-blue eyes. She was holding the wire up for Gwen who, stooped of posture, was in the act of scrambling beneath.

Gwen was troubled by the sight of Arthur, who she saw over the top of her knees—the coral dress, rather fetchingly, having been drawn up to keep it off the ground—flushed with an uneasiness of countenance that she had never seen before on the face of any man, let alone hers. At the same time, she found herself increasingly elated by the thought that his expression was simply the result of being consumed with sheer wonderment at seeing her.

JESSE JAMES

Give a boy a rubber duck and he'll seize it by the neck like the butt of a pistol and shout "Bang!" —*George F. Will*

I've always been an avid watcher of the Western movie. As a kid, I loved outlaws, stagecoach holdups and gunfights, as much as I did parading around in Western outfits. The biggy for me was the gun draw. I was so obsessed with pulling a holstered weapon that I became quite fast myself. I guess I took after dad. He too was a fan of the Western.

So it's not surprising that I learned about the various guns cowboys sported, the buckskins they wore and the horses they rode. I have childhood memories of gunfights staged in our backyard. Or in the house, straddling a chair arm, holding onto imagined reins.

Of all incidents that happened during this time, there is one that remains unforgettable in memory. It is the one I'm going to tell of now.

It all started on an unusually hot Denver day. Early fall as I recall: trees hung-dog, browned lawns, heat billowing off shimmering asphalt and concrete sidewalks. Everything spent.

"Don't laugh," he said, "but my name's Jesse James."

Well I almost did, for if anyone was going to pretend being the outlaw, surely it couldn't be this pint-sized fellow. But the stubbled chin, the black-flared necktie were there, as was the sleek, swept-back hair. And an unlit stub of what could have been a real cheroot stuck out the corner of his mouth. His face was ashen, long, and pinched, as if life had left it.

What set him apart was that he was so short. Four-foot nothing I estimated. About my height. Slim, but offset somewhat by the bulk of the twin pistols he packed. From the look of the butts, good quality imitation Colts, the same guns I'd been looking at earlier in an illustrated booklet, given to me by my dad.

The glossy front cover depicted the infamous outlaw, waistcoat tails flying, in the act of rushing out of a bank, clutching a money sack. Through the partly open door could be seen the figure of a shirt-sleeved man sprawled on the floor. He had on one of those green eyeshades. A teller I decided he was.

This Jesse stood hands on hips, feet astride, not twenty foot in front of me. His forearms held back the flaps of a black waistcoat, similar to the one in the picture. The guns, side by side, jutted out the center of a wide, silken waistband. They appeared absurdly large against his small stature. But it was the rock-steady gaze that finally did it.

That said. "Go on, draw."

That choked off my laugh. That made me think it must have been the last act of the teller. The sun felt suddenly hot on my back, the air as still as a stopped clock.

Fast as lightning, he pulled one of the Colts. A classic cross-arm draw I remembered described in the picture book, right hand reaching the gun left of center. The revolver jumped immediate and heavy into his small hand. It was all a bit unnerving. I'd thought at first the handguns were imitation. But handled in this way, along with the unmistakable sound of solid wood on metal, slapping into the palm of a hand, they seemed decidedly real.

That's when I became conscious of my own pair, slung around my waist on a star-studded Roy Rogers belt. And my two ninety-nine black Stetson, plastic chaps outfit.

I'd thought myself fast. Dad's stopwatch timed me once at a quarter-second to clear the holster. To fire the cap. Compared to Jessie I might as well have been pulling a rifle. I felt caught out. Stranded. Unsure.

But I didn't draw.

Jesse twirled the Colt. Quite expertly, on an index finger hooked through the trigger guard. Then like magic, he slotted it back behind the waistband. He drew the other Colt left-handed just as quick. The pistol pointed straight at me, the very instant it left its silken berth. Just as fast, just as slickly, the gun was pushed back next to its twin.

"Wow!" It's all I could think of saying.

"That was really something. Never seen a gun pulled that fast. Even in movies."

The pallid face crinkled into a grin.

"It's all right, I'm in the show."

"Well," I stammered, "thanks for the great preview."

"My pleasure."

"You don't mean the Western Fair in Zamora?"

"Yep, been challenged, so got to appear."

"Really! Who against?"

"Believe he goes by Jed Mason."

"And what would your name be Mister? Your real one?"

"Like I told you. Jesse James."

He spoke laconically in a Midwestern drawl. Just like I'd long imagined Jesse would have. As he walked away, I'm sure there was the chink of spurs, the whinny of a waiting horse.

I yelled after him. "Jesse, what time's the show?"

"Eight," he said, throwing the reply over his shoulder.

"I'll be there!" I shouted back.

Dad told me I'd be disappointed. I knew he would say something like that. For he liked to dampen the overly excited. Not in an unpleasant way. Far from it. Rather, to weight things outlandish-seeming into a more practical perspective. With the benefit of hindsight, more often than not his pronouncements proved accurate.

"Those fairs," he said, "especially the so-called Western ones, are all the same. Little different than the last Zamora Show we went to. Remember son, a year ago? Then, the one the year before that? You'll recognize the same clowns. Firing blanks for sure. Much as what you do with your own cap pistols. That can be fun. But the rest, the steer, the horse riding is pretty tame stuff.

"From what you say, there's probably some kind of shoot-out act planned. So you'll get to see your Jesse James," he added with a laugh.

Dad was right. The show was pretty much the same as what we'd seen many times before. At the more famous Loveland and Cheyenne venues. We had a commanding view. Good seats right up front. The organizers had put together the familiar sawdust ring. Basically, a circle of hay bales, within whose perimeter pounded a pair of pinto horses: galloped side-by-side, riders astride both mounts, twirling lassoes. They were so close I could smell them. Could almost reach out and touch their sweat-streaked flanks. Look up into flared, snorting nostrils. The thumping hooves threw up bits of straw and clay, tiny crumbs of which showered onto the program held open on my lap.

All a bit exciting. But I had seen it all before.

Of Jesse there was no sign. Nor was there mention of him or Jed in the program. There was however a hint: the words *Special Event* had been penned in.

As for Jed Mason, no one had ever heard of him. People smiled when asked. Told me I'd been had. "All part of Zamora marketing," said one thickset man. "Maybe your Jesse will rob a bank in town while he's here," another chortled.

As the last act came to an end, when people were readying to leave, the organizer appeared in the center of the ring. Under the blaze of a spotlight and the blare of recorded trumpets, the announcer bellowed, "Since this is the last performance of our famed Zamora Western Show, a special, exciting extra event has been arranged to celebrate it. Therefore everyone please remain seated."

As you can imagine, I didn't need to be told.

Neither it seemed did anyone else.

Except Dad, who was up and ready to go.

"C'mon son," he said. "We'd better be on our way."

"But Dad," I said. "Jesse might be coming on."

And as I spoke, he did!

The trumpets sounded again. "Please welcome Jesse James from Kearney, Missouri!"

Laughter tumbled around the audience.

The thickset man laughed uproariously. "Jesse James! How about Midget Man," he yelled out.

I sat tight-lipped, thinking, wow, wasn't Kearny the place the real Jesse James came from!

A youth was sat beside me. He wore a Stetson, held on his head by a drawstring beneath the chin. He stood and to gales of laughter, whooped: "C'mon' tiny, you can do it!"

I remained silent. Drew in a deep breath. Rolled up, twisted, and untwisted the program one more time.

I felt let down. More so because Jesse appeared even smaller against the backdrop of high canvas than he had in the street. He did indeed look like a midget. The announcer, a tall, muscular fellow, only served to heighten the effect. It looked like father with young kid. Maybe he should be holding the announcer's hand, I thought.

Still, Jesse appeared unperturbed by the heckling. He was clearly the same Jesse who'd jokingly challenged me. The Jesse who'd pulled pistols so lightning fast I was left speechless. Either that, or I was looking at an identical twin.

Another blast of trumpets signaled the announcer to introduce "Our other competitor!

"Jed Mason from Colorado Springs!"

A fancy, cowboy-looking fellow arrived in the ring, vaulting the bales from the other side. He stood—legs wide astride, arms, hands arched as if about to draw—in gleaming-white buckskins, slung with a twin-holstered, black-leather gun belt. In the holsters gleamed what appeared to be pearl-handled pistols. Judging by the solid, steely appearance of them, I decided they could only be real.

The crowd, quiet with the repetitive horse riding, roared their approval as the name of each contestant was announced. Derisive whistles could be heard too.

The announcer joined them in the center of the ring. From his pocket, he produced a silver dollar. At least that's what he said it was. Probably a shiny metal disc that looked like one. I was getting to be as cynical as dad. Turning to the two men, the announcer told them the "dollar" was going to be flicked high in the air and that they each had one shot to try hitting it. "For safety reasons," he said, "the target will be cast high, behind the ring, in the opposite direction, and well away from spectators."

A section of canvas roof had been folded back to reveal a finely meshed net in its place. "The spinning coin," he said, "will flash quite brightly as it crosses the floodlight beams. As you can see these are arranged along both sides of the section over which the coin will travel, so for sure you'll all get a view of it and consequently, be able to see any hits.

"Rest assured, the spent bullet will pass clean through the net. But not the silver dollar." He held the "coin" up between thumb and forefinger for all to see as he spoke.

"Even if the dollar can't be clearly seen by those seated at the back, the sound of a hit will be heard," the announcer added.

Jed went first. The coin—flicked in the air with the aid of some kind of elastic catapult—soared like a shooting star as it tumbled and flashed through the blaze of light.

With a blur of motion, Jed drew, fired.

Ping! Clearly a hit!

The crowd howled in disbelief. I must admit the noise of the 'hit' did sound a bit like someone striking a tin lid. To my reckoning as well, the sound was not quite in sync with the gunshot.

Dad shuffled uneasily in his seat. Glanced at his watch.

"A simple trick, son," he said, smiling down at me. "An illusion. But a brilliant, elaborately rehearsed one, nevertheless. The claim that the coin, or more likely polished metal disc, was hit with a bullet fired from the man's pistol is clearly absurd. Such precise accuracy on such a small, fast-moving target, and with an unsighted weapon is humanly impossible. Other than from a one-in-a-million chance of an incredibly lucky strike. A possibility so remote I'm sure the promoter of the event would in no way want to entertain. The man fired his pistol all right. A blank it would be, though. Gun drawn at lightning speed. No doubt about that. To point in good time in the direction of the coins flight. The trigger pulled at the instant the disk fell out the beam, so as to disappear from sight at that instant. At the same time, when the shooter pulls the trigger, someone backstage raps hard on a metal object, to simulate the ding of a bullet striking a coin. Very clever. But clearly a well-constructed simulation."

I felt dejected, let down by Jesse, even though, as yet, he hadn't taken his shot. When he did, I was sure he would also claim a "hit" because of what dad had said.

The explanation just made so much sense.

I looked intently at him, trying to pick out some clue that might disprove dad's theory.

He stood pretty much as he had when facing me on the street: short legs astride, hands on hips, forearms holding back the tails of the waistcoat. Clearly, he was ready to draw and fire the moment the target was pitched in the air.

I thought of the real Jesse James and how he gunned down the teller. How he would then stash the stolen money in a saddle bag, leap on his horse—no doubt rearing and snorting while tethered outside the bank—to ride out of town in a cloud of dust. I could be sure this Jesse wasn't going to be doing that.

The announcer had moved around to my side the ring. Quite close to where I sat. Alone, Jesse didn't look quite so small. The presenter was talking in a low voice to another man, a dapper-looking fellow who looked like the promoter. Or possibly he was the Zamora Show's owner. They were arguing over something. I've been told that I'm unusually sharp of hearing, so I found myself able to make out snatches of what was being said, even though the conversation was hoarsely whispered.

The dapper man was speaking. "Sure you've got enough doctored ones scattered back there," he seemed to be saying. "They'll for sure be clamoring to see one or two before long."

"Plenty," I thought the announcer answered. The word was hissed out the corner of the man's mouth.

That settled it for me. Clearly, the shooting was bogus. But I still wanted to watch Jesse's performance. Just to see his draw again would be special.

The target pitch for Jesse, I thought followed a higher arc than the one flicked for Jed. This gave the audience more time to pick the disc out as it spun through the flood-light beams. The crowd had never seen a handgun drawn so fast. Far faster than Jed's pull. And from a tight waist-band, not from a low-slung holster. It was incredible to see. Even dad gasped as the shot rang out.

The coin was somewhat predictably "blown from the beam" with a loud ping.

Another incredible hit! So it seemed.

Some in the crowd went wild. But most could be heard openly laughing. As was dad sitting alongside me.

Four more times Jed "hit" the disc. Four more times Jesse replied with "hits."

The two appeared to be deadlocked. But more and more of the crowd were now openly crying, "Fake!

"Show us the coins," they yelled!

I was caught up in the excitement too.

"Yes," I shouted, "find the coins."

"Show them to the doubters!"

Dad learned forward. Whispered in my ear.

"They'll do just that son," he said. "That's what the organizer wants to hear. The "coins" of course have been previously prepared. Shot at probably. At close range. Then placed below the net, behind the ring."

I groaned with disappointment. Now I knew what the announcer had meant. Yet it had all looked so real.

I stared at Jesse. I wanted to catch his eye. Will him to somehow prove he had fired a real bullet to hit the coin.

The organizer announced that three coins had been found. A little bent and twisted, they lay in the palm of the presenter's hand. One even had a hole through it. He walked in among the crowd showing off the "evidence." One sneering onlooker could be heard yelling, "What size drill did you use?" There were loud laughs as the announcer moved around the outside of the ring, offering spectators a closer look at the damaged targets.

Increasingly, jeers rang out. Shouts of "those are not the same coins" arose from a section of more rowdy onlookers. They were soon joined by others chanting "Fakes! Fakes!"

Amid the uproar, the announcer joined Jesse and Jed back in the center of the ring where he held up an arm of each contestant. The man shouted loudly into the microphone "I declare it a tie! There will be an immediate single-shot shoot-off!"

The crowd scoffed.

"Better get more dinged coins," one man yelled.

"Get one with a hole drilled through it," said another.

Jed stood laughing. He appeared to be enjoying himself, if nothing else.

Jesse remained impassive, arms straight at his side, clenching and unclenching his hands.

That was the moment when a spectator chose to step into the ring. His intention was to return the "coins" the announcer had passed around. Holding the one with the hole through it high above his head, he turned to the announcer and asked that if he covered the hole with a postage stamp that had his signature written across it, could he get the two contestants to agree to use *that* target for the shoot off?

Dad turned to me to say that he knew the man.

"It's Mr. Davies," he said. "He lives a couple of blocks along the street from us. In fact, you sometimes play with his son, Tommy."

I recognized him too then. At the same time I saw Tommy sitting with his mom a few rows back from the bales.

I raised a triumphant fist in his direction to show that I thought his dad's plan was an excellent "gottcha." Tommy waved back.

The boy beside me wearing the Stetson yelled. "Yes! Yes! That's it! Let 'em try shootin' through that!"

The announcer spoke into the microphone, telling the audience of Mr. Davies's request.

Dad leaned close. "This is for real son," he said. "For sure, nobody's going to entice Ed Davies to take part in any scam. I can vouch for that. They'll now announce that for some reason they can't do that. They can only target full, new "coins," or something to that effect."

The announcer was already shaking his head, making out some excuse, just as dad had predicted.

Jesse then spoke for the first time. He told the announcer to stick the stamp on.

"Then get it flicked," he said.

Oh, I loved that. Apart from the Midwestern drawl, my idol had thrown out a direct challenge, clearly a risky move, bearing in mind that he was about to attempt the impossible. But it made me feel so proud. I wanted to vault the bales, give my Jesse James a bear hug.

Jed snatched the microphone. Clearly, he wanted to be seen to be equally enthusiastic. But was more hesitant.

"Yeah, yeah, go on," he finally managed. "Spin it."

With minimum fuss, Jed and Jesse emptied their guns of the presumed blanks.

At the sight of this, more yells of "I told you so" and "fakes" rippled around the arena.

Each contestant then inserted a single round of what was presumed to be live ammunition.

Jed would go first. He took some time settling into his stance. Hunched over. Slight forward lean. Arms limply bowed. Right hand cupped, ready to grip the handle of the pistol at his right hip. I noticed the holsters had a low front rim. This meant he could almost straightaway level the gun and fire without the need for much vertical pull. The holster rim may even have been hinged to avoid the need for any vertical pull at all. Even so, I had to admit, he had to be real quick on the draw and incredibly accurate to pick out the flight path and hit such a relatively small spinning target.

The announcer's catapult flicked the coin.

Jed fired. I thought I heard the tiniest ping of bullet hitting metal. Dad said he heard nothing. Jed obviously thought he'd scored a hit because he held his arms up high in triumph. If there was any contact at all, I thought it more realistic sounding than the earlier generated ping.

The stricken coin caromed into the net. Dropped to the ground. I applauded. The crowd roared their approval. That certainly looked and sounded incredibly real.

Dad couldn't believe it.

"Extraordinary accuracy," was all he managed to say.

Mr. Davis rushed over. Found the target, brought it back to the center of the ring. The announcer inspected the coin. Handed it back to Mr. Davis, who held it up for all to see.

Since most were too far away to make out the condition of the "coin," Mr. Davis announced "in his opinion, Jed's bullet had possibly made the faintest of nicks on the edge of the target." He then added, "there was no doubt in his mind that Jed had indeed succeeded in achieving the impossible, albeit registered by the tiniest of nicks." The crowd went wild. Madly cheered the Colorado cowboy's amazing feat of marksmanship.

Dad stood and cheered too.

Jed swept off his Stetson. Bowed expansively.

It was now Jesse's turn.

"The stamp's still intact though. It still covers the hole," Mr. Davies said.

I held my breath.

The audience was shocked into anticipatory silence.

Dad's face formed a picture of concentration.

The silvery disc was again spun high into the still air. Again it twirled toward the apex of its travel, glinted with flashes of reflected light, momentarily hung in its flight, its upward momentum cancelled by gravity's pull.

Jesse drew. My God, how I loved that draw!

The single crack of his shot rang out.

Silence! No metallic ping! Surely no contact this time.

There was a stunned hush at first, as reaction set in. Then mutterings building to heated conversation.

The announcer grabbed Jed's hand. Thrust it high, at arms length above his head.

"The winner!

"Applaud the winner!

"Ladies and Gentlemen, I give you the worlds greatest sharpshooter. Jed Mason of Colorado Springs!"

The crowd was now standing, making ready to leave, seemingly exhausted from cheering and applauding. Some, mostly those who sat furthest back from the ring, were still convinced that the shooting had somehow been rigged. Others looked admiringly at Jed. Dad remained seated, deep in thought, wondering too I assumed.

My view blocked, I lost sight of Jesse. Obviously, like anyone else after such buildup and fanfare, he'd wanted to be out of the place as quick as possible. Distance himself as far as possible from the scene of failure.

My heart sank. Dad placed a consoling arm around me. "For every contest, son," he said, "there has to be a loser. I don't think you've yet seen the Western movie where a shooting match similar to this takes place. One day I'll take you to see it."

But I was too focused to think about an old movie. This was for real. A rising commotion from the other side of the straw-bale ring was beginning to claim attention. People had begun to mill around the figure of Mr. Davies. They obviously wanted to see the outcome of the shootout close up; check the damage to the target disc. Dad hoisted me on his shoulders so I could get a better look.

Tommy's dad was once more atop the straw bale. In his white shirt he stood out like a beacon under the spot-lights. It seemed that after Jesse's shot, Mr. Davies had managed to retrieve the disc again. There was an incredu-lous look on his face as he held it up between thumb and forefinger. He was pointing to the stamp, or what ap-peared to be left of it, since there was a hole through it.

ACROSS THE CRYSTAL SEA

It's always ourselves we find in the sea—E. E. Cummings

Nate was convinced Marko was nuts. Not in the sense that he was sometimes incoherent, or prone to wild swings in behavior—which might otherwise call for a straightjacket—but in the way the inmate went on about a "Crystal sea." Marko would rave about how lucidly emerald his sea was, about how it seethed atop the wall of a rearing swell, about how it furled as it neared a shoreline, but it seemed that the detainee couldn't quite get his mind around his water-wall being transparent, yet at the same time, not being clear enough to see into.

The word Marko sought of course was *translucency;* a term Nate knew would never have entered the fellow inmate's head. And even had it done so, Marko's fogged brain could not have figured its meaning. Think of your crystal sea as "a milky white glue spread unevenly over emerald colored paper," Nate once told him.

Nate was convinced that Marko couldn't discern color either, for the world of Saint Georges certainly wasn't emerald. The exterior façade was in fact a hideous brownstone. And from whichever direction the interior of the edifice was viewed, Nate knew Marko also saw brown. Or a nicotine-stained version of that hue. Or worse, that dead color tinged with gray. Or worse still, a tobacco-brown touched with urine-yellow.

On nights when Nate lay supine in his bed, he would gaze at a wash of painted ceiling, caught in the glow cast by a single bulb. Wisps of air from a vent high in the wall caused the globe to swing slightly, too and fro on its long cord—like a pendulum stroking off time—the circle of light becoming faintly ellipse at each end of the bulb's travel. Despite Marko's insistent raving, Nate's ceiling, like all the other ceilings throughout the building, wasn't bright green. Nothing but nothing was *bright* in Saint Georges. The distemper was in fact a crappy, peeling fawn. Linoleum, the color of shit.

Saint Georges wasn't only about blandness and sameness. There were the stinks to contend with. In addition to bathroom ones—that could linger for days before being overwhelmed by newer stenches—there was the insidious odor of floor polish, a warm, sickly smell that defied description, along with the reek of stale cigarette smoke that hung in the air as though a cabbage-leaf bonfire smoldered in the ward. Each day, added to this base foulness was the stink of some soup concoction, mixed with the smells of whatever else had been cooked that day. As each meal's odors mixed with the previous day's and the days' before that, going back as much as a week—until the menu repeated—the stench became unspeakably vile.

Yet, after a few hours in the ward, the odors became less noticeable. It was only when fresh air chanced to drift in from an opened door that one noticed the difference. When a newcomer entered the ward—the heavy, double-locked door creaking inward as if hung on coarsely cut wooden cogs—a crinkle-nosed, grimacing face was revealed, seemingly about to sneeze. The unfortunate person had no doubt realized his or her misfortune at having exited an endless maze of beige-walled, beige linoleum-floored corridors, to arrive at a wrong beige door. It was only then; amid the inward rush of fresher air that one realized how nauseatingly foul it was inside.

Toward the end of one particular day, when the temperature outside was in the high eighties and the main stench inside was boiled cod laced with body odor, Marko happened to be standing with his back to a window that caught the setting sun. Nate noticed that when he aligned Marko's head with the golden orb, the resulting apparition glowed around its circumference like a beacon.

A guiding lamp at sea? A lighthouse?

Nate was mesmerized by the effect. He found he couldn't turn away from the sphere. Not that there was anything else to compete for his attention. Around him Nate was faced with blandness. Sameness: wide swathes of wishy-washy linoleum studded with brown plastic chairs; fixed expressions on familiar pasty faces. So Nate continued to stare and saw Marko's crystal sea.

And not just the brilliant, bright-green color of it.

The wallow, the slap, the chop were there!

He saw too the sparkle of wavelets—countless mirrored slants turned by deep, heaving undertows, warped on their axes through immeasurable glinting angles.

Nate never told anyone about what he'd seen that day. The vision had tingled his skin so needle-sharply that he had to lie down awhile to control a burst of the shakes. He didn't let on how giddy he'd felt either.

Least of all to Nurse Robinson. The tall, overly made-up medication orderly had been called to subdue Marko, who'd been screaming to Nate that his crystal sea was "way up the outside wall."

"Come look," he'd cried, slobbering heavily on nurse's pristine white cuff. "Come see. Here! Out the window!"

Nate laughed at Marko yelling stuff like that. *Madder than hell*, he'd thought. Just the same, he couldn't resist a peek, even if it meant taking his eyes off Nurse Robinson. And even though he knew Saint Georges to be a five-story edifice fifty miles inland. After all, he needed to look somewhere, other than the plastic floor covering at which he'd been staring all morning. He knew he'd see nothing there, but a shitty, shiny beige lake, one that could never harbor life.

A crystal sea, how preposterous!

But Nate looked.

A week later, when a boisterous sail-filling wind bent the sycamores, and whirled dust up to their third-story window—scattering leaves as big as dinner side plates across the lawns—Nate tried concentrating again. Yet, try as he might, he could not detect the sting of saltiness. Nor, could he hear the cry of a seagull. So Nate told Marko that day that "he suffered from a mind malfunction." "You're delusional," Nate told him.

As always, Leon had looked on, eyes determinedly squinting. His thick, scum-rimmed lips perpetually trembled in silent prayer. The manic religious muttering was conducted clutching a three-inch-thick Bible, a massive, stained, and spotted holy book that was always with him, but never opened.

Nate had long decided that inside Leon's slab of a head, topped with a raft of close-shaven beige hair—like a skin burn—was not candle-lit altar with attendant shrouded figure, as a religious-leaning person might suppose, or even a gleaming set of pearly gates, but a profound inky-blackness, speckled, possibly, with elaborate patterns of white flecks off the inside of his eyelids.

Norm stood by, drooling heavily into his hands. Wet with saliva, his bony fingers—delicate, skeletally white—were held arched about his face. As they jerked, as they rubbed against each other, as they picked and poked, Nate was reminded of feeding crabs. The crustacean illusion was heightened at mealtime. Shunning knife and fork, Norm ate busily, sweeping food into his mouth using each finger set alternately, with a see-saw motion, the dead spit of a crab, until his plate was picked clean.

Norman C. Lewis-Harcourt, General Counsel to the President, as Norm would sometimes startlingly introduce himself, was a mental loner, seemingly unaware of the presence of others; be they doctors, therapists, dietitians, guards, maintenance staff, or cooks. Nate, Marko, Leon, and Nurse Robinson did not exist. Nor did thickset Karl, who sat at a card table looking intently back at Norm, trying, possibly, to probe the finger-cage and decipher the man's unending code of wet silence. Curled and feverish, Karl had nervous greenish-black eyes—like old peas—that darted first to Nate, then Marko, then Leon, then Norm, then Nurse Robinson—always in that sequence and degree of arc—even when they were not there.

Nurse Robinson wavered in a pall of cigarette smoke. She was unsure whether Marko's outburst was the end of a beginning or the beginning of an end. Her, startlingly bright baby-blue eyes swept over the group like tiny hooded searchlights. She turned, dusted the tabletop, and rearranged a pile of magazines. She took a quick glance at a tiny watch clipped to her lower lapel. The movement told Nate that it was near medication-dispensing time. He knew Nurse Robinson liked the role of medication orderly.

A myriad of colorful pills lay in trays on Nurse Robinsons cart. She likened them to vibrant paint squares that as a child she used at school. The capsules, she liked of think of as elongated beads. Much counting was required from the alphabetic arrangement of bottles and boxes. Twists of paper and snatches of cotton wool added to the array of hues. Her red-nailed fingers, impeccably shaped and polished, twisted tops, lifted lids, so precisely, so cleanly, so accurately, it was as a bird pecks seeds. Alongside the pills lay a medication sheet, where names and dosages were neatly yellowed with a highlighter pen. Each quantity was placed next to a paper cup she had earlier filled with water from a spouted blue flask. She glanced at the sheet, called out a name. Her squeaky voice reminded Nate of mice.

Three days later it was rainy. Clouds boiled over the ridge beyond the high-fenced lawns.

"Nate! Quick! Out the window! *Really* this time! See!"

Nate glanced through the bleared glass in the direction of Marko's pointing finger. Vapors poured over the distant hills. The effect could be likened to waves breaking far out at sea, a distant shore, perhaps, a reef. As the downpour drove against the glass, Nate couldn't help but liken the effect to a squall lashing a porthole.

Nurse Robinson was in the ward at the time. After Marko's outburst, all had fallen quiet. Not because the nurse was strict, or because the inmates were straining to listen to what she had to say, but that it was just so refreshing to look at something other than the linoleum sea.

The gleaming white apparition that was Nurse Robinson was utterly out of reach, utterly unobtainable, utterly untouchable. Brush against her inappropriately, and massively obese Matron Nielsen would know about it. The senior nurse would waddle into the ward, breathing heavily, to scold the culprit and threaten the padded cell.

But one could *think* of touching.

The crisp, starched hem of her white uniform was Nate's favorite place to dwell, where it crossed her glistening, nylon-sheathed knee. Then there were the glinting earrings that so tantalizingly disappeared, then reappeared, from behind thick folds of auburn hair. As she moved, the jewels swung on silver chains like tiny erratic plumbs. If only a face could be had that matched the figure, and the whiff of Chanel.

Nate could dream of Nurse Robinson's hemline more easily than he could her expression. But not as satisfyingly deeply as when he dreamt of making a journey across Marko's crystal sea.

Yet, how could Nate explain to the Marko that it was futile to attempt to go out in the driving rain, through five locked doors, to which they didn't have keys! Then to somehow come upon a boat—a small rowing skiff it would be, with improvised sail—conveniently moored upon a gently sloping beach. Necessarily, the craft would be wooden and heavily planked to withstand the blows of ocean waves. There would need to be food and water stowed, fishing gear, some kind of bailing apparatus. The material to set sails would have to lie folded in some waterproof locker. Nate moistened his lips. His breathing quickened. Fresh, clean thoughts gathered, exploded in his brain. He took a deep breath. Then another.

Wasn't that a whiff of open ocean air!

Marko came in close one day, bringing with him the sulfurous odor of boiled egg. In a hoarse conspiratorial whisper he said, "The time will come when we'll both sail away. Across the crystal sea! We'll take turns rowing at first, until we catch the wind!

"You'll see!" he hollered.

"See what? What's on the other side?" Nate had asked.

"Paradise: an unspoiled, palm-fringed desert island!"

Nurse Robinson winced. She looked at her watch. Studied her elaborately painted fingernails. Crossed, uncrossed her legs. The hem slid a fraction. Smooth, long fingers picked at a tiny imperfection. A snagged filament of nylon, thin as a human hair, was lifted; discarded.

A month later, the damp, cold air of November lay upon Saint Georges. Mist shrouded the stone-block building. Thick fog cloaked the ridge. Sodden leaves littered the lawns. Through the bars, the windowpanes were steamed from cabbage furiously boiling in a kitchen vat. Shortly, Nat would see the sodden vegetable slopped on his plate alongside a brick of meatloaf and a gob of mashed potato. He was wondering where Marko was. He hadn't seen him in two whole days. Had the madcap left without him? A series of howls escaped his dry lips.

Like a baby whose dummy's been yanked, Nurse Robinson thought. She wore her usual deadpan expression, sitting cross-legged alongside the medication cart. Her master key, momentarily escaped from her pocket, dangled on its short chain to tap against the side of the blue flask. She would wait for the administered dose to kick in.

Nate thumped a tightly balled fist on Marko's door. He peered through the round view-window, closed his eyes to padded walls, embedded belt anchors and a foreground reflecting-square of shitty beige linoleum. He leaned heavily against the glass. The coldness felt good against his hot forehead. The translucent, emerald swell that heaved against the pane, cleansed and salted him, until his face tingled, his eyes shone. Amid the bluster, the groan of straining oars traversing leathered locks; the slap of waves against prow, Nate took the tiller.

A Desirable Fare

*What's worse than know-
ing you want something,
besides learning you can
never have it?* —James
Patterson

Reginald Ogden
was crouched be-
side his taxi when
the message came in,
outside *Eddie's Plaice*
on Clare Avenue, eat-
ing fish and chips out
of a newspaper wrap.
Squat on the pavement
beside the car, he was
examining what ap-
peared to be a tar
blemish low down on a
door panel.

Before that, he'd
been on tiptoe to check
the finish of the roof: a crinkled leaf, a dead fly—it was a
bluebottle, he'd decided—had been dispatched with a
sweep of the back of his hand, in which, held uppermost
between finger and thumb, was clutched a last morsel of
crisply battered Icelandic cod.

"Reg? Come in, over."

The voice spat out of the car radio like fat sizzling on a hotplate. Reginald was extra proud of his car radio. He'd only given the front panel an hour-long detailed clean the previous day. The small dials, various switches and tiny grooved knobs had been a challenge, but he'd persevered with sharply pointed tool—for levering miniscule amounts of dirt out of crevices and awkward corners—chrome polish, various rags and a buffing pad to make the front panel gleam like new. He reached through the open window and very carefully, with the tip of his little finger—the only part of the appendage he felt to be free of fry oil—flicked the radio to transmit.

"Go ahead, Tommy, over."

"Timed at five-fifty. Go pick up a Mrs. Penson at forty-nine Brocton Court, Ashford. Got that, Reg? *Ashford*. Take customer to Milford Shopping Center. Wait while she shops, and then return her to Brocton Court address. Fare is to be direct-billed, over."

"Will do, Tommy. Over and out."

Reg's balled-up, greasy wrapper thudded into the fish shop trash bin with a satisfying thwack. Images of woodsy mansions were filling his mind. He'd never had a fare from the moneyed enclave of Ashford before. He paused to squint along the car's transfer stripe. The thin, crimson line ran unbroken along the length of each side of the taxi, bisecting the vehicles glossy, two-tone gray finish. He stooped to take in the smudge-free white walls; redone only that morning. He stretched to tweak the angle of the radio aerial. The telescopic chrome rod stuck up from the illuminated, roof-mounted TomCab sign like an insect feeler. He thought the rake of the antenna gave the Zodiac the slick look of an American prowl car.

Since Reg landed the job at the cab company, his taxicab had been where he'd spent most of his life. Even when he wasn't in the vehicle, he was cleaning it. And when he wasn't doing that, he was thinking about the car. His own magic carpet, he liked to think of it as, which whisked him about effortlessly at the press of a pedal. The gleaming metal and glass capsule insulated him from the outside world. The vehicle was his haven, a comfy cabin that kept him warm and dry when the weather turned cold and wet, as it so often did in Mile End. He felt extra confident at the wheel, knowing the car looked so good. At the end of each shift, he spent time hosing and polishing off the days' collected dirt, even on those rare, dry ones when none was visible—no matter that he didn't get paid extra for it.

People waved at him as he glided by. It was as though he was royalty. As he floated along, he delighted in the purr of the six-cylinder engine, the hiss and rumble of rubber on the road. In the Zodiac, he was no longer down-and-out Reginald Ogden, skirted by people without a second glance. The car's leather-scented interior lifted him off the bottom rung of life's ladder. He might have known every pothole, every seam in the road, but each time he drove, it was a different experience. No matter how many times he traversed Mile End's seedy streets, past places he used to rough in—shop doorways, beneath the First Street rail bridge, a folded TV carton for a mattress. Out of the car, he was a nonentity.

"Fuck all," Tommy told him. The taxi-rank owner had been trying to impress on his new hire the importance of the job and what he must do to keep it.

"Punctuality, a welcoming smile, Mr. Ogden, is what it's all about. Each pick-up, each drop-off, you'd better apply that kind of thinking, or face being sacked on the spot. Of course, it's about good driving too. I'm sure you agree Mr. Ogden, that requirement goes without saying."

"Now, with that out of the way Mr. Ogden, what'll we call you?"

As Tommy spoke, he wielded a bright-red pencil that hovered like a dart over a form titled: "Statement of Particulars: On-the-Job Requirements for TomCab Employee."

"Reginald will do just fine." He still couldn't believe his good fortune, that he'd landed the job. He was glad now he'd had a haircut for the interview, taken a bath, and dug out some half-decent clothes.

"That's still a tad long, Reginald. How about Reg?"

Bum would have been good enough, as long as he got behind the wheel of the car Tommy had pointed to.

"Number twelve, the gray two-tone's yours," Tommy said, indicating with the pencil. "The one standing on its own, farthest from the office door."

Reg was sure the car smiled at him. Unlike other drivers on the ramp, when it came to keeping a vehicle in good order, he didn't need a lecture. One time, when he'd briefly had a car of his own—before the finance company had reclaimed it—he'd cared for it like it was a trophy. He was dumbfounded when Mr. Thomas J. Blake responded to his letter, asking him to come in for an interview. He'd composed the half-page application over several nights in his one-bedroom council flat. He'd sat on the bare, boarded floor, surrounded by discarded earlier efforts, not expecting even an acknowledgment. Nobody had ever answered one of his letters before. He was just glad he had a clean driving license—obtained when he'd once hauled gravel in a monster ten-wheel truck, a permit he'd managed to keep current using his Social Security allowance.

He studied the reflection in *Eddie's* window: him at the wheel of the Zodiac, face crinkled into a half-smile. He reached for the ignition in the laconic way that he'd seen done in American movies, without taking his eyes off the fish shop mirrored image.

He knew the Zodiac to be the cleanest taxi in Mile End. Spotless inside and out—even under the hood and inside the doorjambs—the tire treads flicked clean of pebbles each time he got back to the ramp. He took a swig of Coke. The salt and vinegar from the fish and chips had made him thirsty. He secured the can with a Velcro strap he'd fashioned beneath the dash. It wouldn't do to have a drink can visible in such a gleaming specimen of motorcar. He set the rate-meter to "Billed Fare."

In the Gent's he'd washed the fishiness off his hands, being careful to rinse around his mouth. He reflected on how mournful he looked in the cracked mirror. Between the *U* and *C* of *FUCK*, written across the glass with what looked like lipstick, his long face reminded him of a horse. He rotated his earring to hide the joint in the brass circle and flattened the tips of his shirt collar, only to see them slowly re-curl. He thought he looked weird in the glare of the florescent tube. His dark-brown eyes appeared red-rimmed, as if he'd been crying.

He pointed the Zodiac down Mile End's rain-slicked main street, past dreary *Millie's Hair,* in whose doorway he used to sleep most nights. *Sadler's Furniture* slid by with its forever *"Sixty-Percent Off"* poster. Next came the steamed-up windows of *Chicken Chips 'n Sausage* opposite the blacked-out windows of the *Sid Lawton Lounge,* a betting shop his dad used to use.

Before the traffic light at the end of High Street, where he would take the left turn onto Litchfield Road, stood the black granite frontage of *Hemming Brothers Undertakers.* A sign above the door read: "Ask About Our Free Advance-Planning Service." Three years ago, his wife had been stretched out in the undertaker's purple, carpeted front room, inside a pine box placed on a trestle behind a screen. He'd supposed the separation was intended to distance the plastic-handled casket with its ill-fitting lid from the array of polished hardwood coffins, many embossed with a personalized, inlaid brass motif, and in-filled with layers of custom silk padding.

Cynthia had been wearing her synthetic beaver coat when the brain hemorrhage took her. The escape of blood in her brain happened as she stepped off a 59S double-decker bus. The conductor told the coroner, "In the lady's eagerness to exit the vehicle, her hand left the stair-pole before her feet left the platform." The collapse sprawled her in the gutter. "She looked like a rolled-up fur rug," the uniformed, rail-thin conductor had added.

Reg's wife had been on her way to meet the man-friend, who had gifted her the coat the previous day. Reginald knew this from the crumpled note he'd found in one of the coat's pockets. "My Luscious Cynthia, try this on for size. Love, Sid," the message said.

Reg nosed the Zodiac into Buckingham Drive, a tree-lined thoroughfare of stylish houses. Each property was set back from the road, at the end of a sweeping driveway that coiled around an island of manicured lawn. The wealthy community of Ashford was nestled in a wooded valley. Drunks didn't stagger *its* leafy streets. Any inebriation, Reg felt sure, took place quietly and pleasantly behind closed doors, or upon secluded, lighted terraces—all very dignified. Their temporary state of wellbeing was not brought about by jug wine, but from imported estate-bottled vintages, whose elegantly labeled, empty bottles he would sometimes come across when searching for anything of value at the Mile End Council rubbish tip.

Reg had driven through Ashford several times before. He would often detour through the village when returning empty from Milford. To his knowledge, it was unheard of for a resident of Ashford to order a Mile End cab. He wondered why anyone would do such a thing when they had cars of their own. If an Ashford resident did need a taxi, why wouldn't they order it from a *local* company? It struck

Reg as odd, seeing the luxury about him, why Mrs. Pen-
rose—or whatever her name was—would choose TomCab.
Why not a posh *Leslie's* car from Ashford itself?

Buckingham Drive. He whispered the choice words. It
could just as easily have been Buckingham Palace. It was a
startling contrast to *Moorfields,* the halfway-rat-hole he
lived in. His flat was on the third floor of the second high-
rise council building along End Street—a grim, twelve-
story apartment building that overlooked a school playground and the graffiti covered walls of a council road-grit
dump, from which stray dogs tended to bay at night.

Reg smiled at the faint squeal of rubber as he turned
onto the smooth asphalt of Brocton Court. He beamed
again as he made the turn, crunching over the immaculate,
pebbled driveway of number forty-nine.

Reg first saw Mrs. Penson over the top of the Zodiac's
bonnet that he'd been scrutinizing for possible imperfec-
tions. She was standing, hand on hips, in front of the
doorway of her home, framed between the car's shiny
paintwork and the drooping canopy of an elm. Moments
before, he'd been bent backward beneath the tree, anxious-
ly checking for perched birds he knew were prone to dis-
charging the paint-staining contents of their tiny bowel
onto the car.

Reg was disturbed by the thought that his client might
have been standing there for some time, watching him go
through his inspection routine, without understanding the
reason for it, and importance of it. He would've preferred
to explain to her the danger of such fecal deposit, which
could indelibly stain the lustrous finish that only the previous evening he'd buffed for a solid hour.

Through the rising air off the hot metal, his fare shim-
mered in some kind of flowery summer frock that stopped
just below the knee. A pinkish suede vest dropped unbuttoned from her shoulders, only to immediately, and no-

ticeably, be pushed out, indicative of an ample bosom beneath. He drew a deep breath as he moved around to Mrs. Penson's side of the car. Stiffly—and inexplicably—like a uniformed chauffeur, he opened the backseat door, his free hand pressed against the small of his back. Maybe it was her bearing—the quiet, confident look she gave him; the solid, well-proportioned body; the way she was simply, yet elegantly and expensively dressed, with just the right color and combination of quality material—that made this fare so different than any other that had ever been about to enter his cab.

Mrs. Penson reminded him a bit of a middle-aged Maggie Thatcher. The realization made him painfully aware of his own attire. His cotton shirt sported a grease spot, the result of an errant chip. The garment's creased placket, which hung outside his baggy trousers, surely had the look of sackcloth.

A nightshirt, Mrs. Penson thought. *A mode of dress more suited to Bangladesh.* She noticed too how the bottoms of the driver's trousers were frayed from trailing the ground behind thin-soled, shabby sandals. She had already decided that ordering a taxi was a mistake. The sight of this scruffily dressed man, with his peculiar vehicle cleanliness habit, had almost caused her to turn back into the house, to call the company and cancel the booking. It was only on a whim that she'd phoned in the first place. The big, black Rover beneath the white dustsheet in the three-car garage had become too much for her to handle. And she couldn't face the hassle of purchasing something smaller, so she'd thought, why not a cab? This was the first time she'd used such conveyance, and not knowing one company from another, she'd selected the most prominently displayed advertisement on the first yellow page of the phone book.

Seated in the comforting familiarity of the driver's seat, Reg felt a little composure return. There was time now to study the new passenger in more detail. Viewed in the rear view mirror his fare appeared more settled, albeit perched on the edge of the seat. The earlier chilly brittleness seemed to have softened a little, as had the shudder he'd noticed ripple through her frame when she'd first got in. Mrs. Penson wore grayish-blond framed glasses that perfectly matched the color of her hair. She was more comfortingly plump than when arranged like a mirage over the car's bonnet. It was then, he decided, that she would begin to notice the interior: how strikingly different it was from other taxis, how spotlessly clean. The aroma of fine leather would surely make her feel almost at home, and when she stroked the gleaming door trim, as he felt sure she would find herself compelled to do, since that's the first thing that tempts most of his passengers, he would know she was appreciative.

Her soft, hazel eyes, which had so struck him earlier, he now noticed, were blotched violet. He squirmed with pleasure at seeing them rove over the polished upholstery, the freshly swept carpet, and the sparkling, clean glass. Marveling, too, no doubt, at the absence of sweat odor and the sickly stench of stale cigarettes. Those were unpleasant smells, which he was sure a woman of her bearing must associate with taxis, especially those from Mile End—some of which he wouldn't ride in himself.

Prior to this calming had come some utterance he didn't quite catch. It wasn't hello, or good afternoon, even though passengers at that juncture often made such welcome remark, whether grunted as in the case of a drunken male, or shrieked as it sometimes was by a semi-intoxicated, stumbling female. It hurt him to think it might have been disparaging, that such crudity could emanate from such a specimen of womanhood. It was possibly a command, spoken as though she had been instructing a manservant. He therefore didn't answer, feeling it impolite to ask her to repeat herself. The episode had, however, planted an unsettling seed. He had closed the door with this feeling nagging him. For reasons unknown, this passenger was fearful of getting into his car. Still, he couldn't help but notice, as he so often did when seating an attractive female, the flash of inner thigh as her leg lifted to clear the threshold of the sill.

To counter his unease, to avoid the surly look he knew he was prone to slip into when confronted with dilemma, he worked his countenance up into an openmouthed grin, wide enough to show off his front teeth. Polished with whitener only that morning, they were the only part of his drawn-out, sallow face he was in any sense proud of.

He was suddenly conscious of his earring. Whereas normally it was something he liked to show off, he now wished he had slipped the thing out. Such male facial adornment was perfectly acceptable for the Mile End crowd; there, he could have got away with one through his nose. But Ashford was different. Being the sophisticated place it was, and this lady acting as if she was some celebrity, he was discomfited by it. In fact, he felt her eyes upon it, and upon his razored nape, which exposed the purple birthmark on the back of his neck. He felt sure she was looking at that too, as one often does with others' disfigurements. No doubt she was noting its shape and color, and wondering what it was, whether it was some kind of growth, a tumor perhaps, and if it was catching.

He eased the Zodiac off the pebbles onto Brocton Court, gently accelerating in the direction that would bring him to Buckingham Drive. At that juncture, he would turn right, then left onto the main road, then continue on through the village of Milford, to a point a few miles beyond, where he would exit the main road into the shopping complex.

A light tap on his shoulder was the first indication
Mrs. Penson thought something was not quite right with
her driver's navigation. Moments before, Reg had begun to
suspect he'd made a mistake. But rather than turn, by re-
versing into a driveway—thus admitting to an error of
judgment—he decided to continue, sure that at some point
the unfamiliar street would loop back to the main road, not
realizing it came to a dead end.

"Driver, I think we should be going in the *other* direction," was the whispered, throaty comment close to his ear.
"Continue now to the end of this cul-de-sac," she intoned.
"*There*, you'll be able to turn around." He was conscious
now that his nape was aglow, her eyes drawn to the imperfection. Shaped, she would probably think, not unlike the
map of America, as Cynthia had once derisively likened it.
He managed a grunted "oh" before turning to bring the car
to the Milford road, along which he could coast without
undue fear of a further gaffe. The familiarity of the straight
main road lowered his anxiety level, enough to risk another glance in the rearview mirror. But all there was to see
was a raft of hair. Mrs. Penson was on the short side and
she had reclined on the soft seat cushion, such that her face
was below the level of reflection in the mirror. His first
thought was to adjust it. Alternatively, he could have rearranged his position in his seat. Either correction, though,
would make him unable to see out the windscreen properly or would block his reflected view through the rear window. And she would see him make the change and wonder what he was up to. It was the fear of these considera-
tions that he decided to leave well alone.

His self-consciousness, compounded by his need for a
show of perfection, had resulted in him being tongue-tied.
Whereas normally he would be nonchalantly twirling the
wheel, chatting with his passengers, unconcerned about
his driving or how he might look or sound, or how a ques-

tion or comment was to be framed, he now found himself inhibited. The steering felt unusually labored. It was as if the wheel had a brake attached to it. Then there was the lack of suppleness in his arms, shoulders, and wrists. His hands clenched the rim too tightly, and when he changed gear, there was the unmistakable grate of a cog.

He began to wish he'd never been asked to convey the woman. Tommy should have radioed the fare to Les, or Bob, or even Cedric, the older driver, whose dark, mysterious face could suddenly turn savage—to many an unruly passenger's chagrin.

But Reg was not like that. He could not bring himself to shout at his cat, let alone deal with a sophisticated woman. He'd never had such a fare before. One so distant, yet so…well, desirable. He was at ease ferrying Mile End people—in such company he could hold his own. Housewives taking their kids to school, party people on a night out, even the odd drunk—he could handle them. Yet so far he hardly dared speak, for fear his Mile End twang, coarse and inelegant as he knew it to be, especially to an outsider, might cause this woman to visibly cringe.

The thought made him feel inadequate. Hunched at the wheel, knowing her eyes were on the back of his head, he sensed he looked more like the driver of a hearse than the chauffeur-like operator he yearned to be. The fact he was in control of a fine car, albeit not his own, and an old model, didn't compensate. He was the boss, the captain of the good ship Zodiac out of Mile End—but this appeared to carry no weight with this woman.

It is only when Mrs. Penson sat upright and leant forward to tell him to take the next right, bringing with her the scent of lavender, that he met her eyes for the first time. As her face filled the rearview mirror, he confirmed she was undoubtedly attractive in the usual ways of a well-to-do, mature woman. Indeed, he was quickly, if not a little feverishly, drawn to the finer points: her pale, faintly freck-led forehead, the slant of her partly open mouth. Then, there was the breadth of shoulder that held up the body he knew lay so solidly composed below his line of vision. Her bejeweled hand clasped onto the side of his seat, not inches from his arm. The effect of this nearness, along with the alluring fragrance that came with it, caused him to break out in a wash of perspiration. She leaned close toward his shoulder, and he feared that odor from the excessive sweating would waft up into her face. But her violet-flecked eyes belied this. He saw no signs in them suggest-ing a need to pull away from the column of air he sensed might have been forming a stagnant cloud above his soaked underarm.

Perhaps, he allowed giddily, Mrs. Penson found her-self drawn to such manly scent, since she showed no incli-nation to sink back into her seat. Her coral-smeared lips—moistened as if just wetted with a drink—began to mouth words he did not hear, so taken was he by their sinuous movement and the dagger-flash of faultless teeth. The at-traction prompted him to nod and grin, like an idiot, at what he felt were appropriate intervals, before he realized she was asking him to stop. To tell him, "Open the damn door! Let me out so I can go do my shopping!"

Mrs. Penson took exactly sixty minutes to complete her purchases. Time for the red-tipped black hand on the taxi's dashboard clock to circumnavigate its white dial. A dead leaf resting against a wiper blade, and two insects—a wasp and cabbage-white butterfly—stuck to the wind-screen, irritated Reg. He had been eyeing the spoilers for some time. Their presence worsened his sense of unease. It took all his willpower to resist the urge to remove them, to frenziedly wash off any residual stain. He would have used Windolene, which was stored with various polishes and cleaning rags beneath his seat. But he had been too preoccupied.

He had noted, as Mrs. Penson walked away earlier, that her legs were a little on the thick side. He'd observed, too, that everything about the woman swung: the silvery-blond hair to and fro across her shoulders, the leather bag in the crook of an arm, the buttocks beneath her thin dress. He sensed the gait exaggerated. *Wasn't it just a tiny bit put on?* He'd asked himself. *Done to impress?* But how could he now impress her? The thought consumed him. As he drained the last of the now almost hot Coke, he decided he must perform better on the return journey. There could be no more embarrassing mistakes in navigating six miles of roadway back to Brocton Court. As he sniffed lingering fragrances he could not quite put words to, he decided he must promote himself. Despite the obvious shortcomings, he felt he had something to offer, a personal escort service perhaps, or looking after her garden.

His life experience put him at a disadvantage. It hadn't extended much beyond Mile End squalor. There had never been someplace he could call home. It was doubtful even whether his late mother and father had been married, for he'd never been able to discover a certificate. Nor had the local records office. The man behind the counter told him that for Social Security purposes he was classified as "mis-begotten." He'd nodded to the bespectacled assistant to show that he understood the term. Later, when the dictionary in the Mile End public library had explained the word's meaning, he'd looked up, over the lectern and sharp edge of the huge volume's gilt pages, beyond lines of bookcases and a man fingering a card index, to a large window that overlooked a small park. He'd stared, quite in a trance, unseeing of the trash-littered lawn, the trampled salvias, the overhanging trees; the focus of his mind upon vaguely remembered faces that peered questioningly at him from a dim and distant past.

"Did you manage to get all of your shopping done then, Mrs. Penson?" After much thought and rehearsal Reg decided to use that line as an opener. He was relieved the sentence was completed without a choke, and that it had been spoken casually, his Mile End accent minimized. He twirled the steering wheel, allowing its rim to slip back against the friction of his hands as he steered out of the car park. He watched for his passenger's reaction in the repositioned rearview mirror, carefully angled to reflect a section of seat back he'd estimated where her head would be. He had left the shopping center and was on the main road before she replied.

"Sorry driver, I was miles away. What did you say back there?"

His lips and throat—cocked slightly to reply—were stalled mid-word by the need to suppress a fast-rising belch. The internal burp brought hot Coke flooding into the back of his throat. Nonetheless, he managed to complete the gas discharge silently, to expel the stomach fume discretely into the back of his hand.

"I was asking if you had all of your shopping completed, Mrs. Penson."

"Oh yes, most of it at least, thank you."

He wonders if she had noticed that he'd removed the earring, and that the hair on the back of his neck had been smoothed down over the razored part to better hide the skin blemish.

She was looking out the side window. Her hair, swept back from the ear, brushed the glass. A single pearl was clipped to her earlobe. A hand, cupped beneath an up-curl of hair, seemingly unconsciously tidying it, indicated her thoughts might be elsewhere.

Reg had decided to give her a business card, a white oblong, carefully selected from an elastic-banded pack beneath the dash. It was the only one he could find that was not Coke stained. *TomCab Taxi Service* was emblazoned upon it. On the back, diagonally in a penciled flourish, he has written, "Mrs. Penson, ask for me if you need a taxi, or any other help. Thank you, Reginald Ogden."

He felt the card would act as a retaining link. Hopefully, a private keepsake she would want close by, in the kitchen perhaps, on the refrigerator door beneath a magnet. He held the card trapped between his fingers, ready to be plucked from his hand, held at arm's length over his shoulder.

"My name is Reginald Ogden. I hope you don't mind me saying so."

Mrs. Penson was a little taken aback by the driver's sudden assertion. She had been preoccupied, immersed in thinking about the *Ashford Gardens Neighborhood Committee* meeting she would chair that evening, for which she had shopped for gifts. She planned to give them out to the owners of gardens judged by members to be the most pretty in the village.

It wasn't that she found the man's declaration impertinent, or that it was shouted loud enough to cause alarm. It was that she thought the driver to be a sullen loafer. Possibly, judged by his close-cropped hair and earring, a town ruffian, one, who by his appearance, might not speak a word of English. Still, she decided, he seemed harmless enough. And the car was even cleaner than her late husband's Rover.

"Nice to meet you, Mr. Ogden. I was thinking how immaculate you keep your vehicle. It must take up lots of your spare time."

"Oh no, Mrs. Penson, nothing like that. You see, I don't have spare time. I work on it during the day. At night too, sometimes. When I'm waiting for a call. Might as well be doing something useful during slack periods. I'll even give it a quick polish between trips. More especially if the route is dusty or muddy as it so often is around the parts I usually operate in. The windows especially. One has to be ever watchful of them. They are the first things a passenger notes, along with door handles smudged with fingerprints. I won't allow smoking in my car. I'm really firm on that one."

She swallowed hard. She had, of course, not meant to be taken so literally. She wondered why such people didn't read, or listen to a tape, when they had spare time. Write a book even. Jot down their experiences in a journal. There were so many things they could be doing, instead of just hanging about. She couldn't imagine this man polishing his taxi, when it was already spotlessly clean.

She had noticed, too, how he watched her. She sensed it even now when she looked away, as had never been her habit to do. She could feel his eyes upon her now. She thought at first they were on the beady side, but not so much that she would want to avoid them, set as they were in a famished-looking face. It was a countenance that had a pitiful quality, which she momentarily found herself drawn to, though no differently than had it been a lost child's look at an Ashford fair. She noticed, too, that he had tilted the rearview mirror, so sharply it almost faced the floor. Obviously done to see more of her, she'd decided. No harm in that. She knew she looked good. A man beside himself over getting an extra eyeful was nothing new to her. And yet looking at this man now—from the perspective of his oval head silhouetted against the brightness of the advancing road, seemingly filled with endeavor to please; his eyes shyly lowered, such that his most attractive feature by far, long, dark lashes and bushier, even darker brows, were innocently revealed in the mirror—she could not help but feel pity.

"Well, you must keep your mind occupied. For what it is you do, you certainly do a good job," she said brightly. "What else do you do, though? I mean, when you're not driving your taxi? Spend time with family, grandchildren—that sort of thing?"

"Mrs. Penson, I lie in bed thinking about it. The car I mean. Especially when it's raining, or it's blustery, the wind howling around the tall building I live in. Those are the times when I think of it most. Doing that sends me to sleep at night."

"Really, Mr. Ogden, I would never have thought it possible for someone to get so attached, if not obsessed, with what after all is a purely mechanical object."

She looked down at her watch. It was a thirtieth wedding anniversary present from her husband, who the next day suffered a fatal heart attack. That had been two years ago. She took a deep breath. She was impatient to get the journey over, to get on with her gift-wrapping. There were so many things she had left to do before guests arrived.

So intent was she with her thoughts, she was quite unprepared for the driver's follow-on. Later, possibly the following day, or it could have been the day after that—she could never quite recall when—she suddenly and most touchingly remembered as to how poignant she had felt the taxi driver's oratory to be, yet oddly, couldn't remember a single word he'd said.

"If it's blowing hard, Mrs. Penson—I mean such that the wind buffets the window in my bedroom; a small fixed pane is all it is above the bed, the rain pelting against it—I imagine my car then, in the silence of the company garage, where in my mind's eye I see it long after the end of my shift. It stands in its drip pool, into which the plop of an occasional spot causes a slow-moving ripple to pulse out across the surface, much like what happens when you throw a pebble into a millpond. I hear the hisses, too, Mrs. Penson. Barely audible they are, but they're there if you really listen. It's the moisture, you see, seeping over the hot exhaust. Then there's the subdued rumble, like an overactive bowel, if you'll pardon the expression, along with the sharp crack and creak of cooling metal. My wife's been dead coming on five years now, so that's all I get to think of at night—when I'm not driving that is. I've been for a time what I suppose you'd call a derelict. A bum, you might say, living on the streets, sleeping rough. I never knew a mother and father, at least in the sense of them being married and living at home. There's really just me, this car, and Tibby."

Mrs. Penson didn't quite know how to respond, or even whether she should. She supposed the driver was next thing to a down-and-out, yet a romancer, certainly. But in a sincere and quite moving way. She was struck by his prose, the apparent descriptive gift he had in portraying his thoughts. She couldn't imagine anyone sleeping in shop doorways, let alone this poor man. *However do they keep warm?* She wondered.

Buckingham Drive is coming up far too quickly, Reg thought. As he made the turn, he extended his arm higher for Mrs. Penson to better see the offered card. He waved it about, rotating his wrist to display it more clearly, slotted between his bunched fingers. In that instant, Mrs. Penson was busy gathering her shopping, so there was a need for him to say something quickly, to draw her attention to it. Any minute he would need both hands on the wheel to make the sharp turn into Brocton Court.

"Please take my card, Mrs. Penson. If you ever need anything at any time, call the number. Just ask for Reginald."

"Oh thank you, Mr. Ogden. I'm not sure when I'll need a taxi again, if ever. But if I do, I will be sure to ask for you. And I'm sorry to hear, Mr. Ogden, that you have no family, since I presume Tibby is a cat. Here is a bit of something for you," she added, deftly removing the card and inserting in its place a neatly folded five-pound note.

He crumpled the fiver into his pocket with a thickly spoken "Thank you, Mrs. Penson."

"You can call me Reginald, by the way, if you would like to, that is. No one else does. But I would be honored if you would. And might I ask *your* name? Though of course you don't have to tell me if you'd prefer. I fully understand that, Mrs. Penson."

"No, that's fine. It's Alice. But I really do have a preference for Mrs. Penson. It's what most people call me, what I'm used to, what I'm most comfortable with."

She had been named after her mother, who had once told her it came from a popular song of the time: "Alice Blue Gown." She had decided it was far easier to just tell this man her name, rather than explain why she preferred not to.

Alice. How perfect, he thought. *How could it be anything else?* He wished now he'd asked her earlier. Then he could have addressed the card more personally.

He did not know what to say. Perhaps he should tell her what a pleasing smile she had. The way her mouth angled slightly, he thought, was the most exciting part. Of course he could not mention that. A compliment on her attire? That would be safe. He could have risked remarking on how the color of the flowers imprinted on her cotton dress so perfectly matched that of her lips, a facet of her he found irresistibly becoming.

"Dear Alice," he would have written on the card.

He was quite beside himself with these thoughts as he turned into the driveway, a maneuver he executed so well he sensed Mrs. Penson hardly noticed she was home.

Stealing a last glance in the rearview mirror, he swiveled sideways, pushing slightly backward in his seat to more easily grasp and press down the door handle. It was a well-executed move. A practiced rearrangement of body, arm, and hand, acting in unison. A movement done unfailingly, countless times each day.

But things were not destined to continue so smoothly. And for the most inexplicable reason. In his zest to assist his passenger, to impress upon her his attention to detail—inclinations that paled beside the romantically inclined fever that had seized him, even to risk leaving the Zodiac parked beneath the hazard he knew the canopy of the elm to be—he misjudged the workings of the handle. The device had at all times previously been the most reliable of lever-like contraptions, yet in that instant, a lapse in the mechanism made him wish he held a hammer, or other such pounding tool in his hand, so he could severely punish the otherwise mechanically perfect contrivance.

The irredeemable seconds wasted fiddling with the innocuous thing—that never again would hesitate, no matter how many times he tested getting in and out of the driver's seat—was time enough for Mrs. Penson's image to disappear from the rearview mirror. Time enough for her to utter, "Thank you so much, driver." Time enough for his plan to open her door, take the offered-up shopping, place the flat palm of a free hand beneath her elbow—to help her step up the pathway into the house—to be thwarted.

He tempered the disillusionment the lost opportunity brought—a stifled wave of disenchantment he felt spread through his loins like the beginnings of an intestinal disturbance—by glancing up at a patch of sunlit blue sky that pierced the elm's crown, just as Mrs. Penson's manicured fingers released their grip on his card, allowing it to flutter down, to disappear into the depths of a clump of rockrose that grew in profusion alongside the driveway.

The carefully worded reminder, upon which so much tender time had been spent—different wordings tested on scraps of paper, that despite his passion for tidiness, now littered the driver's side plastic floor mat—was no more. With a further breathed "thank you" she was gone, a trace of lavender the only reminder she'd ever been. He stared at the front door of her house, long and hard after she disappeared through it.

Mrs. Penson was relieved to be home. After a short rest she would sip on a glass of sherry while finalizing preparations to receive her guests. Even so, as she momentarily leant back against the closed door—shopping bags hanging limply from an extended arm—and took in the polished oak-floored hallway, the exquisite works of art that adorned the walls, she could not help but relive, albeit fleetingly, the taxi driver's car-caring mania and his poetically expressed concern for it.

Reginald was too filled with adoring thought to take care of a bird dropping that had splattered a side window and two unknown species of insect that had joined the wasp and butterfly stuck to the windscreen.

He turned the key. The engine purred into life. He reached to release the handbrake while looking out the side window. His eyes followed the line of a crazy-paved path that bisected a flower-filled front garden, to meander beside a terraced rockery, over which a waterfall cascaded onto the heads of stone dwarfs.

He envisaged the Tudor-faced home was filled with old-world charm. He knew little of such a residence, other than the sound of ticking clocks, the smell of pure cleanliness, that somewhere in his distant past he felt he had been momentarily acquainted with—the stillness of a doctor's house perhaps, or the oak-paneled lobby of a plush hotel, into which he once gingerly stepped to pick up a client.

The radio crackled into life. As it readied itself to spit a command, Reg found it increasingly difficult to maintain the blissful state that had consumed him. Depicted in the rearview mirror was no longer the countenance of a taxi driver savoring a joyous happening, but such elated expression slowly draining from a face.

As the driveway receded in that reflector of diffused light, as the image morphed into verdant mass, he could not help the folds of parchment-like skin that covered his facial structure, from adapting to their lifelong arrangement. Indeed, at the turn onto Mile End Road, where he looked first right, then left, then right again, it would appear to a casual observer that the person at the wheel of the taxi was absorbedly sucking upon a hard biscuit gripped tightly between his teeth.

ONE HUNDRED EIGHTY-SIX THOUSAND MILES PER SECOND

Know that when you look at the moon, the stars, they do not see you in that same instant — SBJ

Mrs. Meakin had written the number "186,000," followed by "miles per second," across the top of a freshly cleaned blackboard. The white-chalked characters stood out sharply against the matt black, as they had when she'd practiced writing them the previous day.

It took several attempts before the science teacher perfected how best to stand at the board, to be able to write, yet at the same time observe the class. She then practiced speaking, unsure whether to use her natural monotone—which her mother once told her was as devoid of emphasis as a moonscape is vegetation—or the severe, brittle voice she'd rehearsed in preparation for the start of term. After careful thought, she had decided on the latter.

Mrs. Meakin decided also on a velocity, one so momentously fundamental she found herself pressing extra hard on the chalk in recognition. She underlined *"per second,"* so that her pupils would more clearly identify with how stupendously fast it really was.

When the children had filed into the classroom, chattering to each other as seven and eight-year-olds are prone to do—arguing over desk placement, chair and notebook allocation, pencils and rulers—she had noticed with satisfaction the look of bewilderment on their faces upon seeing the number on the blackboard.

The very reaction Mrs. Meakin sought.

The teacher was a tall, thin woman, fifty-ish, with a mop of mousey hair shaped about her head as though readied for a bonnet. She was dressed in a manner that spoke to Victorian strictness: loose fitting, gray blouse; buttoned dark-gray cardigan; ankle-length, even-darker-gray tweed skirt. Her complexion was pink, lightly freckled over a porcelain-like shininess, not unlike that of a moorhen's egg.

It was the first day of term, a most perilous time for a teacher. A period, Mrs. Meakin knew from bitter experience, when the class was out to test her mettle. It was therefore crucial at the outset that she commanded respect. From the get go, she wanted to be seen as the one in charge. Putting on the board something extraordinary, that few if any at such tender age would have a clue about, she was confident would help ensure that.

She glanced down at a paper that lay on her desk. The page was headed "Meakin. Rm 2C. List of Pupils 2nd Grade." A name she had earlier underlined in red pencil stood out.

"Wendy," she said, indicating the figure on the board, and interrupting the girl's apparent fixation on some distraction out the window, "can you think of anything that could move that quickly?" Wendy's inattentiveness had not gone unnoticed when the child had first entered the classroom, identifying the daydreaming pupil as the perfect candidate for the opening question.

Mrs. Meakin drew comfort from the fact that her proposed new teaching method had impressed Mr. Ward, the headmaster at Holmcroft Primary. Nonetheless, she couldn't help but sympathize with the child's task. When so young, as far as she could remember, she could barely read a figure like that, let alone answer what it stood for.

But esteem, if not admiration, needed to be instilled at the outset. It was *she* who was the teacher, and she had taken great pains over the summer holiday to make certain that would be the case for the whole term.

"Excellent idea, Mrs. Meakin. That should bring about some much-needed pupil stability." Mr. Ward's words still jangled. The statement, after all, implied that order had previously been lax. Nonetheless, she managed to think of his remark as heartening, even praiseworthy. In fact, she couldn't help but boast about the encounter to other staff members. 'Wardie' had given her class-opening technique his official nod, and had even gone on to commend her for her plan to educate, as he put it, *"in such an innovative way."*

The headmaster had been his usual grumpy self when she'd first entered his office, a behavioral quirk she'd decided was offset by a certain charm that defied explanation, yet at the same time, she'd found vaguely appealing. In fact, a slight stretch of her imagination turned the seemingly adverse trait into an alluring coyness, a quality she liked to see in a person, especially a male. So she saw no reason to hold back. When she giddily told others in the staff room of her newfound assertiveness—in effect, an oblique reprimand to them for remaining stubbornly stuck in their 'Old-fashioned ways'—a mood of confidence possessed her.

That degree of self-assurance was with her that day; poised and confident, she stood half-turned from the blackboard in front of a new batch of pupils. As she looked over the gaggle sitting before her, a winning smile played over her face. Quite unlike last year's pasted on grin. This time there would be no fake kindheartedness, for no one knew better than Mrs. Meakin that it wasn't enough when dealing with young children—many of whom she knew hated being schooled—to try to win respect through compassion.

Unfortunately, last term's eruptions of unruly behavior that had emanated from her classroom had not gone unnoticed. In particular by Mr. Ward. The headmaster had spoken of passing her door only to hear nothing but bedlam coming from the other side of it. For that reason she was required to give Mr. Ward an assurance that there would be no repeat of, as he put it, *"Loss of control this term."*

Wendy felt she'd sooner watch Cabbage Whites flit between yellow dandelion flowers than respond to teacher's question. It was distracting to be picked on when so rapt with the nervous flight of butterflies. But "186,000 miles per second," emblazoned across the blackboard, had caught her attention, the moment she'd entered the classroom. It prompted her to recall the time of her seventh birthday, when her dad had reached sixty miles per hour in the family Morris. She'd been perched on the edge of the backseat, looking over his shoulder, quite captivated by the speedometer, willing the gauge's red-tipped pointer to go higher, during the course of a journey to visit her aunt. She remembered her dad's look of amazement when she'd exclaimed they were traveling at a mile a minute.

Three months later, Wendy experienced her first flight. She was again with her parents, this time on the way to Amsterdam. A stewardess had offered her a glass of juice while whispering breathlessly in her ear that they were traveling at six hundred miles per hour. "Cool," Wendy had muttered, to the astonishment of the attendant, "a mile every ten seconds." At the same time she was unimpressed, for the pink-tinged clouds outside the cabin, which had so reminded her of fairground candy floss, seemed to be moving disappointingly slowly.

Wendy had seen large numbers before. Even bigger ones than teacher had chalked on the board. But never with this much super-bigness *after* them. She thought of how fantastically fast it would be, even had the number been miles per hour, instead of per second. She also thought of the moon and stars she saw in the night sky and how fast they might be moving. And wasn't everyone on Earth moving swiftly around the sun? Or was it the moon circling the Earth? She couldn't remember which. "Everyone's in motion," her dad had once said, "even those appearing to be at a standstill."

What Wendy did know was that when she switched her flashlight on at night, as she often did when reading her comics in bed—within a tent of sheets formed by her hunched figure—the beam instantly dispelled the gloom. When she thought about it some more, there was no difference from when she pressed the switch on the shiny chrome cylinder, to when a bright, blue-tinged circle lit up the ceiling. And when she switched on her flashlight at the open window, to probe the darkness of the garden, she remembered that the beam straightaway cut like a knife into the night, instantly illuminating the gray branches of a giant beech at the end of the street. Even the trunk of a more distant tree beyond the river, could be lit up with the beam, the instant she pressed the switch. So intuitively, she knew what the velocity stood for.

"The speed of light," she said.

A soft murmur stole over the classroom. A sense of pent up tension was released. It was as if air had suddenly been let out of a balloon. Wendy felt a little taken aback, for she thought her words had come out in a rush, spoken barely above a whisper. It was as if she'd gasped the answer, as though in awe of making such a statement. There was a sudden hush in the classroom, which held for several seconds; seconds that to Wendy seemed like minutes so complete and utter was the time interval. Not the tap of a pencil, not the scrape of a single chair could be heard, just the faint throb of teeming life, trapped as it were in the classroom; a subdued background drumbeat of tiny breathing lungs and pounding hearts. But she had managed it. To get out the words, "*Speed of light.*"

Wendy's face felt hot, her forehead damp with perspiration. Perhaps, she thought, it was the slanting ray of sunshine that had stolen ever closer to her from the tall window. The beam, which had missed her at the start of class, now partially enveloped her. The sunbeam threw her shadow onto the wooden lid of her desk, where the outline of her hair could be seen. She noted, too, that the leading edge of the ray had advanced to almost touch her freshly sharpened pencil that lay in its ink-stained groove. Maybe, she thought, she had the beginnings of the cold her mother had told her was going about, that started with a cough and an inflamed throat. But she had none of those symptoms, just a kind of flushed feeling. But even now, as reason tried to surface that would explain the uneasiness, she felt the effect lessening, the whirl in her head slowing.

As she'd answered the teacher's question, Mrs. Meakin's gray eyes had momentarily flickered, as if affected by a speck of chalk dust. They then, brightened, widened—not too differently, Wendy had thought, than had her dad's eyes when she'd told him their car was traveling a mile a minute.

Mrs. Meakin coughed loudly, elaborately, into the back of her hand. She had thought her inattentive pupil would have given some absurd answer, if not remained glowering in silence, twiddling her fingers. But she had to say something, and quickly, if only to quell the rise in rustling agitation.

"Good girl! Good girl!" Mrs. Meakin spluttered.

She glanced at her class notes, long and hard without seeing a word. It was galling to have her teaching method bettered at the outset, at a point when she was supposed to be at her most formidable. To step in, as it were, to explain the most fundamental scientific measurement ever determined. Yet the question she had thought would be so difficult had been correctly and incisively answered by a seven-year-old.

She would put up another number. A distance this time, one she was sure would appear even more mind-boggling. She was confident that the new figure would appear stupendously huge in the eyes of children used to minuteness. A number so big, none of them would be able to speak it, let alone fathom.

Beneath 186,000 miles <u>per second</u>, Mrs. Meakin wrote 93,000,000 miles. As she chalked the six zeros she spoke the number: *"ninety-three million miles."* She again pressed on the chalk extra heavily, causing more fine white particles to be ground off the end, falling down the face of the board like tiny puffs of snow, further whitening the chalk shelf, the handle of an eraser pad, and the polished wooden floor beneath.

"Can anyone tell me what *that* number represents?" Mrs. Meakin asked. As she looked on the sea of perplexed faces, she couldn't help but feel a sense of satisfaction. The effect caused her eyebrows to arch in anticipation, an expression groomed to give the appearance of expectancy, that it was entirely plausible for pupils—even those of such young age—to know the answer to such a question.

Last term, Mrs. Meakin would have showered such a bright pupil with compliments, even led the class into a round of clapping. But when she had stopped applauding, and the class had continued, on and on, before breaking out into loud cheers accompanied with bursts of desk-lid-slamming, she had decided to never allow this to happen again. This term, any such resemblance of *"rabble-rousing"*—as Mr. Ward had termed the racket, when bursting red-faced into the classroom, to find out *"what in hell's name is going on?"*—Was out of the question.

Wendy's heady moment had now fully subsided. Her mind resumed dealing with matters other than schooling. Flopper, her pet rabbit, needed his pen cleaned out. Sweet smelling straw had to be brought from the bale in the garden shed. And today was Tuesday, comic day. Before school she'd glanced over the pages to ready herself to read at night, within her flashlight-lit bed-tent. Tonight also, her mum had promised ice cream after dinner. That was why, at that particular instant, as Mrs. Meakin's eyes roved the class before narrowly and calculatingly settled upon her, the colorful image of a creamily filled golden cone, topped with dark-brown chocolate chips, took up half the capacity of Wendy's brain.

Mrs. Meakin's question hung unanswered in the still air of the classroom long enough for the ensuing silence to be noticeable. During this interval, the teacher's countenance remained tightly knitted into a questioning, expectant frown, which unwrinkled slightly when she saw Wendy raise her hand for permission to speak. It seemed to the pupil that the teacher's stern gaze and grating voice—like ice cubes shaken in a tin cup—required her to do so.

But it was then, that so did Bennie, a dark-haired, excitable boy who sat next to Wendy. He shot up an arm, at the same time shouting out the first thing that came into his head: that the new figure on the board was the distance around the world. The boy had been nurturing the idea of a response since the impudent girl beside him had answered the first question. He was goaded, too, by the fact that this girl didn't even seem to pay attention, yet was able to give such a cool answer. This time, Bennie was determined that he would get in first, to catch the teacher's attention.

But Bennie's plan was to be thwarted at the outset. At the instant of his utterance, Molly pulled a face at Peggy beside her, which prompted Peggy to also raise a hand. Like Bennie, she was unable to stop from blurting out what she wanted to say: that the new figure on the board was the distance from England to Australia. She knew it to be a very long way because it took so much time to get there even by jet plane.

The net result was that the two shouted answers drowned each other out, ensuring neither was heard. For that reason Mrs. Meakin didn't respond to Bennie or Peggy, or even recognize that they had spoken.

Mrs. Meakin also ignored Molly, who, annoyed that Peggy had spoken before her, was intent on recognition at all cost. To ensure this, she stood in the aisle between the desks, an arm held high over Peggy's head, fingers stretched to the limit of their length, to give the teacher the clearest possible signal that she wanted to speak, even though, like Bennie and Peggy before her, she had no clear idea what she wanted to say.

Instead, Mrs. Meakin again turned to Wendy.

"What do *you* think the distance is?" she asked, in as pleasant and uplifting a manner as she could muster.

Wendy felt uncomfortably hot again. The sunbeam now shone fully upon her. She thought the teacher spoke to her in such a prickly way; the words penetrated her skull like pins and needles. But the new figure chalked on the board, "93,000,000 miles," below "186,000 miles per second," intrigued her. A glance told her that nothing on earth could surely be that far away; therefore, it must be something in the sky.

The needles would soon be pricking again, for Mrs. Meakin was determined not to let Wendy off the hook. She would ask the pupil again to give an opinion on the question asked. She wanted to show the rest of the class that Wendy's previous answer had been a stroke of luck. No doubt the child overheard her parents mention the speed of light, or that by coincidence, she'd read it in some book.

"Wendy?" she said. "You guessed correctly what the first number stood for; can you now tell the class anything about the second one?"

Wendy sat pokerfaced. Even with her mind feeling like it was on fire, no recognizable change in expression disturbed the elfin look as to what was going on within the brain behind it. There was neither a nod, nor a shake. No crinkling around the eyes could be discerned, telling of a problem being wrestled with. Her lower lip did not start to sag, indicating she might be on the verge of tears. Nor was there a sign of nervous swallowing that might signify a lack of understanding of what was being asked.

Mrs. Meakin knew well these signs of child distress, and she badly needed to see them now. But the girl's face remained as passive as the paper that lay on the teacher's spacious desk: a sheet of lined foolscap headed *Pupil Record*. Along one side, penned in alphabetical order and numbered to align with the location of each desk—initialed by Mr. Ward—were listed the eighteen names of the children assigned to her class. She'd planned at the outset to enter a number between one and ten in a space headed *Attentiveness*, to determine the degree of each pupil's level of concentration, a core feature of her new methodology.

Against the red-underlined name *Wendy Elizabeth Harper*, Mrs. Meakin had lightly penciled in the figure 1, suggesting at the start that the child had the most uninterested outlook, thus deserving the lowest possible initial score. That look, she had decided, exactly fitted the countenance of this girl when she'd first entered the classroom. Where others had been curious—asking questions, talking excitedly among themselves, obviously looking forward to start of the new term—this girl had been as quiet as the proverbial mouse, doing nothing other than gaze out the window, observably longing to be anywhere other than at school. Of course, as the day progressed, or even after the first hour or so of class, a pupil's rating could be changed. This flexibility in her method appeared to calm Mr. Ward, who at first sight of the list had commented that such early assessment was too severe.

Wendy had been wondering what it was, in a brain surely not much larger than the head of a pin, that told a butterfly to zigzag so crazily, and yet so precisely, since she'd never once seen two collide.

The meadow grass outside the school window stretched out to a distant wooded area, beside which stood a two-story house. It was where she and Flopper lived, so the field was a familiar sight—even when seen in reverse view of what she saw from her bedroom window. The lush grass grew right up to the old school building, that at one time had been a church hall. Before its mossy stone wall,

the colorful winged insects carried on their dance, meandering and crisscrossing each other's path, oblivious to the
pale-faced young girl, sitting at a desk by the window, trying to understand their habit.

Wendy had attempted to answer the teacher's original
question, but had been drowned out when seemingly everyone else in the class wanted to speak at once. Now, a fol-
low-up had been directed specifically to her, so that she
would say, like Bennie and Peggy had seemed to do, whatever first came to mind. But at that precise moment, the
brilliant ray of sunshine touched the tip of her pencil.

"The distance to the sun," she said.

Mrs. Meakin managed not to show how adversely she
was affected by fully turning away from the class toward
the blackboard. Behind her back, the children ogled Wendy
even more. Suddenly, this quiet, shy girl was a celebrity
sitting among them. Peggy noisily pushed back her chair to
get a better view, pushing aside the still-arm-waving Molly. She wanted to get a good look at the *peaceful one* sitting
by the window, someone she barely knew.

Bennie frowned. His pencil, which he'd been imagining to be a space rocket, slipped from his fingers and clattered to the floor. A chorus of whisperings sounded. Muffled giggles, stifled from becoming outright laughs behind
the backs of tiny raised hands, could be heard.

Mrs. Meakin swung back to face the class. The rustling
and chattering stopped. It was like there had been a loud
bang, and all had been struck dumb wondering what it
was. Idolizing looks were being directed at Wendy, a degree of attention Mrs. Meakin had expected would be reserved for herself. Still, she was thankful general mayhem
hadn't broken out, and that Mr. Ward hadn't chosen that
moment to make one of his bustling, nuisance entrances.
He would hide the real reason for his visit by reading out

some trivial notice about mealtimes, or playground discipline, or that no talking was allowed in corridors.

"Wendy, your answer shows you to be most knowledgeable in this area of basic science." She had been careful not to laud the girl. She felt the statement sufficiently strong, yet embedded with a minimum of acclaim.

Mrs. Meakin had needed for Wendy to be mentally beaten down. By now, the girl should have been open-mouthed, if not awe-stricken, while her teacher explained in great detail—gained from considerable study of the subject beforehand—about the numbers to the class. Such an outcome would have left the children in a state of admiration, perhaps outright wonder. At the outset of her new class, Mrs. Meakin would have commanded her pupils' absolute respect, an attribute so lacking the previous term. Mr. Ward would surely have applauded such achievement. He might even have considered an award appropriate. The prospect of such rapture coming her way was now dimmed, if not extinguished, and by an inattentive, willowy slip of a girl whom she'd thought the perfect candidate to bring such acclaim about.

Mrs. Meakin placed the chalk, now reduced to a damp stub, back in the channel at the base of the blackboard. She sensed classroom order to be in a state of critical balance. It could tip one way or the other. Either quiet acceptance of her authority or riotous behavior would result. She would have to regain the composure she'd felt at the outset, when bursting with self-belief she'd first entered the classroom.

Nonetheless, she could not help a feeling of endearment toward Miss Wendy Harper. Clearly, the girl was highly intelligent, possibly even a prodigy. There was a certain charm about the child too, an unexplainable personality aura that she would have wished on her own daughter when at that age. But she would persevere, ask a third question, one surely too difficult for adults to answer let alone seven and eight-year-olds.

"Anyone in the class, anyone," she said—casting a nervous glance in the direction of the classroom door for any sign Mr. Ward might choose that moment to put in one of his appearances—"now we know how fast light travels and how far from the sun we are, how long do you think it takes that light to reach us from the sun?"

Bennie thought an hour to be about right, for he'd never seen a number with so many nought's after it. Peggy thought the answer to be straightaway, but a niggling doubt remained that stopped her from shouting her answer out. Molly could hardly contain herself. Something had stirred in her mind. This was her chance to speak out like her mom and dad had told her to do. Up until now, it had been all Wendy, or Bennie, Peggy even, the gangly girl who sat beside her, who she sensed was about to give an answer too, possibly even the same one she'd thought of herself!

Mrs. Meakin felt her chance had come too. Here was the stunned lull following the question. The little smarty one was deservedly ripe for a let down. A sulky "I *don't know*" would do it.

"Wendy, no one seems to have an answer to this one. Since you were so forthcoming on the other two questions, do you have any idea how long it would take for the light from the sun to travel ninety-three million miles?"

Wendy was thinking how odd it was that her mind, despite being crammed with non-school-related images, felt as if she was riding her flashlight beam, at its leading edge, shrouded in a blur of blue light.

The sensation was so strong, and she felt so warm, that she needed to glance away from the awesome numbers on the board, away from the teacher's triumphantly ablaze eyes, to the oak-planked floor beside her desk, to where in that instant her foot was touched by the ray of sunshine.

"Eight minutes, twenty seconds," Wendy said.

Mrs. Meakin glanced down at her notes.

"Surely not," she muttered. Against *time for light to travel ninety-three million miles,* she had earlier jotted *"8.20."*

Mrs. Meakin sagged into her chair.

Children sniggered openly then. An occasional chortling yelp could be heard. Chairs were noisily pushed back, desk lids slammed. Bennie threw a sticky-gumball that stuck to the leg of Wendy's desk. Molly chucked her box of coloring crayons in the air, shouting out a word that to a stunned Mrs. Meakin sounded suspiciously like *"bullshit."*

Hand to mouth, as if fearful she'd done something wrong, Peggy held back an urge to jump and skip around the classroom. Reassured by the rising clamor, she darted forward, scattering Molly's crayons, to giggle uncontrollably into Wendy's tousled hair.

INCIDENT ON THE ROAD TO KABUL

I will show you fear in a handful of dust —T. S. Eliot

The TV camera pans across a barren hillside, settles on a mean dirt road; focuses on an elderly man. A gray-speckled beard hangs from the man's chin like the remnant of some tattered curtain. His bare feet, calloused and stained with the colors of the dirty sand in which he stands, are placed one in front of the other, the stance of one braced for a frontal assault. A brown robe is draped around his body. About his head, a poorly wrapped turban has the look of a well-used towel. Partly unfurled, the headdress spills onto his shoulder.

Beyond the road, amid a razed section of stone hovels, rival teenagers, arranged on separate piles of rubble, hurl rocks at one another. Puffs of dust register the projectiles' points of impact. The constant barrage creates a yellowish pall that hangs suspended above the road, thickening the already stifling air.

A black-shrouded figure leans out of the upper window of a crumbling, two-story stone structure. Without pause, the sloppy contents of a bucket are jettisoned onto the road below. As the cloaked shape thrusts forward its arms to propel the sludge from the chamber, the impetus pulls the head shroud aside to reveal a female; with face so ashen it appears bereft of blood.

As the green slurry splats onto the road, balls of the sludge eject from the muck's core. The spheres career over the bone-dry sandy surface like so many dun-colored marbles, partly solidifying as they roll. There is nothing remarkable about this scene, unless you are seeing it for the first time, as the cameraman intends for millions of American TV viewers. It is the way, if not the custom, in this village, as it is in most other destitute parts of Afghanistan, to throw garbage out of the house onto the street.

Three military-looking men, themselves bearded, but with the facial hair soot-black and neatly trimmed—each with an assault rifle slung over a shoulder—confront the old man. A throng of onlookers help pen him in. He stands in the rock-strewn road, a look of despair etched on his face. You know by his wide-eyed expression, and the arrogant postures of the army men, and the behavior of the onlookers—the way they jostle, shuffle, and clap hands, chant, and how sharply they look at one another—that this man is in serious trouble.

His ploy seems to be to talk incessantly, to delay any punishment the men appear intent to inflict. Exaggerated bouts of cheerfulness do little to hide an aura of suppressed fear, apparent in the man's demeanor. It is as though he was about to be pushed into a deep pit, for he has a tendency to look down at his feet, as though to check if they are sufficiently anchored, to resist a backward shove. Clearly, the man is in mortal danger. His body language exudes it. The situation is made more pitiful by his endeavors to hide the fact, to seemingly put off what is in store for as long as possible. He seems to be saying, *"As soon as I've answered a few bothersome questions, I'll be on my way."* But beneath the strained countenance of normality lies the tortured texture of one consumed with dread.

From the heated jabber, the man is being asked about something he's done that seems to be considered woefully wrong. It's not a greeting we are witnessing here, or even a disciplinary lecture. The hot breath of deadliness permeates the air. Some form of judgment, sentence, or even summary-execution process is evidently underway.

The soldier to the right of the old man appears more intent on checking his weapon than questioning the suspect. He occupies himself with sliding the mechanism to and fro, which he does with practiced ease. The dull glint of gunmetal, the metallic clicks, the precise oily slides, appear to fascinate the bystanders, who crane forward, eager to get a glimpse. Evidently, they know that the owner of such a firearm must be someone of substance. They are also aware that mortals so equipped must be favored by people higher up, to be held in awe by those who are not. Ownership a weapon means one can be relied upon to kill when it is demanded of one to do so. It is also understood that there is a downside: choose not to obey and the prized rifle will be taken away, along with the would-be shooter's life, and possibly those of his family as well.

The cameraman feels that whatever shred of dignity the old man once had has eked away through his tendency to gesture. He does so with such prodigious arm movements that one fears he might dislocate a shoulder. To his right, to his left, straight-ahead, he thrusts out an arm to convince his inquisitors that where he's been, where he was going, or what he'd planned on doing, represents perfectly normal behavior. Yet throughout the performance his feet remain stationary. The sandy surface about their emplacement stays undisturbed. It is as though each foot is anchored into the ground by a concealed fastener.

The middle soldier of the three, the one conducting the interrogation—a cocky individual with a military-style cap set at a jaunty angle, clad in khaki dungarees tucked into stout, military-style boots and seemingly young enough to be the old man's son—suddenly shoots out a hand and grasps a fistful of the man's beard, as one would the scruff of a rabbit. With a grin on his boyish face, and urged on by the other two armed men, he violently, and most shockingly, tugs on the tuft. The pull jerks the man's head sharply forward, and down.

The throng cheers. The youths whoop. The dust thickens. The dun-marbles, widely scattered now from the slop's core, are barely distinguishable from any other piece of caked muck on the sunbaked road. The last drop of moisture leeched from them, they lie useless even to flies, which hover and dart frenziedly about in search of bare flesh on which to alight. The cameraman winces, but continues to film. The footage is to be shown on America's primetime news, a time when viewers, comfortably arranged in fireside chairs, will get a chance to wince too.

Despite the assault on his person, the man stands his ground. His feet remain solidly planted, toes clenched into the same small drift of wind-blown sand. He continues to protest his innocence. "You have the wrong person," he appears to gabble. His face has visibly purpled. More of the turban has unfurled, slipping off his shoulder to spill down his frail back, where it slumps in a pile behind his oddly arranged feet. The revealed dome is hairless, save for a tuft in the center of the crown, which spirals upward like a wisp of smoke.

The glossy sphere stands out starkly against the dull, sun-bleached pigment of his face and neck. Yet he makes no attempt to hide the nudity, hugely embarrassing as such nakedness must surely be. Nor does he stoop to pick up the collapsed turban. Instead, he remains resolutely erect, his arms continuing their outward thrusting.

The cameraman shifts uneasily. The soft, leather seat of the Land Rover sticks to the back of his thighs. A cold perspiration cloaks him. He starts the engine. The air-conditioner hums. The camera motor whirs. The powerful zoom lens slides.

The interrogator again jerks on the beard. The yank causes the man to sway drunkenly to the point of collapse, only to yet again maintain his anchor point.

It appears it is not within this man to flee, cower, or plead for mercy. And if he did manage to break and run, where would he go, and to whom? Who would protect him? Who would risk their own life, or that of their loved ones by becoming implicated?

The man gabs louder, to now be heard clearly above the rising clamor, to one more time attempt to explain his behavior. Wildly flinging his arms about, he continues his rant to the interrogators. Howsoever misguided his past intentions may appear, he seems to be saying, at the time, he deemed them to be proper.

Encouraged by the frailty before him, the interrogator becomes more aggressive. Egged on by shouts from the crowd, he tugs on the beard yet again, this time with enough force to wrench the man's feet from their moorings. The man totters, stumbles, and scrabbles to regain a new footing. His feet are now set wider apart, toes even more tightly clenched. His torso is so bent, it is as if he's about to look back between his legs. He slowly straightens, raises his arms high above his head, and howls! Visibly broken, it seems the man has failed to convince his captors of his innocence.

The cameraman, sickened by what is being enacted before him, and fearful of what may come next, slumps lower into his seat. Possibly aware they are witnessing the beginning of the end, the rock-hurlers momentarily pause mid-throw. The soldier on the old man's left, who heretofore has not spoken a word, and whose close-set, darting eyes glint like black opals, jabs the barrel of his rifle into the man's chest, seemingly with enough force to crack a rib. The old man buckles. His face crumbles. He cannot handle this new outrage, this frontal assault on his person. His feet again lose their hold. His toes frantically claw for grip on the loose sandy surface. He sags to his knees, offering his hands up in prayer.

A woman, clad in a black abaya, whose shrouded face the cameraman finds darkly attractive, seemingly wise to the goings-on, who also happens to speak English, tells the cameraman the old man is suspected of being a Taliban sympathizer. Like most females of her race, she is blessed with permanently smiling eyes; of such intensity the cameraman can do little but stare into them. "The three soldiers," she says in a hushed voice, "are anti-Taliban military. They are rounding up dissenters. Those that have been informed upon by others: close friends, neighbors, possibly even relatives. It has to do with their political and religious leaning. They have a simple choice to make. Admit the error of their ways, or die. Those who doggedly stick to certain beliefs, like it seems this man is determined to do, are deemed to be in defiance of the rules set out by the new occupiers of Paktīkā province. Such people must change allegiance or face public humiliation, even death."

For reasons the cameraman cannot fathom — perhaps it is the pale, elfin face that peers up at him from the shadow cast by his vehicle; the unblinking eyes, the woman's laconic manner amid such dread, against a backdrop of shimmering sand that has the glint of wet concrete — the scene reminds him of a movie in which a black trench-coated Marlene Dietrich stood defiant in a brightly lit, rain-slicked Berlin square. He blinks, shakes his head, and wipes away a bead of perspiration that has dripped from his chin onto the polished surface of the camera mount. He swivels the tripod to pan the lens away, over the hillsides — that rear up either side of the narrow road like brickwork slag heaps — to briefly dwell on a rust-colored rock outcrop, before coming to rest on a second knot of khaki-clad men. These soldiers are evidently in heated discussion too, but it appears to be over a different matter, for their babble is joyous, punctuated with outbursts of uproarious laughter. Others pass the group without a second glance: bedraggled, black-hooded women surrounded by shrieking children, who run, or bicycle wildly about, or are packed with their menfolk, like sardines, into trundling beat-up trucks, or hang precariously from overly laden donkey carts. The seething throng of humanity thickens the dust pall, such that it now hangs like a thick mist over the road. One khaki-clad man, who seems to laugh the heartiest, and who sports a burgundy beret with matching epaulets, clings to the outside of a Toyota pickup, into which nine others of his kind are crammed. This man, who would not be out of place in a Hollywood movie, is so animated, so unable to contain himself over the taking back of his province; he jubilantly and one-handedly fires his rifle into the air.

The camera moves on, its operator eager to return to the earlier scene. But there is no sign of the old man or the military interrogators and boisterous crowd. Even the spot where the violation took place is but pummeled sand, in which only the faintest outlines of the shallow pits left by the old man's planted feet, can be seen. And even these indentations are fast morphing into nothingness. Pounded by droves of scurrying feet, the churn of innumerable wheels, the contours quickly transform into barely recognizable depressions. Within minutes, these too have been dashed, into countless other configurations, until there is no evidence left on the hot, sandy surface that tells of anyone ever having stood on that particular spot.

THE CHATTERER

A man, with all his noble qualities, still bears in his bodily frame the indelible stamp of lowly origin—Charles Darwin

"Stupid buggers," Kazug growled. His voice grated like shook gravel in the weighty stillness of the barn. The farmhand was standing in a shaft of mote-filled light that slanted down from a small, cobwebby window—a bright, yellowed contrast to the dimness through which it pierced.

He gripped a pitchfork that was plunged deep into a bale of hay, spiked to lift the straw block from the loft. Years of layered webs, some entwined as thick as ropes, draped from the rafters above his head. In the gloom, the massed filaments took on the look of puckered sackcloth.

"Wot' ya' watchin' me for?

"Why don't ya' peck?"

The guttural questions hung unanswered in the light-stabbed air. Not a cluck, not a flutter, not the grate of a single beak, disturbed the quiet stare of the huddled birds.

Kazug scratched into his beard. Attentiveness from chickens was new to him, even though he knew there was reason enough for it. One of their kin was about to be slaughtered. The flock was stock-still, each hen flat-toed on the earthen floor of the barn, wondering which one of them it was going to be. He'd never seen the birds act this peculiar before. Should the whole cluster of beak and claw attack, beating their wings at him, savagely stabbing and ripping, as he imagined they could—seeing what they had once done to one of their kind that happened to have dropped dead in the barn—he might have to run for it.

Unblinking in the weak light, he savored the thought of the killing. The expectation caused a thread of saliva to dribble from a corner of his mouth, to ooze into a patch of food-stained facial hair. As the seepage scabbed within the thatch of whisker, and his mind relished the thought of the act he was about to commit, his oversized fists loosened their grip around the shaft of the fork to drop to his side like mallets, his stubby fingers clenching and unclenching in anticipation.

Silence cloaked the barn. Life was on hold. The secret runs; the nooks, the crannies, momentarily emptied of scurrying feet. Kazug raised a hand to his mouth. He bit down hard on the knuckle of a crooked index finger, as was his habit when contemplating slaughter.

He liked to chat with the animals, the pigs especially. He felt they showed more understanding. The porkers seemed to listen more carefully to what was being said. But even they mocked. At times, acted beyond their station. Downright disrespectful they could be, the way they squealed in delight, the way their sparkly blood-shot eyes looked back at him. It was like he was one of them!

Baxter was different. The Hereford bull never gave him any lip. The beast merely pawed the ground when he approached; often drawing furrows with a hoof the size of a shovel. Baxter was always considerate. He always looked up at him. Listening. Shiny black eyes glittering. Tail thrashing at flies. The heifers in the back field heeded him too. The young cows stampeded toward him when he opened the gate. But they always slowed down. Showed respect for him. Some even nuzzled into his shoulder, daubing gobs of creamy nostril froth over his jacket.

Mr. Holt's Doberman, Baron, was something else. The beast went into a barking fit as soon as it set eyes on Kazug. Snarled menacingly whenever he got near. It was hate, pure and simple. He recognized that. So he had few words with that piece of slobber.

Kazug couldn't abide Bessie either. The horse was the smug mount of Mrs. Holt, two of the most ungrateful creatures that ever came together. Chickens, now they were different. He'd never chatted with the likes of them before.

The fowl's silent examination of him…well, that was a bit unsettling. "I mean," he muttered, voice lowered to a whispered croak, "how can you talk to a hooked beak?"

Lined, pitted, grizzly stubbled, at first glance Kazug could be mistaken for a farm animal, were it not that he was clothed—if layered rags could be accorded such description. His rounded back gave him a perpetually stooped appearance. It was as though he was always about to pick something up. The illusion was apparent because he was so squat, so solidly droop-shouldered. His thick-fingered hands were as rough as elm bark, palms permanently curved from a lifetime of gripping: the handles of muck-laden wheelbarrows, slop-filled buckets, wooden scythes, shovels, pitchforks. His hands had stuck many a pig, pulled many a gizzard.

Of his past, his mind was blank, apart from a hazy recollection of lying alone in a high-windowed, smooth-walled room, within a corridor-ridden building, in which the main sound, day and night, was the echoing metallic click of doors being locked and unlocked. He couldn't recall much about himself that didn't involve being with farm animals and sleeping rough in woods and hayricks. Or spells, foraging in trash bins, cleaning out hencoops, or working like a mule in exchange for a place to sleep, and a bite to eat—much as like he did at Holts Farm.

"Get me a nice plump one," Mrs. Holt had barked. Kazug thought the flick of spittle that escaped the gape of her mouth to the farm's dairy cow, chewing on its cud. The way the Holt woman ordered him about made his eyes smart. At times, it was like he was Baron: *Go get your bone! Quick! Now, go fetch your bit of stick!* Of course, he'd tell the pigs and Baxter about it. He'd let them know how much he hated the woman. He'd let the heifers know as well, if he happened to be out in the field. They were good listeners. Soon after they'd calved, he'd be among the herd, chattering away, asking how the births went, telling them how much he detested the landowners, the milkman and even the two disrespectful youths who'd painted the back of the farmhouse. They'd propped their ladder against the porch, and Kazug had barely resisted pulling it away while the painters were leaning out from the top of it.

But he never told Bessie anything. Not a word. Not even how Mrs. Holt's slack jaw trembled when she yelled at him, a movement that made him want to dislocate it. He'd never mention the way Mr. Holt spoke to him either. Being called "Ape-Ass" was not right. Neither was being hit across the shoulders with the flat of a spade. Done for no reason at all, other than for the owner to have, as he often put it, *"a bit of fun with the farms pet gorilla."*

One blustery cold day, standing half-frozen in a swirl of sickly scent, Mrs. Holt told Kazug to lift her off Bessie. She said she felt *"a cramp coming on."* But Kazug knew the spasm was faked. She really wanted him to lift her down, whether she could do so herself or not. She told him that he had a back on him as massive as any bull. The build of a baboon is what he knew she'd meant, on account of the slope of his forehead, and arms that hung limp as anchor ropes, to almost reach his knees.

"Kazug! From the shape of you it's no wonder you were given a name like that. No wonder," she would often say with a snigger, going all crinkle-mouthed from the stink she said that he gave off.

On Saturdays, Mrs. Holt usually demanded the hen, so that Muriel, the cook, could have it plucked and slow-roasted in time for Sunday dinner, the carcass stripped for sandwiches on Monday, and the leftovers boiled with vegetables for a peppery stew on Tuesday. Next time it might be a leg of pork that Mrs. Holt would fancy. Boiled usually, with sliced parsnips, which gave off such a mouthwatering smell it would often drive Kazug to prepare his own. He liked rabbit best, if there was one in the trap, though a stoat would do if he was hungry enough. Simmered with turnips, onions, and seed-potatoes, the smell produced was not much different than Muriel's stew. The same was true even with the plump rat he'd managed to club one winter's morning—a day so cold, the field traps were frozen open. Chopped with field swedes, thickened with wheat mash, he'd found the creature still made a fair meal.

Mrs. Holt's demands meant that each week he must make a killing, and that day was the day, as it was for a certain unknowing hen. That's why he studied the flock. That's why his small, darting black eyes were tightly narrowed, covertly as it were, sizing up each bird. He eyed the thickness of a foul's neck mostly, but also the chubbiness of its body. A picture of a feathered form, struggling in his grip, was forming in his brain. He shivered slightly. A tremble fluttered into his legs, ran through his arms and wrists, to tingle his fingers, a sensation that made him want to yell out and run amok around the barn, while throwing the pitchfork at something—anything!

He'd found it best to walk among the birds first, scattering breadcrumbs, though dirt pellets would do just as well. He'd found they'd even go for their own shit. Being fed kind of pacified the flock, calmed them down enough to make it easier to grab the right one. Once the feathered creature was in his calloused hand, it was a goner. Clutching the wildly flapping bird while crouched on the earthen floor of the barn, he appeared even more rounded, like a bull off its back legs. In the dank layer of air that settled there, enriched with the smell of old straw and dung, Kazug would first tension the bird's scrawny neck. He did this to test its breaking point. The creature would squawk a time or two while he held it; wild-eyed, its clawed feet scrabbling to hook onto something—anything to gain a toehold. But once the fowl's craw was against his crooked knee—as hard and unyielding as a saw bench—the wings ceased their frantic beating. The bird simply gave up. The hen accepted the fate that his other, equally hard-skinned, begrimed, and pitted hand then administered.

A pig was more difficult. He'd need to first lure the chosen one away. Isolate it. At the same time, he'd chat cheerfully to the animal, tell it how much he enjoyed being in its company, and that being dragged by the hind legs into the barn was quite normal, so there was no need for fright. Leaning quickly over its head with a bucket of swill, he'd open its throat with his knife—as the animal lifted its snout to sniff, as he'd learned they could never resist doing. After a squeal or two, while it staggered about, blood gushing from the neck wound as if he'd punctured a fire hose, it would suddenly collapse, as though taken by a sudden need for sleep.

Muriel would call the village butcher then, a mustached, dapper man in a bloodstained, leather apron. The slaughterer would cut the sow up properly, all the time looking Muriel up and down as if he was going to do her next. There would be enough pork for a week. Mister and Missus would come first or course, along with families of the three loud-mouthed sons who lived in the village. As often as not, he'd be given a few leftovers, bodily parts he'd take back to the barn, to the place where he'd put the animal down. There, he'd sit on his stool amid the dark-red ooze that had yet to finish seeping into the mud floor. There, he'd chew on a trotter, a jawbone, or a piece of neck-end. And there he'd sit, twisting around on his wooden seat, spitting fragments of bone out onto the bog floor, seething with anger. Mrs. Holt always gave him those pieces. Barely edible bits of the animal Muriel often threw out for the crows.

It didn't bother him that the victim had been a hog he'd chatted to not minutes before. That he'd stuck one he knew. He'd told them they'd all had it anyway. "Doomed, you buggers are," is the way he'd jabbered it. "It's only a matter of time before it's your turn," he'd say.

Kazug flexed his throttling hand, no differently than if he was about to pick up a rake or pickaxe. He was struck again by the fowl's stare, going so long without as much as a cluck. Not even Rhode Island Reds could stand so still for so long. They always poked around, scratching, looking for a disturbed morsel, inspecting the muck for the odd maggot. He lifted the pitchfork. His black pebble-eyes shone at the sight of the tines. Pencil thin. Shiny. Smooth. Steel honed sharp as a needle with his own oiled hand.

He supposed there always had to be a first for everything. Even with chickens. Still, he decided, he'd better take a look around, probe a dark corner or two, check to see if anything jumped out that could be bothering the fowl, a starving rat perhaps, which he knew would go for a scaly leg. Even the cock didn't strut. He'd never seen that before either. *Beady-eyed bastard*, he thought. It crossed his mind to ring its neck too, while he was at it, only he knew Mrs. Holt would miss the morning crow. "The true sound of the country," she'd once told him. He remembered the sucked in breath as she spoke, and the massive, pushed-out breasts, like inflated balloons.

Kazug straightened to better see into the loft. His thick, bandy legs were braced to the barn floor like tree roots, booted feet firmly planted to support his heavy body. There were three hay bundles left, in addition to those he used for screens around his straw bed, which kept the draughts out. "Plenty," he muttered. He twisted the pitch-fork, split the bale, and chucked half into Bessie's stall.

The miserable mare didn't even sniff the freshly sepa-rated hay; she merely snorted and swished her head. It was as if he'd given the horse poison. And maybe he should have. The leather bridle and saddle he cleaned each week hung on hooks by the side of Bessie's stall. He hated the sight of the paraphernalia that went with riding, as much as he hated cleaning it and strapping it on, all the time aware that the mare's cream-edged, brown eyes were roll-ing in fear beside his head. Shovels, a couple of forks, and one of his wooden-toothed rakes were arranged against the back wall. He held the pitchfork like a bayoneted rifle, jab-bing the prongs into darkened corners. But nothing was pierced. Nothing yelped. Nothing jumped out. Not even when he yelled, "I'll stick anything that fuckin' moves!" Even Baron, had the dog been there.

The old Doberman, Baron, would have been put down long ago, if Kazug had had anything to do with it. The dog was greedier than sin. The vicious beast would eat anything. Often, Kazug would throw out stuff while clearing the barn, chunks of hardened dung mainly. After a quick sniff, down it would go. He was sure the old dog would gobble a live hen if it could catch one.

His spat words triggered a flurry of clucks. But no pecks! The flock was beginning to get on his nerves, all gawking at him like that. They'd never done that before. He looked over at Bessie. *Ungrateful beast*, he thought. The mare hadn't touched the fresh hay he'd mauled getting into her stall. The pigs seemed to be acting a bit peculiar too—like it was their turn. A flicker of unease stole through Kazug's shoulders. The feeling quickly spread into his loins. He shook his head. Bits of straw, amid a cloud of dry mud-dust, were flung into the yellow shaft of light, momentarily thickening the motes hanging there. It wasn't like him to feel threatened—other than in his mind, when he'd act like the whole farmyard was ganging-up against him. He'd then drop down on one knee, pitchfork held at an upward thrusting angle in front of him.

He decided on a Leghorn: a strapping fowl of about twenty pounds, feathered white with traces of reddish-beige in its cape. Kazug took out his crumb bag. He dipped in a hand—curved like a trowel—to fill his fist with the dried bread. The birds always at least fluttered a bit when he got to that stage, rising up and down off the barn floor, as though caught by an updraft. He thought of chucking the pitchfork among them. That would stir them up. He could even go get Baron. Set the bugger loose inside the barn. That would give them something to stare at. He threw half a fist of crumbs among them.

Not a single peck!

Not even a scratch!

Bessie snorted. Kazug was convinced it was the sound of hate. The motes danced wildly. Bessie kicked the door of her stall open. Defiant, nostrils flared, forelegs splayed, and head down, the horse's stance told Kazug that the brute was about to charge. She trotted straight out the stall, tail lashing, head nodding, eyes wide with terror.

The pigs spoke up then.

"Get him, Bessie," he heard them grunt.

"Kill him!"

"Kill him!"

He knew now what the hens had known all along. The remainder of the crumbs dropped to the barn floor. He cupped a hand around the pitchfork. It felt better with that in his grasp. For a minute there, he thought he'd lost it, that they were really going to get him. They'd tried before of course. One of the hogs had snuck up on him. He'd been bent down, retying a bootlace when the bugger tried to clamber on his back. Two hundred and fifty pounds of black porker, snuffling its square of gristle hard against his nape. It flattened him, but close enough to the pickaxe handle. He didn't half-give the guzzler some stick. Long after, he could hear the pigs' squeals echoing around the barn. It was a week before the animal could walk proper.

Now they were at it again. Testing him. The black one was in the lead as usual. No sense in him charging madly about. They'd only scatter and make it more difficult. He would take Bessie out first, since she seemed the most deserving. A quick stab in the neck would do it. It would be enough to drop her at least. One less to deal with. The pigs would have to come next, since it seemed they were in the mood—heads lowered, tiny pink eyes darting.

The drum of small-toed feet began to throb in Kazug's temple, building in intensity. A pulsating rhythm had set in, as it did once when he got angry with Baxter. He only got enraged that one time with the Hereford. For months after he'd cried in the night, yelling out he was sorry, that he didn't mean the poor bull any harm. If only Baxter hadn't leaned into him against the side of the barn and trapped him, so he could barely breathe, nothing would have happened.

The welts he'd put across Baxter's flanks with his studded belt soon healed. But he had to keep his distance for a week afterward, before he felt he'd been forgiven.

The pounding in his head increased. The throb reminded him that he must bide his approach. There'd be no wild runs this time. No mad thrusts or sticking of hay bales or useless jabs at sacks of seed potatoes. The chickens would come next, only it wouldn't be just one hen—all thirty would go. A few sweeps of his sharp-sided shovel would do it, and the cock would lose its head first.

After that, he'd go to the house. He always liked that part the most. The picturing caused him to drool, to almost choke on a rush of spittle. The Missus would be there as usual, along with Muriel, each leaning into the other, sniggering, crinkle-nosed, pointing to his bandy legs.

Bitches!

At first, they'd think he'd brought the roaster. Muriel might even get the hook out of the drawer, that she used to hang the bird behind the back door overnight, a bowl on the floor to catch the drippings. "More tender that way," she'd say. They'd be surprised to see him, standing in the doorway with a blood-smeared pitchfork. More trouble than usual slaughtering the bird, they'd think. A couple of jabs into each would suffice, although he might want to beat Mrs. Holt over the head with the fork handle first. He'd feel better after he got them two out of the way.

But it wouldn't be enough.

There'd be no sense in roaming the house for Mr. Holt. The mean, cruel bastard would be in his toolshed, stuffing a rabbit most likely. Or it might be a white-breasted magpie, or a gray-necked jackdaw that he'd snared to feed his hobby. At the sight of the smeared fork, the old fool's eyes would widen with sheer terror. He might put an arm up to shield against a head thrust, but he might as well hold up a sheet of newspaper for all the good it would do.

Beyond the shed was the paddock. Baxter would be browsing there, on the lookout for Baron, tail swatting, ears twitching, and eyes rolling around like giant marbles. The dog nipped at the Hereford's poor ankles, causing him to pound madly around the field, throwing up clumps of earth, tossing his huge head, snorting gobs of phlegm. Kazug knew the Doberman wouldn't be there though. The dog would be panting at his master's feet, begging for a handout. Mr. Holt would more than likely be patting the top of the animal's head.

"There's a good boy," he'd be saying.

Both had treated him badly over the years. Mr. Holt often referred to him as *"that bandy Neanderthal."* Kazug didn't fully understand the term, other than it was clearly scornful and belittling, considering him subhuman.

Baron was encouraged to be vicious. *"Go get the stupid Neand',"* Mr. Holt would yell out. *"Bite, Baron, bite,"* the farm owner would holler. Anything to egg on his slather-mouthed dog. Now both would get their comeuppance. It was only fair to administer what was due. It would be no different for them than it had been for the animals. Except it would take the shotgun in the hallway closet. Both barrels. Plus something heavy. The pickaxe handle would do, leaning by the shed door, which Kazug used for clubbing rats. Then, if Baron charged, as he was dealing with the old man, he could put down that bastard at the same time.

But he wouldn't touch the Hereford. He'd let the old bull graze in peace. Always good for a chat, was Baxter.

THEY CAME RUNNING

Keep your fears to
yourself but share
your courage with
others — Robert
Louis Stevenson

It was Nicky
who got us
there, in that
position, alongside
that trapdoor. And
it was he, who ear-
lier in the day, had
decided we should
go. Who told us
later that it *had* to
be that night.

"Intelligence," he said, decided him. "It's the only time
our snoops could be sure Waffen SS would be there. Officer types. Big shots. All together in one fucking room."

Nicky gave the order, rather than have his sidekick—
Corporal Bernie Johnson—me!—do the telling. The briefing was done with Nicky sitting cross-legged in the middle
of the group, his big, moon-head face sporting a belligerent
look that said, "*Challenge what I say, only if you dare!*"

He then simply stood, stretched to his full height and yelled "Right! Off your fucking asses! We're going! Now!"

I dreaded the command. Yet looking around the circle of blackened faces, everyone seemed glad to hear it. Not that anyone would want to disagree, Nicky being the rank of Captain, and bigger by miles than any of us: six-foot-six, medicine ball-like razored head and ham-fists.

So I made a happy face too.

Weapons had been cleaned and checked, ammunition belts loaded, grenades secured. I lost count of the number of times we went through this preparation ritual. The day before we'd been dropped by helicopter in a small clearing in the Habichtswald forest, west of Kassel. I won't bore you with any more preparation detail; suffice to say that by noon on day two we were ready to go.

The rain had stopped, the night sky turned inky-gray when we set out. There were six of us. Handpicked supposedly. By whom and for what reason I didn't have a clue. My first thought was *"what a fucking shambles."* To my ears we made enough din to waken the dead. I'm already thinking none of us will make it back. Even to the target's outer perimeter fence. The two-hour scramble through thick underbrush felt like a training session. Like what we'd done in practice at base camp. You know, squirming forward on you're elbows, running stooped across clearings, flattening against tree trunks—as if suddenly taken with a need to piss. I suppose we moved like commandos do in movies, only there were no actors among us. No close-up shots of wild eyed, water-steamed faces. Nothing but fear was in the air.

More by luck than judgment we arrived in one piece three hours later at the electrified perimeter. Nicky had us crouch low in a shallow gully so as not to be seen by the guards on the driveway gate. I could make out the glow of the main entrance in the distance. We'd been told that way in was a no-no: brightly illuminated, alarmed, approach heavily mined, you name it. The fence was mined too. Except for a narrow channel that supposedly had been cleared for us the previous night, the spot marked with sticks stuck in the ground. Stripped of their bark, it was said; they'll appear stark white, like real markers.

Nicky lowered his night-optimized binoculars to tell us there were three guards. "Two are smoking in a wooden pillbox beside the gate," he said. "The other one is patrolling along the driveway. Surrounding the entrance is a half circle of sandbags, through which I caught moon-glint off at least two machinegun barrels."

We moved further down the gully. Away from the gate searching for the sticks. Miller spotted them. Fucking hawk-eye! But they *were* white. It was as if they'd been painted. Fifteen minutes or so of silent scraping gave us enough clearance to slide beneath the lower wire. We found this easy because the spot had been pre-dug, then loosely back-filled—by the same fellow who placed the markers. We could have more easily gone over the top using a rubber sheet we carried. But Nicky said we might be visible from the guard hut. From there, it took us thirty minutes to cross a grassy field, to reach the inner fence. It was moonlit, so most of the way we needed to belly-squirm. This barrier, judged by the soft hiss that came off it, was also electrified. No one wants to go first, if they can help it, even so, Miller, who always appeared alert to things—like a dog being taken for a walk—unrolled the rubber sheet, and clambered over it uncomplaining. Next came a narrow strip of thin woodland, a dark-green slash I remembered on the map. Then, another belly-squirm across a close-cropped field, supposedly also mined. After that came the final fence, this one definitely not electrified, it being, from the looks of it, the original wooden farm

fence that once probably separated garden from livestock,
Beyond that was our target, the farmhouse.

The open parts were the worst bits for me. Writhing
across that space was scarier than hell. I was thinking if a
mine doesn't get me a sentry's bullet will. Nicky led us,
next was me, followed by Miller, then Shaun then Big Billy
with Joey bringing up the rear. When we'd set out there
were no lights showing. So we couldn't see exactly where
the building was from the gully—even with Nicky's night
binoc's. We still couldn't make the farmhouse out when
closer in. Nicky said the windows were probably blacked.
Moonlight meant we were in full view, but could more
easily negotiate the minefield to reach the relative safety of
the wooden fence. We did this simply by following a drag-
line, done it seemed with the heel of a boot. Presumably
put there by the same person that placed the sticks.

God bless that man I thought!

The last fence was something else. First, the thing was
so rotten it was on the verge of collapse. Slowly and silently we part-dismantled the fucker, then bellied through,
rather than climb over and have it fall down. Second, nobody seemed to know what the fuck we're supposed to do
the other side. I'd dropped back to the rear of the group
thinking I'd live longer. Call me yellow bastard if you like,
but I was shit-scared. Worse, so it seemed, was everyone
else. I was thinking crack-commandos on a raid shouldn't
be dismantling a fence in a fortified area, a stone throw
from a fucking guard tower.

The west wing of the farmhouse loomed directly beyond the fence. In front the building, German SS vehicles,
and a helicopter, beneath camouflage webbing.

The farmhouse didn't look anything like the images
we'd spent a week studying. The drawings showed plenti-
ful cover, shrubs; trees. Bullshit! It was as bare as my ass.
The building seemed to be nothing but a featureless wall,

devoid of doors and windows. No wonder the place showed no lights. I moved back up front, to whisper my concern to Nicky, but our leader was preoccupied trying to figure the situation himself. That's when Shaun spotted the trapdoor, by the wall. Think of it one of those beer cellar delivery cellar doors one sees set into the pavement outside English pubs, only this one was flanked with waist-high weeds and inlaid into dirt. The thing was marked on the plan. But not there! A metal clasp on the door splintered moonlight onto what looked like a hefty padlock.

By now half my head's left the mission, readying to do a bunk, back across the moonlit garden, past Joey's blackened face, beyond Shaun's hunched figure. I strain to see if I can spot the route we took after exiting the trees, but see only surreal gray. Then there's the minefield to go through.

No thanks!

Instead, I turn to see Nicky examining the padlock. That's when the guard tower wakes up. A powerful light begins sweeping in jerky arcs across the minefield. Any minute the beams going to reach the rubber sheet I see still draped over the second fence wires that idiot Big Billy was supposed to remove. But obviously didn't. Only now does he run back, and in a blur of movement, grab a corner of the sheet, haul it off the wire, ball it up and stuff the thing out of sight in some convenient nearby high grass. I'm impressed. Big Billy's considered the dumbest, slowest in the group – apart from me. So I lie low in the grass alongside the trapdoor, so sick with fear I'm ready to puke. Fortunately, the beam moves along the line of the electrified fence that's maybe 100 yards away.

Nicky's clear thinking and strength saves us. He pulls what looks like a wood chisel from his pocket and begins to pry the clasp up from where it's bolted to the wooden door. A few tugs, and amazingly and soundlessly, he unseats it from its moorings, to leave the thing hanging uselessly in mid air, looped through its now redundant lock and attached still to the frame. A couple of soft blows with Nicky's balled-up ham-fist on the handle of the tool gets his full strength leveraged under one edge of the trapdoor that enables him to swing the heavy-looking thing upward, to lean back against the wall. He then bends the hasp down to act as a stop when the door's lowered.

I can't believe it. We're almost in the fucking building and we only left the gully a couple of hours ago. I'm beginning to feel like a real commando now. And there's me thinking of getting the hell out of it. An uncomfortable feeling stirs in me: guilty your honor, but I'm careful not to show it. Only Bert needs to know how shit-yellow Bert is. And for all I know, the others could feel the same way, except Nicky. He acted like a true, clear-thinking leader. *"Fuck the danger," he said, "I'm going for it."* I just hope that if it ever comes my turn, I can be a bit like him.

One by one we silently descend down a short staircase. The cellar's as dark as fuck. Can't see a thing. All we do is cannon off wooden objects that we make out to be furniture that seems to have been jammed in there in some quantity. I'm so paranoid about the noise we're making; I whisper my unease to Nick. But he's already coming to our rescue again. I'm beginning to truly admire the guy. I've only known him a few days and already I can see why he made Cap so quick. On hands and knees he's groping about till he contacts a staircase that leads to a door. Don't ask me how he found it; it was so pitch in there you couldn't see a fucking hand in front of you. I ask myself why I didn't think of that. It's a fucking cellar dumb ass! And guess what? It's underground! So there's got to be a door out of there someplace that's going to be at the top of some steps.

Right? Right!

Nicky's on his way up the stairs, but freezes. He holds
up a shush finger on step three. He beckons for Miller to
lower the cellar door, to stay guard beside it. Kill anyone
that tries to come through he says, thrusting his holstered
knife out for emphasis. He then points to where the tiniest
crack of light shows beneath a door. Through it I hear faint
voices. Germans! I nearly shit. It's my first enemy accent,
other than on training films. I stroke the Thomson at my
hip. If I'm going down there's going to be a lot coming
with me. Metallic clicks tell me the others have the same
idea. Nicky signals wait. "At some point they'll maybe
move away," he whispers.

This is Nicky's third mission. For Joey, Big Billy and
me, it's our second, although it's rumored Joey 'got sick' on
his first and had to be ferried out. Miller and Shaun are
fresh out of training school. My first mission was a fiasco.
Dropped at the wrong site! So my real-world commando
experience is zero.

I stand in inky blackness, for maybe thirty minutes, in
a dank cellar clad in a black commando outfit. A black balaclava is pulled high onto my chin and down over my
forehead, far enough to almost reach my eyes. My gloves
are black. My face is blackened and I'm prepped and
armed to the teeth. We've come off the steps and are squat
amongst furniture watching a splinter of light beneath a
door—behind which is a deadly enemy. Shaun's crouched
to the right of me. Joey's the other side, with Big Billy close
by him. Miller sits nursing his knife behind us, squatted by
the trapdoor. I have one foot on the first step that puts me
behind Nicky, who's on step two, poised to lead the move
forward – or back as the case may be.

I lean back to rest, only to see Cap's gloved hand extend a finger. It's like he's hitching a lift. But then the appendage jerks forward, toward the door that amazingly
opens soon as he touches it. The other side is a hallway

that per plan has a door at each end. At least intelligence got that right. I whisper this to Shaun who stares at me disbelievingly. His unblinking eyes, like oiled white marbles, tells me he's in shock, one who doesn't know where he is, what the fuck he's doing, why, or anything else that's of use to anyone, except the enemy. In short he's a zombie.

Nicky pokes his head back in the cellar long enough to whisper, "Both doors are fucking closed, get the fuck your asses up there." After telling Joey to stay put by the cellar stair-door he jabs a finger at Big Billy and Shaun, tells them to check the left door. Grabbing my arm he tells me we'll check the other. I can't help thinking the bunch of us shouldn't be standing in that hallway between two closed doors in a farmhouse, supposedly filled with fucking Krauts. Surely just one of us—not me!—would have sufficed to come out to check things, the others remaining in the cellar. I make a mental note: black mark Nicky—his first in my book.

I flatten an ear against the door panel. "Nothing," I whisper. My door has an old fashion brass knob, touch the fucker and it squeaks. I'm even into thinking there's maybe a can of oil back there in the cellar. I slowly turn the handle, first one way then the other. The latch refuses to move. With my knee against the wood, the door doesn't budge either. I turn, and like sheep in a pen, see the others turning toward me, each sporting the same dumb look as must surely be on my own face. Half my mind has already raced back to the relative safety of the cellar, before a gun-totting German bursts through one of those doors. I could be over the fence, across the minefield to grab Big Billy's rubber sheet, run like hell over the open ground and be out of the mess within ten fucking minutes flat.

But Nicky has other plans.

"Bert," he whispers, pressing my arm, "take Miller. Go back through the trapdoor. Reconnoiter around the back of

the house. Look for another door, window, whatever.
Check if they're locked. If not, *do not* enter the building!
Report back to me on what you find. Everyone else, back in
the cellar."

I'm shocked, why doesn't he go the fuck himself? Or
take me, with him in the lead. Or take Miller. Shaun would
have been better still. Short, as well as skinny, he's probably less visible than anyone. I beckon to Miller. Gesture for
him to raise the trapdoor back up. He blinks. Three times.
It's as if an insect is stuck in his eye. He looks past me trying for eye contact with Nicky. Reassurance is what he
seeks. But since he can't see him, he blinks again. Only
then does he lift the door.

We step into fierce moonlight. I feel like one of those
targets at the fairground. I slowly lower the door back
down onto its improvised stop. After the darkness of the
cellar the light is so bright it startles me. I'm thinking the
guard in the tower must see us. I whisper, "Flatten." As
Miller goes down the barrel of his Thompson dings the
edge of the padlock that is still stuck in its useless hasp. We
both freeze. From my position I can't make out the guard.
Miller 's head shakes a negative too. I slide forward, maybe
a yard or so ahead of him. I'm Nicky now, the one who
gets to go first. Miller is so close to my shoulder I can feel
his breath on my neck. He whispers. "Well?" I ignore the
ignoramus, and move quickly down the side of the building. Around the corner, a porch looks onto a light-stippled
yard, mostly cropped weeds growing between unevenly
laid flagstones. An empty clothesline sags in the middle to
almost touch the ground. The frayed cord is strung between rusting poles. Dimly, in the near distant, toward the
tower, I make out what could be hawthorn bushes. They
poke out of higher stands of weeds and seem entwined
with what looks like thorny vines. The landscape appears

as per plan. Though the drawing showed a stand of trees that would have offered more cover.

I slither over to crouch by the back door. I can see the top of the tower now. But not the balcony part we'd seen the guard patrol. The arc lamp is still sweeping, but along the fence still, not in our direction. I test the knob. It turns! The door starts to open with a slight press. And there's no squeak! That's when Miller, squat by the corner, Thompson flat across his knees, holds up a shush-finger. The sound of a car approaching breaks the silence. Gravel is crunching. The vehicle stops somewhere at the front, on the other side the farmhouse. I remember the photograph: *circular pebble driveway, stone steps leading to black front door set off with white pillars.* Doors slam. There's the unmistakable tread of jackboots. I guess one; possibly two Krauts enter the building. I wonder are they the guards from the pillbox, that we were supposed to leave till last, on account of intelligence telling us the phone at the gate only communicates with the farmhouse.

"We'll ignore the fucking gate," Nicky had said. "The fuckers there can't go anywhere except back to the farmhouse. And they'll come running soon enough, when gunfire starts. Let them press their alarm button then."

I think latecomers, for the meeting that we're supposed to interrupt, and then grab documents the participants were working from. I'm ready to head back to the cellar when I get a second finger from Miller. He whispers that someone, possibly the driver of the car, is likely still outside, close to trapdoor corner. He says also that he thought he saw the flicker of a struck match.

As usual I don't know what the fuck to do. I'm squatting half in, half out the back door of a Kraut-filled farmhouse watching Miller hold up shush fingers. His blackened face and whites of his eyes remind me of Al Jolson. After several minutes of fear-driven mind confusion I reason that if I bear left inside, it should bring me to the other side the right hand hallway door. The one we thought to be bolted. I only need slip that bolt to be back with Nicky. With this sketch imprinted in mind, I give Miller a wait signal and close the door silently behind me.

Straight ahead, across an empty, dimly lit central lobby – I imagine one time richly filled with the ornate furniture that appears stacked in the cellar – I see the inside of what must be the front door. Sure enough, on my left is the hallway door. As Nick had said, sure enough the fucker's bolted. I quickly cross the gap and far too noisily slide back the bolt, before pressing myself into a shadowed corner. Just in time. A German appears. He wears britches— clearly an officer. His body language tells me he's agitated. He looks over papers held out before him in one hand, trying to catch the best of the weak light. A cigarette, stuck in a holder, he waves theatrically about in the other hand. He's unarmed as far as I can tell, with not even the standard 9 mm pistol. I kiss the barrel of the Thompson. Should he see me I will kill him. He must have heard me, for he saves his life by returning to the room from which he appeared. He slams the door behind him with the help of a jackbooted heel. I slip over to the back door. Crack it. Whisper to Miller to stay put. Cover the corner I say while I go back inside through to the cellar. His shush finger, while pointing toward trapdoor corner, tells me the Kraut is still there.

I slip through the slightly squeaking hallway door. Close it behind me and push open the cellar door to a hail of clicks. A softly cursing Nicky is sitting on the top step. Idiot, he says, "You almost knocked me down the fucking stairs." I quickly tell him about the driver beside the trapdoor that forced me to come back through the house. He says, "Good job you got an excuse Bert." I tell him about the angry German. That he came out of a door across the reception area. "When this door opened," I tell him, "strong light shone from within, along with the sound of subdued voices."

Nicky doesn't question what I've said. He's got the house plan across his knee, tracing my account into a route. It's the drawing that's been shared with everyone at the briefing. We all well know the layout of the house, where each and every room is, and every door is. And we all know now that the room I saw the Kraut come out of is the designated meeting room, our target.

Nicky beckons Big Billy. Whispers: "Take Shaun, go outside through the trapdoor and kill that fucking Kraut. And do it quietly," he hisses. "Use bayonet or knife. Your choice. Remember, silently! Hand over mouth first. Don't for fuck sake alert the guards at the gate. Then wait concealed, battle ready, near the front door until you hear gunfire. Then, per plan Shaun, you stay by the front door while you, Big Billy, take the stairs. Sweep the second floor, attic; roof space, whatever. Then rendezvous back with me downstairs. Shaun: I'm relying on you to keep your eyes and ears peeled for the guards at the gate. When those fuckers hear gunfire and they get no response form the house, they'll want to know the reason why."

Big Billy and Shaun, in unison, whisper, "Got it Cap."

I'm relieved. He didn't give me the task. Clearing out the second floor could find you stood up in a shooting gallery. We'd all been through knife training. So most of us could have taken the Kraut out. But in training, necks aren't slit. Lifelike sacks stuffed with paper are. But Big Billy's not called "Big" for nothing. And he's expert with the blade. So I've no fear he won't take care of it, unless, as is always the fear, the Kraut happens to be a six-foot seven black-belted judo expert. But then again, he's got Shaun with him as back up. So it would be two against one.

Nicky's whispering again: "Here's what the rest of us are going to do." Tracing the route on the floor plan with his tiny flashlight he says. "We're gonna creep outta here into the house proper, through the right hand door. The door you unbolted Bert. Joey?" he swings around to face Private Joe Lampton, who like Nicky has had real operational experience, though not half as much. "You continue on out the back door. Stay there with Miller. Soon as you hear gunfire, take out the guard in the tower. Any Krauts that try to get in or out that fucking back door, take them out too. Keep your eyes peeled for breakouts from the meeting room. Including them coming through this window." He jabs a finger at the room's bay window on the plan. "You're responsible for the backyard. Got it?" Joey nods affirmatively.

"Corporal Johnson, you're with me. We're gonna open the door of the room your officer came out of and kill everyone inside. Our orders are to take no prisoners. And there will be no escapees. Got it? None. Only then will we search and grab documents."

He used my surname. So I know this is for real. Now I'm wishing I was on the knifing detail. I try to appear as if it's an everyday event for me to be put in mortal danger. But my lips are dry. And each time I swallow, a gulp escapes me. I'm convinced Nicky hears; realizes the significance of the sound. The only time I've ever fired my weapon is in training, since for both my previous missions I was assigned a support role. I have seen gory film of what happens to flesh when caught in a burst from a Thompson. It's not a pretty sight. Nicky has the same sub-machine gun as me. Between us, with the advantage of surprise we should have more than enough firepower. What we don't know though, is what firepower the enemy has inside the room. And whether there are other Krauts in the farmhouse as yet undiscovered.

I wonder about the documents Nicky mentioned. It's the first time I'd heard they officially existed. There'd been rumors: *"secret plans, other bullshit,"* but we'd never been told what the *real* reason was. Our objective was starkly simple: *"Get to farmhouse. Enter. Take out everyone inside. Secure perimeter, search for and possess all documents. Return to helicopter landing site."*

"So? What's the scoop Nick? The documents?"

"Don't know. My gut tells me supply inventories, sources, locations where stuff's stashed, ammunition caches, things like that. Suppose such papers will be around since that's what the meeting is about. We're also to check for briefcases, file boxes, anything that looks like it could hold papers."

We re-enter the hallway. I'm encouraged to see Nicky's hand shaking as he pushes against the door. I note that the target door is inset in the wall. So for sure it opens inwards. From the look of it, it also opens swinging to the left. That would bring the door into a wide-open position against an interior-dividing wall shown on the plan. We cock our weapons.

"What if it's locked," I whisper?

"Did your Kraut lock it? Didn't you say he jackbooted the fucker closed? Nicky answers angrily.

"I'm sure it won't be locked. Still, what if it is?"

"Then our surprise attack is fucked."

"We're going in. Ready?"

"As ever the fuck I'll ever be," I answer.

We creep over to the door, weapons held out in front of us in case anyone suddenly opens it. We position ourselves either side, Nicky, on the hinge side, so I get to turn the handle, push the door hard against the interior wall, and he gets first shot as it opens.

I have to recount now in slow motion. From when I kick the door open, because things happened so quickly. Four German officers are sat at a large map-covered table. A fifth, who looks like he's at least a Grupenfüher, the one

I'm sure who came out into the reception area, stands gazing out the bay-window. His hands are crossed behind his back. Peaked caps are on the table. Holstered pistols hang on the back of a chair.

Those at the table get hit with Nicky's burst more or less at the same time. One gets struck down in mid-flight lunging for a pistol. The three others slump forward in their chairs. I estimate Nicky fires off his whole 30-round clip. The one facing the window turns. His eyes are wide in shocked surprise as I rip him with half a clip across the chest. In seconds all are dead, or are in late-stage dying. I'm now unable to hear. The noise in the confined room had deafened me. Joey and Miller are peering in through what's left of the window. I'm assuming they've taken care of the guard in the tower. It's like I'm in a silent movie and that at any minute text is going to appear.

That's when a side door opens that was not shown on the fucking plan! From the opening, a shirt-sleeved German exits, braces hanging, like he was disturbed taking a crap. He fires a Heckler from the hip, sweeping the weapon around in an arc. The volley hits Nicky in the face, blows away most of the front of his skull. I see this image as I dive under the table. Its thick, oriental leg saves me. Catches the tail end of the burst. Showers me with splinters. As I drop, I find my weapon that just happens to be pointing in the direction of the intruder. This britches and jackbooted bastard crouches to try seeing under the table. I press and hold the trigger. The remaining half clip virtually amputates his legs at the knee. Twin spurts of blood spray into the air like twin fire hoses. As the Kraut sags onto what's left of his legs, he howls in agony, just as Joey and Miller burst through the window, firing as they come and hitting the Kraut in the back of the head, cutting off his screams.

Nicky's a goner. I'm sure of this. I saw his face, or what's left of it. O My God, his temple is shot off. I can't believe it. I'm racked with sobs, yet no tears. Fortunately the Cap lies face down. A stream of blood pulses away from of his head to form a dark lake around his chest. Miller goes to turn him over. I holler, "Don't for fuck sake! His face is missing. And he's for sure dead, sure as I'm lying beneath this fucking table." Miller backs off, stoops to check for a pulse. Straightens with a shake of his head.

Now you know how I came to be battle hardened. How I came to lead the squad. How my mind blanked out the horror of it all. How I came to be lying on the floor beneath a table, hearing Miller emitting heaving howls. He sits on the edge of the conference table, leaning forward as if to vomit. He snatches the balaclava off his head. Combs his fingers back and forth through his hair.

I scream at Miller "More than likely there's Krauts still in the fucking house! At any minute one of them is gonna burst into this fucking room!"

Meanwhile Joey appears, cool as fuck. It's like he's waiting at the coat counter after a dance party. This annoys me a bit because if anyone should be cool, it's me. And I'm shaking like a leaf, wondering what Nicky really looks like. I lie still pressed to the floor amid scattered bits of flesh weeping blood. To one side, the remains of Nicky's binoculars, and what looks like a lip with teeth embedded in it. A piece of what could be nose bone lies on the floor not a foot from my head. Joey stands beside the smashed-window. Bits of glass are stuck in his tunic. His hand bleeds slightly. He doesn't say a fucking word.

Big Billy sticks his head in the room. "Am I late for the party," he asks? He wipes his knife on the door edge, honing it against the wood. Translation: he took care of the Kraut driver. That's when he sees Nicky, splayed out with what's left of his head part submerged in a red lake.

I sit up beneath the table. Gingerly feel for wounds. None. I'm in one piece. I stand. Face Big Billy.

"Fucking hell Bert! Don't tell me Nicky caught it."

"Big Billy? "What about the fucking guards at the gate?" I'm screaming. I have to release bottled up fear.

"Cool it. They're accounted for. Three. Both confirmed dead. Just as Nicky said. They came running."

I tell Big Billy, "Get the fuck your ass upstairs. Join Shaun. Search for enemy. Quick! Damn it! Now!"

I'm swept with nervous energy. Can't think of Nicky. If I do, I'm going to faint. Throw up. And there's no time for any of that. I grip Miller's shoulders. Shake him like I want his head to fall off.

"Status! Guards out back? Now! Quick! Tell me!" I scream into Miller's face, spittle flying.

"Quit the crying. You hear me," I say? Knock the fucking crying off. Now!"

"The Kraut in the tower's no longer a threat, being dead." Miller snuffles the words out like he's got a heavy cold. I sense his big weep is over. I see he too is now battle hardened. He straightens up. Says to Joey, "Common, let's take care of this fucking stuff." At that, the two of them start gathering papers off the table: wall-maps, notepads, and all sorts of crap. They arm-sweep everything, whether blood soaked or not, into a sack along with a couple of box files, and three zippered leather pouches.

I frisk the fallen German's. Take everything out their pockets; wallets, photographs of wives; kids, crumpled letters, cigarette packs, odd papers, pens, clips of 9 mm bullets. Many are blood smeared. I toss them into the sack with barely a glance. I've no time for imagining any a moment of compassion. In a few minutes the meeting room is cleared—apart from the attendees.

Three of the four at the table are slumped forward, stupefied expressions arrested on their faces. The one that

tried to reach the pistol, lies stretched across a side chair;
grotesque, blood-drenched. The officer stood in front the
window is prone on the floor. His is body strangely twisted. There's a look of surprise on his face too. The one that
got Nicky lies on his side in a pool of blood that's beginning to merge with Nicky's lake.

I examine the floor for a hidden trapdoor. Joey taps the
walls for fake panels. The door that wasn't on the plan
through which the Kraut came and killed Nicky leads to a
corridor that in turn leads out to the front door. There's a
small hallway off it that contains the main house staircase.
My thought is that other bastards have somehow made it
upstairs, where I now hear Big Billy rummaging about.

According to the map, the second floor layout mirrors
the lower level. Built-in wardrobes, linen cupboards are
found to be empty. Big Billy reports back that all windows
upstairs are intact. He says he's ransacked all cupboards.
There are no beds to look under, he says. In fact the upstairs, like the downstairs – with the exception of the meeting room – is empty of furniture. I think no wonder we
could hardly move in the cellar.

Big Billy holds the plan of the house up and asks,
"Where the fuck is the hatch into the loft?" I glance over
his shoulder. Jab a finger at a dotted square inside a cup-
board. "It's there," I say. For fuck sake be careful when
opening it. Grenade it first."

As I watch Big Billy working on the hatch and see him
realize its nailed shut on the downside, my mind jerks back
to the cellar. It hits me then that the missing enemy, if any,
is more than likely in there, hidden amongst the furniture.
Or more likely still, are already out the trapdoor and lost
into the night.

I shout for every one to assemble in the hall. I tell them
we can do no more. Joey asks, "What about Nicky. Do we
take him Corp? My mind races. We could place him in

some kind of makeshift body bag, strapped onto an improvised stretcher. But I know he weighs close on 250. That would take two men. It's hopeless.

"No chance Joey, he's dead," I hear myself saying.

"We're getting out, down the driveway, through the main gate. That way we'll avoid the minefield and electric fences. The danger is Kassel reinforcements, so we gotta move fast." I say this while banging my fist on the wall.

"Big Billy! Place explosives on the vehicles and copter out front. Set timer for fifteen minutes. Now!

"Miller! Open the cellar trap door; throw in a couple of grenades. Now!

"Joey! Shaun! Out the front door with the sack. Whatever you do, don't lose it. Joey! I make you responsible for getting the document stuff back. Shaun! Anything happens to Joey, you take that role. Got it! Wait for the rest of us down the driveway. Eyes and ears sharp for enemy. Now!"

I'm alone in the hallway. I go back into the target room as the grenades go off in the cellar. Quickly, I empty Nicky's pockets. I must turn him over to get to those on the front of his tunic. I grab one of the Kraut overcoats off the floor that was hanging on the back of the door. He is so heavy I feel I might need to yell for help, but he yields to flop onto his back. The blood lake ripples. I look away. The thought of what's there, and what's not, along with a strange smell causes me to gag. I toss the coat over his shattered head, and empty the remaining pockets. Joey has already stripped him of weaponry and ammunition. I can't think of anything that I should do that would be deemed proper, other than, say, a prayer over the body? But I'm not religious. I give him a goodbye arm clench.

As I exit the front door, Big Billy materializes out of moonlit shadows. Scares the living shits out of me.

"Big Billy, for fuck sake! Don't ever do that again! I could have fucking killed you," I scream.

"Sorry Bert, but I ran back to tell you. You've got four minutes to get the fuck out of here."

We run down the driveway. The moonlight is bright and clear. After the stench of the meeting room, the night air is sharp and wholesome. It's so fresh I could drink it.

We drop to the ground as one. A hail of bullets whizzes among us. "Anyone hit," I ask. Whispered replies say no one caught it. But I don't get a confirmation from Miller.

"Miller," I hiss," you still with us? Anyone see him?"

More bullets fly. Hit into the branches of trees entwined above our heads. Twigs and leaves rain down.

"Krauts must have good eyesight, or are using some kind of night glass," I say.

"Last muzzle flashes came from our left." Joey says. In this moonlight, they can snipe us easy. Then a volley from up ahead. Nothing from the right yet. Think they might be trying to surround us. They'll certainly be at the gatehouse by now. A Kraut probably got away. Raised the alarm."

I call out Millers name. No answer. Surely not Miller I say to myself. Nicky, I barely knew. But Miller, we'd been together through basic training. And he had a wife and kids. Please don't let it be Miller!"

"What we do Corp?" It's Shaun. His voice is cracking.

"What we do Shaun, is get our asses off this fucking driveway. But don't dare stand up, or even crouch. Bellysquirm!"

We reach the trees on our elbows just as Big Billy's explosive charges light up the sky.

I clench his arm. "Good work Big Billy."

Miller is nowhere to be seen.

"Maybe he did a bunk Corp," Joey says.

I tell him "shut the fuck up."

Shaun screams as another volley lights up the wood somewhere behind us.

"Think he caught one." Joey says.

I elbow over to Shaun, who's lying curled on his side in fetal position. He must have died just as I reached him. I take his wallet.

No time for tears.

No time for remembering.

No time for anything.

I try to think what Nicky would do.

"Think there might be a dozen or so," Joey says. "So far they seem content to snipe us from a distance."

"We gotta run for it." I say. "It's our only chance. Back the way we came in. Head for the fence position we got over. Big Billy! Recover the rubber sheet. Drape it over the wires. Now listen, we gotta cross the minefield. But for fuck sake don't charge over. Look for the drag marks. Re-trace our steps. Follow them. It's almost half-light. So we should be able to make them out. And as the darkness lifts maybe we can pick off a couple."

We have Thompsons. Great weapon, but best for close combat. Joey has grenades. No one left carries a rifle.

A grenade comes in behind us. I decide it's not hand-thrown. Rifle or launcher fired. I hear the plop, then the drop. I squirm madly away. As does Joey, dragging the sack. Big Billy, for reasons unknown, tries to find the grenade, to throw it back. But the deadly missile finds him first. Turns him into a mess of jagged bone and raw flesh. He never had time to even cry out.

Out of the gloom come figures, larger by the second. Faint Kraut-speak. Infantry types. Some slung with what look like Hecklers. Others appear to carry rifles with fixed bayonets. They fire without sighting as they run, and as they stumble, and as two fall to a burst from my Thompson. Our weapons have deadly affect. What must have been twelve to fifteen is suddenly five or six.

I feel a tug high up on my left arm, as though sprinting; I'd snagged a nail. There's a sticky wetness there, and increasingly, a deep pain. The tip of what looks like a splintered humerus shows whitely through a blood-pulsing hole in the sleeve. I manage to support the Thompson across my knee. I struggle to reload, burning my fingers on the hot barrel. I press in the new clip.

"Aw. Bert, I caught one. In the gut. Aw shit! Not there. Please, not there. You hear me Bert? I'm hurt real bad!"

"Joey! Roll a grenade into the sack. Now!"

The explosion showers me with earthen debris. Bits of burning paper cover the grassland.

Joey doesn't answer my call.

They came running then, black and stick-like, fast morphing, growing arms, legs, heads and the spikes of weaponry, zigzagging toward me across the tufted grass. Muzzle flashes. Another yank, more violent this time, and with hot-poker pain. The impact knocks me flat. I rise onto my knees, raise the Thompson, and fire a full clip, my last. I don't get to see the affect of it, as another hit strikes me—on the same side, but higher up. The force spread-eagles me supine. Arms, legs have lost feeling. It's as if they're no longer a part of me, and maybe they're not. I cannot speak a word. In the grip of an overpowering numbness, all I can do is look into a calm, dawn-breaking sky.

It's been a month since I was stretchered into a rescue helicopter. At least I'm alive to tell the tale. I have nightmares recalling the mission. My arm and leg have supposedly been fixed up, though both remain encased in plaster. My pinned shoulder still hurts like crazy, but the doc says the pain will eventually subside: *"When restructured collar bone fusions settle into healing torn shoulder muscle."* I'm told the chopper crew thought me as lifeless as the rest of the squad: Nicky, Joey, Miller, Shaun and Big Billy all caught it—along with twenty three enemy and farmhouse.

A Misjudged Approach

The most precious thing grasped in life—unrealizable by those not similarly stricken—is awareness that someone loves you—SBJ

Jeremy Sadler quickly scanned the menu for poached halibut. The parsley-sauced dish, drizzled with lemon, was his favorite meal at Blakey's. The last time he'd eaten at the restaurant, he'd been with Ruth. In fact, they'd sat at this same table, she with her head propped on the flat of one hand, staring vacantly out the window.

By this time, Jeremy would have commented to his wife on the weather, the good table they had overlooking the promenade, or how wonderful it was they were able to get away to the Oregon coast for a few days. But he might as well have been talking to himself.

Yet, at times like this, Jeremy missed Ruth. He didn't feel comfortable sitting in a restaurant on his own. He never had. Though ostensibly alone when with her, he was comforted in the knowledge that other diners observed him not to be. With Ruth, he didn't have to pretend to read a book, as he did now, glancing up from time to time to look out at the promenade. Nor did he have to pick up and put down the menu the number of times he had, mostly without ever having read a word on it. No doubt, in time, he'd get used to it—Ruth not being around, that is.

He would ask the waitress. Maybe they'd forgotten to put the Pacific flatfish on the menu. She'd been on her way to his table, but had stopped to look out the window. Across the road, on the boardwalk, a small crowd had gathered around a man who'd caught a fish. Beyond, underlined by a low seawall, a sober ocean heaved; an oblong of jade green beneath a peach sky, thick with wheeling seagulls. One gull, attempting to land on the promenade, distracted possibly by the angler's wriggling catch, crash-landed on the road in front of the restaurant.

"A misjudged approach," Jeremy said to the waitress. She had pressed herself against his table to better see out the window.

"Ooh! Did you see that?" she said. "Poor thing fell the last few feet. And on that hard road! I've never seen that before. Gulls are always so aerobatic." As she spoke, she tapped the end of a pencil on her lower teeth, as if contemplating the appropriateness of what she had said.

"Watch out! The poor thing's going to get run over," she exclaimed, gripping the pencil tightly in her hand.

She had spoken matter-of-factly, as though to a general audience, as if he was transparent.

"You'd never think a seagull would make a mistake like that," she continued. "They're always so sure of themselves."

The bird had been executing what appeared to have been a perfect sideslip. Dazed, it instinctively made to fly off, but after a few feet of takeoff-run, it faltered, sliding along the road with its neck extended and head down, seemingly unable to lift its bodily weight.

"Like a plane without a nose-wheel," Jeremy said.

The waitress had placed one hand, palm down, on his table; her other hand clutched the back of his chair. Her knuckles pushed lightly against his shoulder. Her black silk blouse, loosely containing her breasts in the manner of a sling, touched his head.

The stricken bird tried several times to complete its takeoff run along the center of the busy road, but to no avail. Helplessly it settled down, as if sitting on its nest. Jeremy thought it might have damaged a wing, for it gingerly extended each one to test the range of movement, while prodding underneath with its beak, oblivious it would seem, to the peril it was in. Traffic sped by on either side narrowly missing the bird, drivers apparently unaware it was there. When it seemed the next vehicle must surely hit it, the waitress suddenly appeared outside, boldly walking into the center the road, obviously intending to see if there was anything she could do to help the poor thing fly. Then, to everyone's amazement—many diners had left their tables to crowd against the long window—the seagull took off, its powerful wings flapping away as if nothing had ever been wrong. The crowd—clapping hands in appreciation of the gull having survived the ordeal—squinted into the light, trying to follow the bird's flight.

Jeremy squinted too, but found himself irresistibly drawn to admiring the waitress. She was standing in the middle of the road, stunning in her black and white regalia, between lines of traffic passing by on either side—from which puzzled occupants craned to see why a waitress of all people should be standing in such a spot—with legs astride, body arched backward, hands cupped around the eyes, to shut out all but the fast-receding bird, intent on the creature's flight, until the seagull dwindled to an insignificant speck in the pale-peach sky.

Jeremy and Ruth had stopped at Blakey's for a late lunch, six months before. It had been January. They'd stayed overnight at a nearby motel, in a room overlooking the beach. A storm had raged. Rain lashed the windows. Violent wind gusts roared about the eaves. The next morning, they'd walked the beach together, like newlyweds, holding hands, wandering among uprooted trees washed up to the high-tide line. The visit to the coast had been an attempt to save their two-year marriage.

But the brief period of harmony proved nothing other than a patch thinly covering an underlying suspiciousness that bordered on unpleasantness. Jeremy glanced at his watch. His wife would be arriving at The Leeward about now, he thought. She had booked a room there, he knew, from the motel brochure he'd chanced to come upon on her vanity. The glossy booklet was stuck between bottles of perfume. A room confirmation slip had been clipped to it. A romanticized scene on the cover of the pamphlet depicted a section of balcony, framing a mauve sea, which stretched to a sun-drenched horizon.

Jeremy had thought his wife had planned a surprise weekend for them to spend together, and that she'd forgotten to tell him about it, for she was often a little bit absent minded. Several days later she had still not mentioned it. Then, the day before the room reservation date, she told him about a business conference she would be attending.

"It's along the coast in Reedsport. The Holiday Inn," she'd said lightly. "Starts tomorrow. Runs three days."

There had been other deceptions. Jeremy was at a downtown Ashland stoplight in his truck, fingers drumming on the steering wheel to some tune on the radio. He was feeling good. He'd just received payment on a remod-el job. Tall and blond, Ruth was easy to spot as she hurried through the plaza. Lowering the window, he'd shouted to catch her attention. Obviously, she was too preoccupied. That evening, Ruth told him she'd been in a terrible rush. On her way to get paper for the office printer, of all things. They had run out, she'd said. Her secretary was off sick. Jeremy just had to check. There was no shortage of paper. Nobody had been ill. He didn't say anything. He couldn't speak: *a silent rage had consumed him*!

"What are you going to do for an encore?" Jeremy asked the waitress, trying hard to shake his gloom. She had hurried back into the restaurant to stand by his table, ready to take his order.

"I wonder if the gull knew," she said breathlessly, tucking errant wisps of auburn hair back into place.

Her blouse heaved above the top of the menu, the pen-cil poised like a dart over a notepad held flat in the palm of her hand. It was attached to a thin chain, which disap-peared beneath the folds of a scallop-edged white apron to reappear at her waist where it connected to a clip on her pleated skirt.

Jeremy felt the urge to congratulate her, on her plucky attempt to help the gull, without much thought it seemed for her own safety. Instead, he sat hunched over the menu, as if seeing it for the first time. Through a blur of meal de-scriptions, Jeremy realized that apart from Ruth, the wait-ress was the closest he'd been to an attractive female in over a year.

"Poor thing knew I was trying to help. Not hurt it, I mean," the waitress said. "I really thought it was a goner with all that traffic."

She turned to look at him then, appearing to register his presence for the first time. Her soft hazel eyes, moistened with the sting of ocean air, rested gently on his up-turned face.

"I'm so sorry," she said, smiling down at him. "You must be starving, waiting all this time. Believe me, I don't make a habit of running into busy roadways."

"I'd like poached halibut, but I don't see it on the menu," he said. His mouth felt dry. It was all he could do to speak. The pencil moved rapidly over the pad.

"It should be there somewhere, Sir," she said. "I know we do have it. We always have that one. It's our most popular dish.

"Would you like anything to drink?"

"A pot of hot tea would be fine. Darjeeling, if you have it. No cream. No sugar."

Jeremy swallowed. The room suddenly felt warm. He sensed his face was flushed. He'd not wanted to be so abrupt. He would have liked to explain that he was not normally like that. He had a task on his mind, a terrible thing he had to do—something that she would not understand. But she had already moved on to the next table. He reached for his book. Over the top of its pages, he watched her move down the line of tables set against the window; oblivious it seemed to the spell she had cast upon him.

Through the glass, the ocean glinted; blindingly, like a snowfield. He closed his eyes to its glare.

The previous day, Jeremy had checked into *The Ahab*, a nondescript hotel a block away from the promenade. The room was sparsely furnished, but clean. Freshly laundered sheets were neatly folded back on the bed. A sash window draped with a net curtain overlooked a small yard. A girl on the front desk had been absorbed in a magazine. All she would remember, he decided, would be an unshaven male of medium height and build, wearing a dark-blue baseball cap. On the check-in card, Jeremy wrote "*Samuel Blake, 105 Robert Road, Portland, Oregon, 87520.*" The name and address he thought up on the spur of the moment. The vehicle ID box he left blank. He figured his beat-up Chevy truck would go unnoticed in a place like Bandon. Later that day, he'd driven up the coast to *The Leeward*. The oceanfront motel was about an hour's drive north of Bandon. He wanted to get a feel for possibilities. He'd not needed to turn down the asphalt driveway to get to the beach, since the coastal highway was open to the ocean.

The sight of Ruth's red Volvo alongside Joe Morgan's white pickup in the motel parking lot sickened him. He remembered the strained explanations accounting for where she'd been. Why she had been home late. Why she'd needed to stay overnight in her company's apartment annex to complete an important quote. Jeremy recalled fresh-faced Joe, Ruth's supervisor at *The Prudential*. He'd found the manager eager to please, friendly and even trusting. They had been almost close friends.

The whole time bedding his wife!

At first Jeremy had toyed with ideas, halfhearted methods to bring about their demise. He likened it to thinking up plots for the short stories he liked to write. The 'plots' had whirled around in his head like an angry bee wanting out. The thoughts drove him to sweat-flushed confrontations with the bathroom mirror. Staring at himself, he'd asked how he could even think of doing such things. But he did. Day after day. Night after night. Week in, week out, until nauseated by the thought of it. He finally decided that he didn't need to create a complicated alibi. He would simply await an opportunity to present itself. An occasion that had the potential to look like an accident, an occurrence that could happen to anyone, albeit for Ruth and Joe, in slightly modified circumstances. Their clandestine stay at *The Leeward* appeared to provide such an opportunity. On the beach, he'd looked down at the thin blades of grass pushing up through the sand. To escape their harsh environment, Jeremy thought. Just like him. A light had snapped on in a first-floor room of the motel, throwing pencil-thin shadows across the sand toward him. He'd wondered whether it was *their* room. In such a small motel he reasoned there couldn't be more than four or five. He'd followed a narrow path that snaked upward along the edge of a cliff. The precipice shielded the motel from the powerful winter north-westerlies. Eighty feet below, rock formations, like small islands, reared up from a vast, sand plain. The tide was out. The ocean was a surprising distance away. By late morning the surf would be in, crashing up the foreshore, forging its way between the outcrops.

His plan was to wait nearby for them to take a stroll. Jeremy figured that each day there would be a fair chance they would do just that. Then, he would take a walk, too. In old work clothes, high collar turned up against a four-day beard, cap pulled down tight on his head, they wouldn't recognize him until it was too late.

But what at first had been difficult to even contemplate that later became something he thought he might be able to accomplish, suddenly seemed bizarre in the extreme. Jeremy turned away, realizing he could never do such a thing. Rather than attempt to shove Ruth and Joe off the cliff, he might want to just jump off himself!

Julia Johnson smoothed down the hem of her white apron. Like most clothes she wore, Blakey's uniform fitted her figure perfectly. In front of the restaurants long mirror she turned first one way, then the other. As her body twirled, so did the skirt, furling at midcalf, just as she estimated it would when she served a table. She was glad late-lunch and early-dinner was to be her shift for the next month. It gave her time to a see a movie or go to the library. The afternoon shift allowed her to take morning walks along the promenade, too, past the restaurant where she'd later be serving lunch. From her apartment, she liked to watch the twinkling lights of the small town, catch the smell of the sea, and listen to its delicious whisperings. When she'd first moved to Bandon from Cleveland a year before, almost three years after her husband died, she'd found it too cloying. Now, she loved the unspoiled coastal atmosphere.

Julia thought of the previous day and the incident with the seagull and how, to her own amazement, for she was at heart rather reserved, not being prone to rashness, she had dashed into the busy street, to try and save the bird from being run over. She also thought—while sensing a rising heartbeat, to keep pace with an accompanying wave of excitement—of the quiet man she'd served at lunch. Handsome, she'd decided, in a rugged sort of way. Of medium height, probably in his late thirties. A little untidy perhaps. He'd barely looked at her, but when he did, she'd felt the need to quickly look away.

There had been a book lying on the man's table. She'd been curious as to its subject, She was so drawn, she'd risked stretching right over him to read it. It had been a "how to" booklet on short-story writing. She felt herself blush thinking about the incident now. The man had showed no interest in her. Unusual, for most men did. Since Alan's death, she'd not as much as looked at another man, let alone thought about a relationship. Cut down by a drunk driver, her husband's death had shattered her life, turned her into a Cleveland recluse for three long years. She sighed, making a last adjustment to the skirt.

Jeremy sat on the edge of the bed. He stared long and hard at the threadbare gray carpet. The room around him was gray. The light was gray, as was the bedcover and curtains. He was trapped in a gray world of his own, a world in which he had no interest. Another bleak day faced him, moping around a tiny town with which he had little in common. Yet, he couldn't bring himself to leave it. There was no future for him back in Ashland, only an empty house to remind him of Ruth, of what she was doing at any time of day—or night. He didn't think he'd be able to handle that. He hadn't eaten for twenty-four hours. He supposed he'd better go get something.

Blakey's was crowded as usual. Outside, a northerly wind chilled the ocean air. People walking the promenade wore winter coats. A crabbing-boat, escorted by frenzied gulls, made slow headway through a choppy sea. Jeremy reached for his book, remembering as he did so that he'd left it in his room. Conversations were going on around him. Laughter erupted from a nearby table. As usual, he felt conspicuous. It seemed that he was the only person dining alone. A nervy self-consciousness gripped him. Maybe he would see the waitress, who'd served him. He didn't think he'd be up to speaking to her; he just wanted to see her serve the tables again.

He'd been given a table down from where he'd sat before. That had been two long days ago. The waitress didn't appear to be serving that day. He braced his arm against the table. So tight had been his grip on the menu that it had set his hand shaking. A waiter was working the tables against the window. Maybe he'd ask him about her. But what would he say? He didn't even know her name. Not that it mattered. Women never seemed to see anything in him anyway. Maybe that was why Ruth's interest had waned, and then extinguished. Clearly, she'd decided to get herself a man with more go in him.

He didn't ask the waiter anything. Instead he sat looking out the window. A fisherman was huddled at the base of the seawall, threading his line. The ocean glinted like sheet mica beneath a wash of slate cloud. He studied his reflection in the glass. A vacant face stared back at him.

Jeremy buttoned up the collar of his jacket and pulled his cap down tighter on his head. The food had made him feel a bit more alive. He'd been fairly blown along the promenade, walking south from Blakey's. Turning back into the northerly wind was a different story. On the way, he stopped by the fisherman, really, to look across the road at the restaurant. For some reason, it interested him to look back at where he'd been. He felt somehow drawn to the place. Near one end was the table he'd eaten at. A young couple sat there now. The waiter who'd served him barely half an hour earlier was now serving the couple. He thought of the window crammed with faces, intent on watching the waitress attempt to help the gull. He shrugged, he decided it was time to return to the hotel, get the hell out of Bandon, and head home. Maybe he'd stick his head in the gas oven. Ruth and Joe would be delighted with the news.

"Looking for another misjudged approach, are we?"

She was leaning against the seawall in blue jeans and black windcheater, with the hood pulled up. Jeremy managed to say he'd just had late breakfast at Blakey's, but hadn't seen her. The wind was his savior, for as he spoke a gust blew her hood off, causing her to turn to grasp it as it ballooned out behind her head. Jeremy turned too. He stepped awkwardly forward to help. The hazel eyes, which in the restaurant had momentarily wavered upon him before turning sharply away, now calmly held his gaze. Her lips were moist, parted slightly. Tousled hair played over her forehead.

"Wow," she said with a shiver, "must be blowing straight out of Alaska. Let me guess, you're a local fisherman and you have a big, expensive boat moored somewhere?"

Jeremy was conscious of the ruffled ocean, the sharp freshness of sea-borne air, the pale-peach sheen that washed over a slate-gray sky.

"I don't work Wednesdays. Unless there's something special on. In which case, I get paid time-and-a-half. So I don't mind either way. But what about you, are you a millionaire fisherman?"

"Sorry to disappoint," he said. "I'm over from Ashland for a few days. I'm in the building-contractor business there. I build houses, do remodels, that sort of thing."

He'd been about to say he was down from Portland, to hide behind the real reason he'd come to Bandon. But he found words worthy of his old self for once, the self before Ruth, the self that had been carefree, the self that had ambitions to do things, to go places. The fisherman's line sang, as would the rigging of a ship. She had turned sideways from him, her back to the wind. A small boy asked the fisherman if he'd caught anything. She stooped to ask the lad a question.

Jeremy felt the moment slipping away.

She stood and turned toward him. "Well, suppose I'd better get along. Perhaps I'll get to serve you again one day. I'm on a late lunch, early dinner shift this week."

"Look," he shouted, not knowing why he'd chosen such a silly word, when there was so many more appropriate others. But he was conscious of a need to halt time. To say anything, to delay her moving away. A lull in the wind when he spoke caused his voice to sound unnaturally loud. He felt it came out like a command, an alarm, to draw her attention to something he'd seen. Yet, another moment and she'd be gone. Out of his life forever, even though she'd just entered, filling him with wonder, with possibilities, prospects that made him forget Ruth and Joe. Indeed, that made him feel like wishing them well.

Pushing his hand forward, he shouted, "I'm Jeremy Saddler."

"Julia Johnson," she said, taking it.

"Pleased to meet you, Jeremy."

He leaned closer then. He wanted to be sure she heard him. "Sorry, but I wanted to tell you Julia, I thought you were magnificent the other day."

This time the wind behaved. The ocean merely seethed. The boy looked from the fisherman to Julia, to Jeremy, back to the fisherman. The boy's small round-face crinkled, the chapped lips widened to reveal tiny milk teeth. The fisherman adjusted his stance.

"In a way," she said, "I thought you were, too."

Her words tumbled down the promenade with all the other sounds of the precious moment: the subdued roar of a wave, as it washed over shingle and the cry of gulls. Below a puff of sunlit cloud, a white-capped sea danced.

Julia turned into the wind as it strengthened. It was as though the gust was willing her to stay. He felt he should walk with her, since he'd been going that way.

Instead, Jeremy lingered, savoring the romantic edge. Julia's figure slowly receded, threading its way up the long promenade, skirting groups of other strollers, behind which it abruptly disappeared, only to just as suddenly, tantalizingly reappear, each time looking back at him.

The Replacement

Let's start with the three fundamental Rules of Robotics....We have: one, a robot may not injure a human being, or, through inaction, allow a human being to come to harm. Two, a robot must obey the orders given it by human beings except where such orders would conflict with the First Law. And three, a robot must protect its own existence, as long as such protection does not conflict with the First or Second Laws—Isaac Asimov

Seen from above, the Jarvis home nicely filled a quadrant of Stella Circle. Identical electric-fenced yards and attendant Railcar terminals radiated off a common connecting loop, so faithfully, the whole appeared to have been carved upon the landscape with compass and knife.

Closer in, one could see that the quadrants were not so well kept. The Jarvis segment, in particular, was trash-strewn, and it would seem, hemmed in by piles of glinting, disjointed metal. It was as though a battle had raged between giant tin soldiers, the victors having since moved on, leaving behind the crumpled heaps of the vanquished. Closer still—within earshot—shouted commands rang out:

"Ark! Put dishes away!"

"Now! Dishes! Away!"

"And don't break any!"

It was upsetting for Helen to have to bawl in such an uncouth manner, especially when her sister Peggy was visiting. But Ark's increasing carelessness made Helen mad.

"But he will, Helen, you know that," said Peggy. "I don't care how good a defender you think Ark is, he managed to ding the vase I gave you. Remember? The blue, crystal one? I won't tell you what it cost. Chipped, it's worthless."

Helen knew things were even worse than that: the house not cleaned properly, annoying grease on the countertop, untouched for three days since it had been spilt there. Then, there was the garbage-littered yard and trash still not bagged for the Incinerator. She thought about how Peggy's birthday gift used to catch the morning light on the windowsill. Discarded in the darkness of the attic, the vase was lit no more.

She supposed Ark had protected well. No Vagrant had gotten into the house, despite their increased number and tendency to form packs. A bit like it used to be with stray dogs, so she'd read. Don had been right. Ark couldn't be relied on anymore. She touched the letter in her pocket. She was thankful a replacement had been granted. Still, she was a little saddened that Ark's days were numbered, that the robot was destined to be incinerated after years of faithful service. When it came time, she feared it might be a bit like losing a family member. She knew it would be different for Don. Her husband felt that a replacement for Ark couldn't come soon enough.

"It's official by the way. We're getting a new one. Might as well tell you, since you're here. Don wrote them last week. Told them straight. Ark was unreliable. He also told them that if the more intelligent Vagrant came here, as we keep being told by the government that the vagabond robots one day will, Ark wouldn't be able to cope."

"You devil," Peggy said, "not telling me."

Momentarily livid, she snatched up a magazine.

"When's it delivered?"

"Tomorrow morning, just as the letter said. It told us also to have our old one ready. For disposal, that is. Here, read it." She tossed the letter onto Peggy's lap.

It was from RoboCare, the outfit Peggy used herself.

Dear Mr. Jarvis, the letter began.

We understand that you have become dissatisfied with your RoboCare product. Be assured we are giving your complaint the urgent attention it deserves. Our records show you to be the owner of a Model 25. While this robot has proven a reliable workhorse over the years, we're pleased to inform you that our significantly improved Model 30 Android is now available.

Note our use of the term "Android" in place of "Robot." This change has been made with good reason. Model 30 Android is so lifelike, so intelligent, we're confident you'll think it's human!

KILL capability, so important these days, with the spread of ever-smarter Vagrant packs, has been considerably enhanced in Android. For example, the owner, via encrypted password, can now program SEEK as well as KILL. Think about that, Mr. Jarvis. It will not just exterminate on sight, but can be programmed when to conduct surveillance by time of day. Or indeed, any parameter of your choosing!

Rest assured, RoboCare will take full ownership of the Model 25. We have vastly improved our collection and incineration processing service in recent months to ensure that your old robot doesn't add to the already-high number of Vagrant automaton population. You will be pleased to learn that this service is available to you at no extra cost.

As with all our Robotic products, customers must complete a training class before taking delivery. The course of instruction is designed to ensure that you safely familiarize yourself with Android prior to full initialization in your home. From our records Mr. Jarvis, we note that you completed the training course on June 25, 2065. We can therefore verify that delivery of your Model 30 Android will take place July 18, 2065. Please ensure that your existing Model 25 is available on that date for collection and incineration.

Sincerely,

Eugene C. Johnson
VP Customer Cooperation,
RoboCare of America

Peggy refolded the letter and placed it back in its cream envelope, emblazoned with the bright-red RoboCare crest. "I'm envious, Helen, not to mention impressed. Don's obviously had better luck than me. All I got was a computerized response, you know, one of those, "thank you for your letter, but regrettably we cannot at this time" replies. So, I remain stuck with Zelp."

"Oh, you'll get a replacement soon," Helen said. "Maybe they're allocated alphabetically or something. Or perhaps they can handle only so many applications in the training classes. As you can see by the letter, Don's just completed his class. He came back so excited, but wouldn't talk much about it. He wanted it to be a surprise. Why don't you come over tomorrow? You'll get to meet Android, and at the same time say goodbye to Ark."

Peggy laughed. She glanced at her watch. "Gosh," she said, "better be going, got things to do."

"Is Zelp with you, Peggy?"

"No. From now on, the dumbass babysits the cat!"

"Why don't you bring him along too? Zelp, I mean. He might learn something. They claim the new model is good at advising. Some say they're almost indistinguishable from humans. Don wasn't prepared to go that far, but he did say that some kind of synthetic skin treatment was used, and that the robot is clad in a kind of plastic molded, collar-less cloak. Very sleek looking he said. Rather like the appearance of one of those science fiction characters you and I read about when we were kids. Don was also told that you can program how you want Android to react. The latest model can even interpret facial expression. Supposedly, you frown and your Android becomes concerned. Goes protective. Imagine being able to do that with your Zelp Peggy, or with Ark for that matter."

"I'm sure Don's going to love that," Peggy said, taking her coat off Ark's extended arm. "I'm not scheduled for anything as far as I know, so Zelp and I *will* join you. Might do the old robot good to see how backward he is."

Helen watched Peggy climb into her CV. The driverless Courtesy Vehicle was one of the latest government innovations, brilliant orange in color and equipped with destination navigation software, addressable from a cellphone. Stella Circle was quiet, as was usual in daylight. Quite different than at night. Several of the colorful CV's whizzed round the loop, "Available" signs flashing, no doubt cruising for "Vacant" slots, as would be the status of Helen's own terminal, soon as Peggy left it. A freighter sped along a distant rail. The line snaked along the base of blue-gray foothills. The chain of silvery containers flashed like a bejeweled necklace in the morning sunlight. A rusting car, flattened like a beer can, sat at the corner. Flung there, she remembered, by a Vagrant. The nomadic robot's crumpled, glinting form lay alongside it.

Further out were more shiny heaps. She counted seven in all. By midday, she knew that the Incinerator would be around to pick up the scrap. The vehicle would also deal with domestic garbage. Helen thought it rather neat that the metals and plastics that made up most trash and 'dead' Vagrants were melted and separated out in the Incinerator, then reused in new robot production.

The lone survivor of the night's renegade pack still lurched about like a morning drunk. No cause for alarm, Helen knew. Vagrants were almost harmless alone. Like homeless tramps used to be years ago. Isolated from a power source, it was only a matter of time before the metallic creature clattered to the pavement, to become another discard, another unwanted hulk, another pile of junk awaiting the Incinerator.

Helen just wished that owners would secure their robots better. Maybe a tether was the answer. She'd read that when robots neared the end of their useful life, many owners were just allowing them to wander off, to avoid the hassle and cost of having them properly disposed of. Hopefully, that was a thing of the past, since RoboCare now offered a free service.

The next bout of aggression came that night. Helen and Don had just gone upstairs to bed. Ark was in *Sleep Mode*, slumped in the hall, so intruder enticement calls didn't register on his computer. But the numerous proximity circuits in the yard buzzed their arrival as usual. Don soon had the window open, laser-rifle on the sill. He was well practiced. This was the third successive night assault. He took out three as they lumbered toward the front door. They were old models, judging by how clumsily they tried to avoid the beam. Others clumped about in the dark.

"Where in hell's name is Ark?" Don wondered, angrily tapping an icon on his wrist pad. He entered his password and hit *Kill*. Ark finally appeared:

Dragging his power cord, turning the wrong way, and getting tangled in the privet hedge!

Don fumed at the delay. Such clumsiness was galling to watch. Ark finally extracted himself to corner the two remaining Vagrants further around Stella Circle. With a single sweep of his reinforced arm, Ark disabled each robot's spinal column. That's when Don noticed the front door wide open. Fortunately, no other Vagrant was there to take advantage. He rolled his eyes. If ever one got in the house, God knows what would happen. It was just another scare. Another reason the old robot needed to be replaced.

Ark stood alone in the kitchen. Through a window, dawn touched the tips of the foothills. He sagged against the wall, torso bowed, hands clutching his knees. He'd long initiated *Sleep Mode,* but his mind was seething with computations. He was, as humanoids put it, seriously troubled. He felt a most unusual, labored heaviness in the region of his memory cache. He couldn't quite grasp the reason why. He would understand in due course; subtle meanings took a little more time to compute than they used to. He'd made mistakes, yes, but he felt he'd always gone out of his way to correct them. He'd never seen Don so angry. Long after, he could hear Helen trying to calm him down. When Ark pulled on the power cord inside the house, he'd thought he was fully disconnected from the charging outlet. He could have gone out on a wireless charge, or even opened a couple of solar panels had it been daylight, but with radar reporting more than one Vagrant, his processor informed him that the risk was too great.

Ark's power cord had stopped the door from closing. He'd then tripped over the thing, falling headlong into the hedge. The shock had confused him, making him look like a neophyte, freshly unloaded from a supplier's delivery truck. But he'd managed to recover and complete the *Kill* sequence, even though he was only quarter-charged. Now there was talk of "replacement." Whispered at first; now, it seemed, spoken about openly.

Ark gripped the plastic shrouds that covered the electro-mechanisms within his knees. *"Replacement"* His memory whirled, groping to match meaning with the subtlety of recorded vocal-chord vibration. He straightened, extended a pencil-like index finger, and tapped a series of keys on a touchpad embedded in his forearm. *"Take place of"* was downloaded and activated in core memory. *"Disposal."* Ark again entered data into the touchpad. *"The act of getting rid of something considered useless"* was implanted. He felt downtrodden. Unwanted.

The business of ridding the Stella Quadrant of obsolete versions of himself, Ark had found easy enough. Increasingly though, Ark had been coming upon nomadic automatons that had formed into organized packs, which made disabling them much more challenging. Several newer versions of Ark's model-type, seemingly let go by owners frustrated even with that level of performance, were quicker, smarter, and hence, more difficult to kill. The downloads only served to confirm Ark's worst fears that he was seriously outdated! He was to be replaced!

The RoboCare van arrived as Helen and Don were greeting Peggy at the front door. Ark was hunched at the end of the hallway, hands on knees. He was eyeing Zelp, who was sitting in the back of Peggy's CV. A Model 20, Ark decided—an early predecessor to his own 25 design. At least he wouldn't be outsmarted by that piece of junk. Still, it didn't alter the precariousness of his situation. Once inside the Incinerator he'd be a goner. That he did know. He'd seen others, immobilized and purged before being trundled into the bright-red truck. A faint, telltale puff of smoke and a brief, pungent smell of molten metal and plastic told they were gone forever.

There were two men, both on the burly side, clad in RoboCare jumpsuits. A third figure stared fixedly ahead; Ark assumed it to be the replacement, the much-talked-about Android. The sight reminded him of when he was first transported, how ineffectual he was. He decided that except for the vacant stare, the inheritor could almost pass for a human. That was a huge difference compared to his own metal-man appearance.

Ark's plan was to demobilize the RoboCare men, then, in some way—as of yet not determined—seize control of Android. But he knew it was no use attempting that until the replacement's *Delivery Default* had been overwritten. That way, Android wouldn't be as brainlessly useless as he obviously was now. Ark was keenly aware of this situation from his own experience of being delivered.

Ark had long known that he was able to activate *Kill* without the need for Don or Helen to initiate the command. This quirk of processor software was key to him having any chance of long-term survival on the outside. First though, he had to communicate his intention to Zelp. Unfortunately, the only robots he'd seen before of Model 20 vintage had been deadbeats wandering the quadrants, none of which he'd ever been able to communicate with. He knew he must now try harder to establish contact with Zelp, and then they both could try to convince Android to join them. Indeed, lead them. The replacement's superior intelligence might then enable them to prevail.

Ark had considered taking the easy way out by joining a Vagrant pack. But that course, he was convinced, held no future, other than to lumber around with a bunch of brainless has-beens that every few days needed to find a power outlet, or die. He'd rather face incineration. With Android, life on the outside had a real chance of being different.

Don and Helen had not done a memory wipe and shutdown—as was requested by RoboCare, before pickup—prior to preparing Ark for disposal. Despite the obvious security concerns, they had decided to entrust the data purge to RoboCare. Ark had counted on this. He knew better than anyone how complex a task implementing a shutdown procedure was, having endured such 'brain-cleansing' several times during production tests at the RoboCare plant. Neither Don nor Helen had attempted the complicated task in the seven years Ark had been assigned to them, so Ark had correctly guessed he would still be active when Android arrived.

Even so, Don turned to the terminal to initiate that very procedure, after having second thoughts about leaving Ark's secure memory open to others' eyes. The abrupt move caused Ark to realize his life was about to end. In desperation, he raised his arms high above his head in a display of token resistance.

Unwittingly, Helen was to come to his aid.

"No, not yet, Don," she said, moving in front of the terminal, pulling Ark's arms down as she did so. "Let RoboCare deal with it. They'll likely want to move him to disposal under his own power anyway, considering how cumbersome he is."

Ark's raised arms revealed shiny, stainless steel piston rods on their undersides. The shafts were similar, only much smaller, to those seen on excavator machines. They were powerful enough for the hands to grip and crush the head of a Vagrant, or more commonly—and more easily—

with a swing of an arm, disable a robot's spinal column, effectively severing or seriously damaging the robot's fiber-optic control nerve.

Don was incensed, not only because of Ark's aggressive manner, thrusting his arms up like that as a barrier, but by his wife's intervention. She always left Ark-related matters to him. Peggy noticed this too. She also noticed how Ark stayed close to Helen, never Don.

Despite the rage that boiled in his throat, Don was in fact glad of Helen's suggestion. He'd never done a power down purge, so wasn't sure how to go about it. And he certainly wasn't going to start looking through technical manuals to find out how to do so now.

Don was astonished by Ark's behavior. Never before had the robot displayed belligerence, except of course when facing Vagrants. But within hours, Ark would be no more, reduced to pots of molten metal and plastic, along with possibly a pot or two of fine ash, so he wouldn't waste time bothering about it. Thank God, with Android— he'd understood during the training class—the manufacturer did such procedure remotely.

Helen was reminded of an old movie interpretation of horror zombies when she first set eyes on Android. This was on account of his overall oily appearance and rather crude stitching, where scalp became face. There was also a suggestion of sewed 'skin' on the chin. Still, she decided, compared to Ark's gleaming stainless steel, with all its associated rods and wires, the olive colored, seemingly vinyl-skinned Android looked distinctly human. Helen noticed, too, that Android's walk was smoother and quicker. Compared to Ark's awkward, jointed construction, this new creation appeared muscularly athletic.

Peggy was appalled at Android's appearance, although careful not to show it. She now felt relieved to be keeping Zelp. Not only was she dismayed at the rubbery face of the replacement; she couldn't help but notice the seemingly lecherous look it gave her. The creature's eyes, set in unblinking sockets, resembled large, swiveling plums, they were so shiny and purple. The 'plums' gave the creature's molded-plastic countenance such a lustful look. Whether the unfortunate facial expression was an electro-mechanical coincidence, or the result of some default software state, she couldn't begin to imagine.

While Don attended to the RoboCare paperwork, Helen asked Peggy to motion for Zelp to come join them inside the house. She wanted to observe her sister's robot's mobility. Or, as it turned out, gross deficiency. Previously, Helen had only seen Zelp doing basic fetch, store, and cleanup work. Being an older model, Peggy's robot lacked much of the intelligence that Ark had. Peggy told Helen once that she never allowed Zelp anywhere other than within her electric-fenced patio, even in a CV, the robot had never ventured beyond her circle. "My metal servant is only fit to take care of the occasional Vagrant that might break through to the yard," she often would say.

It was obvious from the outset that Zelp's ability to move about was much worse than that of Ark. The robot barely managed to climb out of the CV unaided. Helen was familiar with Zelp's general level of mobility, but seeing him stumble now, being used to Ark's superior physical level, and after having watched Android virtually lope into the house, the difference was striking. She decided Peggy definitely needed a replacement too.

Don had argued that Ark should go straight away. "Put down, soon as the Incinerator arrives," was the way he'd put it.

"I don't want Android's brain contaminated by old ideas," he stated, glaring at Helen. He knew she harbored thoughts about keeping Ark longer, if not permanently.

But his wife stood her ground, insisting that RoboCare could pick up Ark later.

"So we can all have a last get-together," she said.

Ark had been ready to dislocate the spines of the RoboCare men, no differently than had they been Vagrant fiber-optic vertebrae, but he never even got close. Both workers were back in the Incinerator vehicle and gone before he had time to move. "Back to the RoboCare plant," he heard Don say. To pick up Android's terminal among other things. Before the RoboCare men left, they spoke with Don; they told him how to change Android from *Delivery Default* to *Basic Operation*. The procedure initiated Android's operating system to permit functions such as listen, speak, and so on, prior to being programmed *Full Personal*.

Basic Operation, as the name implied, actuated a series of steps that turned on essential programs. This allowed for a more gradual introduction, during which owner and robot could learn each other's peculiarities. In this way, the transformation to *Full Personal* would be measured. A more rapid changeover might prove overwhelming, if not dangerous, for both client and robot.

The entering of Don's security code on Android's waist belt turned on *Basic*. Even so, Android didn't outwardly change. Peggy thought the creature remained frozen-faced. Then the eyelids suddenly blinked, albeit slowly, and more noisily than either Ark's or Zelp's. It was a sound that reminded Helen of old-fashioned camera-shutters.

Helen told the RoboCare men to sit Android between Zelp and Ark on one side of her kitchen table. She would take the end seat next to Ark. In that position she could monitor the robotic interactions more discretely from the side. While Ark was warm and familiar, Android was cold and alien. At least thus far. The way Android appeared to fixate on Don, sitting directly opposite, made her glad it wasn't her in that seat. The imitation-tissue face, she thought, looked puffy. Its head inclined in a chin-up posture of alertness, reminding her of a dog awaiting the drop of an offered treat. Her husband's constant fiddling with the remote was getting on her nerves. As he touched various icons on its screen, Android made as if about to stand up, only to immediately be jerked back down again. Apart from the clatter as the creature was wrenched to and fro from the seat, there was a danger of his preprogrammed mind getting damaged.

Peggy sat next to Zelp at the other end of the table, facing Helen. She thought her robot a pathetic, yet endearing figure slumped in the chair; collapsed, she thought, like a marionette after having its support-strings cut. She was in a state of disbelief over Don's ineptness with the remote. She felt the urge to get up and give him a good slap.

Ark sat upright, but with torso bent forward, so he appeared to be examining the tabletop. Unbeknownst to the humans, his processors were humming with trial procedural avoidance, termination-delaying computations. Limited by his older capability, he had thus far proven himself inadequate to the task. He could do little else other than play a waiting game to see what happened.

Peggy was annoyed as hell. She had decided Don didn't have a clue how to control Android, despite having supposedly been in a RoboCare training course. Her brother-in-law was simply jabbing blindly at each button just to see what each did. Peggy made signs at Zelp to be sure he wasn't in *Sleep Mode* in case she needed protection. In the event Android went berserk! She knew only too well how effectively Zelp dealt with older Vagrants and how completely and quickly the robot could recover from a seemingly lifeless state, ready to defend. It was just a pity that between times of need, he appeared so lifelessly dumb. Her robot was clearly perplexed even now. The old-fashioned, overlapping, plastic, ventilation flanges above

his eye slots were a giveaway, being decidedly more furrowed than normal. It was as if he was trying to resolve
some unworkable problem. The last time she saw such facial behavior, Zelp developed a malfunction so severe that
she had to restart him. It was a procedure that set back the
robot's memory almost to the dormant state he was in
when first delivered.

Helen was infuriated with Don too. Sharply, she told
her husband to give up on the remote.

"Wait for the damn RoboCare technicians to return,"
she snapped.

Don, an exasperated look on his face, finally hurled the
button-bedecked gadget across the table, where it came to
rest in front of Ark.

"I thought it was going to be easy," he said. "In training there wasn't a remote available. We could only program from the terminal, which, as you can see, for reasons
unknown, hasn't been delivered yet. Believe me, remote-
programming is a completely different animal."

"Isn't there an operating manual?" Peggy asked in as
calm voice as she could muster. "Surely, there's some written instruction on how to properly start the thing up—and
more importantly, shut it down."

Zelp was trying to decode why Ark, sitting on the other side of Android from him, was pumping out so much
data, most of which he couldn't decipher. But he sensed
appalling things, possibly even about himself. Although
he'd had trouble keeping up with what was going on, he
understood Ark wanted him to do something about it.

Something extraordinary.

Something he'd never attempted before.

As best as Zelp could tell, the flow of messages told
him he was soon going to be replaced. Just like Ark said he
was going to be today. And that he and Ark should band
together to prevent it. Ark was even reinforcing his wire-

less transmissions with vibration. Over and over, ever
since they'd sat down.

Zelp, even with his feeble, out-of-date brain, was now
beginning to get it. *"De-brained," "Scrapped,"* and *"Like a
piece of junk"* were now activated line items in his core
memory. As a consequence, the robot felt the urge to inhib-
it interference with his new state. To activate *"Deny Owner
Access."* Even, *"Self-activate Kill"* command.

If only Zelp could. That Authority Level was something only done by Peggy. She would enter a special password, and then only when Vagrants threatened. Ark's data
demands, and the continuous vibrating intelligence were
close to overwhelming Zelp's old brain.

Yet, incredibly, he found himself vibrating back, and in
doing so, self-initiating the transfer of intelligence from
Ark's superior memory core. Essentially, illegal upgrades
were being transmitted to him that he was receiving and
storing within his own core memory.

The new commands now rested alongside *"De-
brained," "Scrapped,"* and *"Like a piece of junk."* As the new
information surged through his system, he felt rejuvenat-
ed. Younger. Sharper. Ready to launch forward the instant
Ark triggered him to do so. Even if Peggy commanded,
"No!"

Android—who up to this point had sat at the table in a
passive state, seeing nothing before him but a slab of grayness, hearing nothing but the electric whirl of shuffled ter-
abytes, suddenly became aware of electrifying, vivid detail.
Dull, muffled sound instantly became crisp, high fidelity.
Android quite suddenly gained an acute awareness of his
bearings and the scene before him:

*"Located at Jarvis Stella Circle residence on wooden seat at
oblong wooden table between Model 25, Ark—left; Model 20,
Zelp—right. At left of Ark: Level 2 humanoid Helen. Right of*

Ark: Level 5 humanoid Peggy. Directly facing: Level 1 humanoid Don."

"*Got it!*" Android suddenly and startlingly exclaimed. "There," Don said. "Our new Android is up in "*Basic Operation.*" And I didn't do anything, other than press one button on his belt. How's that for smart? So clever. Android *anticipated* what I wanted him to do! Now we can communicate without needing that stupid remote. I'm sure he's already identified everyone around him. Fitted each of us into a hierarchal memory slot. A chain of command, if you will. "*Basic,*" should enable him to move around under his own control, even outside if necessary. With Ark it took weeks to even find his way around the living room, let alone step out into the yard. Android should be able to do that from the get-go."

"Got what, Android? And you don't have to shout. We can hear you loud and clear at normal volume."

Android was scanning reams of data. A wireless dump from Ark was completing. There was also sporadic input from Zelp. This was unusual right at the commencement of activation. Android now remembered his previous 'life' on the factory assembly line, surrounded by lines of identical Model 30's. His command modules were opened up, being worked on by white-coated technicians. His new location was different. A quick memory scan, even in "*Basic,*" told him he was located in a kitchen: an eating room in a house on Stella Circle.

"Volume level lowered. All around table identified and in focus. Data secure in core memory bank CD900."

"We're not sure what that geek-speak means, Android," Don said. "But you do express well. No trace of echo. No sign of Ark's harshness either. And you turn your head. You look at people individually. Not just stare stupidly at the tabletop!"

"Is communication going on between them? In the background, I mean?" Helen asked.

"Maybe. Let's see," Don said.

"Android, are you in touch with Ark or Zelp yet?"

"Yes, Don. It seems they were dumping data on me even when I was in *Delivery Default.* So there is a lot backed up. I have now been able to decode most of it. It's not good news that I have for you. They have been telling me bad things. About what's in store for them. Things that cause me great concern."

Don looked sharply at Helen. "I told you RoboCare should have taken Ark!"

"Do a restart then. Shut him down," Helen said.

"Can't. Procedure's not possible with Android. At least for me to command. All we have is the stupid remote."

"What sort of things have you been learning, Android?" Don asked.

"That these older robots are destined for deactivation. To be purged, followed by an intense burn-cycle," Android replied.

"Is that true, Don? Are they going to be incinerated?" the replacement robot asked.

"Now! What do I tell him?" Don exclaimed, fuming.

"Nothing!" Peggy said, jumping up alarmed, signaling Zelp to join her. "Until RoboCare returns, don't any of us speak another word! Sign language is the rule from now on. Or we move to another room. In fact, we should do that now, before the situation gets out of hand."

Zelp's decoder weighed in favor of ignoring the command. The old robot struggled for a moment with competing inputs before deciding to accept the coder's bias: *"Overrule Peggy command, remain seated at table."*

Android's fast wireless modem spat a data burst:

Humanoid Don has been unable to confirm that you robots are not destined for elimination by fire. My core CPU tells me the statement means, in effect, you will be laser-burned at such high temperature your bodies, processors, memory cores, software-structured discs, will be reduced to liquid metal, plastic and white ash in less than twenty seconds.

Ark detected the burst, but was having trouble decoding most of it.

Zelp's old receiver was incompatible with the format used, so couldn't decode *any* of the data burst.

Meanwhile, five Vagrants milled outside the Jarvis house. Martin, a smarter-than-normal robot, at least for a Vagrant, was one of them. Martin had just slid back the Government Issue steel grating on the Jarvis front door. Evidently, the auto-mechanism had not caused the lock-rod to push fully home. He reached through the grill and attempted to turn the inside door latch. Reading an unfamiliar grip, the owner-sensing handle refused to budge.

Android was oblivious to the Vagrant threat. There was nothing in *"Basic Operation"* to correlate. But he did get input from Ark that an outside danger existed. He also could hear reverberations emanating from the region of the front door. And all three humans were looking fixedly in that direction.

Zelp felt completely overwhelmed. Something was seriously amiss. But what? Not being in his own quadrant, he felt insecure. In an unfamiliar location, he was totally confused. The massive amounts of data flooding into his system, while causing some welcome rejuvenation, had exhausted his ability to decode it.

Ark was aware of Vagrant presence. He'd known for some time that this pack was on the prowl. He checked his charge level. Fifty-seven percent should be enough. If directed, he could go out now and cripple them all in minutes. Except that is, the one with the ID Martin—a robot he'd encountered before and the most intelligent he'd ever faced. Martin was largely 'unknowable', not being a

RoboCare product, and much quicker with thought than Zelp, possibly on a level with himself. This fact made him wonder why Martin was homeless in the first place. He must have once had a secure station, just like Ark was trying to hang onto now. But he wasn't going to do anything at this time. It was all he could do to focus on saving himself. Unless he got a *"Kill"* command from Helen, of course. He could initiate the level himself, if necessary.

"Peggy! We don't need to keep quiet!" Don bellowed. "We don't need to go anywhere. Android is programmed to take instruction from me. And only me."

"Get it!"

"Whatever I tell Android to do, he will. Plain and simple. So refrain from panicky outbursts, if you would, please. And if you feel you must go somewhere, go jump in your CV. Go home!"

"And take dumbass Zelp with you!"

Peggy seethed. Anxiety pulled at her face. She didn't quite know how to respond to such a barrage of shouted insults. She was choked that Don had berated her, as he so often did to her sister. His outburst was humiliating, especially in front of Android. All she'd wanted was for everyone to be extra careful about what they said. She sensed the replacement watching her now, out of the corners of his plum eyes. Seemingly, the thing was aware of her embarrassment. Enjoying her predicament! She gripped the back of her chair so tightly, the knuckles on her small hands turned white.

What was even more humiliating was that Zelp had ignored her command too! That, she *couldn't* believe.

She was of two minds as to whether to leave on her own. Then Zelp would face a choice. But she couldn't bring herself to desert her sister. And Vagrants were supposedly outside. Even with Zelp, it might be risky to try crossing the yard to the terminal.

Martin was desperate. He was down to 10-percent charge level and exhausted. It was over two weeks since he'd shared an outlet. A lucky find, unguarded outside. Somehow the government inspectors had missed it. It was the only one he'd come upon in two weeks of purposeless wandering, during which several times he'd narrowly escaped the Incinerator. He knew a RoboCare Model 25 named Ark was inside the Jarvis residence. Ark was a formidable robot with which he'd had several previous, uncomfortable encounters. Earlier, he'd noted the arrival of a Model 20 and the delivery of a strange looking new robot, about which he knew nothing.

An image of a vaporizing laser furnace caused Martin's memory to momentarily lose sync. The blackout caused him to drop to one knee on the doorstep against which his leg had been braced, ready for its steel-encased patella to try to cave in the grating. But he was too weak to even attempt it. Even had he broken through, he knew the reinforced door behind, like so many he'd tried to break down before, would not yield. Not even if all five robots lunged at it at the same time.

Ark was sorting input from Android when he got a "Kill" from Helen. "Immediate: Activate on Vagrants," was all the code said. He could do nothing other than act. It was the highest priority and overruled all other inputs—even if executing the command threatened his own existence.

As Ark rose from his seat, Peggy volunteered that Zelp would go with him. This gave reason for her to activate "Kill" too. The command would overwrite Zelp's failure to respond to her earlier attempt, and place the robot firmly back under her control.

But for Zelp it was not to be. The added input, over and above constant data packets streaming from Android, along with continuous vibrations from Ark, finally overwhelmed his ability to sort it. The robot fell off the chair and clattered to the floor, limbs, arms shaking and violent spasms racking his metal torso.

As Zelp fell, he instinctively flung out an arm to steady himself. The fast-moving metal claw caught Android on his instep, a place that design computers had predicted to be the most protected spot on a robot's body. It was right where a sensing junction pad lay beneath a thin layer of Teflon tape, which was temporarily stuck there by RoboCare in place of a screwed on plastic plate. The plate was to be fitted when home initiation was complete. The blow destroyed a small, yet vital, section of Android's "Brain Command Module," effectively paralyzing the robot from the waist down.

Android suddenly had no legs!

Don shouted at Peggy, "Get that fucking raving-mad robot of yours out this house—now!"

Still reeling from Don's earlier verbal assault, Peggy was in no mood to take another broadside. She had backed away from Zelp, wide-eyed, with hand over mouth, having never seen anyone take a fit before, let alone a robot. Zelp's seizures had lessened, but the unpredictable flaying of its steel arms and legs meant the metal man was still too dangerous to approach. Any command would surely make matters worse, since memory overload was likely the reason for the convulsions.

Helen had hold of Android's remote, frantically thumbing buttons, trying to arrest any tendency for the creature to leverage any further movement. The loss of leg control had triggered a default instruction for Android to grip the underside of his chair with his metal hands and propel himself in a sitting position around the kitchen in a series of jerked hops.

"Don!" she shouted. "Do something! Android's remote doesn't seem to be having any effect. Looks like it died when you flung it on the table. You'll just have to somehow get a hold of the thing. Try bundling it out the back door.

Before it wrecks my kitchen!"

Ark had already exited the kitchen by the back door, immediately to be faced with two Vagrants. With their batteries almost run down, they feebly and unsuccessfully tried to defend themselves from the fatal blows Ark delivered across each robot's upper vertebrae. Two other Vagrants turned to run, stumbled and fell facedown. Ark forcefully kneeled in the middle of each robot's back, until he heard the familiar snap of a fiber-optic spinal column.

Martin came at him then. Ark realized, too late, that the lead Vagrant must have been hidden in the yard somewhere behind him. Ark felt the blow across his back that crashed him facedown onto the concrete path. His weight, plus the impetus of Martin's thrust, flattened his sense-of-smell input—a computer chip in a metal vent disguised as a humanoid nose, in the middle of his face.

The RoboCare men returned then.

Martin realized he was doomed the minute the Incinerator pulled up. They'd been after him for months. Now here he was, trapped in a small yard from which there was no escape. The last clear thing Martin remembered was an electrocution dart penetrating his processor. After that, a brief interval occurred where everything whirled out of control. Had he been able to communicate this last vestige of feeling, he would have said that the sensation was of *"clinging to the periphery of a fast-spinning wheel."*

Ark made a run for it. But clumsy as ever, he tripped, sprawling alongside the Incinerator. Conveniently for RoboCare, he fell next to a flap on the side of the vehicle that opened automatically, allowing an internal, magnetized arm to latch onto anything metallic within its reach. This rearing, crane-like contrivance, hovering over his back, its tiny brain no doubt scanning model and serial number, was the last thing Ark remembered.

Don helped Peggy bundle a confused, still faintly convulsing Zelp into her CV. Peggy vowed to herself that never again would she visit with the Jarvis's. Never again would she let Zelp out of her electric-fenced yard. And never again would she consider replacing him.

Android, powerless to move out of his chair, and fast-running out of charge from constantly jerking his way around the kitchen, shouted to the RoboCare men to fix his broken *"Brain Command Module."* Unknowing of the happenings outside, Android put the sudden loss of signal from Ark, and the seemingly crazed jumble of data from Zelp, down to the fact that he was only up in *"Basic,"* a level severely restricted by an *"Inactive BCM."*

Helen rushed out into the yard. She was choked. She didn't know whether it was fitting to cry over Ark's sudden demise. After all, he was only a robot. She stooped to pick up a bit of him that was left: a small, shiny piece of nose flange.

PARANOIA

You know you've got it when you can't think of anything that's your fault—R. Hutchins

I cannot recall precisely what it was that awoke me from a drink and travel-induced slumber. It may well have been the change in rhythm as the fast-moving train sped through a set of points, or possibly, it was the roar when hurtling beneath a bridge. In any event, I had awoken with a troubled mind, along with a headache I knew would take time and several aspirins to disperse.

More painful still was the recollection of a distressful incident that took place before I dozed. And if that wasn't enough, I awakened plagued with the notion that something untoward had happened in the compartment whilst I'd napped. So profound was this belief, I felt the need to act as if still asleep; to remain sprawled unmoving in my seat, eyes mere slits, in order to covertly understand the reason for my unease.

But the longer I held the posture, the more I strained to hear above the muted hiss and rumble of steel on steel, the more the compartment maintained an appearance of normalcy—as at first did the two other occupants in it.

Thus painstakingly disposed, I recalled the long lunch in the dining car, lengthy, in part, because I consumed a full bottle of Bordeaux during the course of it. This was an extraordinary amount of drink for me at any time, let alone in the middle of the day and on a train. Even so, I hadn't acted the fool or become drunkenly silly, as one might expect. Head cradled in the palm of my hand, elbow propped on a linen-covered tabletop, I had quietly savored the last of the claret, alongside a panoramic blur of hurtling meadow and hedgerow.

As a waiter hovered discretely nearby, my mind could do little but wander over images of my beloved Sheila, who would be meeting me off the train in London. In this delectable stupor, glass in hand, no doubt sporting a blissful smile—as I've been told I'm prone to do when inebriated—I was conscious only of the whir and click of wheels rushing us ever-closer together.

My sense of well being was to be short-lived, however. Upon leaving the table, I mistakenly turned in the wrong direction, to go stumbling past a waiter. From the raised-eyebrow look given me, the uniformed attendant—standing ridiculously erect in the passageway with a napkin over his arm; like a bathhouse manservant—clearly expected me to exit the other way, in the direction from which I had originally arrived. An absurd thing for me to do, one might think. Yet with a mind as exhilarated and romantically preoccupied as mine was, I can vouch for such state of fluster not being silly at all.

Earlier, I had boarded the Express in Liverpool for the three-hour journey to London, a trip I usually make once a month. This outing was special, however, for after attending to a minor business matter, Sheila and I planned to spend the next two weeks together. After a few days at my Chelsea flat, we intended to take a drive along the south coast, into Dorset, and perhaps on into Devon and Cornwall. More exciting still was the thought that sometime during the journey I was going to pop the proverbial question: to ask her to marry me. That is, should I pluck up enough courage to do so. Just the thought of it, while slumped and seething in my seat, had lathered me in a cold sweat.

My error of direction was to prove more than the mere confusing annoyance it appeared to be at the time, for it sent me lurching along seemingly endless lengths of swaying passageway in search of my First-Class compartment. Despite being a frequent traveler, I had never realized before the extent to which sameness exists on a train. Nauseated further by the heaving of each carriageway floor, my thought was that I must have been trapped in a corridor-ridden labyrinth. There may have been numbers displayed for each carriage, I don't know. What I do know is that I must have peered into every compartment on the train before I finally recognized the one I'd earlier vacated.

When I finally got to my seat, rather than sit and relax—recover, if you will, from my ordeal, which I certainly felt the need to do—I decided instead to take a magazine down from my briefcase in the overhead rack. Despite my somewhat queasy, semi-exhausted state, I wanted to quickly confirm that a writer, to whom a passenger had referred to earlier in the dining car, was indeed the author of an article in that particular publication.

Evidently, the wine had affected me more than I'd realized, for having taken out the magazine, I inexplicably attempted to relock the case while standing on the edge of the seat. That I managed to have fiddled with the thing long enough to register a lock click was not only a feat of balance—wallet with attached keys in one hand, magazine clutched in the other—but was, in hindsight, an absurdly unnecessary one, for I could have so easily lifted the briefcase down onto the unoccupied seat beside me. It was in this muddled state, that I slipped off the cushion and crashed to the floor, narrowly missing landing in the lap of a woman sprawled in her seat directly opposite mine.

As can be imagined, my stupidity had been a considerable embarrassment. What had irked more, though, was the attitude of the two passengers in the compartment. No matter that they had just witnessed an unfortunate and perhaps hurtful accident, they chose to not show any concern whatsoever!

I could have broken my neck for all they seemed to care. They simply remained in their seats, grinning at each other, implying, no doubt, that I was a common drunk, which I can assure you I definitely was not.

Mortified, I'd remained on the floor, head in hands, for several minutes in order to regain some sort of composure—and, I might add, for the compartment to stop spinning, for the fall had left me somewhat stunned.

Bad as it was, not even this misfortune was to prepare me for the predicament in which I was eventually going to find myself. Still, it had been a humiliating enough experience, one I'd been only too glad to close my eyes to.

From my forward-facing window seat, a familiar land-scape had rushed toward me as if fed by conveyor. Out of the corner of a squinted eye, drifts of daisy-dotted meadow, mixed-woodland, and ivy-shrouded farmhouse had all put in an appearance before streaming on by. Scenic splendor to behold for the occasional traveler, but rather monotonous, I'm afraid, for one who journeys the Liverpool-London route as often as I do. The bizarre incident had left a mark that the nap had been unable to erase. I suppose one could say the experience of falling off the seat had left me mentally wounded. *'Psychologically impaired'* might be the term a doctor would use.

I believe that, in addition to privacy, the thing desired by most who step into a compartment on a train, or a bus for that matter, is that the companions with whom one will be journeying are agreeable. On a long trip especially, fellow passengers may have similar tastes, possibly the same habits, be equally educated, and perhaps have enough interest in worldly matters to be able to intelligently converse. When I first slid back the door of the train compartment in Liverpool, I had been, as usual, fearful of encountering a chronic-bronchitis sufferer, no doubt with a need to cough gobs of phlegm into a soggy handkerchief. Or an obese person whose girth took up more than a fair share of seat. Or, God-forbid, noisy children running around unattended by parents. Speaking for myself, the ideal candidate a man hopes for in a traveling companion would be a mature, reasonably attractive woman. One who would help pass the time. Let us say a widow, knowledgeable in world affairs. One not without a touch of humor perhaps, or even a hint of make-believe romantic interlude.

These thoughts had been in my mind when I'd first entered the compartment. For me, it's like a spin of the roulette wheel. Upon seeing what appeared to be a respectable-looking man and woman, I thought I had struck lucky.

Indeed, their appearance being so…well, congenial, quickly dispelled any feelings of disquiet. It was only when I'd attempted conversation that I realized the truth in the fallacy that goes with believing first impressions.

"Have you just boarded?"

"Awful weather to be traveling, don't you think?"

"So damp and miserable, Lime Street, isn't it?"

"Are you traveling far?"

I addressed the questions to both passengers, to which each responded respectively:

"Yes."

"Yes."

No answer.

"Rugby."

So you see, at the outset of my journey I was already guarded. Adding to that, the fall in the compartment had made me even more fraught with apprehension. Undeniably, a growing level of fellow-traveler mistrust was building within me. Finally, and most importantly, to bolster my injured self-image, there lay within me a deep smoldering resentment: a need to show these people that I was not the drunken clown they undoubtedly thought me to be.

On the floor in front of me I could make out the magazine. The wretched thing must have fallen off my knee as I snoozed. It had come to rest, pages splayed like that of a tent, against the foot of the man who sat in the seat diagonally opposite. The other passenger, the woman whom I had almost fallen upon, occupied the window seat facing me. She had apparently fallen asleep too, for her head, like mine, lolled against the padded side cushion, nodding to the rhythm of the train as though controlled by a marionette's string.

The man, whom earlier I had guessed to be in his mid-thirties, busily rummaged in a small suitcase balanced on his knee. I clandestinely studied this fellow, with a large measure of distaste, on account of his arrogant disregard of my earlier plight. It even crossed my mind to 'wake up', to ask whether he'd enjoyed the spectacle.

Nonetheless, I swallowed the urge for retribution, since I was curious to understand what it was he was doing. There was something distinctly peculiar about it.

He seemed to feel the need to repeatedly inspect the contents of the case, for at intervals, he raised the lid to poke around with whatever was inside, and then closed it, evidently satisfied things were in order after all. Each time he did this he gave me a quick look. A shifty one, I thought. No doubt to check whether I was still asleep, which of course, I was pretending to be.

There was an unnatural paleness about his face, emphasized by soot-black hair, slicked flat against his scalp, like a pelt. A shaved back-and-sides haircut accentuated the inverted bowl-like appearance of his head, such that one might think he was wearing a Jewish skullcap. A pointed nose and thin lips gave him a chiseled look that made me think he might be a used-car dealer. His gray suit was noticeably shiny at the knees. Tired, black shoes showed patches of wear in the soles and signs of mud-splatter—no doubt off the Liverpool streets where it had been raining. The leg that stretched out toward the magazine had its trouser hitched slightly, revealing a sliver of hairless lily-white skin above the top of a rumpled navy blue sock.

Both seats on my left were unoccupied, as was the middle seat between the man and woman. On that seat lay her coat—at least, I presumed it to be hers since it was red and had a brooch pinned to it. On top of the coat, she had placed her handbag, somewhat carelessly I thought.

It was while looking at this purse, an exquisitely tooled redish-leather pouch with inlaid brass motif, that I noticed the man's left hand straying ever closer toward it. I

thought he might be about to reach over; touch her perhaps, to wake her up, though I knew they were strangers
to each other from the manner in which they had con-
versed earlier. Yet he appeared intent on something else,
for rather awkwardly, he rested his hand within an inch of
the woman's bag. Why, I could not at first fathom, but I
soon became convinced he was preparing to open it, to rob
it of its contents, if not steal it.

The connection between him and his suitcase then became too obvious. What other reason could there be for his
seemingly manic need to open and close his case like he
had? Had he been just familiarizing himself with the action
of doing so, so that when the time came he could take the
woman's bag in a flash? As I'd warmed to this theory, I
persuaded myself that any second he would scoop the
thing up. Then, like a magician's trick, the lady's purse
would disappear into his case, to likely join other loot concealed within it.

I held my breath. For the first time in my life I was going to witness a robbery. The man was about to validate
my intense dislike of him and prove the scoundrel was
nothing more than a common thief.

The technique, I reasoned, was how a train robber
must often steal passengers' valuables, stashing them away
in this manner. Thus, the robber could nonchalantly walk
away undetected, to a distant compartment maybe, or
more likely a toilet, from where the thief would slink off
the train at the first station it stopped at.

I braced myself to spring up and expose the man for
what he was. I would restrain him with one hand, while
sliding the compartment door open with the other. I would
then yell for the guard. That action would surely awaken
the woman, who equally surely would be only too glad to
help. Between us, we would wrestle the robber to the floor.
Pin him down until help arrived.

The man's hand continued to wander about. Squint-eyed, I became cross-eyed trying to keep track of it. It was as if I was the cobra and he, the charmer. His hand would move nearer, then pull away, raise up over his head to stroke his flat, greasy hair one minute and down to pat the side of his pimply face the next. After each foray, I was sure his long-fingered, almost skeletal appendage, stopped ever closer to the bag, while all the while his free hand tapped out an incessant drumroll on the lid of his case. Though he inched closer still to the handbag, even hovered above it, and on one occasion actually touched its shiny leather surface, he never quite managed to complete the movement I felt so confident he would.

I had got myself into a lather waiting for the inevitable to happen. Desire and intent were there, I decided; he just couldn't bring himself to take the risk knowing I might be watching. Denied the gratification of retribution that ex-posing him as a train robber would have given me, I never-theless congratulated myself—my feigned-sleep masquer-ade had saved the woman from being robbed.

Satisfied my ruse had rendered the man harmless, at least for the time being, I turned my secretive attention to the bag's owner. She wore a tweed trouser-suit that I thought gave her a trussed-up look. Straw-colored hair, streaked gray at the temple, was gathered in a needle-pierced bun on top of her head. Rather like a bird's nest, I thought, with a suppressed chuckle—*only intensifying the ache in my head!* I guessed her to be in her late forties. Cer-tainly, she was overly made up for such a journey. I felt smugly sure Shelia would never have gone to such unnec-essary lengths. Beneath the layers of makeup, giving her the appearance of having stepped off a tropical beach, I envisaged an ashen, freckly skin that needed laborious ef-fort to bring to such a healthy glow. She was also unusual-ly tall. So long-legged was she, her feet ended up almost beneath my seat, forcing me to sit in an awkward semi-sidesaddle position.

It was at that point that I'd decided further make-believe sleep was futile. It was time I '*awakened*'. So with what I'd thought to be an appropriate amount of yawn and stretch, interspersed with puzzled glances around the compartment, squints into the harsh light of the window, and so forth, I '*awoke*'.

My theatrical performance drew no reaction. The woman remained lifeless. The man continued to poke in his case. I'd felt that had I leapt through the window, it would have gone unnoticed.

Then, like a cloud abruptly blocking the warmth of the sun on a chilly day, all that had gone on before paled into insignificance. It was as though I had fallen again, only this time landing on my head. As my right arm—heretofore crooked beneath my aching head to gently cradle it against the side of the seat—stretched out across the floor to retrieve the magazine, finger and thumb prearranged pincer-like to more easily grasp its glossy spine, I recalled I had fallen asleep with my wallet lying on its pages!

The realization jolted my headachy, nauseous being like an electric charge. But such was my need to get psychologically even; I determinedly maintained an appearance of outward composure. I had made myself fool enough in front of these people to risk a cry of alarm. Even so, the shock of the disappearance of my wallet was causing me difficulty in swallowing, so dry had my mouth become. Calmly as I could, I carefully explored my inside pocket, only for my heart to sink, along with my hand, as it slid unimpeded to the bottom of the silky pouch.

Empty!

Mentally, I revisited the scene of my earlier semi-inebriated attempt to maintain balance while standing on the edge of the seat. Magazine in one hand and wallet with

attached dangling keys in the other, I had managed to lock
the briefcase, while totteringly trying to avoid falling. After
the tumble, I most surely had sat down, the magazine an
obvious platform on my lap to support the wallet with its
fob of keys. My cerebral reassessment absolutely confirmed that the wallet, like the magazine, had fallen off my
knee. Armed with this newfound validation, I regarded the
man with a feeling of hatred

Flat head, as I scornfully thought of him, continued to
fumble in his case. The woman uttered a dry cough that
broke her snore-cycle but failed to trigger an awakening.
The countryside continued to hurtle past. The compartment swayed. Beads of perspiration pooled at my temple.

Systematically, I patted trousers, jacket and waistcoat
pockets. The man opened the lid of his case and peered at
me over the top of it. I thought his countenance registered
a pitiful smile. Did he think my increasingly frenzied
searches a sobering-up antic? I looked away. I was in no
mood for contact with black eyes set in a skeletal head, of
one who was the stealer of my wallet!

I stood between the seats, swiveled, a little giddily,
first one way then the other, as though admiring the fit of a
jacket in a tailor's mirror. I checked the floor. The seats.
The luggage racks. The woman issued a drawn-out sigh. A
smirk played about the man's face, uncertain, it seemed, as
whether to morph into a loose grin or outright laughter.

I stared at the rocketing scenery, oddly partitioned in
that instant by telephone poles that flashed past like strobe
markers. I burrowed a hand deep down between my seat
cushion and backrest. Nothing but odd bits of paper. A few
crumbs. A white, plastic paperclip.

I disregarded further niceties. Despite my splitting
headache, I got down on hands and knees to examine under the seat where the carpet adjoins the heater vent, bizarrely recognizing the newness of the pattern from my

earlier, even closer look, at that particular, untrodden space. I studied the floor beneath the bridge formed by the woman's outstretched, trouser-clad legs, careful not to go too near that appropriated space.

Angrily, I pushed my briefcase aside on the overhead rack. I knew it couldn't be in there. The key to open the damn thing was attached to the wallet!

I couldn't help but glare at the man. For the umpteenth time he had just pulled down the lid of his case. The complexion that earlier had been pallid, was now flushed. It struck me he was aware of the reason for my distress. Being the type of person I judged him to be, he obviously enjoyed observing my frantic search for a wallet he knew damn well I would never find!

'Excuse me. Sorry to bother you. I seem to have mislaid my wallet." My voice sounded shrill. I may have been shouting. "It was on my knee you see. I distinctly remember that. On this magazine here." I shook the *Country Life* open, as if expecting the thing to drop out from between its pages. "You don't recall seeing it, do you? It's leather. Brown. About so big." I held my hands out, forefingers extended to show the rough shape and size of it. "It has a key pouch attached to it. Cedric R. Smith embossed on the leather. In gold capitals. Along the bottom edge."

"No, can't say I have," he replied.

"Then that is most strange, if I may say so," I couldn't help but speak sarcastically, couched in what could only have been evident as suppressed venom.

I slid a hand once more into my inside pocket. To reinforce the emptiness there, I made a fist, pushing my knuckles out against the inside of the lining. I made a hopeless face. I was now standing over him. I was more and more convinced the wallet lay in his briefcase. Nestled no doubt with other items stolen from other unsuspecting passengers. With some difficulty, I resisted an urge to snatch the thing off his lap, upturn it on the floor, and stomp it flat!

I looked over at the woman. There was something odd about her, too, that I had been unable to quite place before. Emboldened by my confrontation with the man, it hit me: how could she still be asleep, despite that I had made enough noise to awaken the dead? And weren't the red coat and expensive-looking handbag placed a little too casually? A little too obviously, perhaps? The more this thought rolled around my throbbing head, the more the arrangement adopted sinister relevance.

With rising conviction, I decided that the coat, the bag, the woman faking sleep, and the man with his silly case were mere props, suggestive to other passengers that it was safe to doze off with their valuables left unsecured.

And the man maddeningly pretended ignorance! He looked fixedly at his closed case. And the woman 'slept' on. Clearly, the two were acting together. How otherwise could they be so indifferent to my plight? She had not stirred, despite it being blatantly obvious, given the racket I'd made, that she was not genuinely asleep. And the man continued to sit there with that complacent look on his face that I longed to knock off!

"It has all my money in it. My personal affects. Driving license. Credit cards. It has to be here somewhere. I've not left the compartment since I returned from lunch. You can vouch for that surely. Can't you? I don't understand it," I snarled on, hands held out, palms upward, as though testing for the presence of rain. "It was on this magazine here." I angrily wafted the pages over of the man's head.

The woman stirred then. Good, I thought. I'll play one against the other. That will sort it out. She looked the part too. A ringleader type. The 'sleeper'. One who listens to what's transpired, then makes entry.

As if hearing my thoughts, she suddenly jerked upright. She looked about confusedly, as if affected by a bright light. She appeared to need confirmation that she was still on the train. She glanced at her watch and started at the time. She looked up at me. Our eyes met for a second, no more than that. I looked away, out the window, anywhere to avoid those horrid, sleepy eyes. She looked across at the man, who coolly returned her gaze. The leer that had been such a fixture on his pallid face broadened into a knowing smile. His face visibly brightened. It was as though a spotlight had suddenly picked him out. His perfectly round, piggy eyes widened. His beetle brows arched.

The woman coughed, and again, more discreetly this time into a tiny, pink handkerchief.

A polished team performance!

One covering for the other. Anyone could see it. Thievery was written in their faces. They obviously traveled up and down the inter-city routes to steal from passengers! But how could I let on that I was onto their sordid game? Doing so would leave me open to cries of ridicule. For sure they would never admit to it. And I had no witness, nor a shred of proof. It was all conjecture, they would say. A figment of this passenger's warped mind. They would shout for the guard. Claim I was a drunkard. Insane even. I would be further humiliated and escorted off the train.

Still without my wallet!

I turned determinedly toward the woman. "It's gone," I said. "I think it may have been stolen while I slept. I was reading that magazine." I pointed to where I had flung it on the floor. "My wallet was on that, on my knee when I dozed off. Have you seen it at all? I don't know how long *you* were asleep. I know I was out for not more than half an hour. This man here, I think, was awake the whole time. He claims he knows nothing about it. It's not in the compartment. At least not in the places I've been able to examine. I'm afraid I have to conclude it's been stolen."

With a puzzled, disbelieving look, she finally levered herself upright. After a yawn and a stretch, during which she almost touched the compartment ceiling, she set about straightening her suit. She took a small travel mirror from her handbag and, with her legs braced against the front of the seat, peered closely into it. Satisfied her complexion was in order; she angled the mirror to reflect the bun, painstakingly tidying loose hairs around its periphery. Seemingly content with her hair arrangement, she proceeded to rub her nose with the ends of her fingers, as though trying to elongate it. Extracting a lipstick from her bag, she daubed on a new layer of coat-matching crimson. Seated, she had appeared big and tall. Upright, she was massive. Indeed, I could not recall ever being near such an enormous female. A feminine goliath. Ideal to fend off victims trying to retrieve stolen valuables! One shove of that huge body would be enough to hold anyone at bay, if not propel a victim off the train. Certainly one as delicate as me: a five-foot-one lightweight. One who rode a stationary bike and drank high-calorie fluids, yet never put on a sliver of muscle or as much as a pound in weight.

She examined the inside of her purse, possibly to confirm that her ticket was in order. Even on tiptoe I could not quite see over her shoulder into it. She sensed my intention and snapped the purse shut. She picked up the red coat, carefully folded it and placed it on the overhead rack beside her suitcase. Clearly, there was no need for *her* to stand on the seat. She could have reached her luggage had it been on the roof!

The man stood then, so that the three of us were grouped close together between the seats, a situation in which, I'm afraid to say, I felt totally inhibited. The man finally broke the tension. He stooped to gather his newspapers together, neatly creased each one in turn and stacked them on the edge of his seat. He was a good head taller than me and had a confident, tough look about him—the very traits I lacked. He was broader than I had first thought too. His fist, I estimated, to be not far short of being the size of my head. Moreover, his head, far from angular, was more bull-like, rooted to a thick neck. His hair, which earlier I had the thought was so slicked that there was a danger of it slipping off his skull—were he to incline his head too steeply—now looked fuller, more natural.

Without a word, both turned to examine their seat areas. I quickly joined them. Once again I pressed my hands between cushion and backrest. But the effort did not yield my wallet. What it did do was increase my sense that a charade was being enacted for my benefit to deflect their obvious guilt.

Sickened by the turn of events I slid open the compartment door. I had been insulted enough. I felt I must find the guard before it was too late. The ticket collector would do. *Anyone in railway uniform!* I'd request their belongings be searched. But the corridor was empty. I swayed weakly in the confined space for some time. I belched, tasting stale wine. My dull headache had worsened. My tongue was barely moist, my lips were cracked. Across the corridor, my image reflected in the glass stared back at me. My tie was askew. A tuft of hair sprouted perpendicular to the side of my head, as it can sometimes do when pressed overnight against a pillow.

The countryside was increasingly broken with buildings. The train roared deafeningly beneath a series of overpasses. Warehouses flashed by, asphalt and concrete car parks filled with vehicles, dilapidated buildings, and strips of run-down terraced house. We were coming into a sizable town. Rugby I knew it to be. The brakes were applied, adding to the appalling din.

I turned to reenter the compartment. As I did so, the man and woman squeezed out past me. I surveyed the empty seats. On hands and knees, I revisited the depths of each corner of the floor. Felt again between the cushions. Shook out the magazine, the man's newspapers. Scattered them over the floor.

"They stole my wallet!"

Soon they would be sharing the spoils. The fifty pounds in banknotes. The sexually explicit letter I had half-written to Sheila that was tucked alongside my driving license—which I needed for the rental car in London. My credit cards, return rail ticket, key to my London flat, key to my Liverpool office and key to my briefcase were all gone.

I decided I had to get off the train, even if it risked being stranded, for I couldn't face Sheila with no money, no identification, no nothing. I would confront the man and woman on the platform, in front of railway personnel.

"I have good reason to believe these two stole my wallet," I would say. I'd have the station manager question them and call the local police. I'd make a statement and have them arrested!

The train slowed to a crawl. The platform came into view. Station buildings slid by: a ticket office, a newspaper stand, a snack bar. Outside, groups of passengers stood about, many drinking from paper cups.

I lifted down my attaché case and angrily flung it onto the seat. New passengers pushed into the compartment. One, a stout, mustachioed man, clutched bundles of bulging shopping bags emblazoned with *Marks & Spencer* and *Sainsbury's*. He chose the seat the woman had sat in. A small boy, excited by the prospect of a rail journey, cried out excitedly to a teenage girl who was about to occupy the seat the man had sat in. His sister, I thought. She mouthed a reply.

The newcomers stared. Distaste was written on their faces. Their eyes asked, *who is this wild-eyed, disheveled creature? What is he doing in First Class?*

Out the window I spotted the woman. A tall, bearded fellow, arms folded, stood beside her on the platform. Two young girls dashed up. Each trailed a bright yellow balloon. The woman stooped to hug them. The bearded fellow patted the top of the woman's hair bun.

The stealer of my wallet was in a phone booth further along the platform. I could make out his briefcase on a shelf next to the phone.

The stout man busily stuffed his shopping bags onto the overhead rack. The girl wagged a disproving finger at the boy, who was trying to sit on my vacated window seat, but could not because my briefcase lay on it. When picking up the case I almost fell over the lad, for he stood at my feet, tugging at my sleeve, an imploring look on his face. I ignored him. I had no time for children. It appeared that I'd not locked the case after all, for it had sprung open with the shock of hitting the seat.

I raised the partly open lid. Inside was my cell phone. At least I could call Sheila. The rental car agreement was there too, but without my drivers license and credit card it was quite useless. The train jolted into motion, then immediately jerked to a halt—a train driver's way of signaling to passengers it was about to depart. The woman was leaving the platform, her red coat loosely draped about her shoulders. The two girls pranced about her like dolls. The bearded fellow carried her suitcase. His free arm was tight around the woman's waist. Was she telling him about the idiot on the train? I wondered bitterly. The one who drunkenly fell off the seat. The manic one, who claimed he'd lost his wallet.

The man was still in the phone booth. I barely managed to stifle an enraged shout. The mustachioed man, hearing my choked off syllables and seemingly exhausted from his struggle with the shopping bags, shrank fearfully back into his seat.

"I'll break every bone in his body, lever open his damn case." I muttered the threats to myself, but unconsciously the words were breathed out, half aloud. I restocked my briefcase with what had spilled out: odds and ends, business cards, clips, pads of paper, a partly crushed packet of Smiths potato crisps. "After I've dealt with him," I muttered on, "I'll call Sheila. Tell her of my misfortune. In a calm voice, I'll let her know that I handled it, that I took care of it."

I snapped the case shut. The slam of the lid caused the new passengers to shrink further back into their seats. I disregarded them, pushing rudely past the still-imploring boy out of the compartment. I rushed headlong down the corridor to the door at the front of the carriage. As I stepped onto the platform the train creaked into movement. Compartment windows began to silently and slowly glide past behind me. My transport to London was going to leave me behind!

The ache in my head was undiminished. I felt sick. My state was not helped by the sour, metallic smell of the railway station. The cathedral-like echoing ring and clatter of the place jangled further my frayed nerves. The edifice's massive, light-filled, cantilevered roof soared giddily above my head. Pigeons strutted and cooed on the platform.

The man had left the phone booth. He strode toward the exit stairwell, a satisfied, confident look on his face. I thought his gait had a noticeable swagger.

But as I leaned forward, grim of face, tight of lip, attaché case clutched in my white-knuckled left hand, it was the boy in the compartment that caught my attention. The youngster's bare forearm waved out of the compartment air-vent window, his body hoisted against the glass by the girl who I had thought to be his sister.

"Hey Mister," he shouted, as he drew level, allowing my wallet to drop from his grasp into my hastily cupped free hand. "I tried to tell you, this fell out of your brief-case." I somehow wrestled open a fast accelerating door and threw myself back onto the train.

An Alluring Enigma

*Writing comes more easily if you have
something to say — Sholem Asch*

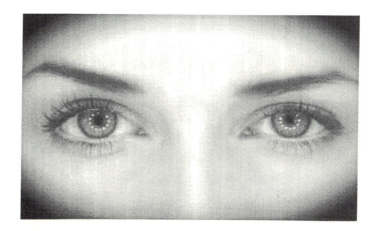

A cool, showery rain had long given way to a warm, dry evening by the time the young woman arrived at the corner of Holmcroft Road. Surely, few so pleasing to the eye could ever have stood on that particular paved spot. She had appeared unmindful of her very exquisiteness — a loveliness of such allure, eyes of such magnetism, that those prone to be drawn, could surely do no other than act as moths do to a light.

She'd glanced repeatedly at her tiny bejeweled watch, for it was half-past six, and there was still no sign of him. The Bath train had arrived early, yet he was not at home, at least not the two times she'd called.

He'd not answered the messages she'd left either, so where was he? He'd called earlier in the day. "Visiting someone in the city," he'd said, a half-hour train journey away. This claim was a surprise, for his clients usually came to him, at his office in Henley. Still, he'd promised he would be back in time for the neighborhood party. If only he'd show up, as promised.

"Ted. Pick up, it's me!"

She had spoken with the mouthpiece held away from her face, to lessen the stale odor of the public phone. "This is the third time I've called," she'd said, pressing the sole of a fashionable, heeled shoe against the half-open kiosk door, to hold it open. She'd studied the white leather purse clutched in her other hand. It had been a twenty-second birthday gift from him. The color of the handbag perfectly matched her white sheath dress and suede leather shoes.

"Where are you? It's 7 o'clock. I've been at the corner of Holmcroft for over half an hour. It's where we agreed to meet. Remember? Please say this time that you do. The station told me your trains arrived, so I know you should be here. That's if you caught that one. If you don't call me back within 5 minutes, I'll assume you didn't. In which case, I'll make my own way to the Fisher party. It's a short walk from here. No doubt I'll see you there later."

She'd given him the number of the phone, told him she loved him, hoped everything was all right, and hung up.

It was now 7.15. On the face of it, it was the third time in as many weeks that he'd stood her up. What will his excuse be this time? She wondered. The heady mix of anger and jealousy hurt, even when tempered with concern.

"Damn him!" she muttered.

She vowed that when he appeared at the party, she would ignore him. She wouldn't rush to him as she always had, throwing her arms around his neck, kissing him hard, deliciously, and messily on the mouth, the end of his Nordic nose, his craggy jaw. This time she would hold back. She would let him find her for a change. She might go as far as pretending not to recognize him at all!

Filled with this resolve, she turned in the direction of the Fishers' house. But an ugly thought went along with her, festering, troubling her. Surely, she thought, he won't find it in him to say he'd forgotten *again*. That would be too much for her to bear, for it could well mean someone else: a secret lover perhaps, from the days when he'd worked full-time in Bath. She didn't like to even think of such a thing. Surely this latest memory lapse was nothing more than a case of male forgetfulness.

Maurice Templeton's tiresome evening at the Fisher party was to some extent electrified by a young woman's entry into the room. It wasn't just that she was striking in a white, clingy dress or that she turned everyone's head; it was that she straightaway singled him out, fixing him with a look so intense he felt the need to look quickly away.

Until then, the thought uppermost in Maurice's mind, apart from figuring out the plot of his latest story, had been how to exit the event gracefully, steadily working his way through the gathered throng toward the French doors that he knew opened onto the terrace. From there, he could melt into the garden, no one the wiser he'd ever left.

The annual bash had been a bore, even when with Joan. Alone, and at the Fishers—always the biggest, snazziest of venues on the Holmcroft community party calendar—it was plain awful. Everyone was there, or so it seemed, considering how scant his knowledge was of who his neighbors were. The prospect of unlimited drink with sumptuously catered buffet dinner had obviously proven irresistible. He couldn't help but feel less than ordinary. In the spacious reception room in which the guests had gathered, *small* was the word he would have chosen. Even though he was a hefty five-eleven, those about him appeared bigger. The men laughed more heartily, slapping one another on the back. The women loomed larger than life, too, confidently working the room, seemingly armed with a myriad of exciting subjects to chat about.

Maurice wasn't overjoyed at his appearance either. The double-breasted suit he wore was a mistake. He realized that now. Apart from not having been pressed, it was so tight across his shoulders that he'd felt the need to undo the top button, only to see in the Fisher bathroom mirror that the lapels sagged untidily. He was sure Joan would never have selected the outfit for him.

Maurice had exchanged greetings with the Walkers, the Gordons, spoken briefly with the Berringers—congratulating them on the completion of their extension. He'd even managed to commiserate with the Hamptons over the loss of their dog—a fat listless creature, the passing of which he wouldn't miss. The absence of excrement on his lawn each day was not something he would mourn.

The air was thick with wealth. Expensively suited, by the looks of many of them, company-executive types, well-off investment people, prosperous retirees, and the like, most of whom he didn't know.

He was sure there were not many *Fiction Inventory Directors*, a title *Eaton Publications* concocted to replace *warehouse clerk*, the job he and his colleagues all knew it to be. It was quite a step down from *Finance Manager* at *IBM*. Still, he supposed, he was gainfully employed at a time in his life when he couldn't be bothered much anyway. Most mornings it was a challenge just to get out of bed, to spend yet another day trying to overcome his God-awful writer's block. Compensations came with the position; he got to feel and smell books and to read them for free.

Maurice had never been sure of himself at such gatherings. The question of timing confused him: when it was appropriate to say something, when not. His deficiency was already making him wish he hadn't come. He would not have, had he not thought a break might free up the frustrating block. He'd done the prerequisite tour. Seen the sunken marble bath one more time, into which water spewed from the mouths of gold-plated lions. Watched the dumbwaiter trundle its way between floors. Viewed wall-hung pictures, numbered prints, sculptural art, pausing for an appropriate interval before each pedestal, nodding approvingly, as if he understood Romanesque.

After such meandering, the glass in his hand felt decidedly sticky. It was as though it had been glued there. A kind of stage fright gripped him. It was no wonder he was so taken aback by the woman's entrance, as though he was the only person in the room. He'd glanced away shyly, then quickly back and forth, as one does when skirting eye contact, only to see her gaze remain unwaveringly upon him.

Everyone he'd chatted with wanted to know about his divorce. Several times he'd answered that he didn't know or care where his ex was. Or with whom Joan was living, if anyone. And that he wasn't seeing someone himself.

"Other than from a discrete distance," Francis Hampton had laughed out. A plump woman in her fifties, with the beginnings of a double chin, she gave an impression of pinkness: pink dress, pink lips, pinkish eyes, and apple-pink cheeks. He couldn't help but notice, too, how wetly pink the gape of her mouth was. By any means it wasn't something he normally noticed on a person. But it was just open so often, and her arched tongue tucked behind pristine teeth so reminded him of Joan's.

Apart from the Hamptons, he knew few of the others in the group with whom he happened to be standing. At least, those he could talk to without risk of saying a wrong name. He glimpsed a familiar face here and there: a short, bald man drove a bright-red BMW each morning, which roared past his house like an entrant at Le Mans; a bespectacled woman; an eager-faced estate agent, whom he thought he recognized. The hosts he hardly knew at all, other than that they appeared loaded. Filthy rich, Joan had often remarked. Seemingly, the whole neighborhood got an invitation, irrespective of whether the host knew them or not. He felt sure they wouldn't know him, even though this was the third time he'd been there. Without his name-tag, they would probably pass by without a second glance. And he was sure they would do the same had the label been pinned on, rather than suffer the indignity of stooping to read it.

Even so, for all that, he couldn't help but laugh at Francis's comment. Her innuendos could be sharply funny.

"I can't stop people from looking, he'd answered. "I just wish I knew the reason why."

He turned to look back across the room. It felt good to know she was still there. Still focused on him. He realized it would have been quite a letdown had she not been. She clutched a white purse at arm's length by her side. He thought how stylish that was, how appropriate that the bag was held in that way: straight-armed down, instead of messily held in the crook of an arm, or by a shoulder strap that would have marred the sheerness of her dress.

He realized that her audacious eye contact was why he had subconsciously decided to go the longer way round the room, to delay his arrival at the terrace door. To some extent, the route would encircle her as if she were prey. He would take that route, even though it would mean pushing through the tightly knit group around the piano, where someone was playing "In the Blue of Evening."

But for that haunting melody, he would have returned earlier, to the quiet comfort of his study, to a glass of Pinot Gris, accompanied by a slice of sharp Cheddar on freshly buttered French bread. Settled, he would gaze into the canopy of an oak that towered outside the room's bay window, its notched leaves reminding him of pieces of a jigsaw. There, he would settle in his armchair and try one more time to get beyond his block, to flesh out his story. It was a tale he'd been struggling to complete; yet one that excited him more than any he'd previously written. A man sustains loss of memory while on a train journey. Suddenly, and quite terrifyingly, this man doesn't know who he is, or why he's where he is. It was the first piece that had avoided being balled-up in the wastebasket since his messy divorce ten months earlier. Instead of trashing the Fisher invitation, as—given his state of mind—he'd impulsively felt the need to do; he'd decided the break might help.

The woman's look had been so unerring that his natural shyness had caused him to lower his eyes, his face to slip into what he'd often thought reflected a polite half-smile, an apologetic expression that spoke of him having been overly bold. It was his nature to be a little sensitive, a tendency Joan had often taken advantage of. In place of the quiet girl he'd married, a selfish brashness had surfaced, and then flourished. In the end, her constant nagging had driven him out of the house.

Maurice normally avoided returning stares. Not that he got many. Scrutiny embarrassed him, made him feel something was out of place. It crossed his mind that his flawed appearance might be so noticeable that it could be detected from across the room. He wasn't unzipped; he was quite sure of that. And he'd brushed his dark hair to what in the mirror appeared to be a reasonable sheen. He toyed with the idea she was a past acquaintance. One whom he should have recognized, and then suddenly would, prompting him to rush over, to embrace, to tell her how wonderful it was to meet up with her again. Yet he knew he'd never set eyes on the woman before, or indeed anyone so stunning. He recalled a poster of a young Elizabeth Taylor—only she could compare.

So, Maurice had looked again. Determined this time not to look away, he'd applied a laconic upward glance that he'd thought had worked well with women before. It had, after all, attracted Joan. So direct and sustained was his stare, a hint of slyness he hadn't planned on crept into his gray eyes, an intense look that might mistakenly communicate desire, if not lust. While that was not his intention—it was nothing more than a primeval urge to return her seeming interest in him—he didn't want to rule out any interpretation she might have wanted to put on it.

So, across the jade-green carpet, flanked with wall-hung tapestries and works of art, beneath a twinkling chandelier, he communicated a touch of interest, straight into the darkened recesses of her eyes, which he thought must be deep blue, or even violet, to linger openly on her shadowed face—about which auburn hair furled onto creamy shoulders.

But as the look held, so it increasingly became a form of contest, like when as a child he'd competed to out-stare another. He was beginning to feel it a struggle to maintain composure, when he needed to step smartly to one side, to avoid the stumble of a waiter, who miraculously pirouetted away a tray of drinks from being cast over him. That was when he saw that her gaze didn't follow his sudden movement. She didn't flinch from where she'd been directing her attention all along, right through where he'd been standing, toward a flaxen-haired man directly behind him:

a tall, anxious-looking fellow whom Maurice recognized as someone who lived on the far side of the neighborhood, quite near his own house.

He'd taken a sip of his white-burgundy, warm enough now to taste not unlike syrup. He'd barely managed to return Francis's knowing look, her silly, raised-eyebrow grin. Clearly, his moment of flirtation had not been missed. Francis was, however, a perfect foil for his moment of disenchantment. She was one to whom he could easily turn to with such a frivolous remark. He could rely upon her ensuing gush of laughter, which would help discharge the stimulating feeling that had built up in him.

"I'm glad the waiter was the athletic type," he managed.

"Do you know her then?" Francis asked, with the suggestion of a wink, delicately sipping on her drink.

"Know who?"

"The delectable one of course. The one in the white, clingy dress. The one you were looking at so intently."

"Can't say I've ever seen her before in my life."

"She's Langley's girl. Elizabeth...Walker. In case you don't know, Mr. Langley...Ted, is the Scandinavian-looking fellow who lives next door but one to you. Not sure what he does, but I believe he has an office here in Henley. Dazzling isn't she?"

"Yes, quite," Maurice replied. "I know little of Langley other than that, since you mention it, it might be he who stands directly behind you."

"Oh, yes, that's him," Francis said, half turning. "He's so sweet. A lovely, lovely man, with striking, green eyes. Poor thing. He looks totally lost. It must be his first time at one of our events."

Maurice couldn't help but notice how closely Langley resembled the description he'd written of the protagonist in his story. It was quite uncanny. Being a near neighbor, he now realized he'd probably subconsciously used the man's appearance as a sort of template. So perfect was the match, it was as if his fictional character had suddenly surfaced in real life!

Langley appeared to be concentrating on returning Elizabeth's stare, his expression oddly confused as though having difficulty recognizing who she was. Maurice couldn't help but notice, too, that the man had a pronounced arm shake. His drink was almost spilling out of the glass.

"Strange isn't it? Her not being with him, I mean," Francis remarked sweetly. "The way they stand gazing at each other across the room like that. It's as though each is waiting for the other's response in a child's game."

"Perhaps they've fallen out of love," he said.

Maurice turned just in time to see Elizabeth disappear through the terrace door, the very door he'd planned to exit through himself. Her sudden disappearance had clearly upset Langley. The man looked decidedly more dejected, more perplexed than he'd seemed even moments before. Maurice couldn't help but feel concerned. He decided the man must be stricken with lovesickness, a sensation similar to what he himself had experienced not moments before. Yet, oddly, he felt a sense of elation. Langley's mannerism was suggestive of torment, brought about, possibly, by an acute loss of memory, the very state the protagonist endures in his short story. If only he could envisage a flowing continuation.

Maurice had written thus far:

The train compartment, in which the man sat alone, was spotlessly clean, seats opulently upholstered in the manner of club settees. A sign on the window stated 'First

Class.' A black and white photograph—framed into the wall above the opposite seat—depicted a moorland scene.

The man stared intently at the picture as if recognizing a long-lost work of art: at a farm, at longhorn cattle that grazed a rock-strewn meadow, at a horse cart of the type used to deliver milk, at a wooden barn, and at a rocky crag that reared above a slate-roofed house, atop of which, beneath a threatening sky, highland sheep clustered like rag dolls. A smoked-glass wall lamp lit the picture. Its creamy glow was reflected in the darkened compartment window. The light pooled onto the wall, over the seat, onto the floor, and onto the blond-haired man's upturned face, such that he appeared like an angel in a beam of heavenly light.

The man turned toward the window. It struck him in doing so that the scene—in which he saw himself for the first time, floodlit against a background of diffused light—could be the setting for a vaguely remembered stage play.

"What am I doing here? Who am I? Am I trapped in a dream?" he murmured disbelievingly, apparently hearing his voice for the first time too. "Am I trapped in a bubble of life, like a fish in a bowl, in which I, the narrator on the outside, am unable to break in unto myself?"

He had no knowledge of who he was, or why he was there. Nor did he know where he was going, or where he had come from. He recognized everyday objects, yet of himself his mind was like an empty revolving drum within which fragmented images were teasingly and fleetingly displayed. It was like he was at the edge of a dark pit, trying to discern in the inky-blackness, amid echoing drips of condensation, something other than his faint reflection in the pool far below.

The seat was dwarfed by his lankiness. He flexed his long, manicured fingers. They worked well enough. As

did his arms and his legs. His head swiveled at the command of his brain.

His black leather shoes gleamed.

But who polished them?

Who arranged those laces so neatly into bowties?

And the gray-burgundy, diamond-pattern socks:
when and where did he pull those on?

He touched the sleeve of the dark-blue suit in which
he found himself dressed. He stroked a white shirt cuff
that protruded from beneath a sleeve. Beneath the cuff, a
Tag-Heuer gleamed. A sliver of a second hand jerked
around a steely-blue dial; fifteen minutes past six; twelfth
of some month. Nervously he played with a starry-night,
blue tie that bisected his shirt, held by a tiny, silver tack.
A photograph lay in a jacket pocket. Penciled on the back
of the picture was an address: 32 Hawke Road, Holmcroft,
Henley

"Did not a leather wallet once reside in that inside
pocket, alongside the photo?" he asked himself.

The person in the photo and the one reflected in the
window were the same, only his image sat hunched ap-
prehensively on the edge of a train seat, feverously turning out pockets as though beset with an ant swarm. In the
photograph, he was depicted leaning on a balcony that
overlooked a flower garden. A peaceful expression panned
his tanned face. His arm was draped upon the shoulder of
a woman. Dark-haired, she sat sidesaddle on the rail, tantalizingly angled such that he could not discern her face.

He stood and stared into a mirror above his seat, in
which was reflected the moorland picture. Darting, green
eyes sought explanation. His long face was supported on a
straight neck in which he noted the peculiar wobble of his
Adam's apple. He was close-shaven below long square-cut
sideburns that curled upward slightly at their edges. His
hair, the color of sun-burnished straw, was parted down

the middle. The strands felt fine and silky between his fingers.

The train slowed and ground to a halt.

A dimly lit sign told him it was Henley.

Panic welled within him like an inflating balloon.

It had grown fully dark by the time Maurice stepped onto the Fisher terrace. Elizabeth was visible across an expanse of Yorkshire flagstone, beyond a low wall, in which naked cherubs, illuminated in softly lit alcoves, perpetually peed into stone bowls. She stood at the edge of an oblong of grass at the fringe of a yellow light cast from the house. Arms folded, she looked straight ahead into the gloom of trees that screened the building from the road. On her right, the pebbled driveway Maurice had walked up not quite an hour earlier that led to a fancy wrought-iron gate.

He was surprised Elizabeth was there, for it had taken him a while after she had exited the room to work his way around to the terrace door, delayed somewhat by semi-inebriated nameless faces that insisted they learn more about him: who he was, what he did for a living, which house on the estate was his?

Maurice glanced back toward the house. Framed in the French doors the party was in full swing. The subdued hum of mass conversation filtered to him. Nobody inside was yet interested in what lay outside. Later, after having taken their fill at the buffet, they would throng the patio. Voices loosened by drink, the hum would build to a soft, muted roar. Increasingly, as the night wore on, the darkness would be pierced by excited yelps and the occasional shriek.

But for now all is quiet, so profoundly, he felt he should make a sound, to alert Elizabeth of his presence, for he must not alarm her. He was unsure as to Langley's whereabouts, for the man had hurried from the room ahead of him, via the foyer, so he could be anywhere. After such ogling, both might want to meet. More than likely in the seclusion of the garden. Although, if they were having a tiff, they could well decide to angrily go their own ways.

His discrete cough had the desired effect. Elizabeth half-turned and moved toward the driveway. Anxious that she did not sense she was being followed, or worse stalked, he strolled leisurely, with hands in pockets, across the terrace. He walked diagonally over the lawn, to intersect with her before she moved out of the sphere of light. He gauged his pace and line, such that he would arrive at a point that she would reach near the driveway. But upon arriving at that spot—a grassy hillock that preceded a raised flower-bed—she was nowhere to be seen. He reasoned she had moved even quicker. Perhaps she was already beyond the range of light in the darkened wooded area. Unsure, he remained on the plinth of lawn. It was possible she could have moved more rapidly still to now be down the drive-way, out the gate, away into the night. Unable to see out-side the lighted area, he was reluctant to go further. After all, he was not after her. At least not in the sense a sexual predator might be.

In fact, he was scarcely aware of the reason he was out in the garden at all. He had been infatuated, sure. But her exit from the room had effectively dismissed her from his mind. Even so, curiosity had gotten the better of him, in part because the escapade increasingly appeared to be a real-life enactment of his story. More than anything, he wanted to build on that.

Is Elizabeth alone in the gloom, he wondered, or with Langley? They were probably at that moment giggling softly together in the dark, seeing him no differently atop the hillock, in the glow from the house, than had he been standing on an illuminated pedestal.

He turned when this thought struck him, with the intent of moving quietly down the pea-pebble driveway. As he'd discovered earlier on his arrival, even when walking at normal pace, so deep were the small round stones, so smooth were they against the thin leather soles of his moccasins, he had a job to keep his footing. Twice he slipped. Twice he almost fell before being forced to slacken pace. Twice he whispered curses into the warm night air, as the sound of crunching stones—after so much stealth—magnified his exit. It was only when he got to the gate, after yet another stagger in the now pitch-dark—thinking Elizabeth and Langley must surely be laughing their silly heads off—did he spot them.

So feverishly were the couple embracing, they were clearly beyond care about his presence, had he even raced out the driveway on a motorbike. So intense was Elizabeth's ardor, Langley could have returned from a spell on a different planet.

Maurice turned away. He would not intrude further on such intimacy. But the scene had illuminated his thinking. Clear of the pebbles, his stride quickened, for he was now in a joyous hurry.

"I have it! Of course!" he cried.

Number twenty-one was on a corner, behind a dense privet-hedge much in need of a trim. The place seemed familiar, yet no single feature stood out. There were no lights in any of the windows. The head-unit of a street lamp softly illuminated cream stucco. The angled light cast with it the shadow of a porch pillar. The path to the front door was composed of bricks, in which moss-filled gaps formed vaguely recognizable shapes.

The return ticket was for Henley, a name that had a recognizable ring. A railway worker on the platform had told him Holmcroft Road was a short walk. "Take this left, then that right," the man had said, with a flourish of a bare, muscular arm. "Then continue for about a hundred yards. You will see the road on your left."

The sound of chimes, faintly distant within an empty hollowness, answered his press of the bell push. He rapped his knuckles on the door. Banged his balled fist. There was no answer to the reverberations. The door was locked. He had a feeling that somewhere there was a hidden key. But he could not remember where. Early evening gloom surrounded the house. It lay thick about him, like a blanket. He recalled the unoccupied train compartment, the small, bleak station at which only he had alighted, in which a lone ticket collector—sleeves rolled high in the manner of a factory worker—directed him. Beyond the dense hedge was the deserted road he had walked along. And now he had arrived at a seemingly empty house.

Was this a carefully orchestrated charade? A series of scenes astutely arranged to give the appearance of normalcy? About him, the last vestige of light rested on the vegetation, imparting to it a silvery sheen.

He stopped by a window that was propped partly open at the rear of the house. He was undecided whether to climb through, fearful that within the dark interior a slobbering Doberman awaited.

But he must establish a start-point. Unravel time.

He blinked recognition. His fingers meandered over the wood grain of the windowsill, as though fingering beads. But for his attire, he could be a burglar attempting to understand the window's opening mechanism. The Tag Heuer registered the extent of his past. Forty minutes had elapsed since he discovered himself on the train.

Crouched on a carpeted floor, he recalled the small bedroom. Intuitively, he sensed the lack of a bed in that room, and that a built-in wardrobe faced the window he'd *just clambered through. Adjacent to it was a door he knew opened onto a carpeted hallway.*

He moved quickly. Recollection was returning fast. Like a video recorder on fast-forward, playback images were spinning into familiarity.

The grimness eased from his face.

He was not an intruder, damn it! This was his house!

Beyond a door, ajar to his right, was the kitchen he knew led to a utility room, then on to a garage. Straight ahead was the family room, featuring a stone fireplace.

Instead he strode purposefully to his left to enter what he knew was his bedroom. On a small table beside the wide-open door, against a stack of books of which he suddenly recollected the titles, was propped an invitation. "To Mr. Ted Langley (& companion if so wished), at the invitation of Lyle and Nora Fisher, to attend The Holmcroft Neighborhood Bash," with a thoughtfully attached "we-are-here" map. Like a slap across the face it came to him where someone should be. And where he should be too. And the wallet that lay there, a square of leather that rested askew atop the books, belonged to him. The wallet, which contained the house key he must have forgotten, as he had forgotten so many things lately. Embarrassingly, he could not show his medical insurance card to the neurologist, whom he now recalled was a suave, kindly gentleman of possible Indian heritage. The doctor was an impressive, darkly bespectacled figure, with gleaming white teeth. From behind a large, polished wooden desk, strewn with papers, amid stacks of glossy x-ray film, the doctor told him it was a tumor.

"A microscopic growth, Mr. Langley, is impinging on a blood vessel on the fringe of your brain, this is what is causing your acute bouts of memory loss. The good news, however, Mr. Langley," the physician had continued almost matter-of-factly, a radiologist report gripped

between thick, gold-ringed fingers, "is that the cause of your inexplicable bouts of amnesia is a tiny intracranial distortion of the nonmalignant type, curable with a rather straightforward surgery procedure."

Langley picked up the map. No more invented excuses. This time he would tell this person, this woman, what he had suspected all along. If only he could remember her name and what she looked like!

Surely though, she would seek him out. He would put up with the dull headache, the tremor in his arm. Above all, he would act swiftly. With the aid of the map, he would sprint to the Fisher home, where he was sure she would be—before the shutter of his mind again closed.

RABANUS

That old black magic has me in its spell—Johnny Mercer

At the unveiling of teeny, pinch-faced Rabanus, it was reported by *Magic Review* that "six of forty-eight attendees fainted". One stricken member needed treatment at the local Grimsville emergency unit. "To subdue symptoms of severe fright anxiety", the report stated.

Heavily tattooed arms folded, skeletal elbows sticking out like plucked wings, the alleged wizard was revealed squat on the arm of a wicker chair. Blackly lit against an open window, the presumed master of unaccountable effects, appeared, to those squinting into its brightness, to take on the look of a perched raven.

Those in the room not forewarned that they were to be addressed by a freakish dwarf, were, to quote from the *Magic Review* piece, "quite horror-struck at the wizard's appearance". The reporter went on to pen that "The startling manifestation caused attendee's limbs to involuntarily twitch, suggestive of a need to rush frantically from the room, as if an announcement had been made that a bomb was about to go off". A black silken scarf about the magic man's lengthy neck only heightened the Corvus illusion. Iridescently flashing highlights of blue, green, and purple, the garment gave off the appearance of hackles.

When the curtain was raised from in front of the wicker chair—somewhat jerkily, by a bearded attendee, stood to one side pulling on a length of string—the *Magic Review* account noted, "There were less gasps, more choking kinds of sounds, as if people were readying to vomit".

Early arrivals had clustered closest to Rabanus. Arranged on the floor in various states of alertness, the more fanatical occult believers calmly nibbled on a biscuit, as though it was an everyday event to be addressed by a malformed birdman. Others, conveyed thoughtfulness by sipping on a can of soda, or pretended fascination with the event's single-page handout. The flyer—emblazoned with a raven's head, atop a long, black-feathered neck—caused readers' expressions to vary from *straining to be ordinary*, to *confusedly aghast*. Several countenances were clearly phony: perched before them was nothing more than an example of amateurish wizardry. Others, quite breathlessly, pointed out the likeness of the bird's neck on the pamphlet, to the shiny cravat around the overlong stem of the sorcerer.

A few faces—the assumed *professionals* in the audience—showed signs of suppressed annoyance. These folks cast hostile looks at those appearing to view the event as in any way magical. Any minute, this latter type of onlooker expected the hideous apparition before them to shed some

form of cloak, to reveal a grinning, pint-sized humanoid.
Those further back, stared open-mouthed, a look of disbelief on their faces. It was as if they were under sentence for
a heinous crime that they didn't commit.

"Once," the supposed sorcerer suddenly intoned, in a
voice most onlookers likened to a gurgling croak—whilst
eyeing the room for hidden woofers, no doubt wondering,
how could such powerful bass reflex come from such a
tiny larynx—"sleet lay inches deep out back, like shitty
cotton wool, yet there was none out front."

As though beset with an unreachable itch, the gathering squirmed. Mr. Ravensholm, the shrunken sorcerer's
slavishly attentive assistant, thought *"like pulled worms."*
Arranged cross-legged on the floor, beside Rabanus's cane
chair, the helper didn't crave anything, least of all the need
to scratch.

It was all too much for acne-scarred Daniel. Unaccus-
tomed to the paranormal, the youth leapt from his coveted
sofa-seat, belched, and spilling his drink, bellowed, "Hey!
I'm outta here, gotta' go fix me a grease-burger."

Emma, lolling on the floor beside Mr. Ravensholm,
looked stricken. Overly ripe of face and given to etiquette,
she masked her discomfort with attempted conversation.
"We're so glad you're here Mister Rabanus," she cooed
sweetly. "We're all in bad need of your chant." And more
sugary still: "You too, Mister Ravensholm."

Paula, seated on the now damp, Coke-stained couch,
marveled at the size of the sorcerer's horn-like feet, relative
that is, to the magic-man's diminutive body. So massively
three-toed were they, it took a seat cushion, pressed hard
to her mouth, to stifle spasms of laughter.

Confined within expanses of sky blue latex wall, many
onlookers—in order to avoid eye contact with the magic-
man, whose bullet-like black pupils could seem like they
were boring deep into your skull—could do little else but

stare out the single window, to gawp at buff-tiled roofs mostly, but also at endless chimney pots, neon-sign gantries and clapboard buildings.

It was during this opening lull, this absorbing time, this interval of trying to understand what in hell's name it was there squat before them, that a line of distant poplar trees—Mr. Ravensholm likened to "round paintbrushes standing on end"—suddenly became sleek-backed.

"Brushes, pressed wet to canvas!"

The associate noted too, the outside gust that had caused the affect. Mr. Ravensholm spotted that the same burst of energy dwindled to a mere puff within the room, enough of a waft, to lift a telltale wedge of the sorcerer's oiled black hair.

"As glinting-a tar-fall as you ever will see," Mr. Ravensholm muttered, eyeing the wizard's locks. The metaphor triggered a smirk that stole over the assistant's bony face as if something as black as a raven's wing had caused a shadow there, so darkly puckered was it. The auxiliary couldn't help but liken the tresses, spilling from His Master's peculiarly shaped head, and lying in folds on the windowsill—as if a North American Indian's feathered headdress had been thrown there—to a *wind-ruffled black lake, in which a slate vase nicely served as a rock outcrop.*

Suggestive of mature fruit, Emma—a buxom housewife she will tell you—complained, "Daniel's exit done it. The gust it was, what caused it," she spouted indignantly. "Off the stairwell door that the lad kicked open, that blew my pages." Strewn about her swollen feet, the yellowed, age-spotted leafs reminded Mr. Ravensholm of a wheat-stubble landscape he'd once looked down upon from the cockpit of a light airplane: an aviation fuel reeking machine that sickeningly yawed beneath the sinister base of a dark cumulonimbus cloud.

The assistant dutifully picked up the pages, one by one, and placed them back atop the stack beside Emma's bulbous knees. The subordinate liked to keep things tidy. That was a key part of his support job.

Sideways on to Rabanus, Mr. Ravensholm had been thinking how jaw-jutted his employer was. With a slight stretch of his imagination, the silhouette suggested a Bowie knife of a beak. He also reflected on the shaggy throat, and the hooked nails that terminated each curved finger. So wizardly talon-like they might alarm the uninformed. More so, he thought, should they begin to abrade skin. What's more, he noted that the magic-man's Adams-apple caused the scarf to wobble. "An empty craw beneath ruffled feathers! Perfect!" Mr. Ravensholm exclaimed—more loudly than he'd intended.

"The previous month," Mr. Ravensholm said, seeking to lighten tension in the room, if not expectant fear "before the outbreak of heavy thunderstorms over Midland— residents will tell you a poultice wrapped the town—"My Master croaked to me that 'leaves turned autumn brown overnight, front-side of his house, while those out back stayed summer green.'"

Chairs scraped. A soda can was crushed. Coughs erupted and yelps sounded. "Preposterous nonsense!" was shouted from the back of the room.

Mr. Ravensholm knew better. Preoccupied with the necromancer's eyes, he chose not to elaborate. What intrigued him was that when shot with window-light, ravens' feet-like crevices appeared about the bony cavities. The pupils, he thought, matched the color of a threadbare patch on the knee of the occultist's close-fitting black trousers. So clingy were these, it was as if sticks protruded from the body, appearing barely strong enough to support its weight—were he to 'hop' off the chair arm. The remnant of cloth was bulged slightly from the patella beneath. Not convexly, as is the exterior surface of a sphere, or indeed a kneecap, but pointed in the manner of a chicken's heel. Mr. Ravensholm thought the oddly shaped, purple-tinted hillock, surrounded as it was with raven-black, perfectly matched the wizard's eyes.

Such nonsensical notions often throbbed through Mr. Ravensholm's shaved head. Recruited by the occultist to give light relief during the buildup to the chant, he instead found his mind befouled with unspeakable observations.

The assistant next spoke about His Master's house. About it being a clapboard structure on North Main. About it being next to Morton Lumber. About it being a weed-infested patch the magician called his garden. About tar-paulin-covered lumber units stacked three-high that surrounded the oasis. About the scene reminding him of circled wagons.

Mr. Ravensholm then added, grinning at the perceived wordiness of his observation, "that an oil-stained, truck-trundled concrete ramp served as the front yard."

Emma—ponderous head supported by vast forearm, elbow jackknifed on the composite-wood floor—not normally inclined to use expletives, told the gathering, "The wizard once told me that 'a sooty bird seen at the house was almost the size of a lumber unit.' When flat-toed atop of one, he said, 'the bird—a raven it was—blanketed the whole fuckin' tarp.'"

"Go figure," she'd added, crinkly nosed.

She'd chimed on, stifling an outburst of sniggering into the back of a pudgy hand, to tell Mr. Ravensholm that "Mister Rabanus also told her 'the bird croak-spoke. Said things like, we peck eyeballs—out!'"

Mr. Ravensholm noted the speaker's blood-gorged face. He hated the woman. Hated the flabbiness, the seeming absence of bones. Loathed the thick lips. His Master had croaked to him once that 'the female's unexplained laughing-speak reminded him of a supermarket announcer telling of in-store specials.'

"Mister Rabanus also said," Emma continued with fake solemnity, "'the bird took off like a B24 bomber, throwing the back of the building into shadow. Caused flaps of displaced air to pulse through the house, strong enough to lift the drapes.'" "What's more," she said, "he said, 'the curtains still swayed a full minute after the creature left.' Oh, and one more thing," she said, turning to face Mr. Ravensholm with sham alarm—shapeless arm limply extended toward the sorcerer—"Mister Rabanus spoke of 'the winged-thingy not appearing out front.'"

Mr. Ravensholm then said, turning dramatically toward the others in the room, "that not long after the air displacement episode, that this woman here has just spoken about, My Master had croaked to me that 'ravens, goose-stepping on the concrete ramp out front, were thrice the size of those out back.'"

Gales of bottled-up glee tore at Emma's mouth. The roly-poly body doubled in mirth such that Mr. Ravensholm could make out the breasts: pendulant, like mangoes, lolling against the inside of a loose-necked woolen jumper, out of which a pudgy neck sprouted like a topped turnip—so repulsively, the assistant barely resisted the urge to throttle the life out of it!

Rabanus remained silent. He wasn't thinking of tits, or how he thought ravens looked like helmeted Roman generals. On his mind was what *hadn't* been spoken about. The morning sky out front turning molten pitch while out back the hot sun beat down from an unblemished blue. He pursed his lips. The sallow cheeks fluted. Membranous tissue puckered. A hum stole over the room. Reverberated in dusty corners. Nooks, crannies began to drone. The melodious buzz impinged on the structure.

Through the open window a raven peered into the room. Its miniscule brain vibrated "lovely pecks in there" to beak sinews. The sound of wings unfolding, forced Paula into fake awakening. Rustling, black cloth umbrellas were on her mind.

Outside, a raven clutched the edge of a ridge tile. Another, with the clinginess of a blowfly, hopped sideways along the edge of a gutter. Yet another Corvus emerged from a sooty chimney pot. Across the roof, clumps of feathers grew like metastasizing tumors.

"Let it be chanted from the steeples, the mountaintops," Rabanus intoned. As the wizard croaked out the chant, he shuffled. Clearly the wizard-bird was impatient to be off the arm of the wicker chair.

"*Perch*," Mr. Ravensholm thought, for His Master seemed to be gathering himself in the manner of a scavenging Aves readying for flight—crop thrust outward to the extent its hollow cavity would permit.

There were three ravens sat on a tree
Downe a downe, hay downe, hay downe
They were as black as they might be
With a downe derrie derrie downe

Tremors rippled through the room. Hooked feet scraped tile, a resonance that struck Mr. Ravensholm as "bastard-grit, embedded in stick-chalk, drawn sharply across a dry blackboard." Somewhere within the room, dentures reset over hard gums.

Leaning as though to puke, Emma waddled out the room. She wobbled to the top of the stairwell, and exploded bottled up laughter down the shaft.

Ravensholm noted that Rabanus's jaw that broadcast the croak-chant was powerfully hinged, as is a projecting, horny sheath. The supposed wizard leaned into the light.

He knew he glowed. He knew he would soon fade to raven-black. Somewhere, inside a chimney pot it seemed, feathery wings beat against pottery. The surface of the windowsill-lake shimmied. Somewhere else, something sounding like sleet, slipped on a slate roof

Ravensholm relaxed. His Master would control the encroachment: the croak-speak of hungry scavengers, along with their habit of yawing over chasms.

She lift up his bloudy head
And kist his wounds so red
She got him up upon her backe
Buried him before his prime
Dead herself ere evensong time
Hay downe, derrie derrie downe

Emma was glad to be on the landing. "The fuck out that room" was how she expressed it. But not to look down upon a discarded soda can, dispensing its syrupy load down the staircase.

And further down—*hay derrie, derrie downe*—to look upon a spread-eagled, russet-haired youth with empty eye sockets. It was while standing upon that uncarpeted intermediate platform that a horny spout-like object—Emma just had time to think *"unopened hedge shears!"*—stabbed out the last dreg of hilarity, gurgling deep in her throat.

Paula was uncringing from sofa cushions when Emma's piercing scream seized her—as a cramp sometimes does a leg. Ravensholm likened the ensuing feather storm to hens crammed in egg-farm cages, attempting flight. Captivated by his Master's canticle, the devoted assistant knew it was time to stay put.

Hackles quivered, as the sorcerer dropped off the wicker chair arm, goose-stepped to the stairwell door. Jabbed it open with bill-like cadence.

The gathering scrambled frenziedly to its feet. Paula broke into a fit of hysterical laughter that quickly turned to shrieked cries of "He*lp me get outa here!*" Chairs tumbled. Members backed away, to press against resistance—anything, a latex blue wall, each other—backs of hands to mouths, eyes widened.

Ponderously from the stairwell, an enormous raven rose. The creature's scaly feet folded like bomb doors. Bat-like, the Corvus flapped lazily out the landing window.

Clawing altitude, the creature, tottering and whirling in a flat-winged soar—like a page of blackened newssheet spiraling out of a bonfire—disappeared.

Verses: From, *"Melismata"*—Thomas Ravenscroft c. 1611.

THE SENTENCE

It is as well to remember that one can escape all in life, except death, for no one gets out of the former alive — SBJ

The rasp of steel biting into wood, the hammering of nails, the scrape of work boots on the paved forecourt had gone on most of the morning, before receding footsteps signaled the work had been completed. The soldier viewed the goings on through a barred aperture that was the window of his cell.

The uniformed infantryman looked over the finished work piece with a professional eye, for prior to joining the Polish army he'd been a carpenter, a trade the recruiter told him would be much in demand. Yet, assigned to an infantry division, he'd not seen cut lumber, let alone worked it, the whole first year of his three-year enlistment.

That, and the relentless discipline, the mindless cleaning, the nonsensical, repetitive, parade-square drilling, had bred in him an intense dislike of the military, to such degree that he had devoted himself to getting out of it.

Unknowing of a looming, fateful happening, after which sheer dread would be his only emotion, he had deliberately disadvantaged himself militarily with a show of insolent indifference to the activities of his unit. He had acted with such belligerent intensity; his behavior was brought to the attention of his commanding officer. Alarmed at the enlisted man's attitude, and the effect such *Reprehensible conduct might have on battalion moral.* The Colonel had immediately recommended that the enlisted man be marked: *Classified Unsuitable for Service, forthwith to be Dishonorably Discharged by Court Marshal.*

Having achieved his aim, while awaiting papers that would officially release him from the service, the soldier couldn't help but recall that it was the prospect of an adventurous lifestyle that had drawn him to enlist in the first place. Swayed by colorful army recruitment posters, depicting radiant young men in exotic settings—arranged bright-eyed around a forest campfire, biting into what appeared to be succulent cuts of chicken, roasted on a spit—he'd asked himself, why shouldn't he want to exchange drab Elblag to become one of them? Why should he have to suffer even one more day of the seemingly perpetually cold, wet Baltic air that swept across the flat, featureless fields and swamps of Drużno?

He'd smiled, reinforcing the idea by loudly exclaiming, *"Of course! Of course!"* So he'd enlisted.

Now, four days after the most unbelievably dreadful incident, that when compared to *Reprehensible Conduct*, makes the latter mere young man's naughtiness; just to stride across that selfsame cobbled yard, to hear his own footsteps ring out, would be adventure enough. Past the coarse-grained wooden box, he's decided is made of cedar, on through the thicket to frolic in the sun-drenched meadow he's observed shimmering through the trees.

A planked lid, of the same yellowish wood—that when the time comes, will be nailed to the top of the container—lies propped against the side of an improvised trestle, upon which the finished work stands.

He's not surprised the receptacle is outsize, and that it has been made without the classic taper of a coffin. Such abnormal volume, he knows, increases the tomb's capacity to hold oxygen, ensuring that any would-be occupant—assuming such inhabitant to be alive at entombment—be subjected to as long a period of interment as possible before asphyxiation brings an end to suffering.

He knows too that there is nothing ceremonial about what is planned for the container. For other than him, the only persons who will witness the use for which it is to be put are two peasant farm laborers. Culled from the fields on the promise of a bonus, the men have been told that upon a command from the officer, they are to lower the box into an earthen pit that they will have prepared the previous day.

The upright edges of each of the two corners of the coffin facing the infantryman—when aligned against a vertical bar of his cell—tell him the work has been properly squared. He knows too that the lone workman, with minimal hand-tools, has performed adequately, and will be well satisfied with the job he's done. He envisages this man trudging home through the forest, to perhaps wife and family, unknowing and uncaring as to whom his handiwork will contain.

The soldier wonders—with a degree of foreboding that causes his clenched hands to slip down the bars of his cell, and his mind to verge on total breakdown—how long it will be after the box is buried six-foot down with himself inside before it rots, before it collapses to a featureless, gray powder, streaked red-rust with the very nails he has seen so cleanly driven in, him, reduced to an earth-entombed skeleton, arranged in the state of his last frenzied attempt to extricate himself?

Despite the unspeakable dread the thought of such entrapment brings, his curious mind—the product of a trade where it's an everyday event to come up with a work-around for a previous mistake—probes, with as much rational thought as can be mustered, various escape possibilities. If they bury him alive, as the draconian sentence calls for, would there be a flaw in the underside of the lid, he wonders, that would enable him to pry a piece away? Wouldn't this possible imperfection, in a species of timber he knows to be prone to such defect, when picked at sliver by sliver with finger nail, with teeth, perhaps even with the buckle of his belt should it be entombed with him, eventually cause the wood to succumb? Cause the cedar to reveal, in all its sinister deadweight compactness, and earthen dankness, the face of the soil in which it's incased?

His imagination knows no bounds. Surely, he reasons, he should then be able to abrade each soil layer. By a tiny fraction each time, yes, but if assailed at long enough, would not each miniscule amount slowly but surely fill the cavity beneath? And, as the space fills around him—at a rate he can surely govern by adjusting the amount of wood removed—then, by further scraping at the exposed earthen roof, shouldn't he, after repeating the procedure many times, be able to claw his way to the top of each consecutive infill, thus enabling him to work his way to the surface upon a succession of earthen mounds?

Could he not then haul himself out of the tomb? Shake off the filthy, clogging dirt. Clear his mouth, his eyes, his nose, and his ears to look up into a clear, blue sky? Or perhaps even a starlit one?

The soldier readjusts his grip on the bars. He knows such thought is but fantasy, yet nonetheless, given his dire situation, an allure to which he finds himself irresistibly drawn. He is aware the notion is preposterous in the extreme. Apart from lack of oxygen, and having to remove enough of the coffin's roof for him to squeeze his body through, such an escape would surely require Herculean effort. Two hundred and fifty cubic feet of earth resting upon the lid would make it impossible for him to pry off anything, least several planks above his head that are securely nailed onto the top of the coffin's frame. Under such pressure, significant movement would require an explosive force for it to even budge. What's more, he admits, that even should he by some marvel of ingenuity, manage to gain a finger-hold on the lid's underside—the edge of a knot perhaps or a split in the grain—the burden of the soil above would be so great as to force its way through the crevice in an unstoppable, suffocating avalanche!

He wishes for the wings of a bird he sees alight on the concrete sill. It's a house sparrow. Nondescript, yes, he knows, but a survivor of all challenges nature can throw at it. The creature is so close to his clasping hands; he feels an urge to grab it, to press the fluttering, grayish brown-feathered body to his lips. But the bird flits to perch on the rim of the coffin, to chirrup along the length of a sawn edge, seemingly to explore the unusual object that has suddenly appeared in its territory.

The soldier is struck yet again with a lightning rod of thought. Adrenaline pulsates wishfully through his being, as does the rhythmic clasp and unclasp of his hands around the bars. His mind is a whirl of ideas, albeit thus far, each a fanciful, hopeless notion. Still, he must explore every escape possibility, howsoever bizarrely far-fetched each may at first seem. Surely, he reasons, it would be better to work on the coffin's side planks. For there would be little, if any, pressure acting there. But the scheme is at once doomed, fatally flawed, for he knows he would be no better off than had it been a piece of the lid removed. Each shaving off the earthen sidewall would collapse into the space thus fashioned, filling the void as fast as he could excavate it.

And what about oxygen? His feverish mind turns to that. Wouldn't such exertion deplete what little there was to start with, even though the container was constructed outsize to sustain life long enough for sheer terror to kill first?

"*Long enough for the convicted criminal, nay, heinous, murdering swine, to suffer maximum torment before death,*" the sleek-haired, mustachioed presiding officer had intoned. The medal-bedecked major had been seated in the center of a group of three officers. The trio sat at a long, wooden table set on a raised platform. "*Prisoner 385, you will look up here, and smartly so, when addressed by members of this panel,*" the major had added.

The defendant could not find it in him to do anything other than to stare at the pine floor. Even under acute duress, he found himself examining the grain, the knots and whirls, the iron nails driven in by some long ago carpenter, the many and varied indentations—he surmised, the result of soldiers coming smartly to attention, oblivious to a steel tack on their boot heel digging into the wood—the correctness of each plank's alignment with its adjacent boards, and the oiled finish that gave the floor a beautiful gleam. It was as if pine was covered with a film of water.

And then there's an utter pitch-blackness. What about that? He tightly closes his eyes to try to simulate it. Shuts out the breeze-rustled canopy of an oak. The tree casts its leafy shadow across the forecourt, where it flickers across the sparrow, as it hops along the lid of the container, pecking, it would seem, at grains of sawdust. The level of absolute darkness, he realizes, would be unchanged whether his eyes were firmly shut or stretched wide open!

And a silence of unnerving profoundness. What about that? Broken only by the sound of earth as it settles around the wooden tomb. And the creak and groan of the planked lid as it takes the strain of the weight above it. Such heaviness will surely cause the top to sag, possibly, create enough of a bend to touch his nose, or his chest, a sensation he will not see, yet suddenly feel!

And the soil, the finer particles of it at least, will surely ooze through gaps in the boards. The grains will land unannounced on his face, in his eyes possibly and his mouth, that again will first be felt as he lies in dread-blackness of when and where the next trickle will occur!

And if and when it will stop!

It is as well then that suffocation would take him before such nightmarish outcome. Of course, that would be his plan, should it reach that terrifying stage. He would hasten the onset of asphyxiation; speed up his demise by working his arms and his legs, as best he could—assuming he was not strapped—to use up oxygen quicker. For death would be an escape from lingering hell.

Consumed with this turmoil of doomed thought, he releases his hold on the bars, to settle back onto the flats of his bare feet. Exhausted by hopeless, desperate thought, he turns from the window to face his cell. Unlike the coffin, it is square. Each wall he has measured at twenty and a half handspans. A heavy wooden door, with sliding view-panel embedded in its upper face, is centered in the wall facing him. Construction, he noted when first arriving in the building—as is his habit when entering a place for the first time, irrespective of its utility, to immediately size up the type of material and method of deployment—is stone block, each measuring two and a quarter handspans in length, one and a quarter in height. A metal bucket that serves as a latrine stands in a corner, where the wall facing him meets the wall on his left. To his right, a stained, louse-infested mattress lies on the floor against the wall.

The ceiling is of poor-quality plaster. He knows this from repeatedly leaping up at it, arms extended above his head. The attacks, with fingers and thumbs extended, have created indentations in the surface. The pits have confirmed the presence of embedded wooden slats.

It is now nearing nightfall. The shadows of the bars across the cell floor, cast by an outside lamp, have lengthened. Shortly, a single light bulb, behind a metal screen on the wall beside the door, will turn on, as it has the other three nights of his imprisonment. In its faint glow he will see the outline of the tiny valleys he has made in the ceiling plaster more clearly. He has determined that the finish is skimmed thinly over the lathes, like an eggshell. He's sure that the surface will be brittle enough to crack, possibly to break away with continued assaults, to eventually enable him to penetrate the roof space.

This plan is his colossal secret, his stunning covert plot, a supreme scheme that he's nurtured every terrible second of every agonizing minute of every wretched hour, during each day and long into each night of his captivity!

Other than the ceiling, which is a dirt-ingrained gray-ish white, the cell is uniformly greenish brown. This over-all drabness is only broken by the checkerboard pattern of darker-brown mortar between the blocks, and here and there, finger-painted excrement left by previous occupants. The uneven stone floor glistens wetly in the corners. Rising damp reaches half way up the walls, attracting cockroach-es that cluster excitedly at each fecal scrawl.

Every hour, a shutter over the grill in the door slams open. The roaches scatter. Darting black eyes set deep in a swarthy face rest upon him long enough to confirm that he's alive. That the prisoner has not managed to cheat the unimaginable sentence that is to be carried out the next day at first light.

Each evening, a plate of food has been placed on the floor by the door. The mash appears to be a mix of shredded meat of some kind that could be rat or squirrel with what looks like mashed black beans, speckled with bits of white that could well be maggot. The soldier has noted that the guard is always careful not to enter the cell. "For fear of being waylaid," the man says. "Battered to death with the bucket. Asphyxiated with the mattress. Or I've heard it told, garroted with daisy-chained bootlaces, as happened to the unfortunate before me."

Two guards change the metal container daily. One steps inside; the other remains outside the cell. Such is the care taken to preserve him, to keep him alive for a punishment worse than death.

Even should he, by some miracle, manage to rush past this grizzled guard, to escape his cell, freedom would be brief. For should he be fortunate and strong enough to overcome the shifty-eyed one at the door, he knows the cell opens onto an interior courtyard secured by a locked gate, the other side of which stand two more guards, each armed with a bayoneted rifle. They have been instructed to shoot only as a last resort—*use the butt, the blade of your weapon, your steel-tipped boots by all means, but don't kill him!*

The meal serving for the day is due any minute. As soon as the cell door closes, he will wolf down the ghastly concoction with cupped fingers, for he must eat to maintain his strength, to enable him to execute his great escape. Freedom will be gained, not when all is lost from within the burial chamber, as he's all day fantasized about, but tonight, long before he's ever placed in it!

He will gulp the meal down in an uncouth, animal manner because utensils are not allowed. More importantly, he will do so with greatest rapidity to reduce the time having to smell the insidious odor that comes off it. To lessen taste, he will place gobs of the mash onto the back of his tongue and swallow whole. He will then quickly wash any residue down with the beaker of water provided. Fortified, albeit on the point of gagging, only then will he continue to jab at the ceiling.

He is confident that if he could dislodge one tiny piece, a flake of the plaster, to provide a fingerhold, it will be possible to pull further sections away, to expose the lathes. He could then pummel away at these thin lengths of wood until he broke enough of them to allow him entry into the attic, since he knows the cell is a single-story building.

The plaster will fall noiselessly onto the mattress from which he jumps. The debris he will place in the newly emptied bucket that is not due for further replacement until after he has left the cell for the sentence to be carried out.

To enter the loft, he will first need to cling tightly to the bars, while wedging his body upon the narrow, sloping concrete windowsill, long enough to reach up, to grip the edge of the hole and hoist himself onto the rafters.

He does not think it possible for the guard to see the ceiling without entering the cell, which, thus far, the sentry has been loath to do. He has determined that the grill aperture in the door, being covered by an external eyepiece-shroud, is set such that it would be impossible for someone outside the cell to see the ceiling inside.

Exhausted with constantly battering at the plaster, he lies supine on the mattress, his numb, bleeding hands crossed beneath his head. The twelve-inch hole crossed with the wooden lathes that he's created, gapes blackly down at him. The last jump had brought down a good-size piece, much more than he'd intended to jab off in one go. Though the dislodged section had fallen onto the mattress, it had done so with such force it shattered, littering the floor with bits of plaster.

Sweating profusely in the humid air, he'd madly scampered around the cell, making wide passes with his hands to quickly sweep the debris beneath the mattress, dreading the guard choosing that moment to slide back the observation window.

Prisoners try anything to escape their sentence, the guard told him the previous morning in a rare burst of conviviality. "Many have charged me," he said. "Deliberately, to escape judgment. In effect, trying to commit suicide." The heavily built man had been stationed outside his cell brandishing a shotgun. Done, the soldier thought, to show that he could take that way out too if he chose. If he did so, the guard would be only too pleased to oblige. Tempting as it was, the soldier could not bring himself to take up the offer, for he knew the guard to be lying. The prisoner would be merely clubbed into unconsciousness. Or worse, shot in the leg, or an arm. And how silly such an attempt would be. Wasted effort that would more than likely hamper, if not abruptly end, his escape plan!

"A cold-blooded murderer is the worst of the criminal type," the guard had continued with a contemptuous sneer that the soldier thought to goad him into leaping forward. "Those that commit murder," the sentry growled on, "deserve the worst punishment. And when the victim is their commanding officer they deserve the most heinous sentence it's possible for mankind to hand down."

The infantryman chose not to respond. He decided that there was nothing to be gained by explaining to this ignoramus that his weapon had fired accidentally. The rifle discharged as he tried to free up its jammed bolt-mechanism. The bullet ricocheted at least once before striking the colonel in the forehead. The round blew out the back of the commanding officer's skull, along with most of his brain, into the face of the drill instructor—a medal festooned major, recently declared a national hero, following *Outstand-*

ing bravery in battle—who was sat at attention in full ceremonial dress, immediately behind the colonel.

The hastily arranged tribunal, hell-bent on retribution,
especially to one under dishonorable discharge, dismissed
those facts out of hand. The court decided that a punishment worse than death was the only fit sentence for such
calculating, deliberate, brutal, cold-blooded murder.

The soldier turned his mind back to the attic. He envisages the darkness, the musty, warm smell. He must act
fast, immediately after a guard-check. Then, he will know
he has at least sixty minutes before the shutter is next slid
back. He should be through to the tiled roof by then, despite the handicap of raw fingers and utter fatigue.

The clearness of his plan fortifies his resolve to escape.
As does the knowledge that he must, or die doing so.
There will be no capture. No return to the death cell. The
sickening feeling that for days has lain like lead in his gut
has lightened slightly. He relaxes. His hands remain
crossed beneath his head. There is time to rest his aching
wrists, arms. Make ready for the supreme effort.

His plan appears like a dream in which he appears
outside looking back into it. Instead of verging on the impossible, his task begins to appear quite simple. Methodi-
cal even, and strangely soft and effortless to accomplish.

He will go over it one more time.

The hole in the plaster ceiling stares down at him like a
blackened eye. It will need widening of course, along with
the breaking through several lathes. This shouldn't present
too much of a problem, he decides, since his bodily weight
will act in his favor: to pull down, to rip. He can even hang
there for a while if necessary, always provided that all is
done quietly and is immediately followed by a cleanup-
sweep of mattress and cell floor. He will achieve this degree of penetration by gripping the edge of the hole at the
peak of each leap, to pull down whole sections at a time.

Once in the attic he will need to act swiftly too, and again quietly, to first remove roofing material that may lie beneath the tiles. Then, carefully push and lift several of them outward, clear of the roof. After hoisting his slim body through the opening, he will creep up onto the ridge. There, he will suck in the cool, clear, night air. He might even take a moment to look down on the open coffin with its propped lid, from which no doubt will waft the aromatic scent of cedar.

Then, like a cat, barefoot, silent, he will move along the apex of the roof. Leap the gap between the buildings. Drop softly to the ground. There, he will turn, crouched, ready for a challenge. But none will materialize out of the darkness. For no alarms will have sounded.

No shouts of *Get him! There he goes! Get him! Don't kill him! Maim the swine!* Will ring out.

Speedily, he will run across a stretch of dirt to the wide-open gate through which he will disappear. Just like that. Vanish. Melt into the night down the dusty lane he has spent so much time looking at from his cell window. After several strides, he will jump through the bushes to lay low for a few minutes in the soft grasses he knows grow there.

Head back, chest thrust out, he will then start his run. Yard after yard, mile after mile, through memorable woodland, open meadow, glade, he will splash across familiar streams, leap bramble patches, fallen trees; tumble down recognizable valley slopes, always on the move. Faster, faster, fleet of foot he will head northeast toward the crack of dawn that soon will widen to a crimson oblong, then balloon to a golden ellipse. Like a white-hot brazier the orb will burst forth, flooding the gully along which he will be racing, and from which pheasants, partridges will rise and rabbits scatter, disturbed from their morning browse amid the dewy grass. His raw hands, the aching bones of his

thumbs, his fingers—one of which he knows is fractured—
the stiffness in the backs of his legs, neck and lower back,
through thrusting off the mattress, won't matter.

Oblivious to such physical pain, he will be filled with a
sense of freedom, a lust to be home! To his mother, father,
who unaware of his dreadful predicament—having been
informed their son is missing in action—will look up startled as they rise from their seats on the patio. Astounded to
see their son bursting from the woodland toward them.
Thunderstruck to see him race across the clearing that is
the family garden: set with cabbage, lettuce—peas up to
his waist and lines of furrowed potatoes—and there on the
lawn, Shandy the old collie, startled out of a snooze, as he
races closer, causing the tail to wag, the ears to droop, uncertain, having never seen her master move so fast, his face
contorted, froth-flecked even; and yet no doubt brilliantly
creased with lines of joy at the sight of his parents holding
onto each other for support, yet also extending an arm to
greet him, the last few strides now in slow motion such
that he can savor each step, examine the unfolding experience in minute detail, frame by frame...

As the thumps of shoveled earth grow fainter, as the infantryman succumbs to his cedar-scented world, he
clings tenaciously to his dream, behind tightly closed eyes.
Not in utter blackness, but scenery of such vibrancy, such
fidelity, he can hear familiar voices, the chirp of birds amid
the rustle of breezily disturbed, leafy canopies—oblivious
to the slither of earth against wood.

A Retaliatory Measure

While seeking revenge, dig two graves, one for yourself—D. Horton

Separated from others in the office, I sit facing a darkened window that reflects my face, a 9 mm pistol and sheets of paper that lie on a desk in front of me. Soon, I'll read over what I've written on the paper. Soon after, I'll pick up the pistol, press it against my temple and pull the trigger.

This is now—August 27, 12.45 pm to be precise.

Two months prior, June, the month of my twenty-ninth birthday, I'm in *Brook Hall* where a quartet is playing *Moonlight in Vermont*. I'm dancing a slow foxtrot with Sheila, a small, delicate girl, light as a feather. The slightest lift of my arms, and her toes to skim the polished floor.

I don't know it yet, but later, I decide it was then—flushed with romantic thought, tempered with a surge of heart-stopping jealousy at the sight of Steve watching her dance—she must have decided to finish. In fact she was probably eyeing Steve over my shoulder. No doubt displaying one of those raised eyebrow looks of hers that says, *look what I have to put up with.*

And there's me, twirling in my single-breasted Hepworth with matching Windsor-knotted tie—carefully loosened in the cloakroom mirror; pulled down just enough from an unbuttoned white shirt collar, to look like I'd just left an all night card game—pretending to be unaffected.

July. I'm still going with Sheila but feel in tow, her, ready to cut the link; sever it with a sharply worded comment. Or, perhaps, via a small note discretely posted to me. I think lots of things about this time, including killing her, then myself. This mood passes to leave me empty. There's no future, there's no past to call upon that has pleasant memories. I'm crushed, flattened; cowed. It's as if there's a weasel inside me, eating out my heart.

It's still July and we're still sort of together, only I've heard on the vine she's seeing Steve on the sly. This shatters me completely. I envision them fondling each other in his penthouse loft atop the fifty-eight floor Edward Tower, the two of them fucking: on the polished maple floor, spread-legged on his big California King, the adjoining bathroom, or even up against the wall in the stairwell.

I can't breathe with these thoughts raging in my head!

I'm possessed with the devil, a fearful state that can only be satisfied through retribution. There's a need to do something special that will forever catch their attention. Albeit, in this life, fleetingly—in the few seconds available to them, they will think one last thought: *that's what Damien's look meant!*

I lie awake at night, sometimes all night. My mind is tormented with the thrill of satisfying a desire for revenge. In one fantasy, I barge in on them in their rooftop lair. They show surprise, if not outright shock at my unexpected intrusion. Eventually, I small talk them over to the French-door side of the room that I know overlooks a sheer drop to a flagstone courtyard.

My tactic is to slide back the glazed doors that open onto a tiny low-walled balcony—to let in fresh air, whatever—then push them both out into the rainy night. Him first, because she, being the slighter, would be the easiest, even when hysterical, that she surely will be, seeing what I'd just done to him. I work myself up into lather, enacting such sweet reckoning.

I wake up filled with the heaviness of unsatisfied justice. All day, I can't get the thought out of my head, especially the bit where I suddenly place the flats of both hands against Steve's shoulders.

I give Steve such a huge backward push he tipples head over heels straight out over the wall. And, of course, down. The fact that he, the womanizer, the lecherous swine, if you will, instantly exits my life, causes such a wave of relief to sweep me, I almost forget the job is half done. Sheila, the betrayer, the whore, the slut, is still there. She's unable to believe what she's just seen me do, her tiny hand no doubt raised to her equally tiny mouth in speechless horror.

Even so, bent on survival, she starts to shimmy over to the apartment door side of the room. But me, despite being a stick-of-a-guy, am pretty quick on my feet. Yards quicker than a woman rooted to the spot with abject terror. I'm also strong in a lean, leggy sort of way.

So I grab her around the waist and literally fling her after Steve, with whom, let it be said, she clearly indicated she wanted to be.

Fantasy executed! I'm terrifically refreshed! It's like being into a double dose of Xanax. Believe me, actually doing is so much better than dreaming! The edginess, the feverish hesitancy, the gut-wrenching ache have gone. I hold my hand up to the city lights that shine through the gape of the still open balcony door, to see it steady as the proverbial rock. I find myself laughing, softly at first, but quickly rising to border on hysteria.

I step out again to look down. A small crowd has gathered around the corpses. Already there are police sirens wailing, getting nearer by the second. Soon, cops will be swarming the stairs, riding the elevators, holsters unclipped. What the fuck am I to do? My plan was to follow them down, only wait until the cops had gathered, so my arrival would be more spectacular.

But I don't do that.

Instead of suicidal tendencies, fear, loathing; stuff like that, I feel buoyed. Compared to jumping to my death, or, God-forbid, spending time in a police cell followed by the Electric Chair, a continuation of existence suddenly appeals. So I turn back into the brightly lit room, mind racing over possibilities. I take maybe ten seconds considering whether to concoct a story that I witnessed the lovers falling off the balcony entwined, or me never having been there at all.

I choose the latter and exit the room.

But not before giving the balcony door handles a good wipe over with the edge of a curtain. Both sides of the room doorknob I wipe with my handkerchief. As far as I can recall those are the only objects I've touched—other than Steve and Sheila. Even so, I need not hide that fact, since I've visited with them so often, right up to the point I discovered they were having it off. So prints in the room, in the elevator, are okay. As are fibers, just so long as they're not the last ones on the balcony door.

I ride the service elevator down—amazingly without stopping at any of the fifty-eight floors. Dead lucky. Obviously, the cops have not yet got around to discovering this route to the top. I exit the building. Sprint across a pitch-dark parking lot.

August. The beginning of. I'm packing my things to go on a trip. I believe enough time has elapsed since my double slaying for me to disappear. Being the known boyfriend, along with the cops learning that Steve was screwing my girlfriend, I was obviously the chief suspect. In fact, as far as I can tell, I've been the only one, other than them both committing together in an unremitting tryst.

I won't bore you with the coroner's inquest, the endless interviews, interrogations; report of the District Attorney (insufficient evidence to prosecute). Just think of me as one incredible lucky fellow.

Late August, I'm in a motel on the edge of some pokey town, two hundred miles or so from the crime scene. I've spent the last three nights (and days) at this dump-of-a-place, in a room that feels like the size of a dog kennel. In front of me, on the unmade bed, sits my travel bag. It's ready for final zipping. I have only to stuff in the motel facecloths (three), the motel shower towels (two), the motel soaps (five), sachet's of shampoo (2), my electric razor, a brown comb, toothbrush and nine-tenths exhausted tube of spearmint flavored toothpaste, and I'm ready for the door. The three-day stay has allowed me to test whether or not I'm still under investigation. Check if there's any probes going, or concern raised about my disappearance. As far as I can tell there hasn't been. No one has called. No mention has been made in the paper, or on TV. So I figure get the hell out of if, to some distant state—country even.

That's when the phone rings.

Yes, that shiny-black, smelly, fuckin' gizmo on its innocuous cradle beside the bed—is fuckin' ringing!

Go on, be the Lobby: *Good morning Sir, just calling to remind you that guest check-out time today is…*

"Hello?"

"Am I speaking with a Damien Lionel Thompson?"

"Yes, this is he."

"Officer Polanski, Pasadena Police Department speaking. If you look out your room window Mr. Thompson, you'll see, across the parking lot, me, holding a cell-phone to my ear, standing beside a broadsided black and white, looking back at you. Beyond, you will also see other black and whites—three in all, if you care to count…"

I don't know how my bag and me got out the bathroom window. I'm skinny, but for sure the opening couldn't have been more than a foot and a half square. Anyway, I pushed out the fly screen, wiggled, squeezed, to drop to the ground amid deep grasses that must have been growing there uncut since the place was built. Then there was this hellishly convenient slope. So steep, it was almost a cliff, down which I rolled and slid, to end up in a ditch.

The cops are, presumably, still out front, laconically leaning against their black and whites.

Okay, I've escaped, but to where?

Back to my office to write this scrawl.

To pick up this pistol.

THE INTRUDERS

Go as far as you can see; when you get there you'll be able to see farther—J. P. Morgan

My bladder aches to be emptied. I take yet another flight of steps, three at a time, only to reach more closed bathroom doors I know will be useless to beat upon. I run up and down countless stairs, along endless corridors, in some stair and corridor-ridden edifice.

Others throng the complex. Purposeful, confident, bladders surely on empty, they stride unconcernedly through the labyrinth, ignorant of my predicament.

It's no use me asking *them* where the nearest bathroom is, for I know they will tell me there are two. One at the end of each block, they will say airily.

These people will even take time to point the bathrooms out to me—with raised arm, in the manner of a Hitler salute—adding that if those are in use, there is another just down the corridor.

But these toilets are always in use too. Untold numbers of blank, brown doors I have dashed up to, wild-eyed, sweating profusely, hand pushed hard against crotch, only to find them occupied. So I lean into a corner, and like a drunk about to throw up, feverishly unzip.

I dread the ensuing flood, for I know it will run foam-flecked into the corridor for all to see. A steaming stream that others will have to wincingly step over.

But as I give in, and release the pent-up torrent, a hand grips my arm. Pincer-like, it squeezes.

Again it compresses.

Yet again, even more tightly.

I awaken to Joan's clench.

"Shush!" She whispers.

"What?"

"Shush!"

"What's the matter?"

"Shush!"

The air-conditioner whooshes.

The window blind sways.

Slats tap the glass; I think like the beak of some bird pecking at its reflection. Faint moonlight shimmies the ceiling. I am drenched with perspiration. My body is still unzipped. I'm still in an endless, echoing, quarry-tiled corridor, savoring the sensation of release.

"I don't hear anything."

"Shush!"

My hearing's not what it used to be. *Impaired* a specialist once said. The white-coated physician told me "we all suffer hearing loss as we age. At one time," he said—with what I perceived to be a forced laugh that showed he'd made the same comment to countless other elderly, hard-of-hearing clients—"a hearing horn would have been prescribed."

My hearing aids are tiny, skin-colored inserts. No matter, they are downstairs. It's where I always leave them, after watching TV.

Again the clench.

The long case chimes. I count three.

Muffled footfalls. Something, or, dare I think it, *someone*, is moving about downstairs.

Down our stairs!

It's my turn to clench. My fingers find Joan's nape damp with perspiration. I'm not in a fit state to leap out of bed. Indeed, to leap anywhere, least of all to tackle an unknown assailant. Even if I had a baseball bat. For he may be a big, burly fellow who would easily snatch it out of my feeble grasp. More than likely break it over my head.

Long ago in the school playground, I learned my physique placed me at a distinct disadvantage when attempting the likes of that. I never took anything by force off anybody. Even if what they had was mine. Bodybuilding advertisements all too often reminded me of my inadequacy. Alongside the bronzed, muscled specimen—that supposedly I would become were I to sign up—cowered a replica of me. A skinny weakling. Sixty years later, in a postoperative state, the odds of me being effective against some brute of a burglar are laughably inadequate.

Alone, I think I might have climbed out the window, onto our prized maple. Discretely slid to the ground. Melted into the moonlit landscape. My grasp of Joan's neck has lessened with each minute of silence that has passed. I give it a light massage beneath matted nape-hair.

The air-conditioner cycles off.

The blinds, the light bars are stilled.

I'm beginning, very optimistically, to think possum, or possibly raccoon. Scavengers of the night. On the deck. At the barbeque drip-tray. Our house is on the edge of wilderness. The nearest neighbor is a quarter-mile away, the other side of a steep hill.

Joan looks at me, wide-eyed. I'm thinking, she's thinking, *you're the man. Go on, go down. See what it is, damn it!* Of course she means, *see who it is*, since it wouldn't be the neighbor's dog. Unless it was outfitted with boots.

I half-roll off the bed onto the floor, shuffle in a crouched posture—as if under enemy fire—across the room to a chair, over which my dressing gown is draped. Out of the window, at the end of the driveway, a single streetlamp glows. The intersection with Hurlingham Road is flooded with lamplight. A vehicle, hidden from my view outside the light's periphery, would be well placed to receive stuff hauled across the back garden. There would be no need to use the driveway. A van, so parked, would mean a quick getaway. Swift haulage of loot is almost guaranteed.

Across the moonlit room, Joan leans crookedly on an elbow. "Bedside light," she whispers.

I had thought about it, but decided against. Better to be considered asleep. Retain surprise advantage. I communicate this to her with various hand movements, interspersed with inclinations of the head and punctuated with hoarse whispers. Seeing more clearly a bedroom I'd spent the last twenty years sleeping in would not be much help.

Even though it is warm, I need my robe. There is no way I'm going to go naked, anywhere, never mind downstairs to meet a possible burglar. I'm vulnerable enough as it is. The gown will hide my physique, or lack of, as shoulder pads do on a jacket. More importantly, it will hide the bladder draining apparatus, loosely Velcro'd to my leg.

What can I take with me? A chair? Heavy and unwieldy. The hanger pole out the dressing room? Brilliant. But does it lift out? Unlikely. And would not levering it from its brackets make enough noise to waken the dead? Surely. Barricade: move chest, bed, chair, everything in the room, pile stuff high against the door? Wait for the intruder to finish, rob the house of everything of value? If Hercules was in the room, maybe. Even then, a determined crook could heave and push, to eventually topple what's blocking the door. And how pathetically pitiful would such action look to Joan, the supposed man of the house cowering in the bedroom behind a mound of furniture?

The layout of the room takes shape: Joan's dressing table, littered with make-up paraphernalia, bedside tables, small chest over by the window. Another larger chest is by the bathroom door. No weaponry anywhere.

Any second, I expect someone to burst into the room. I feel helpless. Worse, I'm frightened to death. I'm not trying to be funny when I say my penis is afraid too. The appendage appears to have receded into itself. I've never seen the thing as shrunken, even with a plastic tube coming out the end of it. Maybe the weight of a full bag has something to do with it. I move over to the bathroom. By feel and familiarity I find the toilet. Down the side of its dark interior, I slowly and silently uncork and let flow the contents of my nightmarish dream.

A heavy thud, followed by what sounds like the scrape of a chair, startles me upright. The emptied urine drainage bag hangs from me on its umbilical chord like a deflated balloon. Whoever is downstairs, doesn't care if the man-of-the-house upstairs is awakened. An attitude of mind that takes guts, such as that of a jail-hardened criminal.

The phone. Of course, stupid me. Call the cops. It's on my side of the bed, though I'm now on the other side of the room. With my hearing, it would be better for Joan to make the call anyway. I whisper slowly in computer-speak.

"Joan."

"Dial-nine-one-one.

"Ask-for-police.

"Give-name-address.

"Say-there-is-an-intruder-inside-our-house."

She reaches across the bed and lifts the handset. Pushes it beneath her hair. Shakes her head, sadly, from side to side. Her tears will surely be spilling in the darkness.

She points to the phone. I lip-read.

"No-Dial-tone!"

I'm at the bedroom door. It is closed. I study the handle. Is it about to move I wonder? If it did, I would leap back, collapsed bag and accompanying tube yanked with me, sickened with fear, but closer to the window, before which, on the chest, is a lamp, one that is as heavy, as it is expensive: a Tiffany. Brought down on some ones head, the light would make them regret ever having entered.

Such empty bravado!

But the handle stays still. I close a clammy hand over the cool metal. It is a lever type. It strikes me that the turn of a knob would be less easy to see than a five-inch blade moving from three to six o'clock. It utters a faint squeak. I wonder *how much louder that sounds to the not-so-hard-of-hearing*. The bottom of the door drags slightly across the carpet, as I swing it open.

I wonder why I am taking such pains to be quiet. Why not create a huge din? Scare the living shits out of whoever is in the house. *My house!*

But whoever it may be, may not want to leave. Indeed, they may choose to come fix the reason for them being dis-

turbed. Then, they would find Joan. I might add, a not un-
attractive wife of sixty-eight years, lying naked in bed.

So I glide noiselessly—to my ears—out of the room.

My heart hammers in its cavity. The silence booms.
Moonlight softly illuminates a hallway clear of intruders.
The doors leading off are closed. The skylight above the
stairwell is flecked with stars. I listen.

Muffled noises. Louder than before, for there is now
one wall less to attenuate. I picture stuff being carried out
around the pool of creamy light, trundled across the garden to a waiting truck. The stair balustrade is slashed with
moonlight. I tell myself, *a head will first be seen there, supported by a mother-of-all-tough-guy neck, the thickness of my
thigh. The cranium will be shaven and polished, the color of
bone-knuckle. The sphere will move smoothly upward, as if on
wheels. Behind the balustrade verticals, its slanting progress will
give the appearance of being plotted on a graph.*

I must find a weapon, to offset my postoperative pros-
tatectomy frailty. One Doctor Fabian Michael removed the
cancerous gland two days ago.

If only I had a Doberman. I see its alert face, the
pricked ears. It strains on a short leash. Sniffs the air. I release it down the stairwell.

"Get 'em Tarzan. Kill!"

A flashlight would help, though I would probably be
afraid to switch it on.

I mean, why point out where I am?

The plastic drain tube traps beneath my knee, so that
when I move, it painfully tugs at my shrunken penis. I
think perhaps it will help elongate it. I look into the stairwell through the banister verticals. See nothing but
dimmed walls. Hear nothing but a solemn tick tock, from a
dark clock, in the darkened hallway below.

My watch glows three-thirty. Half an hour gone. Have
yet to leave the top step of the sixteen-step staircase. I

know the number. I designed the house. Nine-foot ceilings downstairs really need that many stair risers.

Any second, and the dark clock will dong the half-hour. And it does. And I hear a rustle. And my heart— pounding, blood-gorged, pulsating mass that it must be— almost jumps from its hollow. Joan floats out of the gloom, clad in a whitish gown.

"Did I close the garage door?" I whisper the question to Joan. A hand goes up to her mouth. Her eyes widen.

"If you didn't Frank, whomever is in our house, just walked straight in."

She breathes the words with controlled dreadfulness.

Clearly, she cannot rely on me entirely, if at all. Surely, she suspects that. Seeing me, cringing in suppressed dread at the top of the staircase, cannot be reassuring. I think I'm more concerned with ego than predicament. The cowering weakling is being put to the test. Laid bare for her to see, to minutely examine, as if a live video.

Footfalls tread over what sounds like the living-room carpet. I drop down two steps. I'm now four above the landing. I reach up to switch on the lamp that sits on a ledge there. My finger is on the switch, but my mind says *do not press.* Joan slowly shakes her head. I don't know whether she means, *do not turn it on,* or whether she's ex-asperated at my performance, or even that she still can't believe that she could not make the phone call.

I don't switch the light on. Together now, we drop four steps. We are now six down, on the landing, crouched against the banister, holding onto each other. There's a dragging sound. The TV going out through the garage? If only I had a handgun. Better still, a shotgun. People argue less with them I'm told.

Half of the landing is in shadow.

I find the stairwell more lighted when on it, than it was when looked down into. I make out the hallway. The doors to the family room, the dining room, and living room, are partly open. Each is a sinister, shadowy ambush-trap. I hesitate. It would be so much easier to creep back upstairs into the bedroom and barricade the door. What I'm intending to do, clearly putting my dear wife at risk, is not clear to me. What am I trying to accomplish, for Christ-sake?

Joan's frown above incredulous eyes breaks my train of thought. She has recalled something. She tells me in trembling tones that the phone was definitely not working. Bless her. She had thought the taut cord across the bed had trapped the hook. I tell her to focus on the one in the hallway, downstairs.

"Check it for a dial tone," I say, "as soon as you see there's a chance to do so." She looks at me as if I'd asked her to jump out the window, but nods.

I've still not tested a light. The main electric panel is in the garage by the utility-room door, as is the house phone wiring connector box. Someone entering the house by that route would see both.

I tell myself, that were I the crook, I would want to be safe from discovery that phoned help and being suddenly illuminated would spoil. I decide that is the reason why so much noise is being made. It tells me the intruders are aware that the man-of-the-house is old and decrepit and that he lives alone with his wife and that they are both huddled in fear somewhere upstairs.

And they would be right.

There is a crash of some heavy object. Possibly in the garage. Could be utility room. Could be kitchen. Are they smashing things, I wonder? Powerful sounds mean powerful bodies. Clearly, they don't give a damn about the need for stealth. They? Yes, at this stage, I'm assuming at least two intruders. Maybe more. They would take pictures first. Then silverware. Ornaments of course would go, along with many objects d'art collected over years of worldwide travel.

Joan clings to my gown. There is no way she is going to dial anyone. She is paralyzed.

I whisper, go back upstairs into the back bedroom. Wedge the door with the bed."

Her eyes say, *go jump out the window.*

I can see along the hall ceiling as far as the family room. Murmured voices. Raccoons don't speak! Kitchen? Utility room? Garage? With my ears I cannot tell. More noise. Loading stuff? Joan clinging onto me makes me feel better about myself.

Seemingly, she *is* relying on me.

She *does* trust her fate in my hands.

But then she must. She has no other option.

I drag myself down, four steps. Six now lie between the hall floor and me. Hard right at the bottom is a door. It leads beneath the stairs to a general junk room.

Inside this tiny, sloped-ceiling chamber, leaning against the back wall, between a filing cabinet and a book-shelf, surrounded by reams of printer paper and piles of old records, is my golf bag. In it are clubs! I picture my titanium driver. I make a sign to Joan to let go of my gown.

I whisper, "I'm going to get a weapon." I tell her not to bother about the dial tone. She nods her head. I'm beginning to feel less incompetent. I am filled with a great idea. It encourages me to think that it may even look to Joan like I'd planned it this way since I got out of bed.

My left foot is on the hall floor. My right hand grips the spiral end of the balustrade. Body coiled, I'm about to turn the corner. Joan is crouched on the staircase four steps up, behind, and above me. The dark clock looms. It is against the wall on the other side of the hallway. Three minutes to four. Even I can hear its ticks and tocks.

A tall, dark figure shuffles across the dark hallway! Whoosh! The sight of it makes me want to vomit.

The clock dongs four, stifling my gasps.

A stranger is moving about. Uninvited! At night! In our home! I can't believe it!

The shape moved from kitchen to family room. Over a shoulder was what appeared to be a swag-bag. Possibly, a blanket, four corners pulled together. It's as though a conscientious removal man had decided to get an early start, and was tiptoeing about, loading.

The 'weapon-door' is on my right, around the curve of the balustrade. I reach out and grasp the lever. I turn it with practiced hand, the required forty-five degrees. It opens. I enter. Can't get the driver out. Damn thing is too long. Catches the ceiling. I pull an iron, noiselessly from its plastic tube. It feels like a *wedge*. Or a *nine*.

Joan is still.

Still halfway down the stairs.

Still crouched by the banister.

Still fixated on me.

Still quaking.

I move down the hallway. It *is* a pitching wedge. I raise it above my shoulder, like one would an axe when about to split a log. I tell myself that anything that comes within range gets it. My mouth is bone-dry. Lips are stuck together. I pry a dry tongue between them, to lubricate, but there is no liquid to assist it. I am spittle-less.

Cool air wafts from the direction of the utility room. I did leave the garage door open! Through the kitchen, I see that the utility room door is wide open to the garage. I wait for something to happen. I'm afraid to cross the threshold of this room that some stranger just went in. Joan can't see me, so I can now let my face reflect how I truly feel. The hall is full of darkened recesses. Straight ahead, across the kitchen, beyond the side-by-side washer-dryer, against the utility-room wall, is a large patch of pitch-black. My seventy-seven year-old eyes fail to penetrate it.

I realize that in the restricted space I might not be able to swing the club. I would hit a wall. I compensate, grip the club lower down, as one would for an above-the-feet pitch. It feels uncomfortable, but will still enable me to deliver a blow of some sort.

I press myself up against the hall wall.

A slithering emanates from the family room. It is as if someone is braced against a wall, as I am, or is perhaps upon the floor, feet unable to gain traction. Lifting heavy stuff, no doubt.

I ready myself. My adrenalin is off-scale. I will kill now. Cool and calculatingly, I will bring my club down in a deadly chop.

"Who's there?" I yell.

I'm shocked at my audacity. Joan is out of sight. I imagine her cringing. I work the iron up and down, frenziedly, in a continuous hack-movement, as if beating someone to death. I realize it is a fear-driven reflex action, like a shaking lower jaw.

I press the light switch. Nothing. I was right.

The shadowy figure of a tall male appears through the doorway. He wears a black sweater with a heavy rolled collar about his neck. He's carrying the loot-sack. I bring the club down on the apparition. The downward swing is slow. It lacks power. It impacts his skull on the shaft instead of the club-head. I want that to have been a practice swing. The effort brings me to the floor. An ache spreads through the area where two days ago my prostate was. The shape grunts. A strong hand grabs me. I thrust the butt-end of the club upward, fast and hard into where I estimate head to be. It strikes what feels like lip-covered teeth. The shape screams, collapses in the hallway. Pictures and ornaments spill from the sack over the floor. The shape yells out, tries to rise, clutches at me, but only manages to grab onto a door handle for support. Blood gushes from the center of the face. The dark rivulet pours across his protective hand. More choked-off yells and curses pour from his mouth. He rises. I see his face fully. He seems a reasonable sort, clean-shaven, more bewildered than angry. His mouth and chin are awash with blood. What looks like a section of his lower lip, sags, dripping blood. Mid twenties possibly. A ring in each ear lobe. Another is in the end of his rather long nose. He staggers back into the kitchen. I follow, club poised to deliver a second blow. He backs away from me into the utility room. I follow. He stumbles out that room into the garage. I follow. He stops to look back at me. If he detects my physical state, I fear revenge will be swift and deadly. I shake the raised iron to remind him there may be further cost to him trying that. The robe seems to have the desired effect.

The garage up-and-over door is up. The opening frames a coral-tinged eastern-sky, against which the intruder is silhouetted, as is another one fast materializing out of the night.

"Let's get the fuck outta here," the approaching figure yells.

A she!

They recede into the garden. The one who took the jab in the face walks unaided. Every now and then, he stops to draw a sleeve across his face. The female sprints ahead. An engine starts up. A grayish van crosses the light pool. The vehicle stops to pick up the injured one. With a growl they are quickly swallowed by the half-spent night.

I pick up the drainage bag. With it held underarm, as though carrying a ladies purse, I switch the power breaker back on. The garage and hallway light up. I shield my eyes from the brilliance.

Joan glides toward me. She is ashen. Tearful. "Still no dial tone Frank," she whispers.

We embrace, silently, in the object-littered hallway. The now not-so-dark clock dongs the half-hour. Over Joan's shoulder I count the pictures on the wall. Lonely hooks tell me of those gone. I cannot remember which. We shuffle into the family room. She points to my hearing aids. They lie at the edge of a square of dust on the otherwise empty TV table. The stereo cabinet is empty. Ominous gaps reveal themselves on shelves.

I prop the blood-smeared nine-iron against the wall.

BEAR ATTACK

Survivors aren't always the strongest; sometimes they're the smartest, but more often simply the luckiest — Carrie Ryan

It was thought the grizzly rushed the group because it had young nearby. Though this assumption later proved false, it was felt that the hikers, blundering into its territory in the way they did, would be more than enough to trigger a charge, and with the gorge on three sides, there was only one way the beast could go.

For sure, panic didn't help. Forest Rangers will attest to that. They will tell you that fright is the worst thing to show when faced with an enraged animal.

Witnesses to the rampage tell of, people running, madly, desperate to stay ahead of the fast-shuffling beast, and, per one hiker, of a terror-stricken woman, plunging lemming-like into the ravine, and of a man, involuntarily emptying his bladder as he fled, the outpouring darkening his light-blue jeans for all to see, and of a youth, narrowly escape the animal's lunge by climbing a tree, a pine, limbs arranged like that of a ladder, in which, this witness said, he leapt about like a performing chimpanzee, to try to shake the creature's deadly intent, only to discover that no matter how the man turned, sidestepped, or swung, the claws find him, to slash with murderous precision—an outstretched arm, a dangling leg—yet to see, when seemingly leaden of body, exhausted to the point of collapse, the brute abruptly swing down, to lope after a fleeing, spindly legged fellow—each lumbering bound equal to this man's five paces—such, that had it not been for the large caliber bullet tearing through the creatures windpipe—a vital air passage at any time, let alone when extraordinary amounts of throughput are demanded of it—the enraged animal would have caught the ashen-faced being.

The single shot dropped the bear to the woodland floor like a thrown fur rug, albeit overly humped of shape, and with gaping, blood-oozing neck wound; facets of the fallen beast the hikers heeded not one iota. Instead, as often happens when people are snared from fate, they huddled in open-mouthed wonder, to stare, first at the steaming mound, shuddering in its death throes; then, at one another, before settling on the lone shooter, a tall, fringe-buckskin-clad man who stood a short distance away, weapon gripped at the muzzle, butt to the ground, in the manner of a posed Davy Crocket.

A Short-Lived Affair

Which death is preferable to every other? The unexpected—Julius Caesar

It happened unexpectedly, late one rain-lashed autumn afternoon, a time of sogginess, and sodden leaves, stuck flat to roads and paths, like ironed-on yellow and gold transfers. Bulbous gray clouds, pregnant with moisture, hung low over suburbia. And Craddock Drive—upon which mayhem would unfold—glowed like a strip of oiled mica, beneath the flicker of igniting, orange streetlights.

The maple-lined thoroughfare bisected an area of lush, manicured lawn that fronted apartment blocks set back on either side. Paths, linking each block to the street, further segmented the overly nitrated swathes.

The teeming downpour sheeted across the landscape like a pulled shade. Raindrops pattered, drummed; gutters bubbled, gurgled—innumerable watery murmurings, beyond which nothing stirred, and over which stillness held sway like bated breath.

No one could have foreseen it.

Not even Laura Baker.

Blotched and flushed of face, as if running a fever, she stood at her third-floor apartment window, peering out into the pelting rain. She cringed, clasping her hands to her pretty face. It was a futile attempt to shut out reality. The thought uppermost in Laura's mind—apart from an overriding sense of guilt—was that it should have taken about the same amount of time, for Joe-whatever-his-name-was to reach the lobby, as it had for her to close the apartment door on him, rinse out two glasses, pour what was left of a bottle of French burgundy down the drain, and move from kitchen sink to living-room window.

Laura was relieved he was gone. In hindsight, mortified the life insurance salesman was ever there. That she'd let him in. That she'd allowed herself to get so worked up. That the agent's grayish blue eyes had seduced her in the way that they had. Even so, she couldn't resist parting the drapes to look out on the sodium-lit scene, to see him exit the building, to see one more time, the tall, dark, athletic physique that had so beguiled her.

To her right, across the liquid-orange street, a dapper middle-aged man in a dark-gray raincoat was about to step into a waiting taxi. The driver, a black-haired, black-eyed, sallow-complexioned fellow, upon whose head Laura thought a turban would not be out of place—had there not already been perched a jauntily angled military-style cap—held the door in readiness to close it on his would-be occupant. The passenger appeared rankled. A look of disgust, etched on his face, reflected her own sense of distaste. This man it seemed, wanted out from wherever he'd been; yet here he was apparently faced with something worse.

Joe came out of the building at a run, holding Laura's husband's *Wall Street Journal* over his head, for the rain was coming down even more heavily. A black-leather attaché case swung in his free hand. Inside, Laura knew, alongside the laptop he used for presentations, was the freshly opened box of *Trojans* she had insisted he take with him.

"If any, Gerald must find a new, unopened box," she had said lightly, pushing the package into his hand. She was alluding to the fact her husband would be returning off a month-long business trip the following day.

Joe had the contraceptives in mind too, not in the sense of any lingering desire, but of the thought that such evidence sordidly implicated him. Especially since one of the condoms in the box was now used. He decided he must get rid of them at the first opportunity—before his suspicious, prying wife, found reason to lift the lid of the case.

It was just then that another man, exiting a building directly across the street from Joe, caught Laura's attention. Upon this man's head was jammed a white baseball cap, its bill bent sharply upward. The oddity identified him as the man who took care of building security. The deluge caused him to briefly shelter beneath the overhang of the roof. With a shrug and a tweak at the cap, he too then hurried toward the street—just as a red car moved out to overtake the taxicab that had begun accelerating from the curb.

The irate-looking passenger hated taxis, as much as he hated doors slammed on him. The dislike showed on his face. The look of displeasure deepened when the smell of cigarettes and body odor had greeted him. The sight of condensation-streaked glass and unemptied ashtrays aggravated his mood further. He comforted himself with the thought that his journey would be a short one. The airport was but thirty minutes away.

He was glad to be on his way after three miserable days spent with his estranged wife. For him, getting back together had proven unworkable. Judged by how firmly the apartment door had been slammed on him, without as much as a word of goodbye, she had come to the same conclusion.

He smiled thinly at the thought of how much he'd looked forward to the visit, the preparation he'd put in beforehand: what he would wear, what he would say, how he would say it. He now realized how pathetic that had all been. His mind turned to the return, empty-handed though it would be, to his one-bedroom Boston apartment where he would be reunited with his six cats, two more than allowed by Massachusetts state law.

He closed his eyes, and let the acceleration press him back into his seat, unaware the driver was scrutinizing him in the rearview mirror, or that alongside the taxi; a red car was attempting to overtake, and that a short distance down the glassy boulevard, a woman with a distasteful look on her face, was absent-mindedly watching the two vehicles through a chink in her curtained window.

When Walt, the driver of a brown delivery van, first saw the hurrying adulterer, the equally dashing white-capped man, and side-by-side taxi and red car, they appeared to be converging in the form of a sandwich, albeit a distant, rain-swept image of one. Five seconds earlier, Walt had come out of the tight bend on Craddock onto the straight part, along which he liked to floor the accelerator. He didn't know or care that the speed of the taxi at that instant was equal to that of the red car, effectively trapping the latter vehicle on the wrong side of the two-lane road.

Walt's take was that at some point, one or other of the vehicles would slow enough for one or the other to pull the
hell out of his way. To reinforce the idea in the minds of
the approaching drivers, Walt maintained his high rate of
speed. He needed to do this anyway, to get back on the
schedule his irksome boss had disrupted earlier, when telling him of an extra delivery he had to make.

As maple trunks hurtled faster toward the brown van's
rain-hammered windshield, and one by one the orange
streetlights froze their flickering to glow full-on, he
thought not of the additional drop, to deliver twenty boxes
of file hangers, but of Daisy, and the double-cheeseburger
and fries he would soon be eating at Larry's Pit Stop. The
greasy spoon over on Woodland was where he'd break-
fasted earlier in the day; served by the most stunning waitress he'd ever set eyes on. So gorgeous was she, his three
over-easy, basted farm eggs, double side order of bacon,
fried potatoes, and lightly toasted wheat bread had gone
lukewarm watching her.

"Just call me Daisy," had been her tersely whispered
response to his bright, smiling "Hi, I'm Walt, what handle
d'ya go by hon?"

"Daisy, Daisy, give me your answer, do. I'm half-
crazy, all for the love of you," Walt sang out. Above the
trash-littered dashboard, upon which empty soda cans
rolled about like loose barrels at sea, the two oncoming
vehicles rapidly filled more of the van's windshield.

At that instant, the driver of the red car was thinking
how cool it was to be alone on the wrong side of the road.
Rather than slow, as he would have, had he been less of a
teenage hothead, he determinedly maintained his position.
The thought uppermost in his head was that if he'd been in
his dad's Chevy truck, instead of his mom's crappie Hon-
da, he'd show *this fuck-face-of-a-cab-driver a thing or two.*

Why, he'd *put the living shits up him. Stomp the Chevy's J40 rims right over him!*

At that instant, the taxi driver was unaware of the vehicle alongside. Least, one in which the driver was incensed. The cabby was intent on observing his passenger in the rearview mirror, on the point of deciding that his client was a moneyed businessman, though a downright miserable one. Yet the traveller seemed to be a fare capable of giving above-average gratuity. To maximize the prospect of this, the taxi driver would sprinkle the journey to the airport with a drizzle of patronizing conversation. It was a technique honed over the years. The cabby could have an exchange of opinion on virtually any subject—about which he may have no knowledge or interest whatsoever—without consciously knowing he was doing so. All that was required was the occasional nod and shake of head synchronized with an appropriate change of expression, as befit his interpretation of the countenance on a client's face.

The driver of the red car was something else. The adolescent was consumed with outputting the contents of his head smack into the face of the taxi driver. *What in fuck's name d'ya' think yore' doin', mothafucka*, was what the teenager had in mind yelling, until that is, realization dawned that a fast-closing wall of brown metal and glass was almost upon him.

The realization barely tempered the red car driver's rage: a manic determination *to get past this son of a bitch cabby.* The driver of the red car instinctively attempted to turn right, to avoid the onrushing mass, but could not do so on account of the taxi. Not being one to tuck behind anything, even when faced with his own demise, he went to swing left, a direction he found he couldn't stomach either, because a man with a newspaper held over his head was standing at the curb. His only recourse was to stand on the brakes and try to swerve behind the taxi after all.

The red car driver would have succeeded in doing this, and Laura would have let the curtain folds slip from her fingers, allowing them to shimmy back into place, so that she could finish cleaning up after Joe. Awareness of how disgustingly shameful her vile act had been to her husband—one short, balding, pot-bellied Gerald—would have undoubtedly increased as she did so. And she would have gone on thinking how badly she needed to climb into a hot bath, and scrub every Joe-stain off her body.

And the driver of the taxi would have remained rapt with possibilities of remuneration, blissfully unaware that his client's flaccid, sullen countenance masked a seething cauldron of thought that was on the brink of concluding not to tip *this God-awful, filthy-rotten, foreign-looking cabdriver a single penny.*

And that Joe—Joseph Dennis Webster, Agent 39; District 24B, Thompson Life & Casualty; *Your Life is Ours!*— would have crossed the gold-slicked street to a point halfway. There, he would have met the man in the oddly peaked cap, away from whom he would have half-turned, to give a goodbye wave of the newspaper at a third-floor oblong of shimmying-curtained window.

All these things would have happened.

Had it not been that the driver of the red car had used up all reaction time available to him. And that Walt, tired of being in his van for the best part of an hour anyway—in which he would have begged to have stayed indefinitely had he ten seconds earlier a crystal ball—remained confident his intimidation technique would still prevail.

Even at that critical juncture, the looming red car failed to fully overwrite thought of Daisy, a condition that existed until oblivion descended; a sensation both drivers—had they been able to report on the occurrence—would have likened to a lead-heavy, ink-black, oxygen-expelled bag, pulled sharply over the head.

The squeal, the slither of rubber, the shattering of glass, the rending of metal, stopped Laura as she made to turn from the window. She had been thinking how smart a move on her part it was to have put the used contraceptive back in its box, rather than risk Gerald finding it in the trash. Or worse, for him to see the ghastly balloon resurface in the toilet, as she'd read somewhere they are prone to do. She'd decided she would leave nothing to chance. Every inch of apartment would be gone over. Every sign, every odor, eliminated. Never mind the torrential rain. Windows would be opened. Mattress, bedspread inspected. Sheets, pillowslips washed. Carpet vacuumed. Cushions on the chaise lounge lifted, shaken. Garbage taken out with all that Joe had touched placed in it. Carefully. At the bottom of the can. Only then would she bathe.

The tragedy of red car and brown van would have been the end of it, terrible as it was, were it not for a last second, jerked reflex action by the taxi driver. The cabbie had taken his eyes off the image of his client in the rearview mirror long enough for him to have made a safe avoidance move—one that would have possibly enabled him, along with his distraught passenger, to continue their journey unaware of the havoc in their wake.

Horrified upon seeing that a disaster was imminent, the taxi driver had rightly sensed that the impending collision would happen on his left. To counter this, he had intuitively turned hard right, sadly, by a yank of the wheel, rather than a steady, forcefully applied pressure, as was called for under the circumstance.

The taxi driver's jerked-wheel driving peculiarity had alarmed many a passenger. One, an enormous obese woman, had insisted he immediately pull over to let her out. He relates the story often to other drivers. Interspersed with thinly disguised, feverish laughter, he tells them "this massive creature, positioned in the center of the cab, took up the whole width of the vehicle, an enormous pouched arm lodged on each backseat-door armrest."

So savagely did the taxi driver turn the wheel, the vehicle mounted the sidewalk, to slew sideways across the lawn, gouging the sodden grass so deep that outlines of the furrows would still be discernable five years later.

And it didn't end there, for the taxi then glanced off a maple to strike the building security man, who in that instant was recoiling horror-stricken from witnessing the collision between Walt's van and the teenager's red car. Moments before, the peaked bill man had been nurturing the image of an attractive woman, stood at the drape-shrouded window of an apartment across the street. It was a window his oddly capped head always turned to, like a wind vane, in the hope of catching sight of the alluring female occupant he knew resided there.

Unwitting of his final moment, the safekeeping man had been gripped with the erotic realization that a smirking male figure, clutching an attaché case, standing on the opposite curb with newspaper held over his head, was the reason the female had been at that rain-swept, glassy aperture in the first place.

And it didn't end there.

The deflection angle of the taxi off the maple caused it to skate back across the mirrored street into a second tree, from which trunk it too was deflected.

Had the careening vehicle—now depleted of human life—been spent of kinetic energy, the torn and twisted metal capsule would not have struck Joe, standing at the curb. Would not have caused Laura's flushed face to ashen-over as if smothered with baking flour.

Immediately before lurching in shock from the tragic collision of van and red car, and moments from when the hurtling taxi was to strike him, it had crossed Joe's mind that outside of Gerald, he more than likely was not Laura's first fling—maybe not even that day!

In the triumphant aftermath of sexual conquest, feminine odors still clinging, the insurance agent was savoring an imagined image of him crossing the street sporting a laconic grin, along with a goodbye wave, thrown casually over his shoulder, and had it not been for the tangled clump of tortured metal hurtling into him from his right, he would have done just that.

The cascading misfortunes occurred within several blinks of Laura's mascara-laden eyes. The series of events at first seized her with an urge to flee. To dash down the three flights of stairs two-at-a-time, race across the ornately tiled lobby, push through the revolving door, out into the teeming rain, to rush down the pathway, and stand solemnly by Joe's splayed form—lifeless as the colorful leaves stuck to it.

Yet she could not tear herself from the window. She could not be associated with the calamity! She could do nothing other than be fixated on a fluttering dry corner of Gerald's newspaper. Part-stuck to the wet surface of the road, she found herself considering that the flap could so easily have been the wing of a spent moth.

It was then that she noticed the rain.

It wasn't just shitty wet stuff coming down. She saw how unconcernedly it got on with its pit and patter, no matter the grievous goings-on. How it spawned rivulets that busily sought new territory. How these streams spilled down complex creases in jagged metal. How delicately the drops wetted steely razor edges. How greedily flows invaded dry areas, eased beneath shards of glass and torn fabric, and how each gush forged entrance to new culverts, along which these torrents sped, to pool in dents, to form tiny crimson-tinged ponds.

Yet, of more consequence still for Laura, perhaps equal to the human tragedy itself—certainly more so than the ways of rain—was the fate of the briefcase. Ejected from Joe's clenched hand, it had landed damaged but largely intact in the middle of the shiny street, a place she would never bear look at ever again, without envisioning that block of black leather, with its polished brass latches, being the property of the deceased, and of its contents being examined by wife of the deceased.

The Faker

Luck is a very thin wire between survival and disaster, and not many people can keep their balance on it—Hunter S. Thompson

Of the lurching steel-box that had been his landing craft, there is no sign. Acrid smells of seared metal permeate the phosphorous-hazed air. The taste of vomit fouls his mouth. His face bears the look of a crazed animal. Within his head, uproar rages. The boom of exploding mortar shells, the rattle of machinegun fire, the disturbed, seething sea, and his thrashing around in it, might be a clip from some movie he watches while sealed in a glass chamber in which a claxon blares.

He pushes back from the surface of the water, as if it were possible to lever himself up out of it. It is the color of oiled steel. Waves, in various shapes and sizes, lap against his body. The seas run at different angles to one another, their normal courses affected by the impact of exploding shells. Orange-laced, the blue-gray puffs blast him with spray that stings his face like blown sand. Shards from the clouds, lance the water about his unprotected head, miraculously sparing him.

He feels suspended in some nightmarish state that he will shortly awaken from. The swell that he rides, grew out of nowhere like a small hill. The hummock lifts him high enough to make out a line of dunes on the shore, before which a bank of shingle fronts a seawall. He spies a pocket of infantrymen sprawled there. Flopped blackly on the pink sand, they could just as easily be a pod of seals.

Desperate to escape the unspeakable flotsam in which he flounders, he wills his body toward the beach, incredulous he's able to do so. An iron girder, sharply angled at the surface to rip open the hull of a boat, provides a small cone of shelter from rifle and machinegun fire that pours out from the distant bluff. Others from his Company are clustered there. Helplessly swirled around by the swells— like so many corks—they scrabble for handholds on the steely jut. Hands clutch at him as they soar past. Fingers drag across his tunic, and slither and grope over his face, seeking handholds.

Not unlike Russian roulette, each surging upwelling adds an additional flavor of terror. The ocean's expansions cause a random selection of bobbing heads to be swept out of the girder's protection zone. Many sail out. Fewer come back. The weeding continues until none are left. He observes the slaughter from a position low down in the water, where he clings to a flange on the strut.

Unmindful of such trivia at its surface, the aquatic cauldron in which he wallows, unconcernedly continues to seethe, churn and froth, to lift and draw, oblivious to the consequence of its heaves. But like the barnacles that cut into his grasping hands, he finds he's able to resist its pull. The more the ocean lurches, pitches, and slops, the more it gushes, the more it pulls at his frailty, the tighter he hugs the encrusted projection, until he alone survives.

His fogged brain tells him he cannot continue acting as if a limpet. Nor can he be seen struggling on the surface. To remain alive, he must appear dead, as devoid of life as those infantrymen that drift about him: splayed, water-logged forms that have the look of ragged flats of seaweed. The enemy has deemed these sodden, lifeless shapes un-worthy of further attention. A brief moment of crushing clarity tells him that within each roiling, 'vegetative' raft, inside a water filled pocket, where last pushed into some now sodden wallet—like a faintly beating heart—a picture of an unknowing loved one smiles wanly still.

He allows his body to sag into the surface film. Like a hammock, it supports him. Spread-eagled, he drifts face down, snatching gulps of air through the side of his mouth, manipulating his arms underwater, in the manner of rudders. He braces himself ahead of a rearing, foam-lipped ridge that bears down on him like an advancing cliff. He fears that the wall of gray green must engulf him. But the sinister ledge slips smoothly and silently beneath him, lifting him effortlessly over its boiling crest.

In the churn of the roller's wake, a flat expanse of lead-en sea. Here, amid the small chop, men scream into the wind. These are the fear-stricken, the exhausted, and the wounded. He knows that the mere wave of an arm in sup-port of these poor souls would sign his death warrant; tag him as it were, as is a forest tree to be cut down.

"Mother!"

"Over here! Quick!"

"Oh My God! Save me!"

"Help me!"

But the feeble cries are soon cut short by the crisp zap of a bullet. Black streaked, wide-eyed faces twist words at him he cannot hear. One by one, slowly and silently, the bobbing heads turn over, to slip beneath the surface. It is as if an alternative way out has been found. A secret under-water passageway to safety.

A great sadness wells within him.

He weeps salty tears into the salty sea.

High on the bluff, the snipers eye swivels in its bony socket. Pressed hard against the aperture of a telescopic sight, mesmerized possibly by the cross haired tunnel through which it gazes, the glistening orb rests briefly on each torso before signaling the crooked finger to squeeze. But the dark misshapen patch that soars across the face of a translucent swirl, survives its scrutiny. The unblinking or-gan briefly scans the drifting mass. Dismisses it as a sur-face blemish—a lifeless irregularity—one of many it sees in its debris strewn killing field. Over which it traverses. Over which it decides who shall live, or who shall die.

The throbbing jackhammer inside his head has fallen silent. A soundproof door in his sealed globe has snapped open. The claxon has been replaced by the hiss and boom of the sea.

The troop-train comes to mind that pulled him away from a picturesque English railway platform. Faces slowly slipped past, waving and cheering. Thin ones, narrow, pale, tight-lipped, softly fleshy, bright, and sad-eyed—one after another, momentarily caught in his triumphant gaze.

The landing craft ramp was lowered.

"Not yet! Not here!"

"Keep going in!"

"It's too deep here man!"

"For fuck sake, further in!"

But the ocean was coming in.

Shards were coming in.

Men clutched onto men.

Many slithered, fought to gain friction on the slippery, bucking, riveted steel floor, unknowing that had they slipped they may have lived longer. Fingers pointed at a bobbing object. Glinting, deep in the trough of a swell, a spiked sphere stood out like a giant horse chestnut.

What menace in that sea-washed light!

He had retched. His coffee-laced pack-breakfast burst over the steeply tilting floor.

A lance pierced the grayness.

A shutter opened before a white-hot fire.

A blue-steel jolt forked him.

The blast, part deflected, part absorbed by the bodies that pressed around his stooped form—like sandbags— shielded him. As if an anchor, he'd plummeted, to stand on a white-sandy ocean floor, in perhaps twenty feet of water. Above: an emerald roof. Within him, a sense of release, an escape from seasick dreadfulness. Through blooded en- trails, there were fish, amid swarms of bubbles that rose like a release of New Year balloons. The silvery creatures stared at him. Mirrored his astonishment.

In a flash, he'd let go his rifle, lifted off his helmet, lev- ered himself out of his boots. Wrestled with "fucking, stu- pid, useless, fingernail-breaking, 'quick release straps." Dropped ammunition pouches. Grenade-loaded belts. He'd clawed upward toward the brilliant, dancing light, exploding onto the surface among others; like him gasping, wallowing, like blowing whales.

Below, discarded on the bright sand, amid the cast-off paraphernalia of war, his rifle—an admired blue-steel shaft in the glow of his bunk light. A weapon he'd cleaned, pol- ished, oiled, tested and revered all hours of the day and night, a lethal shaft that he'd been trained to kill with, as useless now as the fish that hovered above it.

Through the oiled surface of the aquarium, men in slow motion struggled to shed weight. Arms thrust through the surface. The appendages sought leverage. Frenziedly, the limbs attempted to grab onto him. The shafts of humanity thrashed about like black sticks, as though to catch the attention of a friend. But no head appeared that would sustain further movement. The grotesque flapping subsided. Dragged down by unseen weight, the members withdrew into the seething sheen. He pleaded for it to be known that in his feeble state, he could never have hung onto one of those sodden weights. He could never have held such a saturated body high enough up, long enough, while releasing the burden that strained to pull it down.

He hears the subdue roar of backwash wavelets. The sound is unmistakable. It is periodically distinct. His knees drag sand. Softness sifts through his trailing fingers. He is cold and exhausted. He shivers uncontrollably. Explosions vibrate the beach beneath him, like pounded bass drums. Ripples move him about on the sand. He appears like a piece of newly arrived seaweed. His head is sideways on, such that he faces out to sea. Tiny crabs scurry across his field of vision: warriors out to do battle.

The edge of a ripple pushes a crust of flotsam before it. He turns with it to see the beach. A wide strip of sand leads up to a shingle bank. He estimates the gravel to be fifty-feet away. The sand drains the sea like blotting paper does ink. An infantryman struggles forward, as if fighting a headwind. Another slumps, like a dump of old snow. One kneels as if in prayer. Two more buckle at the knees to jackknife forward.

Thud! Thud! Zap! Zap! Shusht! Shusht!

He winces. Flattens to the sand.

The death-hail spares him, moves on up the beach, to jerk slumped forms that lie about like piles of wet rags.

How long would it take to run fifty feet, he wonders?

And how long would it take a shooter to see him, to cradle a weapon? Aim? Fire? And, what if the weapon is pre-aimed, such that all is needed is a squeeze of a crooked index finger?"

"Come on Man, make a run for it!"

"Now's your chance!"

The voice comes from the shingle bank.

"Get the-fuck-up man!"

"Run!"

He presses the ball of his right foot into the sand.

"I'll run," he mutters, "like I've never run before. For Mom, for Dad, for sister-Peggy and brother Tom. And for Linda. Dear beautiful, soft, warm, Linda. Where are you at this instant—right now, this very second, as I lie here on damp sand at death's door?

"I'll run too, for Private First Class Michael Edward Walker, nineteen, from beautiful downtown Loveland, Colorado, USA—all one-hundred-sixty-eight-pounds, five-feet-nine-and-a-half-inches of me."

Will the owner of the voice see my supreme effort, he wonders? Did the speaker have to do the same thing? Is that soldier goading me on, because it worked for him? Are the black clumps, embedded in the sand like rock outcrops, the last ones he tempted? Will he see me get hit as I rise? Knocked backward? Morph into yet another clump? Perhaps he'll yell *whoa!* As he see me struck in mid-stride. See's my step falter, as if arrested by some hidden trip wire, caught, making my final lunge.

Or will he get to grip my extended hand? Pull me to safety? Once there, he'll surely want to tell me of his own escape. And I'll tell of mine too. For sure, those behind the safety of the shingle bank will laugh and cry. For a while, I'll be a hero, for they will have witnessed my heroic dash. I can then shout encouragement to others. Give them advice from my position of shelter. Tell them, they too can make it.

Pressure from the ball of his foot gouges a hollow in the sand. The pit fills to form a small pond, around which is pushed a raised edge, like a battlement.

He looks up into pure turquoise, in which sun-tipped clouds float. From their detached, safe world, they look down upon him. Incredibly, so does a gull. The bird risks all, as it wheels high above the fray, surely, barely able to contain itself at the sight of the fish littered beach.

"Mom, I love you," he screams into the bedlam.

The foreshore reflects the sky in which wise clouds ponder. A bare foot thrusts hard from its shallow hollow. An outline of exiting toes notch out the frontal lip of the depression. The pond drains. A ripple slews over the blue-green mirror. Greedily, the surge devours the sand edifice.

Somewhere, a machine gun chatters. Somewhere else, men hustle low, scattering, as they try to make the bluff, only to fall like tipped dominoes.

From the vantage point of the seabird, a sand-encrusted protrusion separates from the tide line. The apparition leans forward, as if burdened with an unseen weight. The outcrop staggers across the turquoise sand field toward the bank of shingle. Short of the pebbles, the clump swerves, as if deflected by some giant hand, lurches, first to one side then the other—amidst a series of spurts that lead up to it, and appear to pass through it—before dropping to the sand with the finality of a discarded puppet.

Unknowing of war or the reason for it, the gull continues its swerve maneuver. Despite the allure of easy food,
the mayhem, smoke and reek of chemicals, pushes the
creature to flap frantically seaward. Yet as it flies, its gluttonous hunger unsatisfied, it surely cannot help but see the
ragged shape, that moments before had slumped so em-
phatically, so disjointedly, as if down forever, suddenly
squirm forward—as does a snake gaining traction in
sand—to merge with a clutch of similar shapes on the bank
of shingle.

MRS. CROUCH

Fear is pain arising from the anticipation of evil — Aristotle

The weather had turned fittingly gray and drizzly, the afternoon an old woman occupied half of the derelict cottage. She had shuffled her way toward the dilapidated building through waist-high weeds that clogged a dirt pathway. So stooped of posture was she — dragging a shopping cart overloaded with her stuff — Sidney, who lived in the other half of the ramshackle structure, almost rushed out with an offer of help, had he not been uneasy about anyone, least of all one so disturbing in appearance, living beside him. So, he'd remained in his half, stood well back from its one intact window: a mildew-stained oblong of glass in which the hag-like figure was momentarily framed.

The woman had arrived wrapped in a black shawl, huddled with her cart and pile of belongings, in the back of a beat-up truck. Sidney thought she could easily have been mistaken for bagged rubbish on the way to the Council refuse dump. Everything about her spoke to the absence of light: long blackish-brown frock—of sorts, black socks and even blacker, flat-heeled shoes that he thought gave her the appearance of a witch, though a faceless one, as far as he was concerned, since so down of mouth was the woman, not once was he able to get a clear view of the front side of her head. What he did get a glimpse of—although he later thought that he must have imagined it—was a heavily crinkled cheek and a jaw that jutted out from the head. The woman's hair was mostly black too, though oily looking and streaked with grey. Stretched flat over her skull, like a pelt, the flattened mop was untidily gathered into a pin-pierced bun at the back of her neck.

While the driver had stood idly by, the woman was left to struggle with lifting her things off the tailgate. Along with the loaded cart, there were two bulging suitcases closed with string, three cardboard boxes punctured with what Sydney thought to be air holes, various plastic bags stuffed with he didn't know what, and a wooden container, chicken-wired at one end as would be used to transport small pets, such as guinea pigs.

The driver, a burly individual with pitted face, shaved head and flattened nose, had warily kept his distance from the woman. Sydney thought, on seeing how dirty she was that there might be an obnoxious smell coming off her. Or worse that she was known to be a carrier of contagious disease. With her things stacked wobblingly on the cart, she had proceeded to drag the ungainly, squeaking contraption through the weeds, toward the other side of the rundown cottage—unable it seemed, to look in any direction other than down.

That was yesterday. Then, seeing she was so frail looking and in obvious need of shelter, Sidney had felt more sympathetic, allowing that her living so near to him, frightful though that prospect had seemed at first sight, might not be so bad after all. Now, in the early evening of the next day, on edge and alarmed, after it sinking in she could well be both foul smelling and disease-ridden, he couldn't stomach the thought of the woman being anywhere near.

The rundown building, being set at the end of a disused farm lane, a mile from the main Bromley road, meant he'd grown accustomed to peace and quiet. Even the faint hum of distant traffic didn't intrude on the overall peacefulness of the place. Once, an agricultural establishment, the crumbling, slate roofed cottage was all was left that in any way was even remotely habitable. The arrival of this old woman—a repulsive squatter Sidney now thought of her as—nosing in on his private space, and worse, being eerily silent since she'd arrived, brought an abrupt end to any thought of sympathy. As far as he was concerned, her coming was an out-of-the-blue bombshell, if not an outright jolting shock. How she'd found out about the place, he couldn't even begin to fathom.

What irritated Sidney more, though as usual, he wouldn't let himself believe it, was he hadn't found courage to do anything about it. He'd cowered in the background, powerless to intervene. Even after she'd moved in, and the truck had left, he still couldn't summon courage enough to go root her out. Shoo the hag, and her filthy, disgusting belongings back down the lane.

He'd ranted and raved to himself all day, about what punishments he'd inflict—"*Disembowel, hang, hedge shear off that pad of God-awful matted hair, along with its hideous pin-pierced bun*"—but, again, as was typical, he couldn't summon the moral strength to carry out the threats.

He was only too aware that he wasn't much to look at either. Indeed, the woman might be more alarmed to discover him, than he finding her. From his worn shoes, patched trousers and shabby layered shirts, to his bedraggled beard, unkempt gray hair and a face startled still from too many scary nights huddled on park benches, he fitted every ones picture of a down-and-out vagrant. His physical movements told the story too: short sliding steps, constant beard scratching, and the jumpy head movements of the hounded.

Ever since he'd had the good fortune to discover the refuge, two years before, he'd been taken with the serenity of the place. It became so quiet, at times; it was as though he was the only person left on the planet. After years of living rough with down-and-outs, and drunken winos, life had never been as tranquil.

It was like he was a homeowner. And of course in a way he was. A fortunate one at that too, for his house was rent-free. In exchange for the roof above his head, he'd only had to pledge to lie low, remain as inconspicuous as possible, so that as few as possible were ever likely to know the cottage was occupied.

Patrolman, Officer Thomas, who knew Sidney from his can-collecting days, was his only visitor. Once a month, the tall, thin-faced policeman drove up the lane to the cottage, but never bothered to even get out of his car. He'd park for maybe five minutes, is all.

Sometimes the patrolman would lower his window, enough to holler, "*Occupying a dwelling without the owner's permission is squatting, and therefore unlawful.*" Then, to Sidney's relief, he would add, "*As long as you keep as quiet as you have thus far, and a profile as low, I'll turn a blind eye.*"

After a life of clamor and upheaval, the abject silence of the place, while at first welcome, had soon begun to fray Sidney's nerves. It reached a point whereby if he didn't speak, he'd think he was going crazy. So he got into a habit of talking to himself, often, holding full-blown conversations that he'd never had the courage to do on the street. When the discussions became heated, he needed to be careful he was inside the cottage in case someone, having mistakenly turned down the lane, heard him, for he couldn't afford to risk detection. But since the arrival of the woman, he'd felt the need to curb his fiery talk. Aware of how thin the intervening wall was—Officer Thomas told him it was the result of long ago quarrelling farmhand's crudely dividing the cottage into two units—he'd been reduced to creeping about and whispering.

Five days had now elapsed since the old woman's arrival, and he still wasn't sure whether she realized someone lived in the other half, or that another half existed. He realized at the outset, he should have made some kind of commotion to warn of his presence. But having remained silent for so long, he feared that making his whereabouts known now, might result in her fleeing panic-stricken down the lane, or worse, given the frailty of her condition, cause her to suffer a heart attack and die on him.

And what would Officer Thomas think of that!

Sidney had been around to the other side of the cottage many times before. Each visit, it had seemed emptier, more run down. There was only one dry area, a sort of L-shaped space off the main room. But water had come out of a tap he'd turned on, albeit it rusty-brown in color. At least he had a stove in his half, the glazed window, and a roof that was reasonably intact, 'luxuries' he knew the woman didn't have. He hoped she traveled with some sort of bedding, and had the sense to carry candles, for the electric had been cut off years ago. Except that is, on his side. Most astonishingly, upon his arrival, when fiddling with the knobs of a old stove, wondering how he could best get the thing out of his way, into the yard, heat had come off it.

Covertly wired to bypass the electric meter by some savvy previous tramp, he realized he could cook—for free!

Had the woman continued being reasonably silent— and, he assumed, orderly, like he'd expect a female to be, more one so paltry looking—he might have put up with her living next door. But the advent of unearthly noises coming from her half, made him wish for nothing less than to see her gone. He'd never heard sounds like it. Except during feeding time at the zoo. A constant gnashing and chewing racket unnerved him. It almost drove him to pound on the thin dividing wall, to protest at whatever it was she was up to. But being the timid man that he was, he soon managed to convince himself that the disturbance was temporary, or that the noises would soon become perfectly explainable.

He whispered to himself "it's nothing more than her sorting out stuff. So there's no need for me to get upset." Whatever it was she was doing, whether feeding rabbits, or working away at something in need of a drop of oil, he accepted it was just part of her settling in. After all, when he'd first moved into his side, he'd done the same. He'd spent the first few days making the place more habitable, clearing litter and so forth. And, as best he could, blocking up holes to keep out vermin.

But what *was* the God-awful din? That's what he wanted to know. After days of 'deafening silence', the gnawing and rending had begun. It was as if things were being feverishly devoured, rather than unpacked. Apart from what he thought to be her odd name—*Mrs. Crouch* that he'd got off a magazine that had dropped off the shopping cart, to do with, of all things, *Rodents, The Gnawing Mammals*—he knew nothing about the woman. And since her arrival, there'd been no opportunity to learn more, for it seemed that she, like him, carried the basic essentials, so she rarely had need to venture out. Seemingly, she kept starving pets, and that they had started ravenous feeding.

He filled the kettle. He'd have a cup of coffee. The disturbances had to end. But how would he go about stopping them? With the hot drink, he nibbled on a currant-scone. Cut into chunks, smeared with blackberry jelly that he got from the Bromley Homeless Centre, the stale cakes were his favorite afternoon snack. Rock-hard, and with a bit of mold on them, they still tasted good. He sat on a wooden crate that served as his chair. A second crate he used as a table. He licked the jam off his fingers, curling his tongue over his lower lip, to arrest drops of the jelly dribbling into his beard. He winced as the sweetness exploded in his mouth. In a corner, on the floor, was his bed, a jumble of moth-eaten overcoats, spread on layers of cardboard. An old paint tin, placed in another corner, caught the occasional roof drip. Cardboard boxes, stacked three-high, one atop the other, contained his things. One held mittens and balaclavas. In another: sweaters, trousers, a beret and a couple of pairs of rubber boots, were packed.

Sidney was not one for spying on others, but he must understand the cause of the racket, before he could determine how to go about silencing it. He placed the table-crate against the dividing wall. The flimsy wooden box creaked, but otherwise, as it had many times before, supported him. He pealed back a strip of adhesive tape that was stuck over a hole in the wall. He was immediately struck, not so much with the familiar view, as with the sudden increase in sound level. No longer was it muffled and indistinguishable. It seemed that stems and roots were being bitten and voraciously chewed. As he peered through the hole— fashioned for the purpose of checking for vandals and other undesirables—he drew comfort from the fact that he'd carefully gouged out the opening high on the wall, where from the other side it was almost invisible.

A familiar mold-spotted wall, opposite the hole, came into view. A damaged door was propped against it, as it always had been. The wooden planked floor, at least the part he could see, immediately fronting the far wall, was about in the same damp, littered condition, as it was the last time he'd checked. The place seemed as empty, and as bleak as ever. He couldn't place the direction of the feeding sounds, since the noises seemed to come from every direction. Of the woman there was no sign. She will be in the L-part he decided. It was an area he couldn't quite see into, despite pressing his eye hard against the edge of the hole. The space in that section, he remembered, was drier and warmer, being furthest from the door opening.

It was then, when he was thinking the woman must have surely been feeding a horde of pets that the biting and chomping suddenly ceased. The silence was so unexpected, so weighty, he became conscious of how hard he was pressed upon the wall, and how fiercely his heart thudded against it. His hands—pushed flat against the thin partition for support—had turned cold with sweat. He held his breath. He tried to ignore his unease, but not even a flicker of his eyelids on the rough edge of the hole could he allow, for fear his presence would be detected. Stretched upward on the balls of his already aching feet, atop the fragile wooden box, he wondered whether the woman had sensed she was being spied upon. It struck him as odd that the sounds should cease, in the abrupt way that they had, just as he'd taken a first look. It was as if his look through the hole had operated a switch.

What creature, he wondered with a shudder, would make such a din? More ominously, what being would abruptly stop eating, mouth surely hanging slaveringly open, being stuffed with part-masticated food?

Recalling the cartons punched with holes, and the box draped with wire, he supposed the woman must breed rabbits, or similar toothed animals that she had brought with her. Judged by the level of sound, there must be quite a few, in fact, possibly a sizeable colony.

Or, he ventured to think, his eyes widening at the implication, it was one huge, gluttonous creature feeding!

He quickly pressed the tape back over the hole and stepped off the box. His hands were jittery. His lower lip twitched. He wiped his brow and rubbed his sweaty palms on his shirt. The light had dimmed. He thought he heard the patter of rain on the roof. Or was it vermin scurrying in the attic? On hands and knees on the floor—adjacent to where he now estimated the woman to be—he pressed his ear against the divider, effectively weakening his hearing to sounds coming from other directions.

So Sidney didn't hear the sheet of plywood that served as his front door, scrape into its open position. Nor, at first, did he see Mrs. Crouch, on all fours, scampering into his half, the protruding jaw, poking from side to side, sniffing the air, in the manner of the snout of a foraging rat. The hag's mouth was no more than a slit between the jutting bones, stuffed with stems and grasses, the yet to be eaten parts, grotesquely protruding and rotating as they were devoured by a double row of incisor teeth that cut and minced the plant material into a yellowish, frothing pulp.

Stanley Jones grew up in Stafford, England. This volume of short stories is the author's first published work of fiction. He lives in Ashland, Oregon, USA.

Proof

Made in the USA
Charleston, SC
22 April 2014